A HOME FOR THE HEART

A HOME FOR THE HEART

MICHAEL PHILLIPS

BETHANY HOUSE PUBLISHERS
MINNEAPOLIS, MINNESOTA 55438

Published by Bethany House Publishers
A Ministry of Bethany Fellowship, Inc.
11300 Hampshire Avenue South
Minneapolis, Minnesota 55438

Printed in the United States of America

Library of Congress Cataloging-in-Publication Data

Phillips, Michael R., 1946–
    A home for the heart / Michael Phillips.
        p. cm. — (The journals of Corrie Belle Hollister ; v. 8)

    1. Man-woman relationships—United States—Fiction.
2. Women—United States—Fiction. I. Title. II. Series: Phillips,
Michael R., 1946–   Journals of Corrie Belle Hollister ; 8.
PS3566.H492H66   1994
813'.54—dc20   94–4893
ISBN 1–55661–440–3   CIP

To
Cherokee Louise and John Robert Carter,
the father and mother of my wife, Judy—
affectionately known to the many who love them
as Bob and Cherry . . .

Know, dear ones, that your daughter,
your son-in-law, and your three grandsons
all love you and esteem you greatly.

CONTENTS

CHAPTER 1

HAPPY CORRESPONDENCE

Dear Christopher!

I just finished the letter you gave me through Sister Janette! What a surprise!

The train is still in Pennsylvania somewhere—I haven't even traveled through one state yet, and already I am writing to you.

As I read your words, you should have seen it—the people in the coach around me looked and stared. I was crying so!

The conductor came up and asked me if I needed help. He was so kind. I told him I was just so happy I couldn't keep from crying!

And I was!

Christopher, you have made me so very, very happy—happier than ever I think a girl has been. Happier than it seems I deserve.

I know I am babbling on. I feel like such a child! I am crying again just to think of you—I can hardly write the words.

Oh, *Christopher, Christopher*—just to feel your name on my tongue, and to write it with my pen, feels so wonderful! Christopher, Christopher—I cannot stop! Forgive your Corrie for being a fool just this once!

Oh, Christopher, do you truly mean what you said?!

How can I ask such a question? Man of honor and uprightness and truth that I know you for, how can I doubt a word that might fall from your lips? But I am compelled to ask it. I know you mean it, but I cannot believe it!

Will I really see you in California . . . in Miracle Springs! And will your mission there truly be what you say—to ask my father—

I cannot bring myself even to say it!

I will use your words: *husband . . . consent to call you my husband!*

Oh, Christopher, must you even ask?

You have made me so happy! That a man such as you would want to live his life with me—such a thing is beyond all the wildest dreams of my fanciful feminine imagination!

I dare not think about the prospect but to make myself crazy for not being able to share with you the wonderful joy I feel at this moment!

Consent? Oh, Christopher, Christopher—don't you know?

I love you too!

Yes, I will say it for all the world to see and to hear—I love you . . . I love Christopher Braxton!

Do you hear me, world?

Do you hear me, the rest of this train!

I love Christopher Braxton!

> And I, too, am yours forever!
> Corrie Hollister—*Your* Corrie!

Dear Christopher,

The brief pages I wrote immediately after finishing your letter are already an embarrassment to me. I could not stop the gushing of what I felt inside!

It is now an hour later. The happiness has not gone away, only settled into deeper places in my heart so that now I can write you a little more calmly. I would throw away what I wrote an hour ago if it were not for the fact that—if we are to share life together—I want to withhold nothing of myself from you. I want you to know every tiniest and hidden part of my being—the good and the bad, the calm and thoughtful, as well as the light-hearted and emotional. So I am sending it along with this letter, as a token of just what I said—I am yours forever . . . *all* of me. Even the embarrassing parts that I might have tried to hide from other people's eyes before.

I want to be all that God made me to be—as a writer, as a woman, as a wife, as a daughter of God, maybe even as a mother someday, or even a grandmother. If you are to be my husband—there again is that wonderful word, that word I can hardly believe!—then I want you to *help* me become all that God made me to be. How can you do that if I withhold little parts of myself from the gaze of your wise eyes?

So I will not withhold, even that letter. Here it is. Though I am embarrassed—it is *me*.

The train is clacking along steadily, and I am calmer now. My fit of crying is over, and the people who were wondering about me earlier have gone back to their newspapers and conversations. I read your letter again, every word from start to finish, and that made me start crying all over again, though I tried to keep it more to myself.

The conductor was just by and told me that we will be in Pittsburgh soon. . . .

After reading your letter—twice now, and I shall probably read it two dozen times before reaching home!—I do not see how I will be able to stand not seeing you for as long as it takes for you to get to California.

I know what you would tell me. You would say, "Corrie, the best things cannot be hastened. Nor does God rush when he purposes to build something of lasting value."

Is that what you would say?

Oh, Christopher, how I wish I could hear your voice saying it! The words would be so much more eloquent than when they come out of my imagination. But when I put even *my* words into the memory of your voice, it is *almost* like hearing you talk to me! In any case, I shall have to satisfy myself with it for now.

"Corrie," I imagine you saying to me, "the days and weeks we are apart will only deepen our love. In God's time, you will see my face again, and I yours."

I know it is true. Even as I write the words, my heart tells me they are true. For so long, all my life, I have imagined that I would never marry. It was so wise of you to know that there were things I had to think and pray about and resolve before I would be able to think clearly about marriage.

I admit that I didn't understand your silence. I was so afraid to let myself think about you because it seemed that my thoughts were only girlish fancies. Now I see why you were constrained to silence.

You did what you did . . . for me! As difficult as it was at the time, now my heart is full of more than just love for you. I feel such thankfulness too, knowing that you loved me and yet were willing to say goodbye to me and never see me again . . . if that was what God wanted for me. I knew you were a giving man, but that you would do that for me makes me love you all the more.

I know some people could not understand my saying that I know you loved me enough not to have me for your wife, but I understand. And I think I hear your voice saying again to me that you can't really love something in the way God means love to be unless you are willing to give that thing up—otherwise what you call love is really selfish.

Would you say that, Christopher—that love is always giving, always sacrificing, and that you cannot truly love what you only want to possess? Anyway, even if you wouldn't say just that, I do know that you love me all the more because you didn't want me only for your own, but you wanted God's best for me.

Thank you, thank you! But now I want to be yours too!

The train is pulling into Pittsburgh. I am going to stop for now and put this letter in an envelope so that I can ask the conductor to have it mailed from here. I will keep writing more, but I can't bear the thought of not being as close to you as I can, and that means sending this to you right away.

I wish I could send myself in this envelope too!

Yours,
Corrie

Dear Christopher,

The time is passing so slowly and quickly all at once. As I gaze out the window at the passing countryside of Ohio and now Indiana, it seems we are going ever so slowly and that I will never reach California.

At the same time, my thoughts are so occupied with everything I want to say to you, and with writing in my journal, and my daydreams, that suddenly I find another half day has passed and I have lost track of time altogether.

My thoughts dwell more and more upon Miracle Springs

and all my family. I can hardly believe it has been two whole years since I have seen them! They will all be so changed. And what about me—have I changed too? They will probably say so, but I do not see it, though I think they must be right. So much has happened in the two years I have been gone—how can it not show?

Of course they know about you. I have written them letters telling all that you and Mrs. Timms did for me. But they do not really know about you and me. How could they? I would not have known what to tell them before now.

What should I tell them?

Perhaps I should say nothing and wait until you and I can tell them together. I think I shall wait to hear from you first. I imagine that you are writing to me even now, though I will have to wait until I get home to find out.

It seems strange that I must travel away from you in order to hear from you again!

Corrie

CHAPTER 2

THOUGHTS ABOUT HOME

I rode the train all the way west from Pennsylvania to Omaha, Nebraska.

Now that a certain man named Christopher was involved in my life, suddenly it became very, very difficult to write in my journal as I had been doing for so many years. All I wanted to do was write to Christopher! But gradually I began picking up my journal again. There was so much I needed to write about what had happened to me when I visited my birthplace in Bridgeville. And yet I could only write a page or two before my thoughts would turn to Christopher again and I'd take out another sheet of paper and start another letter. It seemed that I mailed off a letter to him at nearly every stop we made!

Much of my time, too, I spent riding quietly, thinking thoughts that I wasn't ready to put on paper yet. When I was in New York visiting our old home, I had gone back and relived some of my childhood memories. Now on the train and then the stagecoach ride west, I was reliving so much of what happened when the five of us kids first went to California with Ma.

Of course, I had thought about that trip many times before, but the memories seemed different now. I suppose I had changed more than I realized. I was twenty-eight, and for the first time in my life I felt like an adult. I'd been on my own for two years, and that can't help but grow a person up in a lot of ways. The time in Bridgeville had put a lot of my past and my childhood into a grown-up perspective too. But probably most of all, it was knowing Christopher—and now talking with him about getting married—that made me realize how much my life had changed and *was going* to change!

It was with a quiet, inward, peaceful sense of getting ready to start my adult life that I rode home, thinking about all that had happened thirteen years earlier in 1852. The realization stole over me that then I'd still been a child, but now I was going to California, not so much to return to my father's home, but rather to begin the second half of my own life, establishing my *own* home.

Then, especially with Ma dead, we'd been looking for some place to call our own, to think of as home. Now Miracle Springs was home, there was family there, a sense of belonging. But there was also a new feeling within me that "home" has to be established anew for every generation.

And now the time was coming when it would be my turn to establish a home—with Christopher, I hoped. I could not know when or where that would be—maybe California, maybe Richmond, Virginia, or maybe someplace in between. But wherever it turned out to be, and however the circumstances came about, it would be *my* home, for *my* family, with my husband and—who could tell?—maybe even someday with children of our own.

I don't know how to describe the feelings all these thoughts prompted within me. I suppose it was a good feeling, in a quiet sort of way, though I looked back on childhood times with a kind of nostalgia too. It was not a sadness exactly, but a slightly melancholy awareness that a former time in life is receding into the past and giving way to a new era. And with that awareness is also an excitement that so much life lay ahead of me, filled with opportunities and new challenges to face.

These feelings were prompted by more than my age, I think, though that was surely part of it. Returning home after being away a long time also can't help but make a person reflective. You think about how things were when you left, and about what kind of person you were yourself, and about all the family and friends you have there. Then you find yourself thinking about how they have changed, but even more about what changes have taken place inside your own self. Coming home is a time for taking stock of your life, looking at how you have matured and grown.

I had found that kind of introspection happening whenever I

was gone from Miracle Springs, even for a short time, like the time I'd traveled to Mariposa and the several trips I'd taken to San Francisco and Sacramento and the long trek Pa and I had made out to Nevada looking for Zack. But this time I'd been gone two years and I'd matured in so many ways, so I couldn't help thinking about all this much more, especially the closer to California I got.

But there was another factor, too, besides my age and my returning home after a long absence. That factor was Christopher.

This is something I would never have known about or been able to anticipate ahead of time. But now that I was riding home, I came to realize what a maturing and growing thing it is just to know that another human being loves you—really loves you—and wants to spend his life with you.

What an incredible thought! That a man like Christopher would want to spend his life with *me*! Every time I thought of it, I had to remind myself all over again that it wasn't a dream. It made me feel giddy like a schoolgirl, and yet it also brought a quiet inward calm that I can only describe as a feeling of growing up and being made ready for the next season of my life.

All these things made me feel so changed inside.

Then I wondered—would anybody else be able to see the changes? Would I look any different to my family's eyes? Would I act different? Does being in love—I still couldn't believe I was writing those words about *me*!—change how you seem to people?

That was a question I never did get altogether resolved, even after I arrived back in California. I don't suppose you ever know exactly what other people think of you, and worrying about it too much will drive you crazy and make you more introspective and self-centered than is healthy. All I knew was that I felt different inside. Only two years had passed, but inside I felt ten years older.

This was the third time I'd crossed this huge land. And I felt as different now from when I'd started east two years ago as I had felt then from all the years that had passed after my first journey west in 1852, when I was just fifteen. Yet different as I felt, I was still hungry to be home. Knowing I was getting closer to California every day made the hard seats on the train easier to tolerate.

All along the way, people were talking about the war. Men got on and got off that I could tell had been part of it, some still wearing their uniforms, many with slings and bandages or limping with canes. None of them wore happy expressions. I don't think that war made anyone feel happy.

I overheard people talking about the war, about President Lincoln and General Grant and General Lee, and about so many things having to do with the war. I even heard Clara Barton's name mentioned.

I didn't talk to many of my fellow passengers, though, nor let on that I knew any of the people they were talking about or had had anything to do with the war effort. Not that I wanted to keep it from them, but my mood was quiet and thoughtful, and I just didn't feel like talking about it all.

That was another way in which I sensed that a new era or chapter of my life was beginning. The war was over and my thoughts were already turning in new directions. I didn't even feel like writing an article about my thoughts, though I knew Mr. Kemble at the *Alta* in San Francisco would surely have printed it.

Everything just felt so changed. Me most of all.

The train took me through Ohio and Indiana, across Iowa and to Omaha. They were working on the transcontinental railroad beyond that, but the stretch from Omaha to Cheyenne, Wyoming, was still not complete. So I boarded the stagecoach in Omaha.

The coach seemed so slow after riding railroads throughout the East. This part of the journey reminded me again how huge the country was and how wild parts of it still were.

I suppose after five years of civil war in the East, you could hardly consider the East more civilized than the West. More people had been killed by civilized and refined northerners and southerners in just a few years than by all the gunfighters and cattle rustlers and train robbers throughout the West in fifty years. But I guess you could still say the West was wild in the sense of being big and pretty much empty and untamed.

I rode the stage the rest of the way to Sacramento.

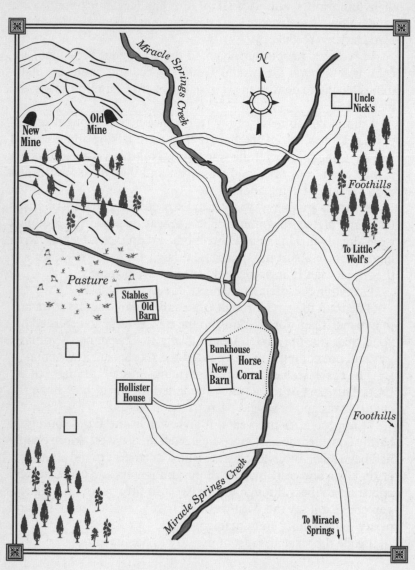

The Hollister Claim

CHAPTER 3

REUNION

I'd telegraphed home telling my family when I was to arrive. The train line was being extended northward and westward from Sacramento, making it possible to get to Sacramento, depending on which way you went to meet the train, in one day. But since I had no way of hearing from them, I didn't know if they might come to Sacramento or just wait for me in Miracle Springs.

I didn't have to wait long to find out!

The moment I stepped out onto the platform in Sacramento, all of a sudden I heard shrieks and shouts and people calling my name, and then I saw six yelling, laughing, waving bodies running toward me.

"Look . . . there she is!"

"Corrie . . . Corrie . . ."

"It's Corrie!"

"Corrie!"

Before I even had a chance to fix my eyes on who they all were, I was engulfed in arms and faces and hands and hair and wet cheeks and hugs and a dozen welcoming smiles and shouts and kisses all at once!

"Welcome home, Corrie Belle!" came a deep voice from behind all the hugs.

I knew the voice but still looked around to focus on where it had come from. The others stepped back just enough to let Pa wrap his big arms around me.

"Oh, Pa . . ." was all I could say before I started crying like a baby.

All of a sudden I was a little girl again, come to California to find my father. I stretched my arms around him and melted into his embrace.

We stood in each other's arms for just a minute. If the others were still making noise I didn't hear it. Everything faded into silence while I was wrapped up in Pa's arms. Years and years of memories with this most wonderful of men flew through my brain, from that fateful day when we'd first arrived in Miracle Springs until today—twelve years of memories. I just hung on to him—I didn't want to let go. It felt so good to have his arms around me again.

Almeda told me later that Pa was crying too, but with my own tears pouring out against his chest, I never saw it.

After a bit he stepped back, put his two big hands onto my shoulders, looked me up and down, and then peered straight into my eyes. Then he smiled.

"Tarnation, Corrie Belle, if you ain't turned into a grown-up woman—and a dang fine-looking one at that!"

Then he leaned down and kissed me, right on the lips.

"Welcome home, girl," he added. "It's mighty good to have you back!"

Before I could say anything in reply—even if I could have found my voice amid the choking sensations in my throat!—all at once the other voices came clamoring into my ears again. There was Becky and Tad and Zack and my little sister Ruth Agatha, who was seven years old! Now I found myself in Almeda's arms, both of us crying and laughing so that we could hardly say a word.

"Oh, Corrie, Corrie . . . I've missed you so!" she whispered and cried and laughed into my ear all at once.

"I'm so happy to be here," I said. "It's so good to see you again!"

Now all the others crowded in for their share of the greetings.

"Zack!" I exclaimed.

"Howdy, Corrie."

"When did you start looking so much like Pa? Why, you're a grown man! And you, Tad—"

"Hi, Corrie."

"When did you get so tall?"

"I was this tall when you left."

"Not that I remember!" I laughed. "Oh, Becky, I'm so happy to see you—"

We embraced. It was so special! Suddenly we were sisters who loved each other as young adults.

Growing up together year after year never gives you the chance to step back and take stock of where you are each going. All along you are aware of changes taking place within yourself, but you don't really think that the same kinds of changes are taking place inside your brothers and sisters too. But when there's a time of separation and then you see them again, all at once you realize that they've grown up too. Here I was with my two brothers and my younger sister, and they were all in their twenties just like me, though Tad was just barely twenty!

We were all so much closer to each other now. The years between us didn't make as much a difference as they had when we'd been younger.

I especially noticed it with Becky. When we stepped back, she was weeping just like me. And I knew the tears said she loved me, just like I loved her.

"I've missed having a sister at home," she said. "I'm so glad you're back!"

"Me too, Becky," I replied. "We have a lot of catching up to do."

I felt a tug on my coat. I looked down. There was little Ruth looking up into my face.

"Oh, Ruth, how are you?" I said, scooping her off the ground with a big hug.

"Good, Corrie," she said. "Mama says we're going to have ice cream when you get home."

I laughed, and all the others joined in. Pretty soon I was engulfed in a new round of hugs, followed by everyone talking at once. Only Pa seemed to keep a clear and practical head in the midst of it all.

"Let's go get your bags, Corrie," he said, "so we can be on our way. How many you got?"

"Just two, Pa."

We all turned and made our way in a single cluster to the stage office. Ten minutes later we were heading outside to enjoy the rest of our reunion.

The whole rest of the day was one of the happiest I remember in my whole life.

Pa took us all out to dinner at a fancy restaurant, and we talked and talked and talked! We stayed that night at a boardinghouse—though not Miss Baxter's, who'd got married and left Sacramento since I'd been away—and then got up real early the next day to go home.

What a trip home it was! We took two days, staying over in Auburn. And such talks we had! We talked practically the whole way. I told them just about everything that had happened in my life from the day I'd left California right up to the present, although I left out the most personal parts about Christopher. I still wasn't used enough to that situation to know quite how to talk about it. No doubt I'd have to get used to the idea by sharing it a little bit at a time with Almeda.

I'd written letters home about most of my experiences, of course, and they had seen some of the articles I wrote while I was away, but still there's something different about telling it and hearing the stories in person. I told them about meeting Sister Janette and then visiting the convent, about Gettysburg and how horrible it had been, then about living in Washington, D.C., and meeting President Lincoln. I also told about writing articles in support of the Union, going to Gettysburg again with the President and hearing his speech about working with the Sanitary Commission in fund-raising, then going farther south and working with Clara Barton to help the wounded. I told them all about Mr. Lincoln's campaign, and about overhearing the plot against General Grant and trying to warn him.

And when time for it came I did explain about being wounded and about Christopher's finding me and nursing me back to health at Mrs. Timms' farm. By the time we pulled into Miracle Springs I guess I had said quite a bit about Christopher himself, and I don't think there was any doubt that I thought him a pretty fine man.

But I didn't do all the talking! All six of them had just about as many stories to tell about those two years as I did—Pa about the town and his involvements in Sacramento, Almeda about home and changes in the business she knew I'd be interested in, Zack and Tad and Becky about their lives, and of course Ruth and all she had been learning.

When Pa talked about his work in the state legislature, I noticed that there wasn't the same enthusiasm in his voice as before. I got the feeling he didn't like being away from home so much and that he missed mining and working with his hands. When we were in Sacramento, he hadn't said a word about his work or even gone by the capitol building. We had just headed straight north out of the city.

Zack and his friend Little Wolf were training and raising horses both at our place and up the hill at Little Wolf's. Little Wolf's father, Jack Lame Pony, was getting too old to do much breaking, but he'd built up a good enough business that it kept both the young men busy. According to Pa, it made them decent money too.

Tad was working some of the time for Zack and Little Wolf and some of the time at the livery stable in town.

Becky helped Almeda at home and worked at the Supply Company a little, like I had. She also had become an assistant to the schoolteacher, Mrs. Nilsen, and taught if she was sick. Mrs. Nilsen had taken over the school when Harriet Rutledge quit to take care of their newborn daughter six years ago.

By the time we got home, in the evening of the second day, I think I was as tired from the talking as from the riding! By then everybody was pretty well caught up-to-date on everyone else's lives.

We rode through Miracle but didn't stop. What emotions I went through seeing the town again!

So much was new, so much looked exactly the same. Not many people were out. The Gold Nugget wasn't as busy these days as back during the gold rush, but we could still hear the familiar saloon sounds coming from behind its swinging doors as we rode quietly past, then out of town and on toward our place a couple miles away.

"Oh, I'd completely forgotten," said Almeda as we rattled up to the house. "There are several letters waiting for you, Corrie. They're postmarked from Richmond, Virginia."

My heart immediately began to pound, but I did my best not to show it!

CHAPTER 4

LETTERS

Dear Christopher,

I am home!

Can you believe it? I cannot!

It has been two years and a little over a month since I left Miracle Springs. How fast time goes, yet also how slow. May 1863 to June 1865 . . . but it seems like ten years!

I hadn't realized how much I missed everyone until suddenly there their faces were in front of me.

Oh, I cried and cried! I'm sorry, Christopher, but I hardly thought of you for an hour once they all were gathered around.

It used to be we'd go into Sacramento either by stage, once the line extended all the way north to Miracle Springs, or in a bouncy old wooden wagon. But while I was gone Pa'd bought a big new open carriage that seated six and was as comfortable as any Butterfield coach. We took the train north as far as the line extended, then squeezed into Pa's waiting carriage and had the most wonderful ride back from the capital.

How could I have been gone so long!

Once we rode into town earlier this evening, I started crying all over again. I love Miracle Springs so much, yet I had stayed away from it for two whole years! I could hardly imagine I had done that.

Then tonight when I sat down to write this letter to you, I realized that if I hadn't been away all that time, I would never have had so many experiences that I'm glad I had.

24

And most importantly, I wouldn't have met you! So I'm glad I went away, yet coming home is hard in its own way too.

It's late, probably past eleven o'clock. After we got home we went up and visited Uncle Nick and Aunt Katie for a while. Then we came back, and everybody was so tired they practically fell straight into their beds. I'm tired too, but I just can't end the day without visiting with you.

I'm back in my old room. It's just the same as always, like I was never gone. I don't think I'll be able to sleep for hours. Now that everything is quiet after the exciting day, my thoughts again are filled with you.

Several of your letters were waiting for me, but I promised myself I wouldn't open them until I was all alone and that I would try to save a few for the next day and answer them one by one.

So now I'm sitting here, writing and thinking of you, but still looking at the first envelope with my name written in your hand. Why do I feel so shy, even afraid, to open it? I know I am not afraid of *you,* dear Christopher! Why am I timid to open your letter?

I will begin . . . right now! Goodbye for now. I am going to let you speak to me for a while. . . .

Dear Corrie,

Words cannot express my excitement and relief at receiving the letter that you mailed from the train in Pittsburgh!

It was like being with you as you were riding along in the train.

I know you will not receive this until you reach home. I wish there could be a letter waiting for you at every station, but I have little choice but to address them to Miracle Springs, even though I am thinking of you still riding along west in the train.

I do not know if you can fully imagine my trepidation in hearing from you. I cannot truthfully say that my reservations and fears reached such a point that I seriously considered trying to retrieve my letter from Sister Janette before she gave it to you. But I did not sleep as well as usual for a week after mailing it, being anxious over what might be your response.

I hoped I knew you well enough to know that what I felt in my heart was mutual between us. But one is never sure about such matters of the heart. And my natural timidity kept my heart beating more rapidly than usual whenever the postman approached Mrs. Timms' farm.

What if you should take offense by the boldness of my words? What if your time in New York should have been used by our Lord to clarify a direction in your life different than what I hoped might be the case? What if your future was not to include me and the prayers I found welling up from within my heart were not in accordance with the will of the Lord as I hoped they might be?

So many *what ifs* filled my anxious thoughts . . . until today!

As my perspiring fingers fumbled with the envelope, I was fearful of tearing the precious letter inside—all the time my heart pounding in anticipation of seeing the familiar writing from your hand once again—and wondering what you would say.

Even as I tore at the envelope, I hastened into my room and closed the door. Mrs. Timms said something to me, but I don't remember my reply. She knew the letter was from you, for she had met the postman. I wanted to ride out to the hill where we went together on that wonderful Christmas Day we shared and read your letter there and imagine you were with me again. But alas, I couldn't wait. I had to know your reply!

Ah, Corrie, what a tremendous burden your letter released from my mind! Your *two* letters, I should say! I laughed and cried together as I read them both!

I dared hope . . . but now it is my turn to ask you—did you really mean what you said? Can it be that . . . that you love me too?

Oh, if only I could see you!

Yet it is best this way. I know that. Yes, I would say what you said I would. And so would you, because you *did* say it!

Christopher

. . . Christopher,
It's just a few minutes later. I read your letter.

You cannot imagine the joy it brought to my heart to see your hand flowing across the page! Oh, I do miss seeing you, but reading your words and imagining your voice speaking them was nearly the next best thing.

And your smiling, thoughtful, friendly, earnest face! The expressions of your mouth and eyes filled my mind as I read too.

Oh, I am being so silly! What will you think of me?

Yes, yes, Christopher, I meant the words I wrote! I do love you and can think of no greater joy and privilege than to be able to share life with you.

I must stop for now. It is late, though I do not know if I will sleep a wink tonight.

Good-night, dear Christopher!

Yours,
Corrie

Dear Corrie,

It is only three days after I wrote you my previous letter, and already I have received two more from you.

What joy you bring me! Are you sending me letters from every stop the train makes? Though even as I ask, I know you will not read this until after you are home. But keep writing! Write me every day if you can!

If this letter reaches you soon enough after you arrive home and you have not yet spoken with your family about our correspondence, I ask you please not to divulge my intentions. It is right and proper that I speak with your father before you and I presume to plan a future together. I must not seem to determine either my course or ours before consulting him.

You see, Corrie, I take his fatherhood over the one I love with great seriousness, and I would do nothing to remove from his hand a decision and counsel that I feel belongs to him. Though you are a grown woman, ultimate responsibility for you still remains not in your hands nor mine, but in your father's. He has been given that solemn obligation by God, and I honor that position. Until such a day that he passes authority for your life on to me, it is my prayer and intent to walk humbly and respectfully before him.

You will not be mine until your father gives you to me. I hope you understand.

You ask when I will come. I cannot say with certainty, although I hardly need say that you shall be the first to know my every plan, my every step.

I have been with Mrs. Timms a good long while now, and I cannot leave her without making provision for her farm, the animals, the work, and she herself. She is a stout woman but steadily aging, and I must take care in finding someone reliable to take my place here. With the war now over, there are many men who would be grateful for honest work. Sadly, however, there are even more descending upon the South who seek neither honesty nor work, but only their own opportunistic gain, however they can come by it. Mrs. Timms would be ripe prey for such men, and I must be vigilant on her behalf. Meanwhile, I am in prayer and am hopeful.

There is also the matter of my own history with which I must concern myself. I know I have not told you a great deal about my past other than what concerns only me. I shall do so—soon, I promise. This will not be a problem in whatever timetable the Lord sets for me, but it is of course of some significance when one is contemplating a change that may be of some duration.

In the meantime, I shall begin making plans for a trip west.

Yours,
Christopher

Dear Christopher,

I was trying to save your second letter to read tonight, trying to space your letters out, but I couldn't do it! It is not even midafternoon, and already I have yielded to temptation and torn open the envelope. So I will say to you the same thing you did to me: write me every day if you can!

Yes, I will try to do as you ask and say nothing about our hopes and plans. But may I tell that you will be coming to California?

What *may* I tell them?

I'm afraid they suspect too much already, especially Almeda. She knows me too well, and the way she looks at me when I mention you tells me that she *knows*. Women understand those kinds of things about each other more than men realize. Or *do* men realize it but just don't talk about it? Probably sensitive and thoughtful men like you do.

Sometimes I think my father is more aware of the way women think than he lets on. A twinkle comes into his eye when he looks at me, and even though he doesn't say anything I think he knows what I am thinking. Uncle Nick is different though. Have I told you about Uncle Nick and Aunt Katie and their family? I'm sure I have. Uncle Nick is more what I guess you would call a typical man. Even though he and Pa are such good friends and are a lot alike in many ways, Uncle Nick doesn't understand his Katie the way Pa does me and Almeda and Becky.

I wouldn't doubt if Pa already has figured out the way it is between you and me. But I won't say anything, and I don't think he will ask. Pa's not one to intrude.

Let me tell you a little more about everyone.

They're all older, of course, than they were when I first went east. I notice it the most with the youngest. Tad and Becky seem more than two years older since I left, but that's because it's a bigger change to grow from eighteen to twenty like Tad has than from twenty-six to twenty-eight like me.

Tad's practically a man now, with such a peaceful countenance on his face and such a gentle expression in his eyes. Of all us five Hollister kids that came west thirteen years ago, he seems the least affected by the hardship and the heartache that went along with that journey. He was only seven at the time, and when I ask him about it, he says he only remembers bits and pieces. I'm glad I remember, but in a way his scant memories are a blessing too. It was a hard time, and losing Ma in the desert was something I'll never forget. He has such a sweet and gentle spirit that I am looking forward to getting to know him all over again, but this time as an equal, as friends.

It seems funny now to think back to when I used to call all the others *young'uns*. They don't seem so much younger than me now!

Pa and Almeda's little girl, Ruth Agatha Parrish Hollister (named both after my ma, Pa's first wife, and Almeda's first husband), is already as old as Tad was when we came. It's amazing to think of, but the only life she has ever known is in California. She's I guess what you'd call the first generation of new Californians. She's cute as a bug's ear, and I can see both Pa and Almeda in her. I even imagine I see a hint of me in her too!

Becky's twenty-two, and such a young lady now. She always had spunk, and still does, but she's calmed a lot. We've already had several nice talks. I shouldn't find myself surprised by this, but I have to admit that in a way I am. She has such deep perceptions about people and, well, about all kinds of things. All this time I just wasn't aware of how much she was taking in inside. I suppose all people tend to focus only on their own inner growth. But I guess I thought Becky was too frivolous and gay to pay much attention to spiritual things. Now I find that she's been growing all along, in her own personal way, and is remarkably mature in her outlook.

Almeda has grown closer to Becky in the past two years, just like she did with me when I was Becky's age. Their relationship is different, of course, but with similar bonds. Becky tells me they had lots of special times when I was gone. She missed me, she says, and yet in another way I think my absence has been a blessing, since she and Almeda were able to spend so much time together and grow close as friends and as Christian sisters. Becky had become a true young lady of depth and faith.

I'm so happy for her . . . for them both! All things work for good! Now Becky and I are able to share our "daughterness" with Almeda, and our "sisterness" with each other. Oh, it's just been so rich with the three of us!

Actually, Becky reminds me of our sister Emily, who's twenty-four now and has a little daughter of her own. Emily wrote me with the news shortly after I'd arrived in Washington, D.C., so I've never seen my little niece—her name is Sarah. Neither have I seen Emily and Mike yet. They moved down toward the southern part of the state where Mike says it's going to grow and there will be lots of opportunities. That's what Pa said he said anyway.

Mike hopes to earn enough money to start a ranch of his own. Pa and Almeda hope for the best for Mike and Emily and their young family, but Pa doesn't place much stock in

Mike's dreams and schemes, as he calls them, and doesn't think the southern part of the state, which is mostly desert, has much of a chance to amount to anything. Pa says that if it came up in the legislature again, he'd vote to let them have their own state down there.

Mike's working on a ranch in a little town called Santa Barbara, where one of California's missions is built. It's a long way from here, but I guess not as far as the East Coast, so I ought to be able to figure out a way to see Emily again soon.

Becky still has her youthful energy and a twinkle in her eye, and it wouldn't surprise me at all to find some young man proposing to her real soon. Can you imagine? All three of us Hollister girls may be married before long! Who would have thought it? It seems like just yesterday we were *all* "young'uns"!

I wonder what will happen with Zack and Tad! I can hardly picture either of *them* married—not my brothers! But then I would never in my wildest dreams have thought that any man would ever love *me,* and . . . here I am writing to you!

I still can hardly believe that one day I will see you in Miracle Springs! The very thought is too wonderful to consider!

I will tell you more about Zack and Pa and Almeda later. I am anxious to get this off in today's mail, and the stage is due within an hour, and I need to get it into town.

Oh, Christopher, when do you think you will come?

Corrie

CHAPTER 5

LIFE AGAIN IN MIRACLE SPRINGS

My first day home I slept in longer than I ever thought I would! When I woke up I could tell the sun was already high, and I knew from the sounds around me that everyone else was already up.

I guess I was more exhausted from the long trip than I'd realized, not to mention being up so late the night before writing to Christopher!

It was a wonderful, happy, exciting day, but frustrating too. I wanted to see everything and everybody at once!

Almeda and Becky and I went up to see Aunt Katie again right after breakfast. Then we went into town to see the Rutledges, and Almeda wanted to show me the Supply Company.

I don't know where that first day went. Suddenly it was gone!

The following days were much the same. It was so good to be in a kitchen again, to be able to help Almeda and Becky with the meals. Oh, we laughed and talked and had such a time! The first time I made biscuits, I was so out of practice that they turned out awful. Pa got such a kick out of teasing me—it was almost worth failing just to see the pleasure it brought him!

And to be able to sleep in the same bed night after night, to be able to put my clothes away and not look at my traveling bags again, to be able to set out my books on a shelf . . . I hadn't stopped to think about all the special little things that make a home *homey,* but now suddenly everything about this place felt special in a whole new way!

I didn't have long to just relish in the hominess of it, though, before the question of "What should Corrie Hollister do next?" began to intrude into my thoughts.

As anxiously as I awaited the mail delivery every several days, I had mixed reactions when I read the following:

Dear Miss Hollister,

I have followed your career these past two years with much pride, and we have run as many of your articles from the East as we have been able to obtain—most of them, I think. From your beginnings as the anonymous C.B. Hollister, who I thought was a man, you have indeed begun to make a name for yourself in a man's profession. Your byline is one that the female portion of our readership awaits eagerly.

Word has it that you are due back in California soon. Perhaps you have already arrived. I would hope for an opportunity soon thereafter to discuss your rejoining the *Alta* team of writers and reporters. As San Francisco and the state grow, more and more women read our newspaper, and we find that they identify quite well with your points of view.

I am aware we have had our differences of opinion in the past over the matter of remuneration. However, I am confident we will be able to arrive at a mutually beneficial arrangement.

I remain, Miss Hollister,
Sincerely yours,
Edward Kemble
Editor, California *Alta*

I put down the letter and smiled. What a turn of events, I thought—Mr. Kemble *asking* me to write for his paper, instead of me begging him!

But I wasn't yet ready to think about that nebulous thing called "the future," especially as it concerned my writing career. I'd been doing so much of that kind of thinking during the last two years—at the convent, then in Washington, and when I'd visited Bridgeville—and my brain was tired from that kind of exercise. I found I couldn't even pray or talk to God about it. It was going to take some time to find out what would happen between me and Christopher. I'd given everything in my life over completely to God when I was in New York, and in the meantime I didn't want to waste energy thinking about what I'd already put in his hands.

There was something else too. I couldn't help but notice that Mr. Kemble still couldn't quite bring himself to admit that I was a full-fledged newspaper writer. The implication of what he said was that my writing was only of interest to women and that if it weren't for his "female readership," he wouldn't waste his time on me.

Maybe Mr. Kemble didn't really think that, but that's what it sounded like! And I couldn't help wondering why more men couldn't be like Pa and just come right out and admit that a woman has done a downright good job at something if it is true! Why did it always have to be, "That's pretty good . . . *for a woman*"?

On the other hand, Mr. Kemble was offering me what I'd always dreamed of—now suddenly it was right in front of me! This wasn't going to be an easy decision.

I folded up Mr. Kemble's letter and put it back in the envelope.

"Well, Mr. Kemble," I sighed to myself, "I don't know what to tell you. I think my answer's just going to have to wait a spell."

But even though I didn't reply to it, the letter from Mr. Kemble did cause me to reflect a bit on the various possibilities in front of me . . . besides Christopher, that is! Suddenly, with the end of the war and Mr. Lincoln's assassination, a chapter of my life had closed. What stories would the new chapters have to tell? I didn't yet know.

Did I want to keep writing? Did I want to be involved in politics anymore? Did I want to go back into the business with Almeda? And the biggest question of all was, how did any of these things fit into life as a married lady? Or did they fit at all?

Everything was so different now. Only one thing I was sure of— my future wasn't mine alone to decide about. So I tried not to think about it all too much. I bided my time and waited to see what would be written on the pages of life's book once the Lord turned them over.

CHAPTER 6

REFLECTIONS ON LOVED ONES

Dear Christopher,

I told you before that I would tell you about Zack, Pa, and Almeda later. Well, it's late now. Another day is behind me, and everybody's in bed but me . . . but I'd rather talk to you than sleep.

About those three—in a way, they're the ones who seem to be changed the most. Actually, that's not really true—they're just the three I find myself noticing the most. On the outside, I suppose, they've changed least of all. The changes that I notice have to do with deep inside things.

Almeda is the same as always—sensitive, warm, caring, always trying to serve someone else. As we visit and talk, she treats me so much like an equal that it's hard to think back to our first years together, when I didn't know anything about what it meant to be a Christian. Almeda guided me so wisely through those first years of growing with God that I can't even imagine my life without her help. Now, even though she's still older and wiser and more experienced than I am, there's an evenness to our relationship that makes it seem more like we're on the same level. She's been there longer than me, and I still find myself asking her questions. Yet we're different together now that I'm older, like we're closer to the same age . . . which we are, even though we're not. Do you understand what I'm trying to say?

Almeda is forty-seven now. The thought of her being al-

35

most fifty years old is almost more than I can take in. Yet I will be thirty before she is fifty, and that is all the more astonishing!

I always remember hearing grown-ups talk, when I was little, about how fast the years go. They were right! The older you get, the more they start flying by.

Oh, but what might the years ahead hold for us, dear Christopher? Of course, I don't want to know! Knowing would spoil the adventure of discovering the answers together!

I do see some of the signs of age in Almeda. Of course, it's not a bad or an undesirable thing, because when I look in the mirror I am always amazed at the person staring back at me. The signs of age are happening just as rapidly on *my* face! *What happened to the little girl?* I always want to say to myself.

There are more lines and wrinkles gradually showing themselves around Almeda's eyes and mouth. Her face is still brown from working outside as much as she does, and maybe that makes them show up a little more. Her brown hair has lots more gray streaks than I remember, though on her it looks nice, and she doesn't seem to mind them at all. A smile is always on her lips, and her eyes haven't changed. If anything, they look at you deeper and with more love than before, if that is possible.

I love Almeda so much! God has been so good to our family to arrange it so that she and Pa fell in love after losing Ma and Mr. Parrish.

Pa seems more changed than anyone in the family. It's possible that he was like this when I left in '63 and that I just hadn't noticed. But he seems so different from the hard-working, card-playing outlaw-turned-miner that we found in the Gold Nugget saloon when we first got to California. So different!

He's almost like a city man now. He dresses nicely. He walks tall, like he's comfortable with who he is. People in town call him Mr. Hollister—about the only people who still call him just plain Drum are Uncle Nick and Alkali Jones. Everybody in the whole area is proud of Pa. He was mayor of Miracle Springs for four years, and has now been an assemblyman in the legislature in Sacramento for five.

Maybe coming back makes me realize more than I ever did before that my father is the closest thing to a celebrity there is for miles around. He's an important man! And now all of a sudden I can see it written all over him. He's just so different. He carries himself with poise and stature. Why, he even reminds me of people I met back in Washington, D.C.! But I guess the changes came over him so slowly through the years that I wasn't really struck by them until I went away for a while.

Funny, isn't it, how it's hardest to see when someone right up close to you is gradually becoming important. Everybody else's eyes from farther away knows who they are more than the person's own family and friends. It seems like it ought to be just the opposite.

Pa just turned fifty earlier in the year. He shows the signs of it too, with the wrinkles and the graying of his hair and whiskers. But it all looks so good on Pa!

I'd never quite realized how handsome he is. Distinguished is what you'd call it. He just carries himself like a man who is somebody, but without a hint of putting on airs. He doesn't think too highly of himself, and I don't imagine he ever gives a thought to how he looks or what people think of him. The way he acts seems to come from just the way he is inside, not from anything he is trying to do about it.

Pa's speech is more polished now than it used to be. Of course, mine is too, and Zack's. We have all changed over the years from being around the kind of people who talk in more refined ways. Pa has been in government nine years now, and I've been writing for newspapers even longer. But just like with looks, you don't notice the changes in yourself as much as in other people. My writing has, I suppose, become more polished. At least that's what Mr. MacPherson and Mr. Kemble have told me, but I hardly notice. I just write how it comes out.

But I noticed the change with Pa the day I got back, even though, like I said, it might have already been there long before. Why, Pa sounded almost like an educated man! I could hardly believe it. He still has his own peculiar ways of saying some things, and he still says *ain't* sometimes and words like that. But otherwise, he could fit right in anyplace.

I see Pa reading more now too. He would always read the newspaper, but now he reads books about politics or history, even about mining . . . and of course the Bible.

And though he doesn't talk about it all the time, because he's still one to think first and speak later, I know that a lot of the change in Pa is because of how seriously he takes what being a Christian is to him. He's not one of the kinds of people who gets to a certain point in life and just stays there, just the same year after year. Maybe it's on account of everything that happened in his past and the guilt he had to struggle with for a long time over what he had been and done.

But for whatever reason, I see in Pa a real determination to grow and learn and better himself and to become a more compassionate and giving person. I can tell that he really *works* at trying to do what God wants him to, not just taking things as they happen to come. He's I guess what I would call a determined and forceful Christian, and that's how I want to be too.

Pa's grown over the past few years, just like I have, just like I told you Becky has. He's not just an important man because of politics. He's a deep man too. And maybe that's what has slowly brought about all the changes I seem to notice in him—his time walking with God.

Just two days ago I was up early, going for a walk up past the barn, along the creek, and up to where the old mine is, though it's pretty much played out now and Pa and Uncle Nick aren't mining it anymore. As I went I came upon Pa up there sitting on a rock. Do you know what he was doing? Not working, not planning some project, not writing a political speech, not whittling, not cleaning his gun, not even just thinking. He was reading his Bible—reading it so intently that he didn't hear me when I came up and I startled him. Well, come to think of it, I reckon he *was* thinking! He was really engrossed in his reading, I could tell, trying to find the meaning of some passage.

He put it down and we talked awhile. But before I left him I just picked up his Bible from the rock where he had laid it and I thumbed through it absently. Every page was worn. The book hung limp like it had been used often, and just about every place I looked there were marks on the page in Pa's hand. That was a Bible that had seen a lot of use.

I remember when Pa bought it. He was so proud of that new Bible when he came home with it from Sacramento. Now it was a tired and worn old book!

No wonder he's changed, I found myself thinking. The Bible changes people when they study it and pore through it and try hard to put its principles into practice! Pa was a living example!

It's kind of the same with Zack.

The changes I see in him are like what I've been describing in Pa. Zack is so changed from several years ago—I can tell just from looking at him! There's such a light in his eye and such a steady calmness to the way he walks, I love to look at him! Zack's a man! If I didn't know better, I'd think he was five years older than me!

He was different when he came back home after his year on the Pony Express. Oh, I can't wait for him to tell you about it—it's such a wonderful story. That's why I never have, because it's best when you hear it in his own words.

This is the most wonderful part: I'd told Zack he ought to write down about his time with the Pony Express and Hawk Trumbull—that's the man who took him in out in the desert and taught him so many things.

"I ain't no writer, Corrie," he kept saying to me over and over every time I'd bring it up. But I kept after him, telling him that all the rest of his family would like to read about it, especially Tad, and even his own kids someday.

Well, by golly if he didn't just do it!

Most of the two years I was away—except when he was gone again—he worked on writing down things that had happened and conversations he'd had with Mr. Trumbull.

There's a fellow I would sure like to meet—what a fascinating man. There's hardly a day goes by that Zack doesn't bring him up.

You'd think the rest of us would get sick of hearing about Hawk Trumbull, but we never do. Just like we never get sick of Alkali Jones's stories no matter how many times we've heard them. (Have I told you about my father's old partner Alkali Jones?)

Anyway, Zack's been writing everything down all this time, and on only my second day back, he found a chance to talk to me when I was alone for a minute. He walked up to me with a sheepish expression showing through his beard.

"Corrie," he asked me, "you recollect what you said I oughta do just before you left, about writing down about my time in the desert . . .

"Well, I tried to do it, just like you said . . . would you mind taking a look at it?"

"Mind! Zack, I want to see it immediately!" I said excitedly, starting toward the house.

"I tried to do what you said—you know, telling about your thoughts and feelings, besides all that you're doing. I wrote a lot too about stuff me and Hawk talked about—about God and growing up and being a man. I learned a heap from Hawk, Corrie."

"Oh, Zack," I told him. "I'm so pleased! I can't wait to read it."

I *have* read it, Christopher—all of it. Oh, and it *is* good . . . so good! I can hardly believe that it came from the mouth of my younger brother. I think he's as good a writer as me—certainly better than I was when I first started. And I'd had all those years of keeping a journal too, which gave me lots of practice in expressing my thoughts and feelings. Zack didn't have that—and he's a man besides! So I wonder if there's writing in the Hollister and Belle blood someplace further back than Ma or Pa!

I am just so proud of what Zack's done. I laughed, I cried, and I got frightened, when I read about all that had happened to him. So now he and I are going to work on it together to get it ready to send to Mr. MacPherson, the editor for the publishing house in Chicago. I just know he's going to like it as much as me.*

But, like I already said once . . . this letter is getting long!

My, oh my! I just looked at the time. It's past two o'clock! I've been at my writing table for over two hours . . . or is it three! I must get to bed.

But when the house gets so silent and I start talking to you, even though it's just on paper, I almost feel like you're

*For the story of Zack's adventures, see *Grayfox,* A Companion Reader to the Journals of Corrie Belle Hollister.

right there, and I want to tell you absolutely everything I am thinking about—everything.

Do you ever feel that way?

Oh, Christopher . . . Christopher . . . there is always so much more to say! I could write all day and all night long, and it still wouldn't be enough!

Blessings to you! I think of you nearly all the time!

With Love,
Corrie

CHAPTER 7

DINNER WITH THE RUTLEDGES

When I visited the Rutledges briefly on the Thursday after I arrived home, they invited me to dinner two days later, on Saturday. I was the only one they invited—they wanted to visit . . . just with me. That was another of the many instances of life being different now that I was back home—doing something like that alone instead of as one of the family.

"Hello, Corrie," Harriet greeted me at the door, "come in!"

I smiled and followed her inside.

"It's so nice to see you again, Corrie!" said Rev. Rutledge, giving my hand a friendly shake.

"Thank you. I can hardly believe it's been two whole years!"

"Neither can I," replied Harriet. "As much as everyone missed you, now that you're back, suddenly it seems like only yesterday that you left. Do you remember Corrie?" she asked their daughter, who nodded shyly.

"Hello, Mary," I said. "You have grown since I saw you last."

Still she didn't say anything, but I did manage to coax a smile from her mouth.

"Well, come sit down, Corrie. Supper's all ready."

We sat down at the table.

"Lord," prayed Rev. Rutledge, "we thank you so much for bringing our sister and friend Corrie back safely to Miracle Springs. We pray that your will continues to be supreme in her life, that she continues to grow in stature as your daughter, and that seeking and proclaiming and living your truth continue to be the motivations of her life. Thank you for Corrie, heavenly Father, for all she means to her family and this community . . . and to Harriet and me. Thank you also now for this day, for this opportunity for fellowship, for this food, and for all the abundant provision you make in our lives. In the name of your son, Jesus Christ, we pray these things. Amen."

We lifted our heads. The room was silent just a moment. Harriet began passing the platter of sliced roast beef. I took a slice, then passed it to Rev. Rutledge.

Both Harriet and Avery Rutledge had changed in a different way than my family. Besides being just two years older, they seemed much more tired as well. They smiled and were full of cheerfulness, but neither of them seemed to have quite the energy that they had had before.

Harriet's limp seemed more pronounced to me, and Rev. Rutledge's face appeared to have aged more than just two years' worth. I don't know what his age was, but he was starting to look old, at least to my sight. His face was pale, and he looked several years older than Pa, even though I'd always figured them to be about the same age.

"Thank you," I said after a moment. "Your prayer means a lot to me."

"We are all so proud of you, Corrie," said Harriet. "The whole town . . . what you have done. I suppose we all tended to think of you as our own little Corrie, but then all of a sudden we'd remember that you were back East and involved with important and dangerous things, and then we'd realize what an important lady you had become. Isn't that right, Avery?"

"When one of your articles would be printed in the paper, why, the whole town would be talking about nothing else!" said her husband.

I smiled at the thought.

"Your own father most of all," added Harriet. "You should have seen that man carrying around extra papers and giving them out!"

Now I laughed outright. "He didn't really?"

"He did!" rejoined both Rutledges at once. "And there's no use his denying it because the whole town witnessed it!" added Rev. Rutledge, laughing now too.

"I thought *he* had become the talk of the town, being in the legislature and all," I said.

"To everyone but him, he was," replied Harriet. "But his own pride was more directed toward you than himself."

"Which is precisely why everyone thinks so much of your father," remarked Rev. Rutledge more seriously. "I don't think there's a pompous bone in his body. He's a humble man, and everyone loves him for it."

We continued to talk as we ate, both seriously and lightly, laughing together but also growing pensive at times.

"Do you miss teaching?" I asked Harriet.

"Yes," she answered, "but I have my hands full keeping a home and raising a family. And with the town and community still growing, it's my other job that keeps me busiest."

"Your *other* job?" I asked in surprise.

"She means as my wife," put in Rev. Rutledge.

"I . . . I don't think I understand what you mean," I said, half laughing, but confused.

"There are two ways to be a minister's wife," Rev. Rutledge explained. "Some women take the view that the ministry is only their husband's responsibility. They support and approve of what he does but do not take an active share in the work themselves. Then there is the other way . . . exemplified by my dear wife."

He smiled across the table at Harriet.

"In other words, she's involved in it with you," I said.

"Every step of the way," said Rev. Rutledge.

"Oh, Corrie, there are so many people with so many needs," said Harriet. "How can I not want to be involved in their lives? We've seen the community grow so rapidly, and there are many new families. Avery has begun a midweek service at the church, and I have been instructing some of the women on Saturday mornings here at our home. We had a meeting just this morning. I didn't mention it to you because you were just back, but I hope you will be able to join us. Almeda and Becky usually do."

"I would enjoy that very much," I said.

"There are other things too," Rev. Rutledge went on. "With the growth of the community there are so many more marriages and births . . . and funerals, unfortunately, as well. There are more people with more kinds of difficulties who seek counsel from one of us. And as the church congregation grows, so do its activities— picnics and square dances and money-raising projects. Committees have formed about this and that. There are always decisions to be made. And rarely, if ever, is there unanimity of opinion."

"Leading the church is more complicated than when you left, Corrie," said Harriet. "To be truthful, both Avery and I sometimes miss how it was in the fifties, just after the church was built."

"That's true," added the minister with a wistful tone. "At the same time, we wouldn't trade the growth for anything. The souls of men and women need food, and God has placed us in a position to help bring it to them. We thank him for it all, and we have certainly grown ourselves. But Harriet is right when she says that it is wearying. The ministry is no vocation for the fainthearted."

As they spoke, I could not help thinking of Christopher and the difficulties he had experienced during his time in the pulpit. And I could not keep from wondering what it *would* be like to be a minister's wife, though not once in my hearing had Christopher ever broached the subject of going back into active church ministry.

The conversation slowed, and the three of us fell silent a minute.

"What are you going to do now, Corrie?" Harriet finally asked.

I didn't reply immediately. Though I'd been thinking about nothing else but my future, I still didn't have a ready answer to her question. Besides, my future had two halves—the Christopher half, which I couldn't talk about yet, and the not-Christopher half, which I didn't know what I was going to do about, and which I didn't know how would fit into the Christopher half.

"I . . . I don't really know," I answered slowly after a moment. "All my thoughts were so bound up in just getting home, so now that I am here, I have to think about all the possibilities all over again."

"Will you keep writing?" asked Rev. Rutledge.

I thought a minute.

"I don't know," I said. "Probably . . . how could I *not* keep writing? I'll probably always keep a journal."

"What about newspaper writing?"

"That's what I'm not sure about. I might keep doing it some. But right now writing articles for newspapers just doesn't have the same challenge it did when I first started. I still like to write and express myself and find out about things and tell people about them. I don't know what this change is that I feel. Perhaps it was the war, and Mr. Lincoln's being killed—maybe that took away some of my enthusiasm for it."

It was quiet again around the table.

"At first when I wrote about things," I continued, "I suppose I was pretty idealistic. Maybe that's what comes of being young . . . and being a girl," I added with a laugh. "Mr. Kemble used to tell me that's why women couldn't make good reporters. Now I see that in a way he was right. I *was* pretty idealistic. I'm just thankful he put up with me!

"But seeing the war as close up as I did, and being at Gettysburg and helping Clara Barton and the others with the wounded in the Sanitary Commission brigade, watching men die with my own eyes, and then the assassination . . . how can you live through such experiences and not be changed?

"I still have hopes and dreams and things I'd like to write about. I still want to speak about truth, like you prayed for me, Rev. Rutledge. Yet I doubt I'll ever be quite so idealistic again—not after living through that terrible war. And I'm sure I'll feel differently once some time passes. But right now I'm not burning to get back to newspaper writing. After the war and the President's death, somehow it seems there's not so much worth writing about right now . . . and there are other things I have on my mind."

"Other things . . . like what?" asked Harriet innocently.

I blushed. I hadn't meant to say it like that. How could I tell her that what I'd been thinking about for the last several weeks was getting married and maybe even having children of my own some day!

"I, uh . . ." I fumbled.

"Corrie, there's something you're not telling me, isn't there!" said Harriet, a womanly twinkle in her eye.

I couldn't stop the blushing.

"If there is, I can't tell you about it yet," I said vaguely, but smiling too. "You'll just have to wait along with everybody else. And in the meantime," I went on, trying to change the subject, "I'll answer your question by just saying that maybe I'll go back to work for the Supply Company for a while. But I still haven't made up my mind altogether."

I could tell that Harriet would like to have asked me more, but she respected what I said. Then Rev. Rutledge rescued me from any further awkwardness.

"You will be at church tomorrow morning, won't you, Corrie?"

"Of course. I wouldn't miss it."

"I know everybody's anxious to see you again."

"I feel exactly the same way myself."

The conversation moved toward some of the other people of the community, and as we left the table, they were telling me about the new families who had arrived in the last two years.

The time went by rapidly. A little later we had tea and some cookies. By the time I finally rode home, the evening was thinking about getting dark.

CHAPTER 8

MIRACLE SPRINGS COMMUNITY CHURCH

We squeezed into the big carriage the next morning as best we could. They had probably all been doing it that way every Sunday for the past two years, but for me it was a wonderful and special event! I was reminded of so many past happy times as we rode, the whole family together except for Emily, into town for church.

We got there early enough to greet the other families as they arrived. What a time I had hugging and laughing and visiting and crying with so many old friends! The Wards were there, and Patrick and Chloe Shaw and their family, and Uncle Nick and Aunt Katie and the cousins, and the Peters, Doc Shoemaker, the MacDougalls, Marcus Weber, Sheriff Rafferty, Rolf Douglas and his son, Mr. and Mrs. Ashton, and so many others. Mrs. Gianini hugged me so tight I couldn't breathe. Mr. Bosely from the General Store was there with his new wife, and even Alkali Jones had come, besides lots of new people I didn't know. But when Pa or Almeda or Harriet introduced us, even they greeted me like they'd known me for years.

I was nearly tuckered out by the time Rev. Rutledge rang the bell for the service to start, which it didn't until ten or fifteen minutes late on account of all the visiting!

I can't think of many church services I've enjoyed as much as that first Sunday after my arrival back in Miracle Springs! I don't even remember what hymns we sang, but I know that no congregation had ever sounded so good to my ears.

Such a love for all these people was welling up in my heart that I could hardly contain it. It was as though my skin was size ten but my insides were trying to be a size fourteen! I just knew I was going to burst.

Well, I didn't burst. But I have to admit I was so distracted and so full of happiness and love and memories about the church and the town and the people that I scarcely heard a word of Rev. Rutledge's sermon. I don't even remember what it was about!

I was paying attention enough, however, to think it odd when he began his concluding remarks ten minutes before the hour was over. Considering what a late start we'd had, that wasn't a very long sermon.

Then I was even more astonished when I heard what he said two or three minutes later.

"It will come as no surprise to any of you," he said, "when I tell you that we have a very special person with us this morning. Most of you have already greeted her before the service, but I want to take this opportunity to publicly welcome Corrie Hollister back home to Miracle Springs."

Even though it was in the middle of a church service, everyone started clapping. I could feel myself getting red all over, but I smiled and tried not to show my embarrassment.

"Between you and your father, Corrie," Rev. Rutledge went on, "we've got just about more well-known people than any town the size of Miracle Springs has a right to. And even your father can't lay claim to having personally met Mr. Abraham Lincoln!"

Sitting on the other side of Zack from me, Pa laughed aloud, and the people clapped again.

Rev. Rutledge let it quiet down, then he waited another several seconds.

"We're all real proud of you, Corrie," he went on. "Whenever a newspaper would come with something you'd written, it made us all feel like we were part of important events because we were part of your life. We prayed for you, all of us in this congregation. We prayed that God would watch over you, that he would protect you and guide you and that one day he would bring you back to live among us again. And I'm happy to report that he has answered *all* those prayers!

"So now," he added, "I wonder if you would like to come up here and say a few words about your thoughts on this day."

I sat there between Zack and Becky, too surprised to move. I'd given a few speeches before, working for the Sanitary Fund and for Mr. Lincoln's campaigns, but speaking in church was different.

Before I even had much chance to think it over one way or the other, Zack was nudging me, and Pa was reaching over with his arm and smiling at me to go ahead, and behind me I could hear whispers of encouragement. So all of a sudden I was on my feet and working my way past Becky's and Tad's knees and walking up to where Rev. Rutledge was standing. He had a big smile on his face. As I walked up he hugged me, right there in front of the church.

"Take as much time as you'd like, Corrie," Rev. Rutledge said. "I can't think of anything any of us would rather do than hear what you've learned and would like to share with us." Then he motioned me to stand behind the lectern while he took a seat off to one side.

"I, uh . . . don't quite know what to say," I began. "I had dinner with Harriet and Rev. Rutledge last night, but they didn't warn me about this!"

Everyone chuckled, and a good-natured buzz went through the church. There was a shuffling in the seats, and I started to feel a little more comfortable.

"You can't imagine how good it is to be back . . . to be *home*," I went on. "Not that I didn't have many experiences and meet a lot of people I'm grateful for. I wouldn't trade the last two years for anything. I saw a lot and I learned a lot, some of it not too pleasant. Death is a dreadful thing when it doesn't come the way it's supposed to, that is, from God's hand. I don't think there's anything much worse on this earth than men killing other men, and I've seen more of that from this awful war we've been through than I'll ever be able to erase from my mind.

"So I reckon I did a lot of growing up while I was away, though only my pa'll be able to tell that for certain. . . ."

People turned and glanced toward Pa. He looked around, nodding his head, with a big smile on his face.

"I suppose every young person's got to get out and away from the nest of his parents at some time. I'm not sure what parents think when it happens. My pa and Almeda have always been gracious and supportive of me and all the things I've done, even though now when I look back I realize how foolhardy a lot of those things were. I must have had a pretty strong independent streak to have thought I could be a writer for a newspaper when I was barely more than a child . . . and a girl at that!"

Everyone laughed.

"And to have gone off chasing over half the state during the election of '56 and gotten involved in the election of '60 and then to have gone clear back to the East Coast all by myself—right in the middle of a war!—it's God's mercy I'm still in one piece! Looking back, I can't believe I did all those things! I had no idea how much danger I was always putting myself in.

"My brother Zack and I have been talking some since I got back, and I reckon we both have a heavier dose of that independent spirit than maybe is good for us. Maybe it runs in the family . . . maybe we got it from *you, Pa!*" I added, looking over in Pa's direction.

This brought more laughs, especially from Pa and Zack and Almeda.

"When I think about it, though," I went on, "I suppose my ma had a pretty good dose of it too. Anyway, Zack's been telling me a lot about things he's learned in the last few years about his independence too.

"What I'm getting around to is that young folks have got to get out and try out their independence sometime. Some do it at sixteen or eighteen, though in my opinion that's too young to be ready for it. Others, like Zack, do it when they're twenty-one. Then others like me wait till they're twenty-six to go outside the nest for a spell, and probably others wait till they're thirty or even older.

"So we go out alone and we see what we're made of, and we find out what independence is all about. We find out some good things about ourselves and some things maybe we don't like so much. And we find out about the kind of independence that *isn't* very healthy, like Zack's been telling me he did, because of how it acts toward God.

"Then if we're wise, eventually we learn what we're supposed to. And then we come back older and smarter and more grown up, and maybe more independent in the good way and less independent in the bad way. That's how I'm feeling, anyway—both more independent and less independent at the same time.

"Like I said, I don't know exactly what it's like for a parent to watch this process going on. I don't doubt that it's a mite painful at times. But when you're a young person, you don't have eyes to see that side of it very clearly.

"It's funny—and Zack, I hope you won't mind me saying this—" I said, glancing toward my brother. "The funny thing is, when Zack went away I could see the pain it caused Pa to have him gone. But it never crossed my mind that maybe *my* leaving home for these two years might be hard for him too. You just don't see things like that very clearly until the years and the hand of the Lord working on you gradually open your eyes to it."

I paused and took a deep breath. The church was so quiet you could have heard a pin drop.

"Pa . . . Almeda," I said, looking at them, "I am sorry if I ever had cause to give either of you any pain. I never meant to. At the same time, I want to tell you both, in front of all these friends, how appreciative I am of how you've let me learn and find out things on my own, always guiding and helping and talking to me, but letting me learn about independence too. Along with Ma, you're just about the best father and mother a girl could have. Or a fellow too, for that matter—right, Zack?"

"I'll give an amen to that!" said Zack loudly.

A few scattered amens were added to his from around the room.

"Now here I am again, home again," I went on, looking at the congregation once more. "And never has it felt more like home. Maybe that's something else getting away does—it shows you where your home truly is.

"I reckon that's what I'm trying to say above all—that as thankful as I am for the opportunity to go away and for all the experiences I had, I'm glad to be home. And I'm more thankful for my family than I can possibly say—"

All of a sudden I stopped, because tears had filled my eyes. I blinked hard a few times, then struggled to finish.

"Well," I said, trying to laugh, "that's more than I intended to say . . . and probably more than Rev. Rutledge intended too!"

I looked over at him with a smile. He rose and now walked up, put his arm around me, and stood beside me.

"I just want you all to know how much I love you," I added, "and I'm glad to be with you and among you all again."

I went to sit down beside Zack. To my surprise, everyone started clapping, and it went on for too long to be altogether comfortable.

As it died down, Rev. Rutledge spoke up. "I think that outpouring of sentiment expresses pretty well what the people of Miracle Springs think," he said. Then he looked down at me very earnestly and with a smile on his face. "We all love you too, Corrie!"

Then he bowed his head and gave the benediction.

Immediately after he was through, people started coming up to me and all the rest of the family, greeting and visiting and hugging and talking all over again, even more so than before the service had begun. I think there were more folks gathered around us, and me especially, welcoming me home again, than there were people shaking hands with Rev. Rutledge by the door. By the time everyone had left for home, however, I think most of them had shaken both our hands.

We didn't get home until an hour after the final amen.

CHAPTER 9

A NOVEL AND SURPRISING PROPOSITION

Gradually the days, then the weeks, slipped by, and the newness of being home grew less and less noticeable. I managed to keep busy cooking and cleaning, going into town to the Supply Company with either Becky or Almeda, writing in my journal, and of course writing nearly every day to Christopher.

Toward the middle of September I received a very long letter from Christopher that took me completely by surprise.

I was working at the Supply Company that day, still trying to catch myself up on the changes in the business. I'd been enjoying a good visit with Marcus Weber and Mr. Ashton and Mrs. Virginia Russell, the widow from Sacramento that Almeda had hired part time after Ruth had been born. Mrs. Russell now worked most days with the two men. The four of us were together in the office when the postman arrived. He said he'd seen me come into town so he had brought the letter over to me at the office.

I knew it was from Christopher immediately, and it was so big and thick that I couldn't help being embarrassed when he handed it to me. The others all looked at me, expecting me to open it. But I *couldn't* open it and read it with them all staring at me!

"I'll open it later," I said, trying to busy myself with some work.

But it was no use! That letter burned a hole in my pocketbook where I'd stuffed it with a show of nonchalance. It burned a hole in my brain all morning too. I couldn't think of anything else! Finally, midway through the afternoon, I left for home. I stopped

54

about halfway there in a place where I could read Christopher's letter thoughtfully and all by myself.

At first reading I didn't know quite what to make of it. But the more I thought about it the more it made me appreciate and respect him all the more. That he would be willing to go to such lengths to make sure our marriage was built on a solid foundation made me realize how much he cared about me, not just for right now, but for all the rest of my life!

I don't know if other people would agree, but that's how I took his letter. It made me feel all the more loved and all the more secure, knowing that Christopher was a man who took everything about his life with God seriously.

This is the letter he sent me:

Dear Corrie,

I want to talk to you regarding something I have thought and prayed about for a long time—actually, ever since I was in the pastorate. After considering the implications of our future together, I find that what I once advocated toward others can be no mere abstract teaching, but a policy I must consider carefully as I contemplate the course you and I should pursue. You will presently understand what I am attempting to say.

When I was pastoring in Richmond, as I have told you, my views on the subject of marriage differed widely from those held by most of my parishioners. It was not merely that certain members of my congregation would have liked to see me wed to their daughters, and I had no intention of doing so. The points of contention grew to encompass what many considered my radical notions on the subject—as if taking the holiest and oldest human relationship seriously enough to desire that it be strong, well founded, and giving God glory is "radical"!

As pastor, I was often in the position of having to counsel young people in preparation for marriage. Quite a few were not much younger than myself, actually, and one or two were older, since I was only twenty-five when I entered the ministry in 1859. (Perhaps too young, I now wonder.) Many of the people I was asked to perform marriages for were the sons and daughters of some of Richmond's most notable families. Later, when war loomed, others came wanting me to rush through a ceremony before hostilities took the young man away.

In every case, almost without exception, I found myself discouraged and disheartened, saying to myself, "These two people do not know one another in any depth. Neither do their respective parents have the slightest idea what manner of individual will be joining their family. This young man and young woman are not ready to marry. They are not prepared for the stresses that wedlock will bring to them. They need to pass beyond their present superficial feelings in order to build this marriage on a more solid foundation. They need more time—considerably more time—to prepare themselves."

As you might guess, my attempts to convey these sentiments to the young men and women and their families were not received gladly. The last thing either they or their mothers and fathers wanted was an overly zealous young pastor throwing a bucket of cold water over their euphoria. They did not want spiritual counsel. They did not want me to speak the truth. They did not want to be told that perhaps there was a better way to go about their preparations for matrimony—a way based on Scripture, a way based on God's intent for man and woman. All they wanted from me was a blind acquiescence to their desires so as to give the illusion of spiritual approval to plans about which the will of God could not have been further from their minds.

That was not something I could in good conscience do. I did not enter the ministry to preside over a societal club, but to confront people with the truths of God and his will for our lives. It was another of the several factors that finally made the pulpit untenable for me.

In any event, in my heart I knew that many of these ill-advised marriages could only lead to heartbreak. This is not to say that they all ended in divorce. A few did. But mostly it was a matter of the marriages I performed being built on sand rather than stone. A number of the young men were killed in the war, leaving widows and orphans behind. Even the marriages that did survive for a time could not be said to be strong ones. Almost invariably I saw futures constructed on hopes that could never sustain the giving and commitment and self-sacrifice so necessary between husband and wife if they hope to remain bonded together as one over a lifetime.

I saw marriages founded on mutual attraction, on financial considerations, on ties between important families, on the urgencies of the war. And ego, pride, vanity, and self were ever-present ingredients in the mix of factors—not only in the couples, but also in their parents, whose own social standing demanded the making of what is called a "good marriage" for their offspring. Unfortunately, their view of this so-called "good marriage" was almost always based on the worldly norms of a false set of societal standards—where money, reputation, power, and prestige were the operative factors.

Witnessing these tragic circumstances so frequently—and I do consider it tragic whenever the holy institution of marriage is undertaken with less seriousness than I know from Scripture God intended for it to be—caused me to consider not performing marriages at all. But that did not seem to be the answer. I labored over the question for some time before the Lord began to guide my thinking in a new direction.

As more couples from my congregation came to me for the purpose of being joined in matrimony, I began to encourage them to wait at least a year and to put that twelve months to good use getting to know one another. I even suggested that, if the war allowed it, the young man be invited to join his fiancee's family. My idea was that he would live and work with the future bride's parents for a year, ideally working with and alongside his future father-in-law in whatever activity the latter was engaged in. I suggested that the young woman spend the same period of time with her fiance's parents, living and working daily with her future husband's mother in that woman's home. If the war did not allow it, then I recommended waiting until hostilities were over and then embarking upon such a plan.

What a wonderful setting, I thought, for the parents of both the young man and the young woman to get to know personally and in great depth the individual they would be welcoming into their family!

This plan was such a brainstorm, such a revelation to

me, that I was certain all to whom I told it would be eager to adopt my plan in an instant. Ah, but how wrong I was . . . yet again!

The first young couple to whom I proposed it turned and left my office on the spot, saying that they would find another to marry them. They were not interested in all my spiritual talk on the subject. They only wanted to get married . . . and soon.

I was visited the next day by one of the elders in my church, a powerful man in the community with an attractive daughter of his own approaching marrying age. He had heard of my proposal from the father of the young woman and had come to tell me what he thought of the nonsense, adding that he hoped I was rid of such foolish notions by the time *his* daughter was ready for marriage, because he wanted her married in his own church. Furthermore, he added, he was uninterested in having any business dealings with whatever young man his daughter may decide to marry. If he was of a family of good standing and had means, that was what mattered. He saw no reason for two families to expose their personal lives to one another in such a ridiculous fashion.

This gentleman was far from the only one to react so. In fact, my proposal fell on not a single receptive ear. Again, as in the matter of my stance on the war, my views on marriage threatened to jeopardize my entire ministry. What am I saying? Along with the rest, it *did* jeopardize my ministry, with the result, as you know, of my ultimately leaving the pastorate.

But I was not dissuaded within myself. I continued to ponder the whole subject, and to study what I could find from Scripture. The story of Jacob and Laban's two daughters spoke to me particularly. Jacob loved Rachel so much that he worked not one but *seven* years for her father—only to be deceived in the end and be given her sister Leah instead. But did Jacob despair? No. He served as a faithful husband to Leah, then willingly agreed to work *another* seven years for Rachel. Even though Laban had lied to him, Jacob submitted to him for fourteen years.

After all that time, you can be sure they all knew each other very intimately. Jacob would have known his future father-in-law like a brother. How can one not know a man with whom he has labored side-by-side for fourteen years? Jacob and Rachel, likewise, would have known each other like sister and brother. They surely would not have married solely on the basis of physical attraction or superficial acquaintance! Fourteen years had passed. They must have truly loved each other!

As I pondered the account, I saw that even though Laban played him false, Jacob proved the worth and integrity of his character by being willing to work all those years. Both Rachel and Laban knew what manner of man they were getting!

And what a demonstration of a man's love! I love the passage that reads, "And Jacob served seven years for Rachel, and they seemed unto him but a few days, for the love he had for her." No wonder God was able so to bless Jacob that in time he became more wealthy than Laban himself and eventually gave birth to the twelve patriarchs of Israel!

I cannot say I determined that such a before-marriage apprenticeship with one's future parents-in-law could be termed a scriptural "standard." In the end, however, I *did* become persuaded that it was biblically sound and in line with God's intent. I was certainly convinced that God does intend Christian parents to play a more determinative and aggressive role in training their sons and daughters for marriage than is commonly accepted.

The conclusion of my reflections was the determination that even if I was unable as a pastor to communicate the importance of such preparation effectively, I would do it as a father. If I were ever *myself* blessed by God with a son or a daughter of my own, I decided that I would place such an injunction upon him or her before giving my approval to a marriage that *they* might consider.

Some would consider it a hard thing to exercise such control over his sons and daughters. But is it not the most loving kind of fatherhood imaginable to seek to protect one's own child and spare no effort to obtain the best of all possible future marriages for him or her? Is that not exactly what God is constantly doing for us—watching out for us, helping us, guiding us, instructing us, he the loving and protective father, we his obedient and submissive children? Has he not arranged just such a marriage for us with his own dear Son? Is he not working day and night, all our lives long, to prepare us for that marriage? How can our earthly lives look anywhere but to that coming heavenly marriage as our example?

Some perhaps consider God's overlordship a severe thing. But I say they know not what manner of Father their heavenly Father is! If they knew him, they would rejoice in his authority over every phase of their lives.

"Be it unto me according to your will, Father!" That is my constant prayer. It is the deepest cry of my being: "Oh, Father, watch my steps and guide me in your way in all things!"

But I stray from my purpose in writing to you, my dearest Corrie.

Let me continue. I was speaking of my thoughts if I myself were a father facing the marriage of one of my own.

If a young man were to come to me and say, "Mr. Braxton, I love your daughter, and I want to marry her," I would measure his character and the depth of that love by his willingness to go along with my proposal.

"I would like nothing more, young man," I imagine myself saying, "than to shake your hand as my son, and to give you my daughter as your wife. But first—I'm sure you understand—I must know what manner of Christian young man makes this request of me. So I ask you, do you love my daughter sufficiently to give yourself to me for a year, to live under my roof, to work with me, and talk with me and minister to people alongside me? Do you love her enough to make such a sacrifice—to earn the right to ask for her hand? Do you love her sufficiently to allow me to test your faith, to allow me to get to know you perhaps better than my own daughter knows you or even than you know yourself? Will you allow me to test your character as a man and as a Christian, to determine if I judge you worthy to be called my son-in-law?"

Such a one could well reply, "No, sir, I will be party to no such plan. It is not your right to decide whom your daughter will marry. That should be a decision between her and me alone. I am a free agent, an adult, capable of directing my own life, and I will offer to no other such a complete submission."

If this were his reply, then I would know that he did not understand the most fundamental of all human institutions, that of fatherhood. I would know further that his resistance to my authority and my oversight over his and my daughter's future indicated a flaw in his relationship with his heavenly Father—a flaw that goes by the name of independence. He has not apprehended his role as a child in submission to the heavenly Father's authority, and therefore he takes umbrage at the thought of submission to me as the father of the woman he would make his wife.

I would therefore have no choice, if I wanted the best for my daughter, but to say, "I am sorry, my dear, but I cannot consent to give your hand to this young man. I know you think you love him a great deal at this present time. But in time, believe me, his independence and resistance to authority would inevitably cause you grief as his wife. Because he does not grasp the most fundamental truths of fatherhood or childhood, he is therefore ill-equipped to be a loving and sacrificial husband and even more ill-equipped to step into the proper role as a wise father to your children."

I might hear my daughter reply, "But, Papa, he is young. How can you expect him to share your perspectives when you have been a minister and have been walking with God so much longer than he? He may well grow into all that you say."

"Then he would have been willing," I would reply. "Willingness is the indication of growth yet to come. No, my dear, of course I would not expect him or you to see things altogether as I see them. I look not necessarily for present level of maturity, but rather for *willingness*. A willing spirit is a spirit that *will* grow and *will* mature in time. But your young man was not willing, not even willing to inquire as to my reasons. He did not care to know my heart in the matter. And if he does not love you to that extent now, how much will he love you when the great stresses of life come to your marriage fifteen years from now?"

Oh, Corrie, I pray that you see what is in my heart! *Do* you see it?

During such a period of what I have, for lack of better term, called a marriage *apprenticeship,* all the facades would have time to be peeled away. Both parents would be able to know the quality of belief and the depth of character in the man or woman their son or daughter wants to marry.

What father does not want his daughter well provided for by a husband with foresight, integrity, and common sense? How better to determine whether a young man is capable of sustained work and a healthy outlook than to work alongside him for a year? And what mother does not want her son's home well ordered and his children well raised by a woman with homemaking intuition and skills, a woman who loves children and understands how they are to be trained? What better way for a mother to determine such things than by bringing her future daughter-in-law into her own home to work alongside her?

Perhaps such a plan would not work in every case. Oh, but how many premature marriages between couples ill-suited for one another might be avoided if parents thus took more responsibility upon themselves for a wise and well-thought-out decision?

How wonderful even if the young man and young woman could share time under both parents' roofs, perhaps for three of those twelve months, in an environment highly supervised by the parents. They, too, need to see each other with their hair down, in a family environment where stresses and strains reveal to the often cloudy eyes of love the stark realities of what a fiance may really be like when not on his or her forced best behavior.

Perhaps just as many ill-fated marriages would be avoided by the reconsideration of one of the two young people as from counsel by either set of parents. "I didn't know that's what you were like!" one might say. "I didn't know you were so prone to anger . . . so self-centered . . . so irritable . . . so lazy . . . such a poor cook . . . so moody."

I say, better these things be said, and the stars removed from the eyes now, while there is yet time, than after the marriage has been performed, when it is too late.

Am I too much a radical for you, Corrie!

I admit that mine is a far-reaching proposal, with astounding implications if Christians began practicing it in a widespread way.

I need not worry, for they will not.

Alas, it is the grief of my adult life to realize that most

Christians do not take their faith seriously enough to allow its light to penetrate into all the many and varied corners of their existence. Marriage is a sad case in point, as my short time pastoring in Richmond attests.

But I am one who *does* take his faith seriously. I want the light of God's truth to shine into every corner of my life where I can point it. And I know you share that desire. That is one of the chief reasons why I love you and why I want you to be my wife.

Well, this is not a treatise but an attempt to share with you something that is in my heart to do.

Clearly, what I have been explaining I have not had the opportunity to put into practice. I have no sons or daughters of my own, and none of those whom I counseled in this manner chose to follow my recommendation. All of a sudden I find myself contemplating marriage and realize that I had not given detailed consideration to what might happen in my *own* case! I honestly never expected to face this question, because I honestly never expected to marry. (That I could envision future children without ever considering where those children might come from can only be attributed to the unfathomable mystery of the mind. But that is exactly what I did.)

I have told you before, but I don't know if you can fully appreciate what a huge change you have brought to my life. I am the most surprised of all to find that a young woman as wonderful and as devoted to the Father as you are would love me. And one unforeseen result is that now I suddenly find *myself* right in the middle of my own ponderings, something I had not anticipated!

I have been thinking about this almost from the day I wrote you the letter I sent by way of Sister Janette, and have decided what I want to do. I must live by the same convictions I espouse for others.

Here is my plan:

Your father does not know me. In one sense, Corrie, you do not know me that well either. The time together with which the Lord has blessed us has been relatively quite brief, and there were many unusual circumstances that could have artificially drawn us together. I want both you and your father to know me—really know me in the intimate way in which family members come to know one another. For me to put to your father now the subject of marriage to his daughter would be to place him in a position from which he could not make a wise and prudent decision. How could he? He has no possible way to determine whether I will make a worthy husband.

Don't you see the wonderful protection there is in it, Corrie! Both of us are protected from allowing our love for each other to blind us to practical realities that only one who *is* married is capable of seeing.

I have never been a husband or a father. I cannot say with certainty whether I am capable of carrying out the responsibilities of either with the wisdom and love and sacrificial Christlikeness that both require. I love you too much not to want the very best for you.

What if that best is not me? How can I possibly know? Because men are so easily blinded as to their own motives and abilities, I am the *least* equipped to be able to answer the question insofar as it concerns *me*. And, dear Corrie, as much as I respect your maturity and judgment, neither are you equipped to answer the question as to what kind of husband and father I will make. You and I are both young, and your eyes, too, are clouded with love. If you will forgive my saying so, your judgment is no more to be depended upon than mine.

Similarly, how can either you or I know whether *you* are ready for marriage? How can we know how prepared you are to be a wife and mother? Like me, you have confessed that you did not expect to marry. Neither of us has spent years training and preparing ourselves for marriage. Is it wise for us to proceed?

But there is one whose eyes are not clouded, who is not young, who has been both a husband and a father for many years—a man who is a Christian and who has wide background in making decisions for himself, for his family, for his town, and even for his state. What wisdom such diverse experiences must have instilled in him. He is clearly in a much stronger position than either of us to evaluate the decision we face and to speak wisdom into our lives.

I am, of course, speaking of your father, and along with him your stepmother. If my father or mother were alive, then they too would enter into this process. But as they are not, the decision must rest solely with your parents and with you and me.

I want, therefore, to ask your father for more than your hand in marriage. I am going to ask him to allow me to submit to him in these ways I have spoken of. I will tell him that I do not want him merely to agree to what you and I would like to do, but that we desire to place the decision for what course we should follow fully into *his* hands. I will add that his decision must not be made until he knows me well enough and has seen me in sufficiently diverse circumstances to make a wise judgment concerning me.

Without pushing myself upon him, I want to ask your father if he would consider allowing me to work with him and your stepmother in whatever activities in which they are engaged, be it your father's mine or the freight company you told me about or tending animals or building him a new building, or anything else. As long as I have my daily sustenance and a place to sleep, whether it be a barn or perhaps with some friends of your father's in town, I will consider myself amply provided for.

With both your consent and his, my plan is to state our hopes of marriage, then to submit my way entirely to him for a year, at the end of which time he will be able to give us his decision and advise us in any way he chooses—counsel which you and I will gladly and eagerly receive.

I want to love you with the faithfulness Jacob demonstrated, and I want to prove that faithfulness to both you and your father. I feel it is right and proper and scriptural for me to earn the right to call myself your husband.

So that, my dear Corrie, is what I would like to do when I come to Miracle Springs, which I hope will be soon, before the year is out.

What do you think? Do you consider my plan altogether radical and ridiculous? I hope you do not. But I have been so in the habit of finding my ideas of spirituality looked askance upon by most with whom I share them that I find myself anxious about how you will react. Forgive me. I should trust you more than that. I will learn!

I am of the strong conviction that a man and wife must move together in all things, not separately. It seems that we must begin even at this stage to function as one, and therefore, though I am convinced this is the proper course to follow, I earnestly desire to know your heart on the matter. If it should not be as mine, then I would rethink and repray the whole matter.

I will await your reply to this proposition of mine. Obviously, I do not want to proceed with it if you have objections, though I sincerely think such a course would insure us a much stronger marriage.

My hope is, upon hearing in the affirmative from you, to take my leave of Mrs. Timms by the middle of October or the first of November at the latest. By then I will have all the crops in, she will be set for the winter, and our new man will be well able to take over my responsibilities.

Did I tell you that I found a man whom I have hired as replacement? Being able to rest easy about Mrs. Timms has taken a great load off my mind. Tom McKittrick is with us now and working alongside me, learning everything about the place. I like him very much. He is a Christian and single, like me, with a heart to serve his new employer, which is the primary character quality I was looking for.

In any event, once the farm is well set for winter, then I will travel west by train and stagecoach, planning to arrive in California before the worst of the winter weather sets in. I would hope that would mean before Christmas.

What a delight it is even to contemplate being able to share Christmas with you again!

But I will wait for your answer.

> Yours fondly and
> with anticipation,
> Christopher

I had not been home ten minutes from town before I was in my room, pen in hand, writing my reply to Christopher's letter:

Dear Christopher,

Yours is the most novel proposition about marriage I have ever heard!

Have no anxiety about me or how I might react to something. Even where you and I may differ—I am sure we will from time to time, though the thought of it now seems foreign to me—I know you do nothing without careful thought and prayer. If I do not understand something, or even if I don't agree, I still trust you. I know I can depend on your dialogue with God, and that if you are in error he will show you. And since you want so badly to hear him and to do nothing but what he wants you to do, I know you will be listening whenever he corrects you. So I need worry about nothing at all!

But you especially have nothing to worry about with regard to your proposal. Everything you said makes so much sense I don't know why every Christian family doesn't adopt it. I love the idea!

You're right about my father's experience and wisdom, though he probably wouldn't admit it. I don't think he realizes what a man of God he has become through the years. I have no doubt that he and Almeda will love you, but I understand everything you say and am more than willing to consent to it.

I must admit, however, that perhaps the possibility of your being here for Christmas makes everything else you said seem insignificant in comparison. The year "wait" will not really be a wait—it will be fun! I never anticipated being married, so I'm in no hurry for that. I'm just in a hurry to be with you, my wonderful, wonderful friend, and to know that all my family knows you. I'm excited about the thought of having you here with us for a whole year before we embark on that new phase of our lives.

I am so excited. I can't wait to see you again!

Yours always,
Corrie

CHAPTER 10

THE SAME . . .
YET NOT THE SAME

I kept busy through the autumn. Gradually the oak trees went gold and red, then brown, and the temperature began to cool. Autumn arrived, and the Sierras began to think about snow again.

I was thinking a lot too—of the past, and the future, and what was the same and what was different.

I found that every change in the landscape reminded me so much of former times, of all that God had shown me through his world. I remembered some of the articles I had written, and I dug the papers out of the box where they were stored and read them over again. Then I decided to go visit some of the places that had prompted the articles and also some other places that had been special to me or that had caused me to think about things in a new way.

Walking in the woods above our house, I thought of the time I'd walked there long ago and come across Little Wolf for the first time. That had been right after we'd arrived in California. Now it seemed too long ago.

A few days later, Katie and I had a nice visit and several good laughs reminiscing about when she had come to California, thinking she was going to marry Pa. The article about her and her apple seeds started the conversation, but then we talked about so many things besides. We ended the morning by going out to pick the last of the ripe Virginia apples off the trees. That afternoon we peeled enough for two cobblers—one for each house—and stored away enough for plenty of Christmas pies.

Another day I took a ride up Buck Mountain the way I'd gone with Mr. Jones during the blizzard, and I had a nice visit with the Wards, who still lived in their place up there. Mr. and Mrs. Ward did not seem a day older. And yet the whole visit with them was different because *I* had grown older. They now seemed so much closer to my own age. I had found that was true with all the adults of Miracle Springs.

Riding slowly down off the Buck, I found myself reflecting about all the places and people I was renewing my acquaintance with.

Everything was the same, and yet not the same. Things didn't look or feel quite the way they had before. I thought a lot about that. Did they seem different because they had changed slightly, or was it because I was now looking through the eyes of an adult rather than those of a girl. Even though two years wasn't that long a time to be away, it had been years since I had seen some of the places I was now visiting. How much different might my memories be, after being worked over and over in my mind as I grew, from the reality of what those places really were like?

It probably shouldn't have surprised me that all this reminiscing occupied my mind. I had always liked to think about things and to ponder what they were like and what they meant. But even after I had been home several months, I would still find myself noticing something and saying to myself, "That's different than I remember it."

Also, glad as I was to be home, I was having difficulty settling down into a regular routine. When I left home two years before, I had felt an uneasiness, wondering how long I would be gone and when I would return. Now I found almost the reverse happening. Now that I was back, I couldn't seem to fit comfortably into the life I had known before.

I puzzled over this for some time as I rode down off Buck Mountain.

———

I took a number of long, peaceful walks during the fall. Quiet moods came over me more often. I don't know if it was because of being older and seeing everything through more experienced eyes,

eyes that had seen more of the world. Or perhaps it was from being here in California for the first autumn in more than two years and appreciating it and relishing in it all the more because I'd been away.

I read Mr. Thoreau's book again from cover to cover during the fall, recalling to mind so many places that had looked different after I learned to look at nature through Mr. Thoreau's eyes.

I was returning one day from a long walk in the woods. As I emerged into the clearing up above the house, my eye caught the entrance of the mine, now still and empty. They hadn't worked it much for several years now, though Pa still puttered and clanked about with a pick now and then.

I had not been near the mine since coming home. Now, suddenly, the youthful urge to explore came over me. A lamp was perched on a rock ledge just inside the entry. I had several matches in my pocket, and I tried to light it. There was still some kerosene left, and the wick took. I adjusted the flame, then picked the lamp up by the handle and crept farther into the black mouth that had been the center of our lives so long ago.

The mine cave was like everything else in Miracle Springs— it looked the same but felt different. There were a few changes from how I remembered it, whether from work Pa and the boys had done or my own faulty memory, I didn't know.

It was early in the morning. It had been quiet outside, except for the birds. In the cave, there wasn't a sound.

I walked slowly straight through the open subterrane. Even though my eyes were wide open and there was enough light from the lantern to see by, I wasn't concentrating or focusing my eyes on the rock of the walls.

Suddenly the back wall confronted me. I nearly knocked my head as the roof slanted down to become the end of the cave.

This wasn't where the wall was supposed to be, I thought to myself. It should be farther back. Perhaps the way curved around to lead deeper into the mountain.

I turned and looked all about me.

No, I *had* reached the end. I had walked all the way through the mine.

Puzzled, I turned my light back and held it up, gazing all

around me. The cave was so much narrower and shorter than I remembered. Then again I turned to face the back wall. It had always seemed so huge whenever I'd come in before, when Pa and the others were pounding and chipping and hammering away.

At last it struck me . . . the cave hadn't shrunk—I had grown. Not in body—I was no taller than when I last saw it. But my eyes were bigger . . . my inner eyes, which had seen a great part of a huge and enormous world.

Once more, all I had witnessed came back to me. These eyes of mine had traversed this whole country. They had watched terrible battles and seen blood, anguish, and death. How could something like a little cave not seem smaller after all that?

I thought of all the people I had met who had had influence on my life—President Lincoln, Sister Janette, Clara Barton, the dead boy at Gettysburg whose eyes had seemed to cry out to me . . . and of course, Christopher Braxton.

Those people, those experiences—they had changed me.

Of course, I had known that already, but somehow I knew it more deeply now. Maybe what made me aware of it at a deeper level was realizing that I could never go back and make it the way it had been before. I had seen too much, been too many places, known too many people. Things would never be the same.

A light brightened the cavern behind me, adding to the thin illumination of the lantern I held. I turned.

There stood Zack.

"Breakfast is waiting you, Corrie," he said.

"How did you know where to find me?" I said with a smile.

"I was out in the stables . . . I saw you go in. What are you doing here anyway?"

"Oh, just renewing old memories, I reckon."

Zack nodded as if he understood perfectly what I meant.

"But the mine seems smaller than it once did," I added.

Now it was Zack's turn to smile.

"It happened the same way with me," he said, "after I was away in the desert with Hawk."

Mostly I think my moods during this time were quiet because

everything I saw, every place I went, every thought I had, I wanted to share with Christopher.

Before, I'd been able to appreciate things just for the way they were. But now something was missing when I just looked at them all by myself. Not that I couldn't have told Almeda or Pa or Becky or Zack or Tad about them. But to make the experience complete, I would have to sit down with Christopher and know that he was looking at the things that were so special to me through the same eyes that I was.

Oh, I wanted to show him everything! Every leaf, every twig, every tree, every path through the woods, every rock where I sat, every bend in every stream, every sunset, every sunrise . . . everything! I wanted to take him to all my special places, ride into the mountains together . . . everywhere!

I know the others noticed the quietness about me, and I think they understood. Of course I'd told them about Christopher, and they were certainly aware of the letters flying east and west between Miracle Springs, California, and Richmond, Virginia. Nearly every day that fall, I imagine there was probably a letter from one of us going one way or the other in just about every state between the Atlantic and Pacific!

Out of respect for Christopher's request, I tried to be careful not to say too much when I talked to the family about him. For there to be a man in the life of the girl Ma had as well as predicted would be a spinster was news enough.

Pa teased me a lot about it. Almeda and I had several woman-to-woman talks, and she seemed to understand why I needed not to say too much. Pa, too, and the others, never did ask straight out if we were going to get married. When I told them of Christopher's plans to come for a visit so soon, before the year was out, they knew it was serious enough between us. But still they didn't ask me direct, and I was glad of that. I wouldn't have wanted to face the question!

Gradually news filtered through the town that a young man was coming from the East to see Corrie Belle Hollister.

Then there were those that began to wag their tongues, and I started getting questions and comments about "my beau." With people outside the family I was able to laugh and give a vague answer without too much trouble. Some of the old busybodies who took pleasure in spreading the town gossip didn't like it too much, but it didn't bother me to let them stew. It was none of their business anyway, and they would find out soon enough—that is, if and when Christopher wanted them to.

It wouldn't surprise me if a few of the women in Miracle Springs were having a contest between themselves to see who could be the first to find out "what Corrie's up to!" I had to laugh to myself whenever I'd see one of them coming toward the Supply Company or when one of them would begin talking in confidential tones to me after church. I knew they were going to try to engage me in friendly conversation long enough for me to let something slip that they could then take back to their friends like a precious jewel they'd discovered!

CHAPTER 11

THE FUTURE COMES CALLING SOONER THAN ANTICIPATED

There was an early snowfall in mid-October. It didn't snow in Miracle Springs, of course, but from the cold storm that blew in we knew it had to be snowing in the higher elevations to the east. The last thing Pa said before we went to bed was, "There's gonna be snow in the morning someplace."

Sure enough, next morning you could see white up in the mountains. By then the storm had blown by. It was a brilliant sunny day, and I knew the minute I got up that I wanted to ride up where the snow had fallen.

I didn't have a horse of my own yet. Raspberry, my old favorite, was gone. So I borrowed one of Zack's that he called Blue Star, because of a splotch of dark, almost bluish-black, below his eyes on his pale dun head, and he and I set out up the mountains.

It was a gorgeous day. The remaining chill in the air, so clean from the snowfall and rain, made everything fresh and clean, and just breathing the air into my lungs felt good. I followed one of my favorite trails up through the foothills to the east, along Grouse Ridge and up toward Fall Creek Mountain, where I'd ridden on my twenty-first birthday.

About halfway up I began to encounter snow, and by the time I reached the ridge, Blue Star's hooves were plowing through five or six inches of fresh white powder. Finally I stopped, tied the horse to a tree, and walked about for probably an hour or so—until my feet inside my boots were nearly frozen and I couldn't stand it anymore!

Mostly I remained among the pines where the snow wasn't so deep, just enjoying the absolute stillness of the white and green world about me. Every tree was a perfect Christmas tree, with boughs and branches bending under the weight of the snow. Occasionally one would let go its crystalline burden, which fluttered to the ground with a powdery silent puff.

No revelations came to me. I don't even remember what I was thinking about. The peaceful stillness was enough to enjoy all by itself.

Suddenly ahead of me appeared three deer—all doe, I think, or else a doe and two of her children. They were all about the same size, and one had antlers. I froze in my tracks, trying not to make the slightest movement.

They were walking slowly about in the snow, looking for grass and leaves to eat, and they saw me just as I noticed them. They all stopped, glancing up at me, and held absolutely still, ears cocked.

There we stood, me and the three deer, staring at one another from a distance probably of about twenty feet. No sound disturbed the forest. I don't even remember the single chirp of a bird. I don't know how long I stood, probably five minutes at least, and maybe longer. It was one of those moments when time seems to stop.

There has always been something inside me that wanted to communicate with animals. I don't mean talk to them, but to get inside that place within them where we are alike, to touch that common creatureness that the higher animals must somehow share with man.

There is something indescribable about having eye contact with a wild creature. A peaceful love sort of solidifies the moment, and the memory of it, even days later, can make you smile like you have a secret. You also feel that kind of bond with horses at times, or at least with special horses, like Raspberry, that you've gotten to know and that you feel know you too. It's different than communicating with a human being, but feeling that momentary bond with an animal is wonderful in a completely unique way.

That's how I felt as I was staring at the three deer—a sense of brotherhood and sisterhood from being part of God's creation, part of his huge family of created beings. Somehow, too, it fit in perfectly with my quiet mood.

Then, just as suddenly as I had come upon them, one of the deer lifted its right forepaw and took a step toward me. For a second I thought it was going to approach closer! What a thrill it would be to establish such a trusting bond with a wild animal that it would come up to you without fear! But then it turned its head, set down its foot in the other direction, and took several slow steps through the wood. The other two followed, and the next moment they were gone.

Disappointed, yet with a full feeling of contentment, I sighed, then turned myself and walked back to Blue Star. Like I said, my feet were nearly frozen by then and I was ready to ride back down the mountain.

As I returned, I was in for a real surprise.

I had unsaddled Blue Star and tended to him and was just starting toward the house when Tad came running out to meet me.

"Corrie, Corrie," he called, "you've got a visitor."

My heart skipped at least three beats, and I caught my breath. I felt my face go pale.

"It *can't* be . . . it's . . . it's not—" I stuttered as I broke into a run.

"No, it's not Christopher. How could it be? You just got a letter from him yesterday."

"Who is it then?" I said, gasping for breath and trying to calm myself down.

But by then we were already on our way through the door and inside the house.

There, seated in the family room talking with Pa and Almeda, was the editor of the *Alta* in person!

"Mr. Kemble!"

"Hello, Corrie," he said, rising and walking over to shake my hand.

I couldn't get over my shock. I'd never seen Mr. Kemble anywhere but in his office at the paper in San Francisco. What in the world was he doing in Miracle Springs . . . and in our own family room?

"Mr. Kemble's just been telling us what a fine writer he thinks you are," said Almeda.

"One of the best on his paper," added Pa.

I looked at Almeda, then at Pa, then again at Mr. Kemble, but I still couldn't find any words to say.

"But . . . but what are you doing here?" I said finally.

Mr. Kemble laughed.

"Well, young lady," he said, "I came out here to talk to you."

"Just to see me?"

"That's right. When you didn't reply to my letter, I thought I'd better get myself up to Miracle Springs to see you in person. Do you mind discussing some business with me now . . . today?"

"No . . . no, of course not," I replied, moving toward a chair. Mr. Kemble returned to his seat as well.

"Would you like to speak with Corrie in private?" asked Almeda. "Drummond and I would be happy to—"

"Oh no, Mrs. Hollister, please stay. I'm certain the business proposition I have to discuss with your daughter will be something you will want to discuss as a family—that is, if Corrie has no objection.

I shook my head. "Anything you have to say to me I would be glad for Pa and Almeda to hear."

"Then may I bring you another cup of coffee, Mr. Kemble?" said Almeda, moving toward the kitchen.

"Thank you, yes."

"Drummond?"

Pa handed her his cup.

"Corrie, anything for you?"

"I think I'll make some tea," I said, excusing myself as politely as I could and joining Almeda in the kitchen.

CHAPTER 12

MR. KEMBLE'S OFFER

Once we were all seated again with our cups of coffee and tea, Mr. Kemble started right in.

"As I told you in my letter, Corrie," he began, "since you are back in California, I hope that I will be able to persuade you to join the staff of the *Alta* in a more permanent fashion than has been our arrangement in the past."

Now that I had had a few minutes to get used to the editor's presence in our home, my brain was again working clearly.

"As I recall," I said, "you took the liberty of calling me 'the *Alta*'s own Corrie Belle Hollister' when you printed my story about Gettysburg."

"Well, I . . . er," he said, clearing his throat, "I simply thought that our readers would appreciate knowing our connection."

"And now you would like to make it more official?"

"Yes, that's it exactly."

"At more than two dollars an article?" I said with a smile.

He nodded, though without seeming to see the humor of my statement.

"I only wanted to make sure it wasn't going to be like those first articles I wrote for you," I added, "where I did all the work and you gave me next to nothing for it."

I have to admit I enjoyed needling him a bit. Now that I wasn't quite so feverish in my desire to write, and now that I had traveled in the East and seen so much, and especially now that I had enough confidence to know I could write decently, I wasn't so nervous in talking to him. "You weren't all that generous to aspiring young writers back then, you know," I added with a half-grin.

Mr. Kemble squirmed slightly in his chair. He wasn't enjoying this nearly as much as I was!

I saw Almeda looking at me funny. I think she thought I was being rather hard on poor Mr. Kemble. I would explain it all to her later.

"You, uh . . . you must admit, Miss, uh, Miss Hollister," he said nervously, "that you were young and inexperienced, and you were—"

He stopped abruptly, reconsidering what he had been about to say.

"And I was . . . a girl?" I added. "Is that what you were going to say?"

"You must understand, Miss . . . er, Corrie, that things are different for men and women. A woman simply is not paid the same as a man. I'm certain your stepmother—"

He glanced quickly over toward Almeda, then back again.

"—I'm certain she would agree."

"Even for the same work?" I said. "You once told me yourself, Mr. Kemble, that my writing was as good as some of your men reporters?"

"That is just the way it is, Miss Hollister. I don't see what you can expect me to do to change it."

"In the East, they valued my writing just for what it was."

"As do I, Miss Hollister, I assure you. I would not have come all this distance if I did not think you were a very gifted writer. That is why I want you on the *Alta* staff."

"But . . . at compensation less than what a man's would be?" I said. "Is that why, in your letter, you hinted that my writing was only of interest to your female readers?"

Again Mr. Kemble squirmed.

"I'm sorry if I offended you by anything I said," he returned. "I think we will be able to arrive at a mutually beneficial financial agreement."

"I was not offended," I said, smiling now. "I only wanted to be absolutely clear about what you meant." I think I'd been hard enough on him for one day. I saw Almeda and Pa exchange glances and they each smiled slightly.

Mr. Kemble looked at me, puzzled by the change of my expression. But never one to let an opportunity slip by, he quickly sent the conversation off in a new direction.

"I took the liberty of drawing up a contract," he said, pulling some folded papers out of his coat. "If you're agreeable to it, this will make you an official *Alta* writer with a base salary each month, plus an additional payment for every article of yours the paper publishes."

At first I could hardly believe my ears. He was offering to make me a salaried staff writer! It was more than I could have dreamed of a few years ago.

"Sounds like the man's serious, Corrie Belle," said Pa, speaking now for the first time. "That's a right generous sort of proposition."

"What are the stipulations?" asked Almeda, whose business experiences with men like Franklin Royce kept her eyes open to the strings that were always attached to such agreements.

"No stipulations," he said.

"May I see the contract?"

He handed it to Almeda. She scanned over the first page quickly. "It says here this is an 'exclusive contract for three years,' " she said after a moment.

"Yes, I felt three years to be a reasonable duration."

"My question regards the exclusivity," rejoined Almeda.

"What exactly does that mean?" I asked.

"By signing an exclusive contract," replied Mr. Kemble, "you would agree to write only for the *Alta*. You would be on our staff. That is why you would be given a monthly salary. It's all very standard."

"Standard, perhaps," remarked Almeda, "but restrictive on Corrie."

"What do you mean, Almeda?" I asked.

"You would not be free to take your articles to other papers, even if they might pay more for them. You would have to publish everything with the *Alta*."

"That is true, Mrs. Hollister," said Mr. Kemble. "However,

you must keep in mind that the monthly salary will more than compensate Corrie for the difference."

"Perhaps. But it still places control of Corrie's writing in your hands, not hers."

"Some control, but not absolute control. As her editor, I would look out for her best interests. It is not my objective to be restrictive."

"What about articles of mine you might not want to publish?" I asked. "Would I be able to take them elsewhere?"

"Certainly. If we did not feel them suitable for the *Alta,* I would have no objection to your placing them elsewhere."

As he explained it, the offer did sound almost too good to be true.

"Of course," Mr. Kemble went on, clearing his throat, "if you think this is not a fair proposal, you are free to simply continue writing on your own and hope someone will print what you do, without any guarantees. This contract would make you a member of our staff and guarantees you a regular income. Surely you see the value in such an offer, and surely you realize that I would not make it if I did not want to print your writing. I would anticipate that the *Alta* would publish everything you sent me."

Almeda did not comment further, but simply handed the contract back to Mr. Kemble.

"What would I have to do to earn the salary?" I asked.

"Simply provide us with a minimum of two articles per month."

I thought for a minute before saying anything else.

"To tell you the truth, Mr. Kemble," I said finally, "I'm not sure how much writing I want to do right now."

They were hard words to get out. Part of me wanted to jump at the opportunity right then and sign the contract immediately!

"You're not giving up the profession?" he said with a look of alarm.

"No," I replied. "I'm just thinking about a lot of things and wondering what it is God wants me to be doing right now. I've been writing for so long, maybe I'm just a little tired of it."

"Perhaps the offer of this contract will make you reconsider," he said.

"Perhaps," I replied. "But I have to think and pray about it. I haven't been home very long, and I certainly don't want to make a three-year commitment without much more consideration."

"I understand," he said. "I shall leave the contract with you for your consideration. I sincerely hope you will decide in the affirmative."

"How much is the salary you were talking about?" I asked.

"Twenty dollars a month. That would be for a minimum of two articles. For every article above that, you will be paid an additional fee."

"How much per article?"

"It would depend on the length and subject matter. I would estimate usually between eight and ten dollars."

CHAPTER 13

WHAT TO DO?

After Mr. Kemble left, Pa and Almeda and I talked some more about his offer.

Pa responded to things more from what his gut instinct told him. Almeda tended to analyze things from her business background. I suppose it's just the opposite with some men and women, but that's the way it was with Pa and Almeda. Even when it came to votes he had to make in the Assembly, Pa usually went more by what his heart and conscience told him were the right thing than by what all the facts and figures might say about a certain issue.

"What do you think I ought to do?" I asked both of them.

"I think you should give it a lot of serious thought and prayer," said Almeda. "Once you sign an agreement like that, no matter how good it might seem at the time, it ties you down for a good long time. That can put a lot of pressure on you that might even make it harder for you to write."

"Do you trust this fellow Kemble?" Pa asked me.

"Yes. He's got his views about women not being worth as much. But that's a difference of opinion, not untrustworthiness. I reckon I trust him."

"Even if a man is trustworthy," Almeda said, "or a woman, for that matter, he still has an agenda he's trying to make happen—in a business deal, I mean. Mr. Kemble would not have made this offer unless it benefited *him* and his paper. That is not to say, Corrie, that he isn't to be trusted or that the offer might not be for your good too. It only means that business people make offers that benefit *them* primarily. So you have to be careful to look out for how it's going to affect you."

"So you think I shouldn't do it?"

"No, that's not what I mean—only that you have to make sure you realize what it might mean for you. What if a year from now you didn't want to write two articles a month? If you sign that contract, you'll have to whether you want to or not. That's all I mean—think it through thoroughly."

"What about you, Pa?" I said, turning toward him.

"You want to know what I think?"

I nodded.

"Well then, Corrie Belle, here's what I think," he said. "I think it's a generous offer. Three years ago you might have figured it was about the most exciting thing that could happen to you in the world. But I don't think you have any idea what an important young lady you've become for the folks in California. Unless I miss my guess, you ain't just a celebrity here in Miracle Springs, but a lot of folks in Sacramento and San Francisco have been following your writing too."

"Oh, Pa, I'm no celebrity!"

"You mark my words, Corrie. Kemble ain't the only one that knows you're back in California. My guess is that Kemble understands well enough that folks know who you are, and he's aiming to latch onto you before someone else does."

"You're saying I shouldn't do it?"

"No, I reckon I'm just saying it won't do no harm to bide your time while you're praying for God to show you what he might want you to do."

Both of them had given me good advice.

So I did what Pa had said and bided my time. I read over the two pages Mr. Kemble had left, though half of it didn't make the least sense to me. I guess that's the way contracts are.

Of course, I realized that I couldn't make any decision without Christopher knowing about it and telling me what he thought. I wrote him a long letter telling him everything that had gone on. And I prayed a lot about the decision too.

I was seeing that the older a person gets the more careful you have to be in making decisions. Things carry more consequences.

When you're young, the results of something might last only for an afternoon or a day or a week. But as you grow older, the choices you make have longer and longer results.

I hadn't really considered what the consequences might be when I'd decided to answer President Lincoln's letter and go back east. As it had turned out, I'd gotten involved in the war pretty close up. I could even have been killed. I'd been away from home for two whole years and had more or less supported myself by my writing. And I had met Christopher! So many things had happened that I could not have foreseen—and all as a result of that one decision to travel east to see Mr. Lincoln.

Of course, God had protected me, and most everything had turned out for the good. But there was a lesson to be learned from my experience, and that was, as Pa had said, that it doesn't do any harm to bide your time.

I figured that was pretty sound advice, along with what Almeda had said. Don't rush. Consider the consequences. Pray for God's leading. Think how the decision would affect me, not just today, but next year.

CHAPTER 14

TALKING IT OVER WITH CHRISTOPHER

Dear Christopher,

I told you in my last letter about the visit from Mr. Kemble of the *Alta*. I've talked a lot to Pa and Almeda about it. Their advice was good, but now I find that Mr. Kemble's visit has sent my reflections going off in so many directions.

As badly as I always wanted to write, it is so strange now to find myself apathetic toward it. Especially when what I always dreamed of—newspapers wanting *me* to write for *them* instead of my having to beg somebody, anybody, to pay attention to my passions—has now come to pass.

What is wrong with me? Why have I changed?

I think I know. *You* cannot be the one to answer my question, for you *are* the answer!

You have changed everything!

Because of you, Christopher—will the wonder of your love never cease astonishing me?—I find myself wondering about the future in a new way. I've noticed that choices and decisions carry more weight the older one gets. And of course, at the center of that wondering is what will become of you and me. What will Pa say to your plan? Will you and he like each other? I know you will, yet part of me cannot help being a little frightened.

In any case, I find myself thinking about our future together and thinking about how my choices now might affect that future. For so long, though I have tried to listen to God's leading and to pay attention to Pa and Almeda, my choices have been my own to determine. I suppose I have been even more independent than many young women in their twenties because of my writing and traveling, and because I had no one else to consider.

But now that is all changed. Now I have to—I *want* to—consider you in everything I think, in all I do, in every decision. My life is no longer my own to live by myself.

As this change has come into my thinking, I have to ask myself how everything in my life will fit into yours. If a husband and wife are to be anything, it seems to me, they must be first and foremost *together*. They must be traveling the same life's road as partners and comrades and friends.

Oh, Christopher, do you understand what I am trying to say? It always seems that I am babbling when I try to convey the deep things I am thinking about to you. I hope you occasionally make sense of my words!

Always before, the only thing I considered was whether something seemed right for me to do—for me. I wrote because *I* wanted to write. I went to the East because it seemed right *to me* to go, and I came back to California because that, too, seemed right *to me*.

Now that I am back here, however, and everyone asks me, "What are you going to do now, Corrie?" and I am faced with writing offers and other possibilities—I can no longer decide by asking what seems right *to me*. Now it has to seem right . . . *for us*.

This brings me to the bigger question, "What *is* right for us, Christopher?"

Does marriage have to bring an end to goals and dreams you had before? Should it? Does the larger question of sharing your life with another mean that lesser personal goals disappear? I do not think this is true, yet certainly they must change.

Oh, so many questions!

What do *you* think I should do about Mr. Kemble's offer? I need your help and your prayers. Should I sign the contract? Might God want me to? The staff position he is offering would require a lot of time and work, and I don't want to find myself in the position of having to choose between you and my writing. But that's silly, isn't it? I just don't know where my writing fits in with our future.

I want you to tell me exactly what you think about this. Please be really honest with me.

Christopher, it seems that my thoughts run in circles these days! So many thoughts chase one another, and sometimes I can't seem to make them stand in line.

For example, I feel such a peace about us. You're too much a part of my life for me even to pretend otherwise. Yet I have to confess that sometimes I am overcome with fear that something will happen and I will lose you, Christopher, and then I can't bear it.

I'm sorry for thinking it, yet I am sure it is the Lord leading me in these thoughts. For then I realize I have to be willing to bear anything for God's sake—even losing you. I must be willing to do what he says in all things. Isn't that what it means to be Christ's follower?

I know that is what you want for me, and for yourself too. Yet . . . if I'm truly a disciple, it won't matter whether you want me or not. However, I want to be a disciple . . . *and* your wife. And I really do believe the Lord has brought us together. . . . Do you see what I mean about the circles?

Oh, Christopher, I long so to see you face-to-face.

As much as I like to write, it is sometimes hard to be writing to you, because I want to talk to you directly and ask you questions and tell you things. And I so miss hearing your voice. Do you remember last Good Friday, when you talked to me about choices, and about Jesus' willingly *choosing* to do what he did?

That's what I miss—talking and listening to you. There is so much I want to write, but I can't write all day long!

Where *will* we go together, Christopher? What will be the road the Lord will set us upon to travel together?

Not knowing that, how can I know what the future will hold? Not knowing that, how can I make a wise choice about writing or about Mr. Kemble's offer . . . or about anything?

Maybe I should just ask you: What do *you* think I should do . . . what do you *want* me to do? Whatever you say, I would willingly and eagerly agree to.

I hope you make sense of all this!

Yours,
Corrie

Dear Corrie,

Of course I understand! Everything is different for me, too, now that you are part of my life, though the differences for me are different than the differences for you.

Did I really just say that? Do I sometimes make absolutely no sense to you?

What I meant was that the difference you speak of has to do with your former independence. You are now trying to look anew at your future through interdependent eyes . . . to consider me and our life together as you make your decisions.

For me, however, the change lies in looking toward my future at all. After I left the pulpit and went to work for Mrs. Timms, I did not look ahead in any way. I simply endeavored to be faithful day by day to what was put before me. Envisioning the future was too painful, because I could not do so without the past coming back from my church experience to haunt me.

Now, suddenly, I find the sun has risen over the horizon of my future! Doors have been thrown open wide that I thought were closed to me forever. Far from being too burdensome to contemplate, the thought of sharing my future with another now seems almost too wonderful to be true!

To answer your question—of course you are right in thinking that a husband and wife must first and foremost be *together* in all things. I like what you say, that they must be going along "the same life's road as partners and comrades and friends." That is most certainly what I want to be with you—your partner and comrade and friend, sharing the adventure of life with God!

I'm sorry, though, but I cannot tell you what you ought to do about the newspaper offer. Of course, I want nothing but what is best for you—what makes you happy, and what brings you satisfaction and fulfillment. To achieve that end will be one of my highest objectives in life. But there is always a deeper question than happiness, satisfaction, and fulfillment. You do not need me to tell you what it is, for you already know. The most important question is not what *I* want you to do, but what *God* wants you to do (and what *God* wants me to do . . . and what God wants *us* to do). That is the highest question of all, the one we must ask about everything.

I too am sometimes haunted by fears similar to the ones you confess—fears of losing you. And what you say about it is absolutely right. We must be *willing,* even though we hope and pray such is not the case.

As I see it, willingness is the key to many, many doors of growth. In this life, God is always in the process of pruning away our self-wills. Even though the knife hurts when the branches are cut away, he only does it to strengthen his life within the main trunk of our lives. Don't you love the lessons of John 15?

Still, one of the reasons I am so confident that it *is* God's ultimate will for us to be together is this. If he had said, "Christopher, you put together a woman who has all the qualities you find desirable in a wife, all the characteristics you admire, and a personality which blends with yours completely, and I'll give you that woman," I don't think I would have devised anyone so nearly perfectly suited to me as he did when he made you!

I cannot tell you how happy it makes me to contemplate you as my wife! I get carried away like this whenever I think of you!

As to the specific thing you ask me about, I cannot say whether it be something God wants or does not want. Even if I did know, I am not sure I would say. Perhaps later it will fall to me to make these kinds of decisions for both of us. But right now it seems to me that this is a decision that rests between you and God.

I will pray that God will show us both the answers to the various decisions we are facing.

How good God is to us, is he not! to give us such common goals and visions about what we want our lives to be!

Equally yours,
Christopher

CHAPTER 15

UNEXPECTED MAIL AND NEW QUESTIONS

The week after Mr. Kemble's visit, Pa had to leave for Sacramento for an important session of the legislature. He was gone two weeks.

When he came home, he said, "I told you, Corrie, you're gonna be the most important Hollister in this state!"

"Why's that?" I laughed.

" 'Cause everywhere I went, people were asking about you, asking if you were home yet, asking when I was gonna bring you to Sacramento with me so they could meet you, asking when they were gonna see some more of your writing. You're a celebrity! I tell you, Corrie, I reckon just about everybody knows the name Corrie Belle Hollister."

"Aw, go on, Pa—that can't be true!"

"I wouldn't lie to you!"

Almost as if he had planned it, two days later I got another letter in the mail, this time from the San Francisco *Register*.

Dear Miss Hollister,

We at the *Register* have followed your writing for several years with the keenest interest and respect. You have a very personal method of communicating that would be of great interest to our readership.

With all due respect to your previous relationship with one of our competitors, we would be honored to be allowed to submit an offer for your consideration. For articles printed in the *Register* our minimum fee would be fifteen dollars, and more for those considered of a significant nature.

We would also be honored to discuss with you, during your next visit to the city, the possibility of your joining our permanent staff. Such a position which would carry a monthly stipend of twenty-five dollars, plus an additional payment for each article written.

If such an arrangement would fit into your plans, it could be structured in any manner in which you deemed beneficial.

Respectfully yours,
G. Smythe, Editor
San Francisco *Register*

And then still another letter, similar though not as specific, came the next week from the Sacramento *Bee*.

I couldn't believe it! How had all these papers suddenly found out that I was back in California? Maybe Pa was right, and the articles I had written when I was back East had gotten more attention at home than I'd realized.

I still didn't agree with Pa about being a celebrity, but something was up—that was for sure.

Following the letters from the *Register* and the *Bee* were occasional solicitations from still other papers inquiring about articles I might like to write for them. I also received two invitations to speak, one from the Christian Women's Society of San Francisco, the other from the Legislative Ladies Auxiliary in Sacramento. Both groups said I could speak about anything I wanted, but were especially interested in my experiences during the war and my visits with President Lincoln.

I must admit I was gratified by the offers, but I didn't know what to do about them. Now I had an even longer list of decisions to pray about!

All I would have had to do was agree to even some of the offers, and suddenly I would have been right back into the same kind of busy life I had been living for the past five or six years.

One day I went into my room, closed the door, sat down on my bed, and began to pray.

God, what do you want me to do? All of a sudden it seems that there are so many opportunities staring me right in the face. I always figured before that when something came up, that was a sign that you were behind it and wanted me to do it. But now here are a bunch of things coming along that I'm not sure that's true about. Do you bring things into our lives that you don't want us to do, but you bring them along so that we'll have to think about them and ask you about them?

I stopped.

What a huge new thought that was!

What if God allows things to come along that he *doesn't* want us to do, but that look at first glance like something he *would* want? What if he allows them to come just so that we will think and pray more seriously and consider the consequences more than we have before?

Perhaps that is part of the growing-up process for God's children. Perhaps that is how God intends to make spiritual *men* and *women* of us, by giving us harder and harder decisions to face, decisions with more consequences . . . and giving us a greater share in the making of the decision.

Maybe he intentionally makes his leading more difficult to figure out because he wants us to think about what his purposes might be on deeper levels than we did when we were young.

These were all such new ideas.

I thought about them all the rest of that day, and these ponderings started another whole vein in my correspondence with Christopher. Late that night, I pulled out the letter from him I'd just gotten the previous day, read it over again, then I stayed up past midnight writing back to him. Afterward I could hardly hold in my anxiety in awaiting his reply.

CHAPTER 16

MUTUAL COMMITMENT

Dear Christopher,

You are right, God is so good to us!

I hope you did not misunderstand me before. Laying down my previous independence so that we might share life together is not, as you seemed to think I said, burdensome to me. I rejoice at the thought of it! I only say that it is different than it has been before, and that is an adjustment I must make in ordering my thoughts and decisions.

It seems, however, that I shall have ample practice in making such adjustments. I have already written you about the offers I received from the *Register* and the *Bee*. This week I heard from two other newspapers and also from two groups that want me to come speak. I have not yet responded to any of these offers, but they have certainly sent me to my knees—and now to my writing table, to seek your counsel.

Thinking and praying about the future of my writing from the perspective, as you said, of what God wants has opened a whole new region in my brain. Have you ever considered that perhaps God brings things to us that *look* like they are from him, but that he *doesn't* want us to pursue? That he might give us opportunities that he wants us to say *No* to instead of *Yes*?

At first the very idea of it was perplexing. Why would he do such a thing? Surely God is not one who would intentionally confuse us.

Then I thought, maybe his reason is to help us learn to

distinguish between *good* things . . . and the *best* things.

I have found that in praying about the opportunities I am facing, I have been forced to consider everything from a much larger point of view, looking not just at right now or even next year, but also at what is really important over a whole lifetime.

I have found these thoughts leading to another question: What are the very *best* things in life? What is *the* most important thing to spend one's energy on?

This has caused me to contemplate where God may take us together in life. What *best* things does he want Corrie Hollister and Christopher Braxton to be about?

Will our lives matter?

What will we do that will be significant when we are old? What will we look back on and say, "That counted for something that was a *best* thing, not merely a *good* thing"?

Will we have helped anyone?

Will anyone know God more intimately because of us?

Will we have made any difference in God's kingdom?

What value does life have if we do not do these things?

These questions in turn led me to thinking a new way about all the decisions facing me. They have caused me to ask: Is my writing, for its own sake, of value?

It used to be enough for me just to write about anything, as long as I could communicate something that seemed to me to be true. At first I wrote about blizzards and nature and trees and people. After that I began writing about elections and politics, then about war and the Union cause.

Now, perhaps in all those things I did write about truth. But who will know God better because of what I wrote about Mr. Lincoln or the war? Who will know God better because I wrote in support of Mr. Fremont and Mr. Stanford?

Has this larger perspective come into my consciousness because I am older, or because I know you and we have talked about these things? Wherever it comes from, I now find myself wondering if what we do, in order to be of lasting value, doesn't need to have some connection to helping people . . . and not *just* helping them, but helping them know God better?

That is what I desire my life to be about.

I want to help people with you, Christopher. I want to be

part of your compassion for the men and women that God sends our way. If my writing can do that, then I hope it pleases God to use it. But if it does not serve that end, then perhaps there are other avenues the Lord would have me journey down with you.

You must have considered all these questions. The passion to help people know God burned in you. That is why you went to seminary and entered the ministry.

Now you write that for the first time in years you are considering the future. But what do you think when you look forward? Do you think you will ever go into the pastorate again? What *will* you do? Will you farm, as you have been doing for Mrs. Timms? Will you load sacks of grain on those strong shoulders of yours? What will you and I do together? Where will we live?

How can I possibly commit myself to any plans about my writing when so much is undecided about my life with you? Even though our union may be more than a year away, time passes quickly and I want to begin now ordering my steps *with* you, not on my own.

Am I being too terribly presumptuous to talk so freely of our future together? Forgive me, dear Christopher! But I cannot think of any of these things without you at the center of them.

Yours,
Corrie

Dear Corrie,

Perhaps you are being presumptuous. But who am I to say, for I suffer from the same presumption!

Yes, I do think of the pastorate at times, and yet returning to the pulpit is not something I seek. To tell you the truth, the thought of it frightens me more than excites me. After my previous experience, though I trained for it and desired it in my youth, I would approach such a position now with trepidation. I fear I am not one who could, with good conscience, temper my convictions to please the power brokers of a congregation—and alas, such seems the requirement upon which a so-called "successful pastorate" is based. Thus I cannot at present envision any church having me.

Having said that, however, let me add that my passion

for ministry is undiminished. The *ministry,* in its broader sense, I still seek with my whole heart—ministry to people, to individual men and women and children, the ministry of spreading truth, the ministry of taking cool cups of the water of the gospel to a thirsty world.

The burden of my heart is exactly as you wrote in your last letter—your words ringing with such resonance in my being. Your questions, the cries of your heart, echo mine exactly.

Will our lives matter? you ask. Will we have helped anyone? . . . Will we have made any difference in God's kingdom?

Yes, my dear Corrie—yes to all these questions!

Yes, because we will give our lives to God, and he will use them for his purposes, to accomplish his ends in his kingdom!

Oh, Corrie, let us commit ourselves to live *not* for ourselves, *not* even for each other, *not* for what we can gain in life, *not* for what wealth or pleasures we can amass, *not* for what others may think of us, *not* for what either of us may become in the world's eyes . . . but for our God. Let us commit ourselves to live that God's purposes—not our own—may be accomplished in every corner of our beings. Let us dedicate ourselves to become a man and woman whose characters outshine our achievements. Let us dedicate ourselves to live for others, not ourselves.

Oh, how desperately distant is such a vision of the Christlike nature! Yet my soul longs for nothing else.

I want to be like Jesus, Corrie! Is it too high an objective, too presumptuous a thought? I cannot believe it. Rather, I believe it is the single prayer God most wants his creatures to pray—even though we will never, in this life, attain to that goal.

Do you share the cry of my heart? I know you do, yet I am compelled to ask. I want to hear it from your own lips.

You ask what road God will set us upon to travel down in our life together.

This is the road, dear Corrie—the path of giving him our *selves,* that the nature of Jesus may more and more reflect itself in and through us.

Ah, what a wondrous thought!

It is not what most young couples seek that stirs my passions, my dear Corrie. I seek not the love that sets eyes aflame and hearts aflutter, as I so often witnessed in my congregation. My love for you is not that kind of an emotion, and perhaps is not born in feelings or emotions at all. It is higher and greater (although my heart does smile and skip a beat whenever I think of you). It is the love of the shared journey toward Christlikeness.

God, our Father, carry out that work within us! Father, create in me a new heart, transform my being by your Spirit, make me to become like your Son!

Oh, Corrie, when I think of these things, I ramble on and on! And the vision burns all the brighter because I am so painfully aware of the distance between my own shallow, selfish self and that image of Christ toward which my prayers are directed.

The people in my former church, when I spoke of such a work the Father wants to perform—spoke of it personally and passionately as I am speaking now to you—oh, how utterly they misunderstood my intent! They misconstrued my words to mean that I thought I *did* reflect that Christlikeness which is the focus of my prayers!

"Holier than thou," they accused me of acting. "Who do you think you are?" they said, "to pray such lofty prayers? Are you so much more spiritual than we are?"

They could never understand that it is precisely because of my own weak and fleshly nature—the fact that I am incapable of reflecting my Lord—that I pray so earnestly and diligently for the Father to effect the transformation within me! What I can *never* do, I pray with all the more passion for the Father to do.

I pray you understand, Corrie! But again, my own doubting nature betrays me. You *do* understand, I know it.

And how grateful to God I am to be privileged to share life's road—and the adventure of giving our lives to him to use for his ends—with you, my dear, dear, Corrie Belle Hollister!

As seems inevitable, my plans are finding themselves delayed. Earlier I had hoped to be away from here by early November. Though things are going well, that now appears impossible. How long the delay will be I do not know. I am still hoping to depart Mrs. Timms and Virginia by mid-November, at the latest by the third week of the month.

Is there a boardinghouse in Miracle Springs where I will be able to get a room?

Yours,
Christopher Braxton

Dear Christopher,

Yes . . . yes, Christopher, I do understand!

Here are the words from my own lips—or my own pen!

I too pray to be all that God wants me to be! I share the desire of your heart to be made like Jesus!

Yes, that is the road I want our lives to travel down together, that God might have his complete will in and through us!

I commit myself, with you, to live not for what we can gain in life nor for what others may think of us nor what we may become in the world's eyes. With you, I commit myself to live that *God's* purposes—not mine, not ours—may be accomplished in every corner of my being. I dedicate myself to become a woman whose character outshines my achievements. I dedicate myself to live for others, not myself.

Whatever the people in your church may have thought, I admire you, Christopher Braxton, for your high and lofty aspirations. How could I think of sharing my life with one who did otherwise?

For a Christian young woman like me, there could be no marriage but to a man whose desire in life is to serve his God. But I have had to know you in order to realize that truth. I did not know it before because I had never known a man like you. Knowing you, as I said, has changed everything. The idea of sharing life with someone who does not share these most important of life's goals is now too distant a thought even to contemplate.

Even should you die tomorrow or suddenly forget about me, I have this awareness: It would be a far better thing to spend life single than to marry, even for love, outside the shared commitment of values and purposes that you and I have in common.

I am coming more and more to understand you and what you are trying to stand for and do and be as a man. I have faith in what God is doing in you, in the man he is making of you, in how he is using you in his kingdom. I have faith in your faith—does that make sense? And I am willing and eager to follow you and be part of your life, wherever God leads you.

I also feel more and more that we are being—and maybe already have been—set apart. We have to have faith that God is carrying out something special in us, and we cannot lose sight of that, lest we falter and choose second best. We are being called to stand, and perhaps in some ways to stand alone. It doesn't matter if people don't understand. What matters is whether we are an open channel for God's work.

I am excited about life with you!

I am so thankful to God that I know you!

I cannot wait to lay my eyes upon you again!

Yours,
Corrie

CHAPTER 17

A QUIET DECISION

During this time, as Christopher and I were discussing the future on a new level, sharing our desire to let God's will be done in our lives, I began to realize that the career decisions I'd been wondering about had already been made.

The good wasn't necessarily the best.

Besides, the thought of a lot of travel and activity jarred with the peaceful side of me that was quietly waiting to see a certain Christopher Braxton again. I needed to talk to him about everything and pray with him and to do it face-to-face—before I could feel sure about the choices I was making.

So in the end I decided, like Pa had said, to keep biding my time. What was the hurry? I had a whole lifetime ahead of me. Opportunities would continue to be there. I didn't have to do all there was to do right then.

If writing for newspapers and speaking to women's groups were things that God truly wanted, he would make it clear enough when the time came. But right now was a time to make sure Christopher and I got a good start down God's road together.

So I wrote to the two women's groups, thanked them for their interest, but told them I wouldn't be able to accept their invitations. I also wrote to Mr. Smythe at the *Register* and the editors at the Sacramento *Bee* and the other papers that had contacted me, telling them that my future writing plans were undecided at this time, but that I would keep their offers in mind.

The last letter was hardest of all to write.

It wasn't that there was any doubt left about whether it was the right thing or not. I knew it was. I could even say it was what I wanted now as well.

But the offer represented so much of what I'd always thought I'd wanted. For how many years had I dreamed of just this moment! Even though in my deepest heart I was sure, I couldn't help feeling some lingering pain from the decision at the same time.

It was just after noon on a warm fall day.

Before putting pen to paper I had to take a long walk in the woods—not to think about my decision any further, but just to be alone. Sometimes even when you make what you know is a right choice, a sense of melancholy goes with it.

That's how I felt on this warm fall afternoon. There was a feeling of loss because I was letting go of something, letting go of a dream that had been with me a long time.

I cried a few tears. Quiet tears.

I was giving up something because God had given me something better. I had no second thoughts. I was happy . . . but my happiness had a little melancholy mixed in with it.

I came back to the house, sighed a few last sighs and wiped away the final tears. Then I went to my room, sat down at my desk, and wrote the final letter.

Mr. Edward Kemble
California *Alta*
San Francisco, California

Dear Mr. Kemble,

I appreciate your offer, and am more flattered than I can tell you that you considered it important enough to journey all the way to Miracle Springs to see me in person. I apologize for not answering your first letter. I simply had no answer to give.

I am afraid I still do not. My future writing plans are undetermined at this time. Therefore, I must decline your offer. I am enclosing the unsigned contract with this letter.

I must tell you that I have had other offers as attractive financially as yours. However, I do feel a loyalty both toward you and toward the *Alta*. Therefore, when the time comes that I have an article ready for publication, I shall contact you first.

I am sorry for baiting you when you were here about not paying women enough. Though I consider my writing worthy of consideration on its own merit regardless of my gender, I do understand how things stand. You have always been more than fair with me—except perhaps for a few articles right at first, but I forgive you!—and I am deeply appreciative of all the support you have given me through the years.

Your most recent offer was more than generous. My declining it in no way reflects a dissatisfaction with your proposal. My plans are simply uncertain at this time, and must wait to determine what course my life will take.

Sincerely and with gratitude,
Cornelia Belle Hollister

CHAPTER 18

ANOTHER JOURNEY WEST

November came.

It brought increasingly cold days in our town, snow flurries higher in the mountains . . . and more and more agitation in my heart. For every day brought Christopher nearer!

As my thoughts found it increasingly impossible not to dwell on him, I spent more and more of my time at my desk. The letters were too many and too long to include here—except for a very few, and these only partially.

Dear Christopher,

The time is approaching. I fear I will die of anticipation before you arrive!

I know I will not be able to send you many more letters because you will be gone before they reach Virginia. (I hope you receive this.) I will keep writing you, however, and present you with a great stack of unsent mail the moment you arrive.

Winter is gradually coming. It is not so severe where we are here in the foothills, though nights get very cold. Miracle Springs does not see a great deal of snow, though we are so close to the mountains that the snow is very near.

I have said nothing to Pa or Almeda or the family about your plans other than that you are coming to California to see me. They suspect more, I am sure, than that you will drop by once or twice for afternoon tea and coffee. I have spoken with Mrs. Gianini, who runs a boardinghouse in town, and asked her to keep a room for you. She will get it ready when you have a more certain idea of when you will arrive.

Yesterday I happened to run into two girls I have known for a long time—Jennie Shaw and Laura Douglas. Well, they're hardly girls now, any more than I am, though they are both several years younger than me. I hadn't seen them since I got back, and we had a nice long visit. They both told me about young men they like—Jennie's practically engaged from the sound of it. All they could talk about was how handsome their fellows were, and then they'd start giggling and carrying on.

I felt so out of place.

That must have been one of those "divine appointments" Almeda used to tell me about. Just when I'd written you about people not understanding and having to stand alone, then this conversation came along. I wonder if God was trying to see if I really believed what I'd told you!

I tried to tell Jennie and Laura about you, about the relationship we have, but I could tell they didn't understand. I told them that we were such good friends, and they looked at me strangely. I tried to tell them how we talk (or write) about everything and about how more than anything else we want to grow as Christians together. They *really* couldn't understand that!

I felt both hurt and sorry for them at the same time. I don't mean to say that their two men aren't nice. But it just seemed that they had no idea what a friendship with a man, especially one you're thinking about marrying, ought to be like. What kind of a marriage can they have without the kind of friendship that you and I have?

Later it began to bother me even more that Jennie and Laura couldn't understand about us. I just couldn't explain it to them because by trying I would have had to bring it down to their level where romance is all they think about, not the deeper kinds of relationship. It was so frustrating.

But then I had a revelation—here I go again, you poor man!

When something is right and you know it, you don't forsake it just because no one else can understand it. Even if a million people don't understand our commitment to each other and to the Lord, that doesn't mean we forget about that commitment in order that they might understand us better. Just because another might not understand about what we want in life doesn't mean it isn't worth working for and holding on to.

(Now that I see that written down, it seems so obvious. Oh, sometimes I think God works so slowly in me. I force him to plod through the side roads!)

Then that same night, as I prayed, I found myself thanking God for what he is doing in our lives—and do you know, Christopher, there's no end! He has been so good to us. He has devoted such time and effort to bring us to where we are.

You have spoken of your time of loneliness after you left your pastorate, of how much God used that. My time earlier this year after I left you in Virginia and then when I went up to New York—when I thought I'd never see you again—was much the same. We have both grown when we've been alone.

Thinking of that, I began to wonder if the growing would stop after we were married. (Am I being too terribly bold, dear Christopher!) Then comes my new revelation—it won't!

It won't stop, Christopher. It won't even slow up. Happy or sad, remembering God or even forgetting him for a time, like you wrote about—what we do won't keep *God* from doing what he wants to do!

We'll still be who we are after we are married, though our relationship will no doubt be different than it is now. We'll be one with each other, one with Christ. No, the growing won't stop. It's only begun, and it's picking up momentum.

I wondered for a time when you said your love for me wasn't an emotional feeling. I didn't understand at first. But now I do because I know the same kind of love. It isn't based on the kind of romantic and emotional, heart-fluttering kind of feelings that Laura and Jennie talk about. Those kinds of feelings aren't dependable. What you were describing, and what I now understand, transcends all earthly feelings.

It is a *spiritual* love, isn't it, Christopher? That's what you were trying to get me to see!

It's not less than the other . . . but so much *more*! It is a fulfillment of something so much greater that God intends to flow between a man and a woman. It is something we don't control, because it has been given to us.

I do not mean that it is not emotional, because that is part of it too. Sometimes I long for you to hold me tight and never let me go again. (Oh, I am being *so* bold!) But it is more than *only* this. And I fear young women like Jennie and Laura only know that small part of it, and so therefore cannot know fully what love is meant to be.

You and I are surrounded by love, a love so much greater than what we could ever have for each other. It is greater because all our love is given to God, and all his love is given to us until you can't distinguish any difference.

Oh, Christopher, you mean so much to me because I know you care for me with Christ's love, which is ever so much more than man's alone. Nothing will ever change that. It is good what has happened, and is happening, between us.

> Yours fondly and, right now,
> also very "emotionally"!
> Corrie

Dear Corrie,

Believe it or not, the day is nearly at hand. I leave for California next week!

By the time you read this I will probably be away from Mrs. Timms' farm and on my way to you! So you will be able to reach me no longer. Yet I shall continue to write you, as you did along your way, even if I should outstrip my letters and arrive before they do.

Something inside me simply *must* write. It used to be in my journal, now it takes the form of letters to you. I have always found that my thinking isn't complete unless there's a written component to accompany the mental part. It is as though my brain is incapable of entering into all its functions by itself—my fingers and pen need to be part of the process.

Most preachers, I suppose, are the kind of men who can "think on their feet," who can express themselves eloquently as the ideas first occur in their brains. I do not have that gift. I have always found myself singularly at a loss for what men call "the right word" when first it is demanded.

I have always needed to go through a process of thought—questioning and examining and analyzing some new point of inquiry from many different angles—before a synthesized order begins to dawn into my outlook. Out of this order, conclusions and perspective and a proper course of thought and action gradually begin to reveal themselves. I am rarely able to reach this final point of balanced perspective until I have written down my thoughts on the matter. It is out of the writing that the order and conclusions emerge.

A ready example springs to mind. Even though I had been thinking and praying about it for years, it was not really until I sat down to write you concerning my thoughts on a parentally supervised premarital apprenticeship that the whole plan fit together into a harmonious and scriptural order. That accounts for the length of that letter. (I hope you did not fall asleep reading it!) I was really doing two things at once—yes, I was writing to you, but at the same time I was sifting the ideas and getting them settled within myself.

I have to do that with everything—to think through my ideas on many different levels and from many different angles . . . so that I will know my conclusions are valid. Writing about it—thinking on paper, as it were—helps toward that end.

Do you see what I mean, Corrie? You are a journal keeper and writer too. Is it anything like this for you?

It has caused me no little grief in the past when people have taken my confidence in discussing some disputed spiritual point as evidence of arrogance or pride. Although I must confess to a certain share of human pride, I fail to see the arrogance in my having thought through and prayed about some matter in more depth than another and then expressing my emerging conclusions with boldness. It seems to me that people like to see confidence in those who agree with them but are put off by confidence in a man whose well-constructed views differ from their own half-baked opinions.

I think my assertions have especially confused people because I am not the sort they expect boldness from. I am really more of a timid man than you might realize—often embarrassed and without words when I first meet people, and I have often wondered what they think of me at first meeting.

I am wandering dreadfully from the point at hand—and yet I sense your forgiveness. Oh, but I love writing to you, Corrie. Knowing that you care and are interested in what I think makes more difference than you can possibly realize.

Even what I have been attempting to explain is something I do not recall thinking or writing about in quite this depth before. The process is happening right before your very eyes! It seems I cannot begin to write without ideas emerging onto the page before me that I hadn't previously considered.

And now my time is gone, and I must post this letter.

With anticipation for the journey that will be so soon upon me, I am, as always,

Yours,
Christopher

Dear Corrie,

Now I am on my way to California!

I left Richmond yesterday, traveled north on the *Richmond, Fredericksburg*, and *Potomac*, and then east, no doubt on the very line you took. I am sitting in a relatively quiet coach on the afternoon of my second day, ready at last to set pen to paper again to you.

The many feelings that swept over me as the train pulled out of the Richmond station are impossible to describe.

Mr. McKittrick, the young man who took my place at the farm, drove me into the city with the two cases that contain my few worldly possessions. Mrs. Timms shed a few tears when I left the farm—the poor stoic woman!—and a lump rose in my throat as well. We had become more attached to one another, each in our own way, than perhaps we realized.

But once on my way, with every clack of the great iron wheels along the thick iron rails beneath us, I could feel my past life fading into the distance and new vistas opening before me. I could literally feel former weights and concerns slipping off my shoulders with each mile.

Please do not misunderstand me, I have no regrets for

the path in life I have chosen and where it has led me. Although there were heartaches and times of great loneliness, I would trade none of them for what the Father has shown me of himself through them. Yet how could I not feel a great exhilaration to anticipate walking through these new doors he has opened for us, especially when you will be walking through them with me? How could I not feel a bursting exuberance at the thought of seeing you again?

With all these things on my mind, sifting through the past five years to find meaning in it, at the same time as I was looking excitedly ahead, the miles went by rapidly. . . .

As I read the several pages of rambling thoughts from Christopher's hand, I could sense what he'd written to me about earlier—that he was struggling, even as he wrote to me, to find what he called "perspective" and "order" in this great change that was coming to his life.

I could not help remembering all the thoughts that had filled my own mind both when I'd left Miracle Springs to go east and then when I'd boarded the train in Pennsylvania to begin my journey home. Of course, on that last journey I'd had Christopher's wonderful surprise letter to keep me company, and *he* had occupied most of my thoughts for several days!

For an introspective person, travel is always such a thought-producing thing. Going someplace new has always sent my brain off in a dozen new directions. I could tell Christopher's journey was doing the same for him. He was thinking about me, and about what it meant that he was crossing the entire country. Every mile he described new things he saw and what they made him think about. But traveling also made him look back (as it always did for me) and reflect upon what he was leaving behind. He was wondering if he would see people and places again . . . wondering what the future held. He was excited and expectant, yet thoughtfully and reflectively so.

I received a stack of letters that he'd written three days in a row—pages and pages. How wonderful to get to know someone you love so well! I did nothing but read his letters all afternoon—all of them completely through twice from start to finish.

CHAPTER 19

A SAD LETTER FROM CHICAGO

After Christopher's happy letters of beginning, I hurt for him so when the following one came.

Dear Corrie,

I am sitting in a lonely hotel room in the great city of Chicago, feeling lonelier and more despondent than I think I have ever felt in my life.

Oh, that my Corrie were here! Just to talk to her would comfort me in my hour of desolation.

Traveling far from home can be so sad and lonely. Did you ever feel such things? Some persons are more prone to depression and melancholy than others, and I must confess that I am such a one. Though I love solitude and do not need constant involvement with people, yet there is a sense of loneliness that comes upon me at times and renders me quite disconsolate.

All around are people. The city bustles with activity. But there is no place where one such as myself can feel at home. That the Savior had no place to lay his head takes on a deeper, more poignant meaning.

That is how I feel this morning, Corrie. I have this room where I can lay my head, but it provides no home for my journeying and discouraged soul.

You are far away. God himself is far away. I feel so alone, and all I can do to reach out to you across the miles is put these scratchy marks we call words onto this piece of paper.

It seems it will not satisfy. Alas, it is the only consolation I have.

Early yesterday morning, on the train, I chanced to meet a dear but needy woman with two lovely children. They boarded the eastbound train in Toledo, and immediately my heart went out to them. They were nice looking all three, well dressed, and bore none of the signs a first glance would associate with poverty. The mother could just as well have been a woman of means and gentility. Indeed, she carried herself with a poise and confidence to indicate such.

Somehow—I cannot actually recall how it came about— we engaged each other in conversation. She was a fellow believer, and we began to converse about many subjects of mutual interest about the Christian life—church experiences, favorite passages of scripture, and even a common passion for the world's lost, which drove her, I must say, even more deeply than it does me.

If I did not know better, I would have thought the woman an evangelist herself, even a prophetess. She was astonishingly articulate considering, as she freely shared without the least shame, her lack of formal education. I asked her how she came to be so knowledgeable in the ways of God. She answered that she had sought him in his Word and that he had revealed truth to her in her own spirit.

We had such fellowship, Corrie! It was almost like talking with you. Many of the same bonds seemed to spring up between us. Only later did she begin to share about her personal life. She seemed to trust me entirely, and I felt no awkwardness in it, only joy at the opportunity to help, to be of service to another dear one of my kind. Here was ministry indeed—the chance to bring kindness and acceptance to one who was struggling to walk in her new life, free from bonds still attempting to entrap her from out of her past.

As it turned out, the poor woman—she gave her name as Annie Bowers—was virtually penniless. She had been married, she said, but was not at the moment, though she still spoke of her husband. The circumstances were quite vague, and I did not want to pry too deeply. The two children had different fathers, and once she told me, the fact became clear enough from looking at them. She was attempting to reestablish links with her own relations, from whom she had been estranged for many years, and thus was bound for Chicago. She had spent her last penny for the train passage.

During one of our stops, I bought a meal for Mrs. Bowers and the two youngsters. She was so appreciative that she wept, saying she wished there was something she could do to repay my kindness. I replied that seeing smiles of happiness on each of their faces was compensation enough.

We boarded the train and resumed our journey.

During the afternoon Mrs. Bowers became more and more emotional and began to share more and more personally about her past life. She cried and asked for my help, asked me what she should do about many circumstances, asked for the insight of my spiritual eyes. The woman's earlier poise gave way to the pain of a deeply confused and seeking heart, tormented by a past that had been agonizing and painful. I began to see that there were two women present—the radiant and peaceful Christian who lived confidently in the newness of faith, and the mistreated woman who still suffered from a past she could not entirely escape.

I asked what she planned to do once reaching Chicago. She did not know, she said. The Lord would provide for their needs. Did she have lodgings? I asked. She shook her head. What were her plans? Again she was vague, repeating her conviction that the Lord would take care of them.

We arrived in Chicago midafternoon, and it was there I made a decision I will always wonder about. Though the train was due to continue on, I decided to get off with my new friend. I felt that the meeting had been far from accidental, and that the Lord had certainly brought her my way in order that I might do what I could to help. I spoke with the ticket agent and was able to exchange what remained of my ticket for passage on the next train west, though it would not be for several days. I knew my decision would delay my seeing you, but it was a sacrifice I was willing to make because the need in this young family, without a man to guide them, was so great.

Again, when I explained what was in my heart to do, Mrs. Bowers wept and expressed the profoundest and humblest gratitude.

Retrieving my own bags and hers, I hired a cab, which took us to a hotel in town. I booked a room for her and her son and daughter, paying for a week in advance, and procured a room for myself on the next floor up, paying only for the days necessary until the next train. Then we all ate dinner at the hotel's restaurant and enjoyed the evening together before retiring. I assured her that I would do everything I could to see her reunited with her family before my departure and that she need have no anxiety about anything.

I slept soundly that night, which was last night as I write it now to you, content in the opportunity the Father had given me. I was disturbed in the middle of the night by a faint sound. But I rolled over, sleepily thinking it was a noise from the street outside or perhaps the remnant from some dream. When I awoke it was morning.

I arose and proceeded to dress, noticing nothing amiss other than that it seemed my trousers and coat were thrown upon the back of a chair when I thought I had placed them in the wardrobe. I thought nothing of it, however, but put them on, then went to the room of my friends.

There was no answer to my knock. This I thought strange, for it was still somewhat early. But I descended to the restaurant, thinking perhaps the little family would already be there, for we had agreed to meet for breakfast. There was no sign of them.

I ordered a cup of coffee and sat down to wait. When after some time they still didn't come, I rose from the table and went to pay for my coffee before trying the room once more.

Can you imagine my shock when I pulled out my wallet and found it empty!

I flew back up to my room and searched everywhere, but not a single bill was to be found. It appeared that now I was the one who was penniless!

I raced down again to Mrs. Bowers' room and knocked, I will admit, with a growing feeling of desperation, futility, and a great sense of my own foolhardiness. There was, of course, no answer.

I raced down to the desk clerk and inquired about the woman and two children in room 217. They had checked out hours ago, he said, while it was still dark.

Oh, Corrie . . . Corrie! I cannot tell you what a miserable day I have spent trying to make sense—which I cannot!—

of this unexpected turn of events.

Try as I might, I cannot lay deceit to the poor woman's charge as I recall—even now with fondness—our hours of sharing and talking together on the train. There was a sincerity in her being that I cannot take from her.

What happened, then, to cause her to turn against me? What gave her old ways the upper hand over the new life in God she wanted so badly to live?

I have no answers. I have spent the whole day seeking to sort through the entire episode, and I can find no rational cause to explain how she could have done such a thing to one who had helped her and to whom she had expressed such gratitude. I would have given her whatever would have been in my limited power to give. Why then did she resort to duplicity?

I do not want to grow cynical, but the demons of doubt and mistrust and judgment bark loudly in my ears. Just when I thought I was at last putting to rest difficult attitudes I had wrestled with from my experience in the church, now again I find the hand of help bitten by the very ones I have been trying to feed.

I recall your question of such a short time ago—in fact, I have read that letter of yours over several times today! "What if God puts things in our path that seem like they are from him, but that he *doesn't* want us to do?"

Are there times he wants us to withhold help from another? I cannot believe it could be so. It goes against everything I have always believed. Yet how did I help this woman? Did I really help her at all? Did my presence only put temptation in her path that eventually caused her to forsake the new life trying to blossom, and revert instead to life in the old wineskin of her past?

Hence I cannot escape the question—did I err in what I attempted to do for her and her children?

I do not know, Corrie, and it torments me. Not that I am unwilling to face having done wrong. Nothing could be easier for me than to admit my own sin. That is not the torment.

The agony is rather the blow this experience deals to my heart, which wants to love and give and serve others, and especially my brothers and sisters of faith, but now finds thoughts of self-protection and wariness rising up to guard the flanks of my being lest I be so ill-used again.

I do not want to think such things! I do not want to become self-protective and wary. Yet the pain of being taken advantage of is sometimes too great to keep such motives of self from crying out to be heeded.

What *is* ministry, Corrie? Is this the price that must be paid to be Christ's servant in the lives of others?

Oh, but it is a high price! And sometimes I wonder whether I am willing to pay it!

Do I complain at the cost? Am I yet so lowly and immature? Scarce wonder that I do not yet come anywhere near reflecting the image of him whom it is my prayer to emulate!

Me . . . like Christ! Ha! I am no more like him than those who spat upon him as he carried the cross up the hill to Golgotha.

I pray to be like him. I pray to have my flesh crucified with him. I pray that my life might count for something in his kingdom. And yet at the first opportunity for me to demonstrate my sincerity in all these ways, my flesh rises up with complaint after complaint that I have been ill-treated by those I attempted to serve.

What else is the Christlike life? My Lord gave and gave and gave, only to be rejected by the very recipients of his love. I pray to be like Jesus. But what is it I think such a life might be if not to be rejected and treated as he was?

I should rejoice in what has befallen me. But instead I complain and feel sorry for myself! How little do I deserve to be called by my name, which is so like his!

I am sorry for all those acrid words, Corrie. Were it not that I want you to know every fiber of my being, good and ugly, I would tear up this letter immediately. But you must know me as I am.

After writing the above, I was so distraught that I went out for a long walk. I was gone from my room three or four hours.

I wept. I prayed. I thought. And I searched high and low throughout the city where I thought perhaps I might by chance set eyes again upon the woman who was so in my thoughts. My heart was so sore to see her again, and to look into her eyes and simply ask, "Why?" But nowhere was she to be found.

Gradually my spirit calmed, and I began to pray for her, though I must confess it was with difficulty, for I did not know what to pray. Mostly I knew I had to pray that God would bring forgiveness into my own heart. For did not Jesus himself pray, "Father, forgive them, for they know not what they do"? How could I not pray the same toward her?

Oh, Lord, show me the true ministry of giving without thought of self. You gave your life, and your own best friends betrayed and denied you. They put you to death, while they have only taken from me a few dollars. Father, do not let this blow to my serving heart be lethal. I do not want to grow callous and calculating. Let me be just as willing, the next time you send one in need across my path, to give and give again without thought of what may be the result to me. Help me, Lord. And I pray for that dear tormented woman and her two precious young ones. I do not even know how to pray for them but that you would be a Father to them, that you would love them, and that you would accomplish your purposes in their lives, however and wherever that may lead them—and that you would accomplish your purpose in my heart through this.

Now it is late the same evening. My body is tired and sore, for reasons I will presently explain.

But first I must say that my deepest regret of this day is for you, my own dear Corrie. Though you knew nothing of it, in one respect you are the one who will have to suffer for my having delayed my journey. For now I will be nearly a week later in my arrival than anticipated, and I know this will be difficult for you.

Truly, I am sorry.

I must only trust our Father that he has you in his care, whatever may be my own folly.

Once the train takes me from Chicago, there should be no more delays. In the meantime, I have found it necessary to look for means to sustain myself on the further journey.

I had ten dollars packed away in one of my bags in case of emergency. Also the hotel clerk agreed to refund me the unused portion of Annie Bowers' room. In my walk through town I spoke to a man at a large lumber supply yard. He said that if I was willing to work, he would pay me per day. So until the next train I shall be busy hoisting, not bags of grain, but heavy timbers of pine and fir upon these shoulders of mine.

In that man's generous employ I spent this very afternoon, which explains my physical condition. But honest work is always beneficial to aches of the heart. Soreness notwithstanding, I feel much the better for it.

All in all, I am confident that I shall leave Chicago with sufficient funds for the stagecoach and the last legs of my journey. I may, however, be growing lean by the time you see me, for I will doubtless have to be frugal when it comes to other expenditures, such as food.

I apologize for this dispirited letter. I do feel much better now for having written it. I wish I could throw it away, but I know you would never forgive me if I did.

Pray for me. Sometimes I feel so weak.

                              Christopher

CHAPTER 20

THE NEW DRESS

One of the things that sort of surprised me when I got home was how much Becky had learned from Almeda about what you might call the womanly arts.

Christopher was always so nice to give me compliments, but I had never been as interested in womanly things as most young women. I was always traipsing around the woods, riding horses, tracking down some story, or writing in my journal.

Ma had insisted that I learn the basics of keeping house, though—and Becky hadn't even had that. She wasn't even ten when Ma died, so she had to go all through her growing-up years without a mother at all.

I guess I didn't give it much thought that there might be things that I knew on account of being the oldest that maybe Becky didn't. I got so busy and traveled so much, maybe I didn't pay as much attention to her as I should have. It seemed all I could do to keep the boys and Pa fed and the mud out of the cabin.

Emily got married pretty young—I don't even know if she knew how to make a decent batch of biscuits because I had done most of the cooking. I suppose she did, now that I recall, but Becky was even younger than she was. Then when Pa got married again, Almeda took over most of the cooking and cleaning, and by then I was doing a lot of writing and was gone pretty often, although of course I helped as much as I could.

But now that I was home and seeing Becky as a grown-up and seeing what a homemaker she'd become, I found myself wondering if I really knew enough about being a wife and keeping a home. Ma had never been too much a "wife" while we were growing up because she hadn't had a husband around to be a wife to.

And now it seemed that Becky knew more about these wife kinds of things than I did! She'd been alone with Almeda these last two years, and I was amazed at all the homey and womanly things she knew how to do.

It wasn't just cooking and cleaning, though I was sure she was a better cook than me by now. There was more to it than that. She thought about things like putting flowers on the table and folding the napkins in special ways and laying the knives and forks just so, things I'd never paid much attention to during my years at home before.

The house didn't just look clean now, it had a pretty look. It was more feminine, and that made it pleasant to be in. I noticed all kinds of little things that Becky and Almeda had done to make the house more homey this way.

One of the biggest surprises of all was how well Becky had learned to sew. I certainly wasn't much of a seamstress! Ma had always made our clothes before. And since we'd been in Miracle Springs, Almeda had had Mrs. Gianini make our dresses for us.

I remember that first time when she told Mrs. Gianini to make us all dresses for Christmas. What fun we'd had! We'd never had such pretty things! Then, when I was getting ready to go East, Almeda had told me what I would need, like a traveling suit, a dress for a nice dinner, and a couple of dark skirts with different blouses. But she and Mrs. Gianini had planned it all. I had just stood there while they talked and fitted me. My head had been full of other things besides dresses.

Now, however, clothes were on my mind. Once I knew Christopher really was on his way, I wanted to make a new dress for the occasion. Ma had taught me how to sew a fairly decent seam when I was little, but I had no idea where to start in making a dress. Becky said she'd help me with it.

She took me to the General Store and we looked at the cloth goods and patterns. I was impressed with Becky's knowledge, and she was so careful not to make me feel too stupid for knowing as little as I did.

We picked out a pretty rose-colored calico print. I had been drawn to a yellow material, but Becky suggested that since winter was coming on I might want something a bit darker. She said I could make a yellow dress later for the spring and summer months. So we looked at black and dark blue, but when I saw the dark rose I knew it was the one I wanted.

Next we looked at patterns. I had seen so many pretty dresses in the East, and I had an idea of what I liked and what I didn't care for. I picked out several pictures in the pattern book while Becky was talking to Mr. Bosely, and I showed them to her when she came back. She pointed out to me that two of the patterns would be quite difficult because there were so many pieces and so much detail stitching. She also said the detail wouldn't show up well enough when made with a dark color.

Becky suggested that come spring, when I made the yellow dress, I could pick a fancier pattern. This time, she said, we should select something simpler.

"The fabric you've picked will make any dress look lovely," she added.

I looked at her for a long moment.

"When did you grow up to be so wise?" I said.

We both laughed.

"I guess at the same time you were becoming so famous," she answered.

I didn't know how the dress would turn out, but Becky and I had a wonderful time together making it.

We did settle on a simple pattern—at least that's what she called it. After we had been working on it a week, it didn't seem so simple to me!

We had decided on both a skirt and a blouse. The skirt was full, with a second gathered tier that began about my knees. Becky had insisted that we should make two blouses to go with it. One was of the same dark rose fabric as the skirt, and the other was of a cream-colored sheer fabric that would be trimmed with bits of the dark rose.

The blouse pattern had a yoke in front and back, with gathers just about the bustline. The calico blouse buttoned down the front, with no collar and long sleeves. The cream-colored blouse had the same type of yoke, but it buttoned down the back and had short, puffy sleeves. Its collar was made of the rose material, and it had rose-colored ribbons to gather the sleeves.

I began to get excited as the skirt and two blouses took shape and I was able to visualize what it would look like on me finished. How Becky could tell everything while we were looking at patterns and material to buy, I don't know, but her choices were good ones.

Now the only question was which of the blouses to wear on the day Christopher arrived!

CHAPTER 21

DISAPPOINTMENT

As Christopher got farther and farther west, he knew he would arrive in person before any more letters reached Miracle Springs. So he began sending me brief telegrams of his progress.

The first one came the last week of November from Fremont, Nebraska, where the train line now ended:

CORRIE HOLLISTER MIRACLE SPRINGS CALIFORNIA STOP BOARDING STAGE STOP ONLY TEN MORE DAYS STOP CHRISTOPHER

Another came in from Cheyenne, Wyoming, then one from Salt Lake City in the Utah Territory. Finally, about four days later, I received this message:

ARRIVED CARSON CITY STOP TONIGHT HERE TOMORROW SACRAMENTO STOP ARRIVE THURSDAY STOP CHRISTOPHER

Only three days!

I was beside myself!

It was absolutely worthless to try to do anything, so I tried to do everything. I felt like a teenager again. Holding in my excitement was no use. Everybody knew, from the smile on my face and the giggling laughter erupting out of me every few minutes, that my head was in the clouds.

By Wednesday evening all the rest of the family was laughing and teasing me, but I didn't mind. I think they were nearly as anxious to see Christopher in the flesh as I was.

I hadn't heard from Christopher on Wednesday. I thought I might have another telegram.

I hardly slept that night. Thursday I went to town a little before noon. The northbound stage out of Sacramento wouldn't arrive till late in the afternoon, but I just couldn't stand waiting at home any longer.

I hung around the Supply Company all afternoon, trying to work, but really just waiting for the time to pass.

Finally about four-thirty I heard the familiar sounds of the horses galloping into town and the stagecoach rumbling behind them.

I ran outside. There it was coming down the street!

I ran over to the stage office to meet it. With a great *Whoa!* the driver reined in the horses. Oh, I couldn't stand it!

The stage bounded and bounced to a stop. The driver jumped down. The passenger door opened. A man and two ladies stepped out.

Christopher was nowhere to be seen!

I ran up and looked inside. The coach was empty.

Frantically I approached one of the ladies and asked if there'd been anyone else aboard. She'd come all the way from Auburn, she said, and there had been no one like the man I described.

What could have happened?

I walked back to the office and sat down. I didn't know what to think.

I was still sitting there in a daze ten minutes later when the delivery boy from the telegraph office came in the door.

"Telegram for you, Miss Corrie," he said.

I jumped out of my chair and practically tore it out of the poor boy's hand.

STAGE LOST WHEEL IN SIERRAS STOP DELAYED STOP FRIDAY SOONEST STOP CHRISTOPHER

I sat there staring at the words on the yellow paper.

I had waited all this time. What was another twenty-four hours?

Yet as I sat there, my heart nearly broke.

I didn't think I *could* wait another day!

CHAPTER 22

PLEASANT DREAMS AND
APPLE PIES

How I managed to get through the rest of that Thursday I don't know, but I did.

Time keeps going even when you are miserable. When you're waiting for a certain day to arrive, it always does, slow as it may seem. And fretting about it doesn't speed up the process one bit.

It helped that I hadn't been able to sleep the night before. By suppertime that evening I was dead tired—too tired even to think about getting excited all over again for the next day.

I crawled into bed not knowing whether to smile that I might see Christopher tomorrow or cry because I hadn't seen him today. When I got tired like that, laughing and crying, happiness and sadness, all blended together. My emotions didn't seem to cope with fatigue too well, and I got all mixed up.

But I was too tired even to think about it, and before very long I was sound asleep.

I dreamed of the ride Christopher and I had taken up into the hills around Mrs. Timms' farm on Christmas Day nearly twelve months before. It was one of those lovely dreams you don't ever want to end. Everything happened slowly and peacefully. Even the horses galloped with such slow, drawn-out, and exaggerated motions that their hoofbeats were silent. It was almost like the whole dream was taking place someplace in the clouds where there were no sounds.

Both of us were laughing and smiling and talking, but in my

dream I could hear nothing. Even though it was December, I remember feeling—in the dream, I mean—that the air was like a California summer, warm and fragrant, with but the slightest breeze carrying the scent of the pine trees to our noses.

I don't know if you can smell in a dream, but it felt like smelling. I don't know if you can hear sounds in a dream either, but it seemed like this dream, though slow and quiet, was yet filled with the dream-sounds of happiness.

When I awoke, all my fatigue and sadness from the night before was gone. Sun streamed through my window almost like it was June instead of December.

I lay a few minutes in peaceful half-wakefulness.

Then all of a sudden I remembered.

Christopher!

Today was the day . . . again!

I jumped out of bed. How long had I slept? I looked at the time on my nightstand. It was only eight-forty.

Calm down, I told myself. The stage wouldn't arrive till after four. Sometimes it was as late as six, and the passengers and driver had to spend the night here before going on to Marysville. And Christopher might not even come today. The telegram had said Friday at the *soonest*. I couldn't let myself get as worked up as I did yesterday.

I forced myself to dress slowly and deliberately, then went to the kitchen to help make breakfast. Almeda, Becky, and Ruth were the only ones there. Pa was in Sacramento again, due back tomorrow. Zack and Tad must have already gone out to do their chores.

"Good morning, Corrie," said Almeda. "Will you be going into town bright and early again today?"

"I don't know," I sighed. "I don't think I can survive getting my hopes up again like yesterday. Are you going in?"

"No, Ruth and I are going to spend the whole day today making some decorations for Christmas, aren't we, dear?"

"Yes, Mama," said Ruth.

"What about you, Becky?" I asked.

"I need to go into the office for the morning. I was just about to leave. But I thought I would come back this afternoon and help Almeda fix something nice for supper."

"You *will* bring Christopher home for supper tonight if he arrives today?" said Almeda.

"Of course!"

"I thought it would be good for Almeda and me to take care of it," Becky went on. "The condition you were in yesterday, I don't think you could have made a bowl of porridge."

"What?" I said, laughing. "Are you criticizing my homemaking abilities?"

"No, older sister of mine, you are a very good cook," laughed Becky. "But yesterday you were in a sorry state!"

"I know, I know . . . I was a mess. But today I'm going to be mature and grown-up about it."

"Is that a promise?" laughed Almeda.

"Yes, yes, I promise . . . as long as you don't tell Christopher how I behaved yesterday!"

We all laughed, and they agreed—all except for little Ruth, who kept asking who Christopher was.

Becky left for the office in town shortly, but I decided to go later. After what she'd said I was determined to contribute in *some* way to that evening's supper!

I remembered from last Christmas how much Christopher enjoyed apple pies, so I decided to make some. That would make a perfect welcome!

As soon as I was through with breakfast, I went up to Aunt Katie's and asked if I could have two pies' worth of apples from the stock in her cellar. They were still reasonably fresh. It had only been about three weeks since she and I had picked the last of them off her trees. She let me have them on the condition that I would bring Christopher up to meet them and that we kept enough for Christmas.

"And I'll be on better behavior than when Cal Burton was in your house!" I said. "That much I will promise."

Katie laughed.

"Then take the apples," she said, "and be sure to put plenty of sugar in them. Men like their pies sweet!"

I lugged the apples home. First I made the dough, with plenty of butter. Remembering Katie's advice, I even threw in half a cup of extra sugar with the flour.

Then I set about peeling the apples.

"Would you like some help, Corrie?" asked Almeda.

"Thank you, but if you and Becky are going to make the rest of supper, the least I can do is make the pies all by myself."

"Then the least I can do is make sure the oven will be hot when you need it," she said. "I'll add some wood to the fire."

An hour later I covered over the two pies with a thin layer of crust, made three slits in the top, crimped the thick edges as decoratively as my fingers could manage, sprinkled the tops with a generous snowfall of sugar, and the pies were ready for Almeda's oven.

While waiting for them to cook, I would clean myself up, wash my hair, and get ready to go into town.

Two hours later I was ready. The pies sat on the table cooling. They had turned out perfectly—with the crust lightly browned and just a hint of the gooey apple syrup trying to bubble out from the slits in the middle and here and there around the edge.

I hitched Blue Star to our small carriage, then went back inside to change.

I put on the new dress I'd been making over the last month. I'd worn the calico blouse yesterday. Today I would wear the cream. I felt so happy I could have burst out singing. Maybe I would sing on my way into town, where no one could hear me!

I set out for town a little after one-thirty. About half a mile out of town, I passed Becky on her way back home. She gave me a wave and an understanding smile. But I wondered if anybody could possibly understand how I felt that day.

CHAPTER 23

CHRISTOPHER!

This time the afternoon went by more quickly, and I had my wits more about me too. I didn't feel like I was in quite the same sorry state Becky had said I was in the day before.

Everybody in town seemed to be watching me, wondering why I had come to town with a new dress on for the second day in a row. I noticed that several of the more curious women from church "just happened" to be in town for most of the afternoon, hanging around the General Store and the bank and the dressmaker's longer than any amount of business could possibly account for.

I didn't care.

This was one time none of the gossip and the curiosity would bother me. I didn't care who said what . . . what a fool I made of myself!

About three, the time began to go slower and slower, and I looked at the time more and more. As for my being of help to Mr. Ashton . . . he probably knew he would have to rewrite every invoice I was absently trying to compute at the desk while glancing out the window every five minutes or less.

Three-fifteen . . . three-thirty . . . three-forty . . .

It was hopeless to try to keep my mind on my work!

"Corrie, would you like to go over to the bank for me?" asked Mr. Ashton.

"Yes!" I answered quickly, jumping up. Anything to get out of the office—to be able to *do* something!

He handed me the deposit. I walked outside and up the street as slowly as I could, straining my ear for any hint of the stage.

Suddenly I heard horses!

Yes—from the sound of it—more than one!

I glanced toward the end of town, unconsciously running a few steps in that direction. Here they came!

Then I stopped. It was only Mr. Douglas and Mr. Shaw riding into town. I continued on toward the bank.

When I was finished with my business, I walked back out onto the street and looked at my watch again. Four-ten. Slowly I walked back to the Supply Company.

I went in and again sat down with the stack of invoices.

Four-fifteen . . . four-twenty-five. . . .

I had only gotten through three or four of them when I sat my pencil down, stuck my elbows up on top of the desk, and propped my chin in the palms of my hands.

Are you ever going to come? I thought. What if he *didn't* come today?

I had to be patient. He would be here eventually. What was the harm if it took another day?

Oh no! Suddenly it dawned on me—did the stage run on Saturday? I couldn't remember! And I knew for certain that it didn't operate on Sunday!

Be patient! Don't worry! I told myself. *What would Christopher say if he were here right now? He would tell me not to fret so much.*

Then for some reason I thought of the conversation we had had on our way back to Mrs. Timms' farm from Richmond after I had seen Derrick Gregory. I don't know why I thought of it just then, probably because I was thinking of Christopher. He had become so enthralled with the scenery as we had bounced along in the wagon.

He had become so excited about everything—the grass in the fields we were passing, the trees—and then we'd begun talking about how some people are able to receive what nature is trying to tell them, while others are unseeing and oblivious to it. I could almost remember his exact words: *It is the heart of God that dwells within the essence of nature. He communicates pieces of himself in a very personal way through these things we look upon and say, "I behold beauty therein."*

Vague familiar sounds began to intrude into the back of my mind, but I was too lost in my reverie to pay any attention to them. Not only was I remembering Christopher's words, I could even hear the wagon slowly bouncing along as we went. It was such a vivid daydream!

God is everywhere, Christopher's voice was saying again in my memory, *right in front of our eyes. The very*—

"Miss Corrie," said a voice. "Miss Corrie . . ."

I glanced up. It was Marcus Weber.

"Miss Corrie, wasn't you waitin' on the stage?"

"Oh . . . oh, yes, Marcus—yes, I was."

"Well, it's comin' in, ma'am."

Suddenly I woke up and looked out the window. The sound of horses and a wagon hadn't been part of my daydream at all! The stagecoach was already halfway down the street and heading right toward us!

In two seconds I was flying out the door, leaving a flurry of invoices settling to the floor from off the desk behind me.

I forgot I was wearing a dress. I forgot I had tried to fix my hair so it would look nice. I altogether forgot that I was a grown woman—I felt like an excited little girl again. I picked up the bottom half of my dress and petticoats to get it away from my ankles. My bonnet flew off my head, but I didn't stop for it.

Nothing was going to slow me down!

My boots pounded along the wooden sidewalk for half a block, then I ran off and into the dirt street as fast as my legs could move.

Here came the stage toward me.

There was a head leaning out the open window!

My heart was pounding . . . tears began to cloud my eyes. . . .

It couldn't be . . . *oh, but it was!*

"Corrie . . . Corrie!" cried that wonderful, lovely, strong, tender, manly voice I had waited so long to hear.

I slowed . . . his hand was stretched out toward me . . . I couldn't help it—I could feel myself starting to cry.

His face filled the small stage window, a huge smile spread across it.

"Christopher!" I called, but my voice was drowned out from the approaching din of horses and the clattering carriage.

The stage rumbled past me and, slowing, jostled toward the stage office amid the sounds of hooves and wheels, creaking leather straps, and shouts from the driver.

I ran after it down the middle of the street, tears streaming down my face. Christopher was leaning out the stage window now and waving frantically and yelling to me.

The stage stopped before I could catch it. Before it had even come to a standstill, Christopher had thrown the door open, jumped to the ground, and started running toward me.

"Corrie!" he cried again.

We ran toward each other and met in the middle of the street. Suddenly I was in his arms.

"Oh, Christopher . . . Christopher, I can't believe you're here at last!" I was crying now in earnest.

"It's me . . . and I am really here," he said softly. "Oh, Corrie, words can't say . . . how wonderful you look."

I couldn't say a word, but just wept all the more.

How long we stood there I don't know. There was no place else in the universe I wanted to be.

But then a voice called out from behind us, near the stage.

"Hey, buddy—these bags yours?"

A moment more we stood, then Christopher released me. "I'll be right back," he said. "Don't go anyplace."

He ran back to get his suitcases as the driver handed them down from the top of the stage, then carried the bags over to the stage office. As he did, I wiped my sleeve across my eyes. That's when I noticed probably eight or ten people standing watching from several of the shops. Three women were gawking in front of the dressmaker's, including Mrs. Sinclair, one of the worst of the town's gossips. Everybody would know everything now—probably before sunup tomorrow!

I waved to them with a smile, then walked slowly toward the stage. By now Christopher was running back toward me.

He stopped and walked the last few steps slowly. We stood and held each other's eyes for several moments. Then Christopher took both my hands in his.

"I love you, Corrie," he said softly.

I opened my mouth, but instead of words only more laughter and crying came out.

Gently he stretched his arms around me and pulled me close to his chest. His hand stroked my hair and he leaned his face over the top of my head. I felt him blow a warm breath from his lips through my hair.

I couldn't believe this was happening to me!

CHAPTER 24

CHRISTOPHER IN MIRACLE SPRINGS

"I have a buggy in town," I said as we began walking together slowly back to the stage office. "What do you want to do first—go out to the house and meet everyone . . . or go to Mrs. Gianini's?"

"Who's Mrs. Gianini?" asked Christopher.

"Oh, she has the boardinghouse where you'll be staying."

"She's expecting me?"

I nodded.

"Good. Why don't we get my bags over there then. How far is it?"

"Just down the street."

We'd reached the sidewalk now. Christopher stooped down and laid hold of the two handles of his two bags.

"Do you see those three ladies standing over there in front of that shop?" I said.

Christopher glanced in the direction I'd nodded.

"They're the town gossips. They've been watching me all day, and unless I'm mistaken right now they're positively dying of curiosity about you."

"Then why don't you take me over and introduce me to them?" suggested Christopher.

"You're not serious?" I laughed.

"Certainly. Why not? We might as well give them something substantial to talk about—that is, as long as you don't mind."

"Why should I mind—they've been talking about me anyway . . . all right then!"

Christopher put his bags back down. We turned and began walking briskly up the sidewalk toward Mrs. Hutchens' shop. I couldn't help smiling.

The instant they realized we were headed straight for them, I could see Mrs. Sinclair's eyes widen in panic as she tried to decide what she should do. Should they retreat to the safety of the shop or stand there and wait to see what would happen? Now that the object of her curiosity was walking right for her, she was paralyzed. She hadn't expected this!

"Mrs. Sinclair," I said as we walked boldly up, "I would like you to meet my dear friend, Christopher Braxton. Christopher, may I introduce Mrs. Sinclair, Mrs. Hutchens, who owns this shop, and Mrs. Gilly?"

"Charmed, ladies!" said Christopher in his most polished tone. "I am delighted to meet you."

He bowed slightly. He shook each of their hands gently.

"You . . . you—er . . . are Corrie's . . . *friend?*" asked Mrs. Sinclair, a little nervously but smiling, still unsettled by the turn of events, and emphasizing the last word.

"I would go further than that, Mrs. Sinclair," replied Christopher, playing right into her hand, "I would even go so far as to say we are very *close* friends. We met in Virginia and have been corresponding ever since."

"Oh . . . yes, of course . . . *I see,*" said the more than intrigued Mrs. Sinclair with a significant tone.

"But now, ladies, you must excuse us," said Christopher. "I must make arrangements concerning my lodgings here in your fair town."

Christopher bowed again, I smiled, and we turned and left the three speechless gossips gaping after us. A moment later I heard the door to Mrs. Hutchens' shop close. I glanced back. They had all gone inside.

"I have no doubt all three tongues are wagging now!" I laughed. "How could you have carried on so with a straight face?"

"Remember, I had dealings with women like that all the time when I was pastoring," laughed Christopher. "The best remedy for their affliction is the straightforward approach. If they're going to talk, you might as well let them do it in front of you rather than behind your back."

"Which is exactly what they're doing at this very minute!"

"Some things never change," rejoined Christopher. "Old ladies will forever talk about young people, and I doubt you and I are going to change it!"

He picked up his bags again and we walked off along the sidewalk.

"There's our office," I said, pointing across the street. I could see Marcus and Mr. Ashton inside, looking out the window at us and just as curious as everybody else.

"Hollister Supply Company," said Christopher, reading the sign. "I thought I remember your calling it the Mine and Freight."

"It used to be called Parrish Mine and Freight," I explained. "Almeda and her first husband began the business during the gold rush days. Back then it was mostly mining supplies and freight hauling. As the community grew, gradually the business changed and broadened. When Pa and Almeda were married, they changed it to Hollister-Parrish Mine and Freight, then eventually Almeda decided to drop the Parrish. It's still mostly her business, but she wanted it only to say Hollister. They changed it from 'Mine and Freight' to 'Supply Company' when I was in the East."

"And you all work there?"

"Mostly just Almeda and Becky and I. Pa and Zack and Tad all are familiar with the business and help with deliveries or heavy work when it's too much for Marcus—"

"Marcus? He's a hired man?"

I nodded. "But they're all busy doing their other work most of the time, so besides the people Almeda hires, it's us three women."

"What kind of supplies does a Supply Company sell in California?" asked Christopher.

"Just about anything farmers, ranchers, or miners might need—from seed to saddles to new wagons to wire fencing to shovels, picks and rope, feed, grain . . . hundreds of things."

Now we had reached Mrs. Gianini's. We walked up onto the porch. Christopher set down his suitcases, and I knocked on the door. In a moment it opened.

"Hello, Mrs. Gianini, this is the man I told you about," I said.

"Good afternoon, Mrs. Gianini," said Christopher, extending his hand. "I am Christopher Braxton."

"Come in, Corrie . . . Mr. Braxton. I have your room all ready for you."

We went inside. I waited downstairs while she took Christopher upstairs to the room where he would stay. He took his suitcases up, and in a minute or two they both returned.

"Will you be here for dinner tonight, Mr. Braxton?"

"No," I answered for him. "He will be with us, Mrs. Gianini."

"Breakfast in the morning, then?"

Christopher glanced at me.

I nodded.

"Yes, then—thank you very much," said Christopher.

We moved toward the door.

"Don't be too late, Mr. Braxton," she said behind us. "I lock the door at ten o'clock."

"I'll be sure he's back by then, Mrs. Gianini," I said.

As we walked away, I told Christopher of our first few days in Miracle Springs thirteen years earlier, when we too had stayed at the boardinghouse.

By then it was after five and the sun had just set.

"It's going to be dark before long," I said. "We'd better go get the carriage hitched up and ride out to the house."

CHAPTER 25

SUPPER WITH THE FAMILY

What a wonderful evening it was!

Christopher was so nice and polite and gracious. How could everybody not be taken with him?

Before supper we all went up to Uncle Nick and Aunt Katie's and then came back down the path in the darkness to our own place for supper.

As we walked through the door, I suddenly realized how much I loved this simple home of ours, which Pa had built with his own two hands and added on to twice as his family had grown. The walls had always been only rough wood, though Almeda had done some painting while I was away. Shelves and pictures and other things were hanging about here and there and lanterns hung up several places around. The floor, too, was wood, except for two large rugs Almeda and we girls had made.

There were enough chairs for everybody to sit comfortably, and two sofas gave enough room even for a few guests. Then there was the kitchen and the huge eating table between it and the main living room. It was all so familiar, so homey, so comfortable. Usually there was a fire in the fireplace and in the kitchen stove. But even when there wasn't, it was a warm place to be just because it was home.

I liked it better because it wasn't fancy. I had been in lots of fancy hotels and homes back East—including the White House!— but there was no place I would rather be than right here in our home in Miracle Springs.

Especially now! It felt all the better, all the more *homey,* now that Christopher could share it with me.

We ate the stew and biscuits and sweet potatoes Almeda and Becky had prepared, and we must have stayed at the table two hours.

As well as I thought I knew Christopher, I couldn't help being nervous after what he said in his letter about being shy and not knowing what to say around people when he first met them. What if they didn't like him? What if *Pa* didn't like him? He would soon be home from Sacramento.

But Christopher didn't act timid in the least. Maybe it was because I was there, so he didn't feel like he was among strangers. But from watching him I could hardly believe those things he'd written earlier. The conversation was so lively and fun that the time flew by. After just one evening I think everyone—except Pa, of course—knew Christopher as well as I'd hoped and already realized what a special man he was.

When it came time for dessert, we all stood up and walked around a bit while I cut the pies.

When everyone was seated again, I served Christopher the first slice.

"Do you remember last Christmas dinner," I said, "when you told me all about your preservation methods for Mrs. Timms' apples?"

"Indeed I do," smiled Christopher, looking down at the generous portion I had cut him. "And I see you remembered that apple pie is one of my favorites!"

"Well, I thought to myself—what could I do to make Christopher's coming special?"

"And you decided on apple pie . . . I approve of your decision!"

"But this is no ordinary apple pie," I went on. "Taste it and see if you can tell what I mean."

With everyone watching, Christopher dug in his fork and cut off a big bite, which the next instant disappeared into his mouth.

"That you baked it makes it just about the most special pie I've ever eaten," he said when he had chewed and swallowed it, "and it is every bit the equal of Mrs. Timms'—and she is a truly excellent baker of pies. It's sweet, just the way I like it, with just the right portion of cinnamon and the slightest hint of nutmeg. The apples are soft not hard, a common mistake. But other than that, I'm afraid I am at a loss."

"It's made from Virginia apples," I said.

"Ah yes, I thought I detected the slightest hint of the Atlantic seaboard in it!" remarked Christopher, giving Becky a wink. "But," he added in a puzzled tone, "I'm afraid I don't follow you."

As I served up pie to everyone else, I told him the story of Katie's coming and the apple tree she planted. This led the discussion off into a retelling of Pa's brief engagement to Katie, the wedding, and Uncle Nick's bursting into the middle of it. By the time we had told the whole thing, all of us were laughing so hard our sides hurt.

"I'll have to swap stories with Katie," said Christopher. "As a fellow Virginian, it wouldn't surprise me if she had heard of some of the people in my former congregation. Several of them were rather well known in the state."

"That will have to wait if you're going to get back to Mrs. Gianini's before ten," I said. "It's nine-fifteen now."

"By the way, what sort of provision is there for my return to town?"

"Tad and I will ride you in," said Zack. "I'll saddle up one of my horses, and you can keep it as long as you need it."

"But it's dark."

"Naw, there's plenty of light to see by," rejoined Zack. "Besides, our horses know their way into Miracle with their eyes closed."

CHAPTER 26

WALKING AND TALKING THROUGH TOWN

Now I *really* had a case of sleeplessness! But this time I wasn't kept awake by anticipation, but from contentment and excitement and happiness all rolled up together.

I'm sure that when I finally managed to fall asleep, the smile remained on my face.

As much as we'd talked about Christopher's arrival and planned for it, and as long as I'd anticipated his coming, I still had to pinch myself to make sure I wasn't dreaming.

Christopher Braxton was in Miracle Springs!

He had come all the way across the country . . . *to see me.*

We'd invited Christopher for dinner the next day, Saturday. Pa was due home sometime in the middle of the day, and Almeda was planning dinner for after he got home.

But I didn't wait until afternoon. I persuaded myself that Christopher needed me in town the moment he got up. What could he possibly do all morning at Mrs. Gianini's by himself?

It was just an excuse, and I really wasn't fooling anybody, even myself. I knew Christopher, and I knew that if left to himself he would begin meeting people around town just fine. He had managed thus far in his life without me. But I didn't intend to go a whole morning without seeing him! I had Blue Star saddled up and was on my way into town before nine.

We walked through the whole town, and I showed him everything, introducing him to the people we met. I took him all through the Supply Company office and other buildings. Marcus was working, and the two of them talked for a long time. Christopher seemed to take to him immediately.

We walked around Miracle Springs. I showed him everything, from the church on one end of town to the livery stable where Tad worked on the other. Mostly we just talked—and I felt a great sense of relief.

Yesterday, even though I was thrilled to see Christopher, I had also felt clumsy and awkward, and it had been hard to get into the same flow of conversation we had had when we were together on Mrs. Timms' farm. A fear had begun to steal over me that we had made a terrible mistake, that something had changed between us.

But I guess we just needed time to get comfortable with each other in person again. All the talk and laughter around the table with the rest of the family had been a good beginning. And then this morning, as we walked, gradually the same streams began to open between us, and the conversation began to flow more rapidly. Before long it was just like always.

And there was *so* much to talk about once the floodgates opened! Even though we'd been writing letters almost every day, sharing our thoughts face-to-face was so much easier. Within two hours, we'd said more than in all the letters put together.

"That reminds me!" exclaimed Christopher as we walked back toward town from the church. "I have six or eight more letters to give you that I didn't mail . . . if you still want them."

"Still want them?" I said. "Of course I want them!"

"Then let's go get them. You can have them right now."

"I have probably twenty letters I never sent you," I said sheepishly.

"What? All from the last two weeks?"

"No, from the last six months."

"Why didn't you send them?"

"I don't know. Sometimes I was embarrassed. I didn't know what you'd think."

"What could I think but that they were thoughts from the heart of Corrie Belle Hollister and that makes them dear and precious to me? I want every word!"

"I don't know if I want you to see them all."

"I don't care," insisted Christopher. "I want them anyway."

"Sometimes girls get emotional and personal when they write. I write things in my journal that I don't know if anyone else will ever see."

"Do you think women are the only ones who have emotions? Men can be personal when expressing themselves too."

"Oh, you know what I mean, Christopher. It's different for me."

"Maybe so. But I'm not so sure it's *that* different."

"You're an unusual man."

"You really think so?"

"No," I replied with a smile, "I know so."

"Well, you're as different a woman as I am different a man."

We walked on quietly for a minute.

"Oh, by the way," said Christopher, "I have an embarrassing request to make of you."

"Anything," I said.

"Could I borrow some money? I'm nearly out, and I'll need to pay Mrs. Gianini."

I could not help laughing.

"Of course," I said. "I shall consider it *my* ministry to the penniless and downtrodden!"

Again we walked awhile in silence.

"Well, Corrie," said Christopher after a moment, "how do you find me?"

I was taken aback. His voice sounded like he was serious. I didn't know what to say.

"Uh . . . what do you mean?"

"Do I seem the same? Are you disappointed?"

"No—what?—of course I'm not disappointed!" I exclaimed. "What do you mean? Why . . . are you?"

"Disappointed?"

I nodded.

"In you?"

"Why would you ask if I was . . . if *you* weren't?"

Christopher laughed.

"I'm sorry, Corrie. Certainly I'm not disappointed. It's positively wonderful being here with you."

Then he got serious again.

"But . . . haven't you noticed that it's . . . well, it's a little different?"

I didn't say anything. We kept walking slowly. I was glad Mrs. Hutchins or Mrs. Sinclair didn't happen along *now!*

"Before—in Virginia . . . at the farm—it was all so new between us. New and exciting—getting to know each other, talking about so many things . . . finding out all we had in common."

He paused, and I sensed that a *but* was coming. A sudden fear came over me that he was going to say he'd changed his mind about me!

"But now . . ." he went on, "after the letter I wrote you at the convent and all the letters we've written back and forth to each other since . . . it's all different than before. Even though I don't suppose we *know* what the future holds, we've made a mutual commitment now that . . . that—I don't know—puts our whole relationship on a different footing. Am I making any sense?"

"Some . . . though not completely," I said, breathing easier. "I still don't see why you thought I would be disappointed in you?"

"That was no doubt the wrong word to use. It is just that I feel like there *has* been a difference . . . that now—if I can say it this way—in a sense we have to get to know each other all over again. I mean . . . we've *written* to one another, but now we have to get comfortable *face-to-face* with the sort of things we've been writing about. Maybe you haven't felt it, but I've felt timid, tentative . . . even some of that shyness I told you about in one letter."

"But not toward me! Why would you feel that way toward me?" I asked in surprise.

"I don't know. I didn't expect it myself. Perhaps because when we were together before it was new and there was a sense of wonder to it. But now . . . you are no longer a delightful stranger the Lord sent to me. Now you are the woman I have asked to be my wife. So now, when I look at you, it is through different eyes. It is a new experience . . . one I am having to accustom myself to."

He stopped and let out a long sigh.

"I don't think I said it very well," he went on. "Don't take my words to mean disappointment. That *was* the wrong word for me to use earlier."

"Maybe I do know what you mean," I admitted. "I have been so bold and open in some of my letters, telling you how I feel about so many things. Now that you are actually here, I do feel a little embarrassed. A time or two I have felt like a turtle who wants to retreat back under its shell, wondering if I've stuck my neck too far outside by some of the things I've said."

"That's it exactly!" exclaimed Christopher. "We've been so thoroughly honest in our letters, sticking our necks all the way out, that now we each wonder what the other is thinking. It's that, along with having to adjust to the thought that we may actually be married someday."

I smiled. "I do understand what you've been saying," I said. "Yes, I have felt that same shyness."

This time we walked five or ten minutes without speaking.

"When is your father due home?" Christopher finally asked.

"Probably by one or two. He was going to spend the last night in Auburn. That's what he usually does when he has to be in the capital on Friday."

"I'm anxious to meet him."

"You're not nervous?"

"Why should I be?"

"I don't know, I just thought . . ."

"How could you be the daughter of anything but a sensitive man? I feel a *little* shy perhaps, but I'm not nervous, I'm looking forward to seeing him."

"Shall we ride out to the house pretty soon?" I asked. "I'd like to show you around our place too."

"Whatever you say," he smiled. "I'm all yours!"

CHAPTER 27

PA AND CHRISTOPHER

We were up rummaging around in the old mine shaft when I heard the sound of Pa's horse trotting toward the house.

I'd been telling Christopher about how the mine had caved in on Tad and how the big vein had been discovered and about how Pa and Mr. Jones thought there was still more gold around the other side of the hill. I was just taking him around to show it when I heard the hoofbeats, followed by Pa's shout of greeting.

We hurried down, but we didn't get there till Almeda and the others had already surrounded Pa with hugs and kisses of homecoming.

"Pa, Pa!" I cried, running up and forgetting formalities altogether, "Christopher's here!"

Pa gave me a hug, but before he had much of a chance to say anything, Christopher had caught up to us.

"Hello, Mr. Hollister," he said as he walked up. "I'm Christopher Braxton."

"Drummond Hollister," said Pa as I stepped back.

The two men shook hands and gave each other a good, solid look in the eye. In most circumstances between men, it would have been a look intended to size the other up. But with them, you could tell they each already knew quite a bit about the other, and so the look was one of mutual respect instead. Everybody just stood in kind of a silent circle around them, watching the two men.

"Welcome to Miracle Springs, Mr. Braxton," Pa added after a moment, "and welcome to my home."

146

"I appreciate it, Mr. Hollister. Your wife has already made me more than welcome. I enjoyed a fine supper here yesterday evening."

"When did you arrive?"

"Yesterday's stage from Sacramento."

"Wish I'd have known. I could have fetched you in the capital myself. You got lodgings taken care of?"

"At Mrs. Gianini's."

"A good woman, and she can cook almost as good as my wife and daughters!" laughed Pa. "Well, I'm plumb starvin'! What do you have for vittles, Almeda?"

"Plenty to feed every hungry mouth here!" replied Almeda as we all began moving toward the house.

"You'll join us for dinner, won't you, Braxton?"

"I already invited him, Pa," I said shyly. With Pa and Christopher talking so freely between themselves, I was suddenly reminded of why Christopher had said he needed to come to Miracle Springs in the first place, and I could not help feeling a little self-conscious.

Dinner was much like the night before, though I felt tongue-tied and didn't say much. Toward the end of the meal, Christopher began to get a little quiet too, and I started getting nervous. I was almost relieved when Ruth spilled her glass of milk all over the table. Enough of a stir was created that I didn't have to worry about Christopher and if something was wrong.

"Would you like a piece of pie or cake, Drummond?" asked Almeda once the milky mess was taken care of. "Corrie made two delicious apple pies yesterday, and there are a few pieces left. And today I made a chocolate cake."

"That would be right nice," replied Pa, "but give me some breathing room first. Maybe in about an hour."

He stood up from the table, and the rest of us eased up from our chairs too. Almeda and Becky and I had begun taking away some of the dishes when behind me I heard Christopher speak words that nearly made me die of self-consciousness.

"Mr. Hollister," he said, "I wonder if I might have a few words with you?"

Oh no, I thought. *Christopher—I didn't think you were going to do it this soon! The two of you only just met!*

But then Pa's answer made me die another two or three deaths!

"Sure, Braxton," Pa said, easing into his favorite chair, "have a seat."

No, no . . . not here—not right in front of everybody!

Suddenly a crash sounded, and everybody looked my way. A plate had fallen from my hands onto the hard wood floor. Luckily it didn't break.

My hands were shaking. I had to get out of there! If they were staying inside, I was leaving!

As I stooped down to pick up the plate, I heard Christopher again.

"I mean in private, sir," he said.

"Oh . . . oh yes—why, of course," said Pa, still completely unaware of Christopher's intentions. He stood up again. "How about we take a walk outside?"

Christopher nodded, and they left the house.

I continued to help clean up, but I have never been so agitated or distracted in my life. Every little sound I heard startled me, and I would jump and look toward the door.

Almeda knew, but she kept her peace. Every once in a while she would look at me with a tender, motherly smile and I knew she understood.

"What's wrong with you anyway, Corrie?" Becky said finally. "I've never seen you so nervous."

I glanced away, but I could feel my neck and cheeks getting all red.

Becky kept staring at me. When I didn't answer, suddenly the light dawned on her face.

"*Corrie* . . . really? Is that it!"

But just then, before I could answer, Tad headed for the door.

"I'm going out to see what Pa and Christopher are talking about," he announced.

I spun around to try to stop him, but he was already out the door. Oh, this was all too mortifying! I was simply going to die of embarrassment!

They were gone over an hour. After the kitchen was clean I made an escape to my room, lay down on my bed, and threw my pillow over my head. I didn't want to see anyone!

A while later the outside door opened. I leapt up, crept to the door of my room, and listened. Only one set of footsteps came into the house. It was Tad.

Again I sought refuge on my bed.

Twenty more minutes passed.

Again footsteps approached the house . . . *two sets of steps!*

The door opened. I heard Pa's voice say something to Almeda.

Oh, I would die if I had to go out there now!

What could I do? I wondered if I could escape through the window and make a dash for the safety of the woods.

"Where's Corrie?" I heard Pa ask.

The house was silent a moment, then the door of my room opened. A moment later I felt someone sitting down on the side of my bed. A hand felt under the pillow and laid itself gently on my head.

"Corrie, dear," said Almeda, "I think I have some idea what you are going through, but your father wants you to come out and join the rest of us."

"Oh, but I can't!" I groaned. "I'm too embarrassed."

"I think you must, dear."

A minute more I lay, then slowly turned over. Almeda bent down and gave me a long hug, then kissed my forehead.

She stood up and I joined her, and we walked out into the family room where everyone else was gathered.

Pa's face had a big smile all over it. I knew in an instant that Christopher had asked him.

"Well, what is it, Drummond?" asked Almeda. "You look as if you know something and are dying to tell all the rest of us."

"I reckon I do at that!" said Pa.

"Then tell us, for heaven's sake!" laughed Almeda.

"Well, it's just this, then," said Pa. "Blamed if this young Braxton fellow didn't just ask me if he could make my oldest daughter his wife!"

"*Corrie!*" Almeda exclaimed, bursting into tears.

She spun around and threw her arms around me. Becky too was beside me in an instant, and within seconds they were joined by Tad and Zack whooping and hollering and trying to get to me too. Only Pa and Christopher hung back, chuckling and smiling to themselves.

"Oh, Corrie, I'm so happy for you!" said Almeda, sniffing and wiping her eyes with the dirty apron she still had on. I don't think I'd ever seen such a huge smile on her face.

Meanwhile, Zack and Tad had completed their well-wishing with me and were over shaking Christopher's hand in manly congratulation.

The hubbub slowly died down. Christopher caught my eye and smiled, and I returned it kind of sheepishly. Of course I was happy—wonderfully, deliriously happy!—in spite of my embarrassment. Who wouldn't be happy? And I guess I felt relieved, too, that it was finally all out in the open and we could talk about it. How could I have ever thought that Christopher would change his mind! But I still felt red and hot and was perspiring all over.

"Well . . ." said Almeda impatiently, when the silence became complete and Pa still hadn't said anything.

"Well, what?" asked Pa.

"Well, what answer did you give the man, Drummond, for heaven's sake?" she said, nearly stamping her foot with laughing impatience.

"Didn't give him no answer at all."

"What!" exclaimed two or three voices at once. All the time, Christopher and I stood halfway back watching and listening, and glancing at each other every once in a while.

"He wouldn't let me answer," Pa went on. "Before I could say a word, Christopher here told me he didn't want my answer right yet. Matter of fact . . . he don't want it for a year."

"A year!" exclaimed the same two or three voices again.

"That's right. Seems the young feller's got the notion that it ought to be my decision whether he and Corrie Belle are right for each other. And he don't figure I can say one way or the other till I know him a mite better than two men can who just barely met."

"But what will happen, then, for the whole year?" asked Almeda, bewildered by the whole thing.

Pa shifted on his feet, then glanced over at Christopher.

"You wanna try and explain it to my wife, Braxton," he said. "I ain't sure I more'n half understand it myself."

Christopher laughed.

"I'll try, Mr. Hollister," he said as we all began to take our seats again.

"Are all of you ready for dessert?" asked Almeda. "We can serve it up before Christopher begins."

Nods went around the room, and I sprang up to help. Having something to *do* was better than just standing or sitting while everyone talked about Christopher and me.

Once we all had a piece of pie or cake in front of us, Christopher began, speaking mostly to Almeda, but glancing now and then toward Pa or me. He told them what he had written me—about his church and how he had arrived at his idea.

"I don't know if you'd call it an apprenticeship engagement," he said, "but something like that. During that time I would like to work for your husband, and you too, Mrs. Hollister, and submit myself to you in every way. If I want someday to be called your son-in-law, then I feel I have to earn that right in your eyes. I want the two of you to know me so well that you will know whether you want me for a son or not . . . and whether you feel I'll make a worthy husband for your daughter. After a year, you'll probably know some things about me that I don't even know about myself! And of course, Corrie and I will know each other better too.

"I realize an arrangement like I'm proposing is highly unusual," he went on, "and that probably most folks would consider it just about the craziest thing they'd ever heard. But I happen to think there's wisdom in it, and some scriptural precedent as well. Marriage is too sacred an institution to take lightly, Mr. and Mrs. Hollister. I don't take it lightly myself, and I want to give the two of you and your daughter enough time to make a wise decision among yourselves regarding Corrie's future. I care too much about her to rush into it."

A long silence followed. Neither Pa nor Almeda had ever heard the likes of what Christopher was proposing.

"Well, what do you think about all this, Corrie?" Pa said finally, turning toward me.

"He's a wise man, Pa," I answered softly. "I trust him."

Pa just nodded his head, then rubbed his chin thoughtfully.

"Yep," he said, halfway to himself, "I think I'm starting to see that already."

CHAPTER 28

CHRISTOPHER'S FIRST DAYS

Church the next day was so merry.

Mrs. Sinclair had done her work well. Everyone for miles knew that "Corrie's beau" was in town, and most of them came to church hoping to see him. There was hardly room for everyone, and we had to squeeze in tight.

Rev. Rutledge asked me to introduce Christopher, which I did. As I stood up and turned around, the most visible face in the whole congregation was Mrs. Sinclair's. She sat there beaming, almost gloating, as if she had personally orchestrated the whole relationship between Christopher and me. She glanced around as if to say to one and all, "Do you see? It's just like I told you!" For all I knew, half the people sitting there thought Gertrude Sinclair had introduced Christopher and me and that he would not even be in Miracle Springs had it not been for her!

Gossips are like that, I guess. They like to put themselves into the middle of the news they spread about. I guess it makes them feel important when there's nothing much in their own lives to interest them.

This one time, however, I could forgive Mrs. Sinclair. I was too happy to worry about it.

Christopher seemed highly amused by the whole situation. As we visited after the service, he made such a point of turning on the charm with Mrs. Sinclair, even calling her by her first name, that the poor lady was helpless.

Even as everyone was still emptying out of the church after the

service, Christopher had already approached her even before I
caught up with him outside the church.

" . . . one of the loveliest dresses I have ever seen, Gertrude,"
he was saying. "You must have ordered it from the East."

"Why . . . why, yes, Mr. . . . uh, Mr. Braxton, as a matter of
fact, I did. However did you know?"

"Oh, I know quality and good taste when I see it, Gertrude.
And your hat is positively stunning."

I had walked up to Christopher's side, but I don't think Mrs.
Sinclair even saw me. By now she was blushing—something I
doubt she'd done for years—and struggling to reply, though without much success. At last she noticed me and used my arrival to
escape the unaccustomed awkwardness.

"Corrie, this young man of yours is a charmer!" she said.

"I know quality when I see it too, Mrs. Sinclair," I said. We all
laughed, and then Christopher and I gradually began visiting with
everybody else who was crowding around.

Now they could all see us together in person and could talk all
they wanted. And now that Christopher had spoken with Pa, I
didn't mind nearly so much. The uncertainty was over—at least
some of it.

I knew everyone wanted to know whether Christopher and I
were engaged. But none of us brought it up, and they would never
ask such a forward question right to our faces. It would be up to
Christopher and Pa to tell people how things stood . . . *if* they
wanted to, *when* they wanted to, and in the way they wanted to.

It was another hour before we finally got loaded up and on the
way home! Christopher came with us, of course—to eat dinner and
to talk about the future. He didn't want to waste any time getting
his plan underway.

After we ate, Christopher and Pa and Almeda and I sat down
and talked the whole thing over.

Pa was still a little befuddled by Christopher's proposal. I know
he and Almeda had stayed up late the night before talking about
it, and from their tones—though I was in my bedroom and couldn't
actually hear what they were saying—it was clear that they were
reflecting seriously on what it all might mean.

"So tell me, Braxton," Pa said as we were talking, "is it just that you want to *work* for me—is that all there is to this thing? What if I don't have any work? What if I'm in Sacramento. It ain't exactly as if I'm an employer?"

"I'll do whatever you want me to do," replied Christopher. "It doesn't matter. I want to be around you enough to learn from your wisdom. After all, you're older and more experienced than I am. And you're Corrie's father, and so I figure she must have gotten a lot of what makes her the person she is from you."

Pa sat there taking it in silently. He wasn't used to people talking to him about his wisdom.

"But more than that, sir," Christopher went on, "I feel that it is very important that you know me as well as a man can know another man. You need to know if I'm capable of providing for your daughter, capable of loving her as I know you would want a husband to love her. I hope and pray you'll come to believe I'm the man for her. But if I'm not, then I have to trust you to find that out about me, because the very last thing in the world I would want to do is marry Corrie if I'm not the man you and the Lord feel is best for her."

Pa and Almeda looked at each other silently. I knew they were impressed with Christopher. And I knew they were taking his request very seriously.

"Where will you live?" Pa asked finally.

"Mrs. Gianini's will suit me just fine."

"There is my house in town," suggested Almeda.

Pa looked over at her.

"Hmm," he muttered thoughtfully. "Doesn't seem like it'd be fair to give the Duncans notice. They been there—what?—three or four years?"

"They've always talked about buying a place of their own—since the day I rented it to them."

"I have no need for something large," Christopher broke in. "The room at the boardinghouse is perfect."

"How'll you pay for it?" asked Pa, glancing back toward Christopher. "You got money?" I was a little nervous with him being so abrupt. But that was one thing about Pa. He was as straightforward as Christopher was sincere and open about his thoughts and feelings. I supposed that would help them to get to know each other about as quickly as two men could.

Christopher glanced over at me with a forlorn smile.

"No . . . unfortunately I don't, I'm embarrassed to say. But I'll manage to get by. I'll pick up other work. After all, if I'm going to provide for your daughter and a family someday, I've got to be able to provide for myself now, wouldn't you say."

"Well, I reckon if you're working for me, I oughta be paying you a decent wage for your time."

"Oh no, Mr. Hollister," said Christopher hurriedly. "I hope I haven't given you the wrong impression. In no way do I expect to be paid so much as a cent from you. My working for you—and for you, Mrs. Hollister," he added, glancing over at Almeda, "—that is work I want to do as a member of the family—or at least a member someday. The important thing is that you have the opportunity to know me and observe me and work alongside me. But in no way was I suggesting that there would be any financial obligation on your part. I sincerely apologize if I conveyed such."

"Don't seem right that I don't pay you something."

"I would never suggest this arrangement if I expected pay. That would be highly presumptuous of me. Besides, my pay, if I am found worthy in your estimation, will be the hand of your daughter."

Christopher looked over at me with a smile.

I felt so good and full and content inside to hear him talk so reverently about me to Pa and Almeda. He gave me so much honor and respect that tears sprang to my eyes just thinking about it.

"You think you can make yourself a living around Miracle Springs and work for us at the same time?" asked Pa.

"When a strong young man isn't afraid to work hard," answered Christopher, "work isn't hard to find. And I *am* strong, Mr. Hollister, and I *am* a hard worker. I may have been to seminary and served as a minister, but I also know how to sweat and put my muscles to the purposes God intended for them. Once word gets around that I am willing and available and will ask for only a fair and modest wage in exchange for my services, I have no doubt I will have more work than I can well use. And my needs are modest enough that I shall have plenty of time to work for my own bread and for you as well."

"I see you are confident as well as strong."

Christopher laughed.

"I have been accused of being too confident in myself at times," he said.

"Well, don't apologize for it, son. Too much confidence where it is unfounded has been the undoing of many a man—but a lack of proper confidence keeps many other men from ever making anything of themselves. As long as you stay somewhere in the middle of the two, I reckon you'll do fine. Anyhow, you'll do fine by me."

"Thank you, sir."

Again Pa sat for a spell, listening and trying to absorb all the practical implications.

And I sat there feeling safe and protected. Here were three wise individuals, all older than I was, all of whom I loved and who I knew loved me, discussing my future and my welfare. What security! They all wanted only the best for me. I didn't have to do anything but relax and allow God to speak to them.

"Corrie and I both want to submit ourselves to your insight and wisdom too, Mrs. Hollister," Christopher went on, turning to Almeda. "Corrie has often spoken to me of all she has learned from you as she has matured spiritually. She has a deep love and respect for you, and we both hunger to continue to learn from you as well as your husband."

"Thank you, Christopher," said Almeda. "You are very kind, and I appreciate what you say."

"I agree with everything he said," I added. "I hope you know, Almeda, how big a help you have been to me through the years."

"Thank you, Corrie," she said with a smile. "Yes, I think I do know. We have both meant a great deal to each other. The Lord has been very good to us, hasn't he?"

I nodded.

Gradually the conversation turned toward the specifics of what we would actually do, though both Pa and Christopher agreed that figuring it out would no doubt take some time. Pa said again that he didn't know exactly what he could keep Christopher doing.

Christopher suggested that Pa think of projects he'd like done that he'd been too busy for. Pa said it sounded like a good enough idea. I thought maybe he could learn the Supply Company business too, and Almeda agreed to that.

Bright and early Monday morning Christopher appeared at our place, riding the horse Zack had lent him. By the time we were all up and about, Pa discovered him out in the barn cleaning out some of the stalls and generally tidying the place up.

I don't think at first Pa had realized how much work experience Christopher had had. I'd told him about Mrs. Timms' farm and how Christopher took care of everything for her. But I'm not sure it had all sunk in. The fact that Christopher was from the East, that he was from near a big city like Richmond, and that he had been a minister by profession—I think all that still said to Pa that he was mostly a city man who didn't know how to get his hands dirty.

But by the end of that first day, though, Pa was finding out just what a hard and capable worker Christopher Braxton was.

And I couldn't help being proud whenever I'd see that Pa was pleased with something Christopher had done!

CHAPTER 29

THE NEW CORRAL AND BARN

I wanted that Christmas to be the biggest and most festive one imaginable. Not only was Christopher here, it was also my first Christmas home in two years!

Two weeks before Christmas, Christopher and Tad and I rode up into the hills to cut a Christmas tree. We all spent the next week decorating it, stringing popcorn and berries, and hanging whatever else we could think of on it.

Then Becky and Almeda and I started cooking. If Christopher had lost any weight from the second half of his trip west—which I couldn't notice—Christmas was bound to fatten him up good!

All week we baked breads and pies and cookies and tarts and puddings. And early on Christmas Eve we killed the turkey and plucked him and boiled the rice and cut up bread and vegetables for the stuffing.

And through the whole time there were secrets and whisperings and all kinds of goings-on about what people were buying and making for each other. Christopher had to ask me twice more to borrow money!

He had, like he'd said, already found work. Word in Miracle Springs traveled fast, and even without Gertrude Sinclair's efforts, before that week was out, most of the men around knew Christopher was available. He had helped Mr. Douglas build a new fence around his pasture, and Mr. Bosely at the General Store had hired him to put a fresh coat of paint on the walls of his storeroom. But as yet he was only making enough money to pay his tab at the boardinghouse—that's why he had to borrow money from me for Christmas. I couldn't help laughing to myself at the thought of lending Christopher money to buy *me* a present for Christmas—if indeed that's what he was doing!

Christopher was at the house every day when he wasn't working for somebody else. He stayed so busy that I wasn't able to spend as much time just talking with him as I might have wished, but it was wonderful just to have him nearby.

The legislature was in Christmas recess, so Pa was home all the time, and he and Christopher worked every day together—sometimes just the two of them, sometimes with Zack and Tad. For about a week they just took care of odd jobs around the place that had been put off. And then, suddenly, they were making big plans.

It was only three or four days before Christmas when all four of the men burst into the house together for supper, all talking among themselves so fast and excitedly that none of us knew what was going on.

One thing I was sure of, Christmas was not on their minds right then!

"That ground between the creek and the path up to Uncle Nick's is perfect, Pa," Zack was saying.

"Yep, I like the idea," Pa replied.

"Might even be able to plant it with pasture grass—part of it anyway."

"What was that you were saying about a watering hole, Tad?"

"Just that with the slope of the creek along there, it ought to be easy to dig a trough into the corral with a sluice that we can shut when it's full."

"Why not just let them water in the stream?" asked Christopher.

"Too many folks downstream use it for drinking water. Some of the town too," answered Pa.

"So we'd have to fence off the stream?"

"We'd make the stream the edge, and run a fence all along it, around in both directions to the new barn."

"What are the four of you talking about!" I finally asked.

"We're going to build a new horse corral and barn," beamed

Tad. "We've been walking it off and we've just about got everything figured out."

"But why?" asked Becky.

"So we can get more cattle and more horses," answered Pa.

"Little Wolf's got more'n he can handle up at his place now," Zack explained. "This way I can keep some of the horses down here, and we can get some more besides."

"And I'll be able to bring in some of my own," added Tad.

"And with the other barn and stables empty of the horses, we'll be able to bring in maybe another dozen head of beef cattle," said Pa. "It works out good all the way around."

Almeda suddenly burst out laughing.

"What's so funny?" asked Pa, throwing Christopher a wink.

"I was just thinking about something Zack once said."

"Me? What did I say?"

"Do you remember when you left for the Pony Express—"

"If it was something I said on that day, I'd rather forget about it!" sighed Zack.

"You complained that everything around here had to do with women and babies—don't you remember?"

"Yeah, yeah, I remember—don't remind me!"

"Well, you've turned the tables on me now."

"How do you mean?"

"Now the talk's about all your men things, and we women are the ones left out!"

Everyone had a good laugh over that, and we sat down for supper.

Actually Almeda was right. Pa and Tad and Zack and Christopher were having so much fun working together that I couldn't help envying them a little. Zack was spending less time up at Little Wolf's, and Tad less time at the livery stable. I wanted to go out and be part of it too!

CHAPTER 30

CHRISTMAS EVE

Christopher was invited to celebrate Christmas Eve with us and all of Christmas Day too. I had been wishing he didn't have to stay in town Christmas Eve night, and Uncle Nick must have read my mind, because he invited Christopher to come spend the night with them. Pa and Almeda would have made room for him too, under any other circumstances, but it wouldn't have been proper for him to stay under the same roof with me, even if we hadn't had a houseful.

The biggest surprise of all was that my sister Emily and her husband Mike appeared two days before Christmas with my little niece Sarah. Nobody knew they were coming for a visit, and the excitement still hadn't worn off two weeks later when they had to leave.

Christmas Eve was so wonderful. Our whole family was together again . . . *and* I had Christopher besides!

We ate early and then piled into several wagons—all of us and Christopher and Uncle Nick's family—and headed into town for the community Christmas Eve get-together.

While I'd been gone, the town had built a small building near the church. It served as a town hall and a meeting room and an extra school building all in one.

"You know, Corrie," said Uncle Nick as we got down and began walking toward the hall, "this is going to be the biggest Christmas party Miracle Springs has ever seen."

"Why?"

"Because everybody wants to see your new feller."

"Nah," chimed in Pa behind us, "it's Corrie herself they want to see. Some of the folks still ain't seen her since she's been back."

"Shoot, Corrie," added Zack. "Nobody really wanted to have a Christmas party. They just wanted an excuse to hear about your escapades back East. Heck, they're probably even going to want you to give a speech or something."

"You got a speech ready?" teased Uncle Nick.

"No," I laughed. "Everybody's seen me already at church or one place or another. It's *Emily* they'll be coming to see. But look how nice the hall looks with the windows all lit up!"

"Should be," said Tad. "We all helped build it."

"Yep," added Pa, "bought and paid for by the citizens of Miracle Springs."

"I object t' that remark, hee, hee, hee!" sounded a voice behind us.

"Hey, Alkali!" said Uncle Nick, turning around. "They even invited an old goat like you?"

"Yep, they did, hee, hee, hee. But what you doin' callin' ol' Murphy a citizen, Drum?" he said to Pa. "He weren't one heck of a citizen and you knows it. Why the only reason—"

"We know, Alkali," put in Uncle Nick. "But the extra financing had to come from somewhere, even if it had to be him." He winked over his shoulder at Pa.

We could already hear music coming from the open door, and we walked on inside.

All three of us turned out to be right. I visited with several people I hadn't seen since I'd been back. And since there hadn't been a church service since Mike and Emily had arrived, a lot of people were surprised to see them, and they were the center of attention. But there was still a lot of curiosity about Christopher too, and more than once I saw eyes looking his way from some of the more gossipy groups of women.

The hall looked bright and festive in the lantern light. A few colorful piñatas—red, yellow, and green—hung from the ceiling, donated by the few Mexican families that had moved into the community. A refreshment table off to the side boasted huge bowls full of fresh eggnog some of the women had made, and platters and platters of Christmas cookies. The aroma of refreshments mingled with the faint smell of paint, which you could detect when the hall hadn't been used in a while. The logs in the fireplace were just starting to blaze cheerfully and get the hall nice and warm.

The music we'd heard came from the end of the hall opposite the refreshment table, where Patrick Shaw sat on a stool picking his banjo. Several children had gathered around and were asking him about it. Tad had brought his guitar along, and within another minute or two they had joined together in picking and strumming out "Unclouded Day."

"Still pickin' at that banjo of yours, I see, Pat," said Pa as he walked up.

"Yep—keeps me outta trouble."

Now Christopher joined the small crowd, intrigued. Pa introduced him to Patrick Shaw and they shook hands.

"I've never seen a banjo up close like this, Mr. Shaw," said Christopher.

"Call me Pat."

"All right, Pat." Christopher paused, gazing at the instrument. "What a wonderful sound! How do you get your fingers to move so fast without having them stumble all over each other?"

Mr. Shaw laughed.

"Hours and hours of workin' at it," he answered. "My old man gave me a banjo when I was a boy, and for years I didn't do much else."

He finished off his sentence with a fast-fingered break up the neck of the instrument that ended with higher notes than it seemed any banjo ought to be able to make.

"Play something else," said Christopher.

The fingers on Mr. Shaw's right hand leapt into action again, so fast you could hardly see them, while his left moved up and down and all about the neck for about forty seconds. By the time he was finished, nearly everyone in the hall was clapping and stomping their boots on the floor, and applause exploded when he finished.

"Hey, Pat," said Pa, "I think you're even better'n the last time I heard you!"

Mr. Shaw laughed. "I still manage to learn a new tune or work out some new break every now and then. Once a banjo picker, always a banjo picker, they say!"

"Do you know 'Angel Band'?" asked Christopher.

In answer, Mr. Shaw began to play the old familiar waltz. A moment later and Tad was picking his guitar, and then Christopher began to sing. A few people wandered over and joined in, and pretty soon half the room was singing it with them. When it was over, another began, followed by another.

Then Christopher suggested "Brightest and Best."

Patrick and Tad were so good that it only took them ten or twenty seconds to get into the same key and figure out how they were going to do it, and then they could play just about anything anyone suggested.

For the next hour we all sang Christmas carols, with Mr. Shaw and Christopher leading the whole thing.

I couldn't believe it. For someone who said he was shy, Christopher could sure be the life of the party. He was such an interesting man! I hoped I never got tired of finding out new things about him.

The biggest surprise of all was that I'd never heard him sing before. Not only could he lead singing, he had a wonderful voice.

"That's quite a man you've got there, Corrie," said Rev. Rutledge to me as we were standing off to one side mingling our singing with talk. "A natural-born leader if ever I saw one. If I need any help with my church work, I'll certainly know who to call upon."

"I'm sure he would like that," I said. "His one and only experience with a church wasn't altogether pleasant."

Just then his wife joined us.

"Merry Christmas, Corrie."

"Merry Christmas, Harriet."

"How are you feeling, Avery?" she asked Rev. Rutledge.

"A little better—still tired."

"Are you ready to go?"

"I think so," he answered, then looked back toward me. "I think we are going to go home now, Corrie," he said. "Why don't you and Christopher drop in on us after the Christmas bustle settles down. We would like to get to know him better."

"Good . . . we will."

"Fine. We'll look forward to it."

"And we'll see you out at the house tomorrow?"

"Wouldn't miss it."

"Merry Christmas, then."

"Merry Christmas to you too, Corrie."

"Good-night."

The minister and his wife got their coats, and I watched them as they walked slowly toward the door. Even with her limp, Harriet suddenly seemed to have so much more energy than Rev. Rutledge.

After a moment, I turned and went over to rejoin the boisterous carolers.

CHAPTER 31

THE MOST WONDERFUL CHRISTMAS EVER

I had hoped for a snowy Christmas, but it didn't happen. It was a cold day, but the sun was shining bright and cheery.

Emily, Becky, Tad, Zack, and I were up at the crack of dawn with Ruth and baby Sarah—all excited and eager for the day to begin. Christmas brought out the child in all of us! We five brothers and sisters hadn't all been together for years, much less for Christmas, and it was so wonderful to pretend we were young again. Mike and Christopher watched and laughed, but there was something special between us five. We'd been through a lot together, and the bonds of love between all of us ran deep.

Christmas always unites past with present, bringing with it memories of times that have gone before. I found that all the more true on this particular Christmas.

Pa and Almeda must have sensed what a special occasion it was for us, for when we got up on Christmas morning we found five of Pa's big white stockings hanging from the hearth right along with the stockings we'd hung last night for Ruth and Sarah. Each had one of our names on it and was stuffed to the top with fruits and nuts and candies and other goodies.

I was nearly thirty, but I squealed with delight as I ran into the living room, and so did all the rest. Pa, I think, was happiest of all to see his children part of a family where love was the foundation.

Such a festive spirit filled that whole day!

Delicious aromas had been wafting through the rooms for a

166

week before the day actually arrived, but they were absolutely bursting with the smell of Christmas. Fruitcakes and cookies and fresh bread all had to compete with the fragrance of hot coffee, along with sage and onion for the stuffing and all the other dishes being prepared for the day's feast later in the afternoon.

The house looked like Christmas too. Wreaths we had all made, ribboned in red and sparkled with tinsel, hung on all the doors. The needles of the tree cast a subtle fragrance of the forest about the corner of the room where it stood. A special red and green knit coverlet lay on the sofa.

Uncle Nick and Aunt Katie came with Christopher and the children for a late breakfast about nine. Then the Rutledges and Alkali Jones came about eleven. By then the kitchen was warm and bustling and full of women, all trying to help, but mostly enjoying being together on the day.

I was amazed to see how many children were in the house—a whole new generation was coming up. Life goes by so quickly. You grow up, and before you know it there are youngsters looking up and thinking *you* are one of the adults . . . when it seemed such a short time ago that you were just like they are now.

Uncle Nick and Aunt Katie had brought their three—Erich, who was ten, and seven-year-old Joan, and little four-year-old Jeffrey. The Rutledges brought six-year-old Mary. And of course we had our Ruth, who had turned eight since I had come home, and eighteen-month-old Sarah, who was charming everyone as she enjoyed her first "real" Christmas.

That made six people under ten years old at the dinner table. Then Christopher and Mike and we five Hollister kids would make seven who were between twenty and just barely over thirty. And then there were Pa and Almeda and Uncle Nick and Aunt Katie and Harriet and Rev. Rutledge and Alkali Jones—yet another age group, except that some of them were mixed in with *our* generation. I reckon it would have been a little confusing for a visitor, but it sure made for a lively Christmas!

While the women were working in the kitchen, Pa and Mr. Jones and Uncle Nick and Rev. Rutledge sat in the living room and talked. Mike was busy outside trying to explain the game of baseball to Christopher, who, though he had been in the East, had never heard of it. Before long the two of them, along with Tad and Erich and Zack, were tossing and hitting a ball around. The two younger Belles and the youngest Hollister were running back and forth between all three groups, while Emily did what she could between the kitchen and taking care of Sarah.

"How you feeling, Avery?" I heard Pa asking.

"Little better," answered Rev. Rutledge. "It was a difficult autumn for me, though. I think I'm on the mend."

I glanced over and couldn't help but see on Harriet's face an expression of mingled pain and concern, as if she didn't know whether she agreed. I looked away again and wondered but didn't say anything.

The men's conversation, as so often happened, drifted to mining.

"I take it, then," Rev. Rutledge asked, "that all of you still think there's gold yet to be found."

"We ain't been successful at finding where it is," answered Pa, "but there's reasons to believe that's exactly the case."

"Hee, hee—we been chasin' the blamed vein for years," cackled Mr. Jones, "and if y' ask me, it heads straight into the mountain."

"Or quits right where we did," added Uncle Nick. "If you ask me, we got all we're gonna get outta that hill."

"Why don't you explore farther in?" asked Rev. Rutledge.

"We always planned to," said Pa. "But I'm away so doggone much, and the boys is always doing other things. And who knows but what Nick's right and there ain't no more gold? I reckon we just ain't ever figured it was worth all the work it'd take to find out."

The conversation was interrupted as the door burst open.

"I'm famished!" exclaimed Mike, heading straight for the kitchen to see what he could steal to tide over his still-young appetite.

"You get out of here, young man!" admonished Almeda with a laugh. "You just had breakfast, and dinner's a long way off."

Christopher made a dash for a plate of deviled eggs behind her and caught up two just as she turned around.

"Christopher Braxton!" she cried.

But he was out of reach in an instant, handing one of the eggs to Mike with a wink as they made good their escape from the kitchen.

Zack and Tad followed inside a minute later, but instead of heading for the kitchen they joined the group of men and sat down, breathing hard.

"What have you two rascals been up to?" said Pa.

"Just a little game of chase . . . like the old days," said Tad.

"Except that now I can't outrun you!" rejoined Zack. "When did you get so fast anyway?"

"When you weren't looking!" answered Tad. "Hey—" he exclaimed, "Zack, let's you and me show Mike and Christopher how to play fortress."

"Let me get my breath first—what teams?"

"I'm the youngest, Christopher's the oldest. How about me and him against you and Mike."

"Fair enough," replied Zack. "What about Erich?"

"We could get both him and Ruth—then it'd be even."

"What about Joan?"

"Hold on here—what's fortress?" interrupted Christopher before Zack could answer, approaching closer with a wary but curious expression on his face as he munched down the last of his egg.

"You'll love it," answered Tad. "I'll show you everything."

He leapt up from his chair. "Come on. First thing we gotta do is set up our territories."

"How about the mine?" suggested Zack as all four headed back outside.

"Yeah, the walkway is the boundary. Mike and I claim the space between the big boulder up the hill and the bridge over the creek to Uncle Nick's. You take below."

"All right, and since you're on the hill, it'll be my invasion. Six tags and we have to go back and start over."

"Okay by me."

The door swung shut behind them, and they were off up toward the mine to man the fortress and plan the invasion. As I listened, part of me wanted to go out and play with them. I loved to play fortress and hadn't done it for years! Maybe I'd be able to play after dinner. Right now I still had the apple pies to finish.

I didn't know if the way to a man's heart really was through his stomach. I just knew that Christopher loved apple pie, and I was determined to make the ones this Christmas as good as Mrs. Timms'. The game would have to wait.

CHAPTER 32

A COZY EVENING

When we finally rang the bell signaling that the long-awaited Christmas feast was ready, everyone's appetite was ready to do justice to the long hours of preparation.

Through the door trooped the conquerors and vanquished, laughing and talking and sweating. It was a little harder to get the younger ones inside and settled down, for they had been passionately involved in a game of ball with Mike's equipment, the rules for which would have been anyone's guess. But the aromas from the kitchen finally triumphed over games and balls and contests and discussions, and at length all the seats around the great table and two temporary, makeshift ones were occupied and expectant.

Even though there were two ministers present, Pa stood, reached out his arms, waited for everyone to join hands in a great circle around the room, and then he prayed.

"Our heavenly Father," he prayed, "we're real thankful for all you've done for us. We want to thank you on this special day for our family and friends, for the provision from your hand for everything we need, for our health, and for the laughter of young'uns and the high spirits of young folks and for the wisdom of older folks. Thank you that you've given us all these to enjoy today. Thank you for our visitors from near and far—especially the happy surprise of Emily's visit with Mike and little Sarah. We thank you too for Christopher being here among us. Thank you, God for this day, and for giving your Son for us. We ask that you keep on blessing all the families represented here. Help us to serve you in all that we do. And thank you especially for all the good women who've been working so hard to make this day special. Amen."

Then came the steaming platters and bowls and plates, filled with every kind of holiday food it was possible to imagine!

Turkey and ham provided the foundation, the latter glazed with honey and smelling of the cloves stuck into it all around. There were vegetables in plenty—corn, potatoes, sweet potatoes, and squash. Fresh bread and warm butter came next, followed by crab-apple relish to add color to the display on the table. Already the platters were being emptied onto the plates of the hungry, while Almeda and I continued to bring more—the deviled eggs, another fruit salad, a vegetable and chicken salad, and at last gravy for the potatoes.

Standing ready for later were three apple pies, a cherry pie Aunt Katie had made from her stock of canned cherries, and a dessert that Harriet had brought with crushed berries and cherries, heavily sweetened and mixed with whipped cream, rolled up in a flaky pastry shell.

Never would we be able to eat a fourth of what we had prepared!

The conversation was lively, with Mr. Jones' *hee, hee, hee* of a laugh sounding out now and then. With children around too, there was never any flagging of enthusiasm.

After we had all been sitting for fifteen or twenty minutes, still at the table, wondering why we had eaten so much, Pa rose and slowly made his way to the door. He opened it and peered out.

"What is it, Drum?" asked Almeda.

Pa turned back in and closed the door.

"Sun's gone. Dark clouds coming this way from over the mountains in the east."

"Is it going to snow, Papa?" asked Ruth.

"It just may, little girl . . . it just may."

He sat down again, and we continued to talk and visit. Nobody was in the mood for pie yet.

By five or five-thirty it was pretty dark, and the sky had grown heavy with clouds. There wasn't much wind down on the ground, but the winds must have been high up in the mountains because the storm came on quickly. It was warm, too, not like you'd expect for a winter storm.

Pa piled several more logs onto the fire, went to the door again and stared out, then brought in a store of wood from outside, as if he expected severe weather before morning.

We ate the pies and pastries and cookies, and the men kept nibbling at little scraps of turkey and ham like men do. By seven we could hear the wind starting to pick up. Pa went outside again.

"Temperature's dropping," he announced when he came back in. "Ten degrees lower already, and it could fall even further. If you're going back home tonight, Avery," he added to Rev. Rutledge, "you'd best be going. Not that we wouldn't love to put you up, and we will too if need be, but I thought you oughta know. Rain, or something whiter, ain't far off."

Rev. Rutledge rose. So did Harriet, rousing little Mary, who had dozed off in her lap.

"Then we thank you for your hospitality, and for a wonderful Christmas," Rev. Rutledge said, "but we don't want to impose further. I think we three Rutledges would like to sleep in our own beds tonight."

"Zack," said Pa, "why don't you and Tad saddle up a couple of horses and ride the Reverend into town."

Both boys were on their feet in an instant, grabbing their coats and hats and heading for the door.

"We will be fine, Drummond, I assure you," said Rev. Rutledge.

"I'm sure you will, but I'll rest more comfortably if the boys accompany you. You know as well as anyone how quickly a storm springs up around here. And with you not feelin' well lately . . . well, I'd just feel better."

Rev. Rutledge made no more reply. They said their goodbyes around the room, and in five more minutes they were gone.

"Alkali, Christopher—what about the two of you?" said Pa. "We'd sure like you to stay a spell longer if you want. We might even be able to have another piece of that pie if we wait long enough. But we could have bad weather anytime."

"We're planning to put Christopher up for another night," put in Aunt Katie. "We already arranged it."

"Good, then. Alkali, if you get snowed in, we'll put you up out in the barn."

"Hee, hee, hee—I'll be right at home!"

The conversation settled down again. About eight we heard the boys' horses returning. Five minutes later the door opened and a howl of wind roared through, sending a frigid breeze through the whole room.

"It's nasty out!" said Tad. "I don't know how we could see a thing. Somehow the horses knew the way."

"The Reverend home okay?" asked Pa.

"Yep," said Zack, "and just in time."

"What do you mean?"

"It started snowing almost the minute we turned around and headed back out."

"It's snowing?" exclaimed Ruth, running toward the door.

Everyone else was right behind her. Pa tried to open the door carefully, but again the wind blew so hard it nearly took Ruth off her feet.

Sure enough. Giant white flakes were swirling around outside in the blackness. The storm had kicked up so fast. Now it was emptying the contents of those black clouds right on Miracle Springs!

"A snowy Christmas!" I exclaimed. "It couldn't be more perfect."

After we'd all had a look and had begun to grow cold, we went back in and sat down. Knowing it was snowing outside changed the whole mood of the gathering. The conversation subsided. Even the youngsters seemed to share the peaceful feeling brought on by knowing that a silent blanket of whiteness was gradually spreading itself all over us and that we were cozy and warm inside.

Pa stoked the fire again and added some more logs, but gradually the chill of the night penetrated the walls. Chairs began to inch closer to the fire. Blankets came out and began to be wrapped around shoulders and feet. The peacefulness deepened, almost to a hushed awe. I think somehow the snow made us all think of that first Christmas so long ago when baby Jesus was born in Bethlehem—even though there was no snow on that night, only the stars that God used to light the way to the stable where his Son was being born.

Soon everyone was bundled up and staring into the fire, the quiet and the firelight adding layer upon layer to the coziness.

What a contrast between the inside and the outside! We couldn't hear the snow falling on the roof. But we could hear the wind, and we could *feel* the snow insulating us beneath its frozen crystals. Every once in a while an edge of the wind would catch the chimney and wander down with a moan, as if to remind us that we weren't altogether safe from the storm. But with Pa in the room with us, we were safe from anything. The whole day I had felt like being a child again, and the storm added all the more to that feeling of mystery and security.

As we sat there I thought of the contrast between this cozy, quiet, peaceful evening and all the bustle of the week before, when we were getting ready for Christmas. We had been hurrying about, baking and decorating and planning and making sure everything was perfect. Even though all the Christmasy things were behind us—the party at the town hall, the gifts, conversation, laughter, guests, dinner, dessert—now it seemed like all that had just been preparation for this quiet time in front of the fire. Now we were able to sit back and appreciate the fruit of our labors.

No one thought about what time it was. We just sat, mostly staring into the fire. Every once in a while a brief conversation would flicker into life, just like the flames would rise and brighten occasionally. Then, like the fire, we would settle back again into the contented silence.

The next thing I knew I had dozed off next to Christopher on the sofa, and now I roused back up when I felt him stand. He didn't say a word, just walked over to the hearth and picked up the Bible that always lay there.

I don't know whether Pa had said something to him or he to Pa when I'd been asleep. But no words passed between them now. Christopher just handed the Bible to Pa, and Pa took it as though he'd been expecting it the whole time.

He opened it to the Gospel of Luke and began quietly reading the familiar words.

And it came to pass in those days, that there went out a decree from Caesar Augustus, that all the world should be taxed. (And this taxing was first made when Cyrenius was governor of Syria.) And all went to be taxed, every one into his own city. And Joseph also went up from Galilee, out of the city of Nazareth, into Judaea, unto the city of David, which is called Bethlehem; (because he was of the house and lineage of David:) to be taxed with Mary his espoused wife, being great with child. And so it was, that, while they were there, the days were accomplished that she should be delivered. And she brought forth her firstborn son, and wrapped him in swaddling clothes, and laid him in a manger; because there was no room for them in the inn. . . .

Pa read the whole story.

There could not have been a more perfect way to end a wonderful Christmas Day.

CHAPTER 33

PA'S DECISION

Pa and Christopher and Zack and Tad had started in on the new corral and barn the next day after they'd begun planning, and by the week after Christmas the work was in full swing.

Christopher and Zack spent that whole week felling thin trees from the other side of the creek for the rails, plus a few thicker ones for the posts. (The Supply Company carried what wire and staples and nails they needed.) The lumber for the barn had to be ordered from the mill, and by the time it was ready the fencing for the corral was nearly completed.

It was the third week of January in the year 1866 that Pa told us his decision. He'd been back to Sacramento for a week for the first legislative meetings of the new year. He came back all the way on Friday and got home real late.

The new barn was starting to come up by then. They'd got the foundation pretty well finished before Pa'd left on Monday, and he'd told Zack and Tad and Christopher not to go any further on it till he got back. I think he was afraid he might come home and find the barn completely done. They could have done it too, but Pa didn't want to miss the fun of watching the walls and roof go up and seeing their dream come to life.

Those five days Pa was gone had given everybody a chance to catch up on other work that they'd been neglecting. But it was so dreary and quiet around the place without the sounds of the four of them outside!

The Saturday after Pa got back, he was out of bed at sunup and outside. Christopher rode in from town about the same time, and when he and Pa came inside a little later, he hardly noticed me. They were talking so feverishly about this and that, as they sat down at the table for coffee, that Almeda and I might as well not even have been there! My feelings weren't really hurt, though, because of how wonderful it was to see them hitting it off.

It wasn't long before Zack and Tad rolled out of bed and joined them for a quick breakfast before heading out to work. I think that was the longest day they had put in yet on the place. By suppertime they had all the barn walls nearly raised.

They were exhausted when they came in to supper. But you could tell how much they were enjoying the work—Pa most of all. He hadn't had so much fun in years, and it was even better to be able to work hard alongside his own sons.

It was at supper that he told us what he'd been thinking.

"I been ponderin' over this for a while," he said. "It ain't a sudden decision, though I reckon working out there today like we did made me finally realize it was what I've been wanting to do for a long time. Maybe it's Christopher's coming and saying he wants to work with me, too, that got me thinking more about it. I figure if he's got what it takes to give me a year out of his life, then I oughta have what it takes to give him a good full year on the other side of the fence, instead of only a few days here and there when I have the time. Doesn't seem like it'd quite be a fair bargain if I didn't."

Nobody was quite sure what Pa was getting at, but we waited and let him keep going.

"Anyway," Pa went on, "what I'm trying to say is that the legislature's been a mite boring for me lately. And I been wanting to spend more time with my family. The way it looks to me is that maybe now's a good opportunity to make the kind of change I been wanting to make."

"What kind of change, Pa?" asked Becky.

"Just hear me out, girl, and I'll tell you."

Pa took another drink of his coffee, then set it down and looked all around the table at each of us.

"What kind of work do I love more than anything, Almeda?" he asked.

"Anything, Drummond," she answered, "anything that's working with your hands—probably working the mine."

"You got that right," rejoined Pa. "And I ain't had the chance to do what I like best in years.

"I tell you, Christopher," Pa went on, looking over toward him, "you want to know what kind of a man I am, well, I'll tell you—I'm happiest when I'm working for myself, working hard, and working with my hands. But Alkali's getting too old for mining. Matter of fact, Alkali's getting too dad-blamed old for just about anything! And Nick's time's mostly taken up with his family and them hogs and cattle he keeps thinking he can raise—but actually he's doing a pretty fair job of it. And besides that, our mine played itself out years ago.

"So you see what I'm saying—there just hasn't been much place for me to do the kind of work I like. I reckon some folks might think when a man gets to be my age, he oughta take life a little easier. But I miss it. I miss the hard work. I miss digging gold out of that hill up there. I miss the excitement of always thinking there's gonna be some new vein just where you slammed the end of your pick into the earth. Ain't nothing quite so exciting as mining for gold, Christopher—nothing I ever done, at least. I don't want to take it easy, I want to work all the harder. I got too many good years left in this body of mine to let it waste away surrounded by fancy clothes and speechmaking in Sacramento.

"So what I've decided is this: I ain't gonna run for reelection this year. I'm gonna call it quits to my political career—"

Before he could say any more, exclamations burst out all around the table—more of surprise than anything.

Zack, I think, might have been disappointed at first, because he was proud of Pa.

Almeda and Tad, on the other hand, couldn't hide their immediate reactions in the opposite direction. Neither of them had ever had enough of Pa, and his being around more meant nothing but good news to them!

And Christopher didn't quite know what to think.

CHAPTER 34

PA'S PROPOSED PARTNERSHIP

"Now simmer down, all of you!" laughed Pa as everyone kept talking among themselves about what he'd just said. "Just let me finish.

"What I'm thinking is—seems like this is the perfect time to start thinking about setting in a new mine over on the other side of the mountain. Then by the summertime, when I'm through in Sacramento, the four of us men can get serious about exploring for that vein we've always known came out that side someplace."

Now the exclamations from Tad and Zack were unmistakable! A whoop or two and a shout, and then they were both talking at once.

"What do you think, Braxton?" said Pa above the din. "You game for a little gold mining?"

"You're the boss!"

Pa threw his head back and laughed. "I know that's what you're trying to tell me."

"You tell me what to do, and I'll follow."

"Then I say we tear into that mountain and find us some more gold."

"You sure there's more there?"

"As sure as I am of anything. I can smell it. So can Alkali. But every new line we sent out from the old shaft came up dry. That's why I figure the best way to go about it is to dig a whole new shaft."

"Remember how Mr. Royce was trying to get his hands on that land, Pa?" I said.

"You bet, I do! That's another reason I'm sure there's gold there—Franklin Royce could smell money, even underground!"

Again we all laughed.

"Who's Franklin Royce?" asked Christopher.

"It's a long story," I answered him. "I'll tell you all about it. Better yet, I'll let you read about it in my journals—someday."

"I'm sure you'll get a chance to meet him one of these days," said Almeda. "He's still around."

"Who owns the land now?" asked Christopher. "*Did* he buy it up?"

Pa shook his head. "Nope. Me and Nick own most of it, up almost a mile into the forest. What money we made from the gold we put back into land."

"How much do you have?"

"I don't know. What we got now, Almeda?"

"Something just over twelve hundred acres, Drummond."

Christopher whistled. "That's a big chunk of land."

"God's been good to us," replied Pa. " 'Course most of it's woodland, and some is steep. Anyhow, we own the hill where the gold's most likely to be. I've wanted to put in a new tunnel for years, but the time just never seemed right. I got busy in Sacramento, Zack was gone for a while and then has been involved with his horse business. Nick lost interest, and Tad couldn't do it alone any more than I could. But I figure now, with all four of us working together, we could bore and dynamite and dig our way as far into that mountain as we need to."

"It'll be just like the old days!" said Tad excitedly.

"What do you say, son?" said Pa, turning toward Zack.

"Yeah, Pa, I like it—a lot. I'll have to talk to Little Wolf, though. I got commitments to him too, but I reckon we can work something out. And with the new barn and corral at our place, I'll be able to keep training and breaking ponies here without going up to his place."

"What about you, Christopher?" said Pa.

"Like I said before, you're the boss. Just so long as I can manage enough odd time with other jobs to keep my tab paid with Mrs. Gianini."

"Well, that's another thing I been thinking about," said Pa, then paused. Everybody waited.

"There's one thing that's different about now from the old days," Pa went on, "and that is that my sons are grown men now, or nearly so. Tad, you're twenty . . . Zack, you're twenty-six. What about you, Christopher? How old are you?"

"Thirty-one."

"There, you see. Both my sons, and the feller that'll likely one day be my third son if he don't show himself to be more of a nincompoop than anything I've seen in him yet"—Pa gave me a wink and a smile—"you three aren't just young'uns, you're men. Yeah, you're right, maybe I am the boss and I'm the Pa and the oldest. But it still don't seem like I got the right to ask you all to sacrifice your other jobs, where you're making money just for my mine, which might be nothing but a harebrained idea of somebody who once hit gold and thinks everywhere he digs is gonna turn out the same."

"So what are you proposing we do, Pa?" asked Zack.

"I'm proposing to make the three of you a proposition. I say whoever of you wants to be part of this thing—and I ain't pressuring you, I'm just saying you can if you want, but you don't have to—any rate, whoever wants to, we'll be partners . . . equal partners. We'll share the work, and whatever we find we split up four ways, and the gold will be yours to start your own lives with."

Tad and Zack immediately began whooping and hollering and talking again. They were so excited they were ready to start swinging the picks right then.

Christopher looked over to me. I met his gaze. There was nothing to say. We both knew what an opportunity Pa was giving us.

" 'Course we'll have to talk to Nick, on account of him owning half the mine. I ain't exactly sure where the line is between what him and me claimed before and what Almeda and me has bought and staked claim to since, but we'll want to give him his fair share, too, and invite him into this here partnership if he wants.

"Thing is, finding that vein, and then pulling whatever gold is there out of it—that's gonna take a heap of work. Ain't no work harder than mining. So I want you to think it through from one end to the other—count the cost is what the Good Book calls it, and that's what I want you to do. Then, if you're of a mind to join up with me, then I figure maybe you'll have to let your other work go for a spell—maybe not entirely, but mostly, 'cause we're gonna have a lot a work in front of us."

All three were ready and willing, from the looks on their faces, but Pa wasn't finished. "Tad, that means the livery for you, and I know you like working there for Mr. Simms. He's been good to you. Same for you, Zack. It might mean less work with your ponies for a spell. But if you're gonna be part of a partnership, then hard work and lots of hours is all you got to put into it. So that's a decision the two of you are gonna have to make. Same goes for you, Braxton. Might be too much work for you to have time for much else.

"But for my part of the partnership, I figure it's only fair that I give you all room and board till we find out if there's gonna be any gold there. 'Course, Zack and Tad, you two know that as long as Almeda and I are alive you always got a roof over your head and a plate in front of you without owing no obligation to us. We always made that clear to you. I love the two of you like only a father can love his own boys, and you can live under my roof as long as you like—I hope it's many more years of the same.

"You can bring your wives too—if you ever have them, that is," Pa added with a grin. "This here plan of Christopher's is one I'm starting to like, so I might just *make* you bring your wives here to live with us for a year before I give you my permission to marry them. What do you think of that, Braxton?" said Pa with a laugh.

"I'm happy the arrangement is meeting with your approval," smiled Christopher.

Again we all laughed. I don't know what the boys thought of Pa's suggestion, but they didn't seem shocked by it. And already they were hitting it off well enough with Christopher that I think they saw why he had wanted to do it this way.

"That's the same deal I'm gonna make with you, Christopher," Pa continued. "If you want to be in on this partnership, then I'll take care of your room and board. You don't have to worry none about your bill with Mrs. Gianini."

Now for the first time Christopher began to squirm a little in his chair.

"I said I didn't want you to pay me, sir. I wouldn't feel right taking money from you when I was the one to broach the subject of working with you."

"You said you wanted to work for me."

"But I came to you."

"And I said I agreed with your plan."

"Yes, but not for pay. If you had needed a hand and had hired me, so to speak, but as it was—"

"Well I'm coming to *you* now," insisted Pa. "I'm asking if you want to hire on as my partner. I'm making you the same deal I'm offering to my own two sons."

Christopher thought a moment.

"I see your point," he replied slowly. "However, I feel most strongly that it would not be right for me to accept money from you, which would be the major difference between me and your arrangement with Tad and Zack. They *are* your sons. I am not yet worthy to be called anything except, I hope, a friend to you all. For the sake of our future relationship and the foundation of my hoped-for marriage to your daughter, I must not put you in an obligatory position with regard to me."

He paused for a second. Pa was listening intently.

"It is not that I do not appreciate it," Christopher went on, "but it would not be right at this time. Once Corrie and I are married— if your approval is forthcoming one day—then I would be your son in a spiritual sense, and everything would be different. Until that time, I must not presume upon your kindness and generosity."

Pa nodded his head slowly, trying to piece together everything that Christopher was saying. I could see that he was frustrated, but in a way which only heightened his respect for Christopher's integrity.

Most men are either too proud to receive help from another or else so willing to that they are constantly taking advantage of those around them by not holding up their fair share. Christopher was neither. He only wanted to walk the middle ground between the two so that proper order and integrity was maintained.

"So you absolutely will not take money from me?" asked Pa.

"I'm sorry—I'm afraid that's correct."

"But you have no objection to sharing the proceeds of the mine if we do hit a strike?"

"If I have done my fair share of the work. Though the fact that you do own the land disturbs me about what you are calling a partnership."

"Disturbs you . . . how?"

"Even if we share the work, I would not be entitled to an equal share. It is *your* land . . . *your* gold. You could hire me to dig it out for you, but that does not make me a partner. The gold would still be yours."

"If you're gonna be part of this family, then that brings you in for your share. Besides, until the Assembly lets out, you and the boys will be putting in more work than me. Don't you see? It works out fair for everyone all the way around."

Christopher took in Pa's words reflectively. "You make a good point, Mr. Hollister. But I still cannot allow you to pay for my board at Mrs. Gianini's."

Again Pa nodded silently for a few seconds.

"Well then," he said in a tone of finality, "it seems to me there's only one way out of this little dilemma. We'll just have to add a bunkhouse onto this new barn we're building."

No one said anything at first, not quite understanding what the new barn had to do with Christopher and money and the mine.

"How come, Pa?" asked Tad. "How's that gonna help?"

"Well, we gotta find a place for Christopher here to live besides the boardinghouse, so that we can give him room and board too, but without any money changing hands."

I could hardly believe my ears! Was Pa really suggesting that Christopher move out here onto our property with us? And if he was, what else could it mean but that he liked Christopher and wanted him to be even more part of the family!

"Well, what do you say to that notion, Braxton?"

"I . . . I don't know, Mr. Hollister," replied Christopher with a laugh. "You have succeeded in catching me off guard."

"Can't see as how you'd have any objection to living out here— in a room in the barn—and eating with us if you were working here with me and the boys every day."

"I see your point."

"I'd be showing you the same consideration I'd give to my other two partners here," said Pa, nodding toward Tad and Zack.

Christopher just looked thoughtful.

"Good, then it's settled!" exclaimed Pa. "Before your scruples think of something else you don't like about it, I'm deciding that we'll add a bunkhouse to the new barn."

Again Christopher laughed, not minding Pa's lighthearted fun at his expense.

"Can I live out in the bunkhouse too, Pa . . . with Christopher?" asked Tad.

Pa's face bent itself into a question mark as he thought about it.

"Don't reckon I see nothing wrong with it," replied Pa. "That is, if Christopher's got no objection."

"Of course not," said Christopher. "It's your place, not mine, and I'd welcome the company."

"Me too!" Zack now added boisterously.

"Sounds like this bunkhouse is gonna take over the whole barn!" laughed Pa.

"We can do it, Pa!" said Zack excitedly, "Can't we, Tad . . . Christopher?"

"Sure."

"I guess we can at that."

"The three of us'll build a bunkhouse in the new barn! I know we can do it!"

"Well, it's sure all right by me," said Pa. "The three of you can work on that and finish it up, though we'll likely need more lumber. After you're done and Christopher's moved in—and you other two if you want to—by then we can start in on the new mine cave."

"Yeah!" exclaimed Zack with a yell of excitement, which Tad joined in on the next second.

Christopher glanced over at me with a smile. I could tell he was excited about this turn of events too. I was so happy I couldn't keep my mouth from smiling.

"So . . . we got us a partnership?" asked Pa, looking around at the three young men.

They all nodded.

"Then let's shake hands and make it official."

He held out his hand to Zack first. They shook hands firmly, looking each other in the eye. Then he and Tad did the same thing. Finally he shook Christopher's hand too.

Seeing a father shake a son's hand like that—as two grown men making a pact together—made something leap inside my heart. It seemed so good, so right, so in harmony with God's order of things.

"And one more thing, Mr. Christopher Braxton," said Pa when they'd all shook hands. "If we're going to be partners, and if you're gonna be eating at my table every day and bunking down in my barn, I figure it's about time you started calling me by my name. Folks down in Sacramento can get away with calling me Mr. Hollister. But around here, I'm just plain Drum."

Christopher laughed.

"All right," he said. "I'll do my best to comply with your request. How about Mr. Drum?"

"Nope. Gotta just be Drum."

They laughed.

I could tell they were both having fun with each other, and my heart warmed to hear it.

"It's a deal," said Christopher. "But it goes both ways."

"Fair enough."

CHAPTER 35

THE BUNKHOUSE

If I'd thought the new horse corral and barn was enough to get Zack and Tad excited, it was nothing compared to their enthusiasm now!

I woke up the next morning to the sound of hammering outside. It couldn't have been much past seven—but already Zack and Tad were out in the new barn working away.

I got dressed and went out to see what they were up to. And I was surprised to see that Christopher had already ridden in from town and was working away beside them.

"Corrie!" he said, glancing up, sweat already showing on his face. "Good morning!"

"What are you all doing?" I exclaimed. "It's barely light."

"We're planning where to build the bunkhouse," answered Zack.

"It looks to me like you're already building it."

"We got the planning out of the way in the first ten minutes," laughed Christopher. "Now we're building."

"Building what?"

"A wall right here. Zack and Tad have just about got that section framed already. By noon, there'll be a wall where you're standing right now."

"You're not going to enlarge the barn?"

"No. We already had the walls and roof up. It would have been too much of a structural change."

"It's plenty big, Corrie," said Zack, taking a break from his hammering. "We're just converting a couple of the horse stalls to living quarters."

"My bunk's gonna be right over there!" said Tad, pointing with his hammer toward the far corner of the still-open space.

"You already know where you're going to sleep?" I exclaimed.

"I tell you," said Christopher, "we wasted no time with our planning!"

"I thought Pa said there wasn't enough lumber."

"We'll have to order some more. In the meantime, a few of the horse stalls will just have to remain incomplete."

"Look, Corrie," said Zack, taking my hand and drawing me into the room that would soon be the bunkhouse, "we're going to put a door through here"—he pointed—"to the outside, so we can come and go without going into the barn, and then a window over in that wall, so we'll have the light from the south."

"And over here—" began Tad. But just then Pa walked in.

"Tarnation!" he exclaimed. "Put an idea in you young whippersnappers' minds and you don't waste no time!"

He walked all the way into the barn, looking back and forth, surmising their plan from the boards that were already lying about and from the framework of the future wall lying on the floor, then glanced up and around at the three of them. "Well," he said, "looks like you've got it pretty well figured out. What do you want me to do?"

Immediately all three voices began speaking at once. I excused myself, though I'm not sure any of them even noticed me leave, and went back into the house to help Almeda with breakfast.

She was right. Suddenly everything going on around here was men's activities! I loved it though, because Christopher was one of them—almost like he was already one of the family! To see them all as such friends, and working so hard together and having fun, was sometimes almost more than my heart could absorb. It was so much more than I had ever dreamed of! And it could never have happened if Christopher weren't here with us, working and talking and laughing and figuring things out and sharing with Pa and Zack and Tad hour after hour. The kind of friendship the four of them were forming as men could never have come about any other way.

More and more every day, I was seeing the wisdom of Christopher's plan, and I was so glad he had had the courage to insist, both to me and to Pa, that our engagement—if it could even be called that—be like this. Now that I thought about it, I guess we *weren't* really engaged like most folks think of it. We were just *planning* to be engaged at the end of this year . . . *if* Pa gave his approval.

It was something like that anyway!

It didn't matter to me that it was unusual or even that I didn't know what would happen and didn't even know what to call it. I felt so secure about the relationship Christopher and I had, and watching him and Pa getting to know each other better every day made me trust the two of them all the more to decide what was right and best for us all.

The inside of the barn, particularly the corner of it known as "the bunkhouse," took shape rapidly.

By the end of that same week they had the wall up and sheeted with wider, thinner slabs of pine to block it off from the rest of the barn. They'd put two doors in, one to the outside of the barn and one through the new wall into the main barn area, and the window was already cut out of the south outside wall, though they'd had to order the glass through the Supply Company. They said they'd go to Sacramento to pick it up, along with some other things they wanted to get. Then the trick would be to get the window back to Miracle Springs in one piece, but we'd ordered glass for people before and only twice had we broken it before delivery.

By the first of February, Tad was so excited and so anxious to move in and start sleeping in the new bunkhouse that he was already starting to move some of his things out. He'd never lived away from home before, and even just moving out from under the roof of the main house was a big event in his life.

They built wood-frame bunks alongside the wall, just mattress-size. The new room wasn't all that large, so they built two of them one above the other, and of course Tad wanted the top one. Zack would sleep under him, and Christopher's bunk was built into the adjacent wall. There was room for three or four plain, straight chairs, and Christopher wanted a small desk where he would be able to write. In the southeast corner they slabbed in a brick base for a potbellied wood stove, with a chimney running straight up and through the ceiling.

By the time it was about ready for them to move into, the bunkhouse was starting to have a comfortable feel to it. It was completely rustic—walls and ceiling from rough-hewn fir and pine and the floor of smooth-sawn planks of fir—but still homey in a man-sort of way. When I suggested painting the inside walls, all three of the occupants rejected the idea at once.

"There's an earthiness to the look and feel and smell of rough wood, Corrie," Christopher told me. "The smell of fresh wood always reminds me of Jesus in his father's carpenter shop. It's one of the reasons I love working with wood. No, no paint for me. Anytime you can keep the natural grain of wood, that's what I prefer."

"How about a small rug, then?"

"I would certainly have no objection to that," he said.

"May I make you one?"

"That would be wonderful."

"Then I will! I will braid a rag rug to lay alongside your bed so that your feet will not be cold when you first get up in the morning."

The bunkhouse was completely finished—except for the window—by the middle of February. Tad had already been sleeping there for more than a week by the time Christopher gave up his lodgings at Mrs. Gianini's and transferred his few worldly possessions out to our place.

I think I was more excited about the arrangement than Tad, though I did my best not to show it. Christopher would now be around the place all day and all night and for every meal. I would be able to see him almost whenever I wanted—though I didn't want to make a nuisance of myself! It would be just like it was at Mrs. Timms'.

That first night, knowing that Christopher was sleeping out in the bunkhouse with Zack and Tad, I could hardly stand it. I wanted to be out there with them—listening to them talk, laughing with them, having fun with them.

As strange as it seems to say that I was jealous of my two younger brothers over the man I hoped to marry—that's just what I was. They were so lucky! Maybe I would get to spend a lifetime with him, but they got to have more of him right now than me, and so thinking about the future wasn't much consolation.

And it wasn't just nights. Even during the day, they got to work with him too! I started thinking that maybe I could help them at the mine instead of working at the Supply Company! I wondered if Pa would let me.

The next day, a Saturday, the four of them hauled picks and shovels and timbers up to the location where Pa planned to bore the new mine into the side of the mountain. They spent all that day getting ready to set off the first sticks of dynamite on Monday.

CHAPTER 36

OUR MARRIAGE JOURNAL OF LETTERS

As the weeks went by after Christopher's coming, then turned into months, he and I talked about this time of preparation for what we hoped would be our eventual marriage. And we began to realize what a significant period it was in our lives.

After he'd been in the bunkhouse with Zack and Tad for a week or two, we were walking contentedly together after lunch in the open meadow just east of the house. As we were talking, I happened to say something that put an idea in both of our minds.

"I miss getting letters from you," I said.

We walked on a little farther. Christopher became very silent and pensive. At first I thought I'd offended him, until finally he spoke.

"Now that you mention it," replied Christopher, as if my words had been more profound than I intended them, "I knew there had been something missing . . . I think that's what it is!"

"Missing? What do you mean?" I asked.

"I don't know," he mused. "I hadn't really thought about it specifically until you said what you did. But as happy as I am to be here with you, there was something extraordinary about that time when we were apart too. There was a deeper level to our communication with each other. . . ."

He paused, still thinking it through even as we walked.

"It's not that there's anything wrong with how it is now, but I do miss the other, just like you said. I used to so devour your letters!"

193

"Oh, me too!" I said. "And yours especially were so full of things for me to think about. But we can't keep writing letters now."

"Why not?"

"I don't know—because you just live over there in the bunkhouse. Because we see each other all the time now."

"Who says that has to stop us from writing?"

We talked about it some more and decided to start writing letters to each other again, even though we saw each other every day as well. We wanted to keep track of what we were thinking about and how we were learning to discuss things and communicate with each other in a different way than what we each wrote in our journals and, like Christopher had said, in a different way than we did when we were actually talking with each other. Writing something down forces you to think about it a little more, and writing to somebody presses you to make your thoughts clear. There were *so* many things we were thinking about during that time—especially about our future—that we didn't want to lose sight of any of it.

We felt the letters we exchanged would be like a journal we compiled together of this year when we were learning so much, and growing together in so many ways, and talking together about what kind of people we wanted to be and what we wanted our life together to mean.

In fact, I went into my bedroom early that same night just so I could sit down at my desk and write Christopher a letter! Not too many people would call what we exchanged "love letters"—but then that's because they wouldn't have understood the kind of spiritual love and kinship that was steadily growing between us.

I did love Christopher so much—and the most wonderful thing about it was knowing that he loved me too!

Dear Christopher,

It feels so good to sit down with a clean piece of paper, dip my pen in ink, and write words I know your eyes will read. I'm so glad you thought of it!

I could talk and talk and talk to you all day every day . . . and listen and listen and listen too!

Will we ever tire of each other? Oh, I hope not. We mustn't let ourselves! I promise if you will promise too. I promise never to tire of you, even if you can't make such a promise. Oh, but I am being silly . . . please don't throw my letter away!

I will try to be serious, for a minute anyway, because I know that is why we decided to begin writing again.

Is it wrong of me to think of what we will do after we are married? (That is, if Pa gives his approval.) You have said you don't want to think about it too much until the time comes. Even though you are the kind of person who plans and doesn't let himself get caught off guard by circumstances, you say that you need to live out this present phase before looking ahead and that you can't assume what Pa may or may not say. I think I understand.

But I can't help looking ahead . . . and wondering.

Will we go back to the East, back to Richmond . . . even back to Mrs. Timms'? That seemed so much like home earlier this year, yet that was probably only because you were there. Now it seems so far away. In fact, my whole time in the East suddenly seems distant and long ago. I still can't believe I was gone for so long!

Now that I am here, now that I am "home" again, I feel so good and content and at peace—especially with you here too! I cannot imagine a more wonderful life than what God has given me at this moment, and so it is hard to imagine leaving.

Yet I know that from now on, my home is with you. I have given my heart to you, not to Miracle Springs or to California . . . or to any *place*. Only to you. If you were not here, I would long to be wherever you were. It could be Richmond or Maine or Canada or Mexico! If you were there, then that's where my home would be.

Still, I cannot help wondering what will become of us, what God will do with us, where he might choose to take us.

And still wondering, but at peace and smiling because I am thinking of you, I am going to say good-night . . . and go to bed.

> Good-night,
> my Christopher!
> Corrie

Unknown to me, at the very same time Christopher was also

writing to me from his small desk out in the bunkhouse. His was a longer and more thoughtful letter.

Oh, but how I relished it when he gave it to me the next day! It was like having some solid mental meat to chew on again. I had known I missed his letters, but I hadn't realized just how much.

Christopher had a way of thinking about things and analyzing them from a spiritual point of view that I never tired of listening to (or rather, reading). It didn't matter what the topic was, I loved watching how he tried to get to the bottom of it so that he could do the right and godly thing. Even when it involved something difficult, as this letter did for him, his approach to it made me feel good.

He had been right about the aspect of his plan that involved him and me getting to know each other better. This year wasn't just so *Pa* could get to know him. Every day I was finding out more about the intricate brain of the man known as Christopher Braxton . . . and I liked what I saw!

If I'd had any doubts months earlier, I sure didn't now—I wanted to be this man's wife!

> Dear Corrie,
>
> An unpleasant realization dawned upon me several days ago. I will try to tell you about it and hope you can understand.
>
> Since you happened into my life, I have been so happy and content, and so taken up with *you* in my thoughts, that I suddenly am aware that I have *not* been nearly so conscious of the Lord as before.
>
> Please do not take this wrong, my dear Corrie. In no way is this statement intended to reflect upon you. It refers rather to something amiss in my own soul—or at least I have found myself questioning if such was the case.
>
> Why is it that one turns to God so easily and so naturally in the midst of despondency, confusion, and sadness, but is unable so readily to bring him into all the corners of one's life when all is going well and happiness reigns on the seat of the heart?
>
> When I was going through the worst of my difficulties at my church and even during my sojourn at Mrs. Timms'

farm, which almost seemed like an exile, the Lord was my constant companion. I prayed almost constantly, crying out to him in my uncertainty concerning many aspects of my life. I questioned the past. I sought perspective. I asked my heavenly Father day and night to reveal to me what the ministry was supposed to be, what I might have done differently. I wondered about what was to become of me—what, if anything, I was to do for him with the rest of my life. The pages of my Bible were well worn in my search for answers, consolation, insight, and wisdom. I hungered for the Lord's voice to speak to me, and my thoughts were nearly always turned toward him.

But now everything is so different. The sun has come out upon my existence! All of my life radiates with new joy and purpose.

So much of this, of course, is due to you, dear Corrie. But it is more than only you. Even if you were to be taken from me, my life would still be vastly different than it was for me a year ago. The Lord has renewed my vision of service. So many of the unanswered questions from the past are now fading into a region of the memory where they have no more power to sting and torment and keep me awake.

However—and here we come at last to the source of my new bewilderment—it seems as though the happy change has lessened my moment-by-moment dependence upon the Lord. He is not on my mind nearly so frequently. My Bible sits unopened sometimes for days. My prayers, when I remember to pray at all, are not so urgent and heartfelt as before. Horrible to say—but it does not seem as though I *need* the Father to the same extent as I did before.

Surely this is not so! We need him for every breath we breathe. Most certainly I need him today as much as I did two years ago. But I am less aware of it as I was then.

That is my concern. It worries me, Corrie. I do not want to be one of the Lord's fair-weather friends.

Surely it should not be this way! Why should joy not fill me with such an awareness of the Father's goodness that I walk even *more* closely with him when, as I said, the sun is shining and life seems good?

Life *is* good, Corrie!

It is good because God created it so. I love to reflect upon the Genesis account, in which time and again the Creator says, "It is good," and upon completion of his vast work in the universe proclaims, "It is *very* good"!

Why, then, are we *less* conscious of the Father's nearness the *more* conscious we are of the goodness of life?

A mystery indeed!

Are we supposed to work harder to make the Lord an integral part of our lives at such times as these? Are prayer, Bible reading, trust in God, and growth supposed to require an effort on our part? When I was surrounded by confusion on all sides, seeking the Lord took no special effort. I could do nothing else! And I cannot say I was always aware of growth in those times, yet as I look back now I see that in so many ways the Lord's hand was indeed maturing me. I fear such is not happening now, at least not in the same way.

Is misery necessary for growth? That does not seem reasonable, yet my experience seems to tell me yes.

Well, I am going to worry about it no longer. I am certainly not miserable right now. I am so happy knowing you are so close! And being able to write to you like this has made me feel still closer to you. I have missed communicating with you with my fingers and my brain instead of just with my lips.

I can't wait to give you this tomorrow! This is going to be a much better arrangement than having to wait weeks for an answer!

Bless you, my dear, dear Corrie!

Still yours,
Christopher

P.S. I love your family. I find myself thinking of them almost as often as I do of you! How fortunate you are to be so blessed—and how fortunate am I to love a woman with such a warm and loving family! It's like a precious dowry that makes me want to marry you all the more.

CHAPTER 37

THE NEW MINE

It had been more than seventeen years since gold was first discovered at Sutter's Mill. Since then there'd been hundreds of new innovations in mining equipment, mainly because every year what gold was left got harder to find and a lot harder to extract from the mountains, streams, and rivers.

But Pa was intent on mining the mountain for the new vein just like he and Uncle Nick and Mr. Jones had mined the first one. He didn't want to spend thousands of dollars on expensive new equipment. Also, he was looking forward to doing the hard work with his bare hands, and he didn't want some newfangled metal contraption doing the work for him.

The minute Alkali Jones heard about Pa's decision to reopen the Hollister mine, he was over at our place every day again, just like he had been right at the beginning. Now, of course, he wasn't able to do much work. His beard was grayer and his hair thinner than ever. Pa said Alkali was getting close to seventy or maybe there already.

But even though he was slowing down a lot, Mr. Jones still had the same sense of humor and kept everybody laughing with his stories. And now that he had a new and willing audience in Christopher, he had to tell everyone of his seventy-year supply all over again! There was no end to the teasing he got from Pa and the boys about them, but as long as Christopher was interested, Mr. Jones persisted.

In fact, Christopher showed Mr. Jones such courtesy and listened with such interest to everything he said that before long the two were fast friends. Whenever the old miner came over to the house, he would ask for Christopher, almost like a child asking if a friend could come out to play, and then would follow him around like a devoted puppy all day long.

Pa and Christopher made an effort to make Mr. Jones feel like an important member of the mining team that to listen to them all talk, he was working just as hard as the rest of them. They'd ask him to bring them tools or to fetch some water to drink, and from the times I'd go up to the mine to watch I could see that Pa was always looking out for a softer spot in the rock where he could put Alkali to work with a pick. He let him light the fuse on the first dynamite blast too.

It wouldn't even surprise me, if they did find gold, if Pa gave part of his own share to Mr. Jones. Pa was like that, though he didn't usually let folks see the things he did for other people.

I had always suspected him of giving more than a fair share of the first mine's profits to Mr. Jones, though I know he would have denied that had anybody asked. Even though Mr. Jones didn't do too much regular work as he got older, he still managed to live decently and keep his cabin and have plenty to eat and buy a new mule or horse every so often. There were some who believed Mr. Jones's stories about a big strike he'd had in '48. But I had my own suspicions, and they had Pa's name hooked to them.

I had other suspicions about Pa as well, and about where his money went.

Anyone with two eyes could see that Pa had worked harder and more hours on the first mine than either Mr. Jones or Uncle Nick. Yet when all was said and done, Uncle Nick seemed to have more money than we did. He had bought a lot of cattle and some expensive horses, and he and Aunt Katie traveled quite a bit. I'm not saying Uncle Nick got more than his share. He was a hard worker, and he earned what he got. But for all Pa's efforts, even with Almeda's business to go along with it, we didn't ever have any extra money. They bought land, of course. But I know they also helped a lot of people and probably put more money than anyone else into keeping up the church building and helping support Rev. Rutledge and his family.

I was coming to see that Pa and Christopher were a lot more alike than I think either of them realized. I don't know if it's always true that girls tend to get husbands like their fathers. But I reckon that when you like your father, as I did, you must figure that's a pretty decent place to look when you're sizing up other men.

They bored into the hill from the northeast side, using dynamite to start the shaft, and all of us went up to watch the first blasts. I stood back with Almeda and Becky and Aunt Katie and all the younger children, watching as Pa and Tad and Zack and Uncle Nick explained everything to Christopher about the fuses and the direction the dynamite would blow. It was all new to Christopher, and he was eager to learn all he could.

All Alkali Jones could do was chuckle and cackle at the proceedings—that is, until Pa handed him that first match.

Finally everything was ready. Pa gave the signal, Alkali lit the fuse, everybody backed up well out of the way, I held my hands over my ears . . . and we all waited.

Bang! sounded the great explosion.

Rock shot out of the hillside in what seemed like every direction, but none of it landed near us.

A big cloud of dust and dirt rose up in the air, then gradually settled back down to the earth. Now there was a hole in the mountain, the beginnings of the cavity where the new mine would be.

We all cheered and clapped.

The new mine was underway!

As I stood watching, I remembered the morning some months back that I had gone into the old mine and it had seemed smaller. I thought to myself that the old mine was like my childhood, and now this new one would be the mine of my adulthood.

As all the rock and dust fell, the men ran forward armed with shovels and picks to begin clearing away the debris. They were so anxious to get on with the business of finding gold!

They continued with more dynamiting and picking away all morning. We brought out some lunch about noon. They were all enjoying their work too much to come in. At suppertime we nearly had to drag their filthy, exhausted bodies away, but finally they gave up for the day and walked back down to the house all dirty, sweaty, and laughing.

"Hee, hee, hee," cackled Mr. Jones, who ate with us every day that he came to the mine, which was just about every day. "I done seen a lotta mines in my day. But dangburn it, I never seen one git into a hill so fast as that. Hee, hee."

"We didn't make it all that far, Alkali," said Pa. "But I reckon with five of us, we didn't do too bad at that."

After supper, I took a candle and slipped outside. I wanted to see just how far they had gotten by the day's end.

I wasn't quite as impressed as Mr. Jones. They hadn't even burrowed so far in that you could call it a cave yet, but it was the beginning of one anyway. From now on the work would be slower. I held my candle up, but nothing yellow shone from the walls—only gray and brown dirt and stone.

They continued working on the next day and on every day after that, digging and picking farther into the mountain and then hauling the rocks and gravel and dirt out with wheelbarrows down toward the stream, where they made an arrangement of several sluice boxes in a row to sift it out for the gold.

Gradually they began taking a little gold out too. Pa said all the hills around here had some gold in them. It was just a question of whether there was enough to make it worth all the effort of getting it out. Those first months, all they got was dust and a few pea-sized nuggets.

By the middle of May, the cave was deep enough into the side of the mountain that Pa was getting hopeful they'd find the vein before long. But he didn't want any discoveries made while he was in Sacramento, so he gave the boys and Christopher time off to work at other things when he had to be gone for a whole week or two at a time. Sometimes they'd bring out loads and loads from inside the shaft and wait to sluice it till Pa was gone.

CHAPTER 38

SUMMER 1866

The spring, then the summer came.

The days and weeks went by leisurely yet steadily. Before I knew it, the days were long and hot. The chilly storms of winter were half a year's turn of the earth away and the snow of Christmas night already a fading memory.

Christopher and Rev. Rutledge had by this time become close friends. They lent one another books—although most of the borrowing was done by Christopher, because he had been able to bring only a few favorite books across the country and found Rev. Rutledge's library a great treasure. They also spent a lot of time talking about theological matters, both delighting in the other's mind and spiritual journeys. Pa sometimes accompanied Christopher to the Rutledges' and sat in on those discussions. Before long he was reading more himself than he ever had before.

As the weather warmed, I had shown Christopher nearly everything of the countryside for miles around. All the memorable spots I had renewed acquaintance with after my return to California, I now introduced to Christopher. We walked, we rode, we hiked all over, finding as many places to make new memories about as I had old ones to show him.

It was a happier time than I had ever known in my life.

I don't know what it would have been like if we had tried to have such experiences *after* being married, but I was so glad we weren't doing it that way. Christopher's plan had turned out so wonderful—I couldn't imagine the time being better than it was.

Of course, we continued to write letters to each other for our marriage journal. Even though we delivered the letters in person instead of sending them cross-country, we found that the act of writing helped us think through what we had to say to each other much more thoroughly. Having the year to write letters back and forth and to get so many aspects of our still learning and growing relationship figured out ahead of time was still another reason that this was such a good and growing time for both of us.

One day in the middle of the summer, a strange man rode into Miracle Springs. After he'd made an inquiry or two, he walked right in the door of the Supply Company, where I happened to be working that day, and stood before me.

The man's dark beard was ragged and his face was brown and lined and at first glance he was fearsome to look at. But once his eyes caught hold of me and held mine for a second or two, I knew that gentleness and compassion lived behind the rugged features.

"I'm looking for Zack Hollister," the man said. "They said you might be able to direct me to his place."

"Yes . . . yes, I can," I said. "I'm his sister."

"Which one—Corrie?"

"Why . . . why, *yes!*" I exclaimed. "How did you know?"

Finally the man smiled.

"He told me all about you—he's mighty fond of you, you know."

"And are you . . . Mr. Trumbull?" I asked.

"It seems we each know one another even before being properly introduced. Hawk Trumbull, Miss Hollister," he said, smiling again and holding out a callused hand. "I am very pleased to know you at last by sight."

We shook hands.

"Zack will be so excited to see you!" I said. "He never mentioned that you were coming for a visit."

"He knows nothing about it," said Mr. Trumbull. "It's not exactly what you'd say is a social call."

I told him how to get out to the house and the mine. I wished

I could go with him, but Mr. Ashton was sick that day, and I had to be at the Supply till closing.

There were so many questions I suddenly wanted to ask him, but they didn't come to me until the moment Mr. Trumbull was out of sight. And I didn't get much of a chance to talk with him later. He stayed for supper and the night, but he spent most of the time talking with Zack and Pa.

Early the next morning, the three of them—Zack and Pa and Mr. Trumbull—rode out of town together on the business that had brought Zack's friend from the high desert all the way to Miracle Springs. We didn't see or hear from any one of them for a whole month. But what a story they had to tell when they got back!

While they were gone, Christopher and Tad (with a little help, but mostly verbal encouragement, from Mr. Jones) kept working the mine. But they didn't work quite as long hours as before. They didn't want to make a big strike without Pa and Zack, so they mostly sluiced the gravel and dirt they'd already accumulated.

The month gave Christopher and me more time to spend together and to write to each other. We wrote every day, I think, though it's impossible to tell about *every* letter that passed between us.

Dear Christopher,

Do you recall my telling you about my two friends Jennie and Laura? You've met them at church, I think. Jennie is married now.

I don't really have anything in common with them now, but occasionally I see them and talk a little, and that always makes me reflective. It's funny how you grow up with people, but then the older you get the more the paths of your life diverge. Suddenly you wake up one day to realize you're not at all alike anymore. It always makes me feel melancholy for some reason, although I'm glad for how my life has turned out.

Why is life like that, Christopher? Why do some people go down one road and others another? What makes friends grow apart?

When I told Laura several months ago about you and Pa

and the apprenticeship, she seemed shocked to hear of such a thing.

"How can you stand to wait, Corrie!" she said. "Why would you *want* to wait so long?"

I tried to explain it to her, but she didn't even begin to understand, any more than she had when I'd told her that you and I were best friends.

"You're practically old enough that people will start calling you an old maid if you're not careful," she said. "Aren't you afraid if you wait too long, he'll find out things about you he doesn't like and change his mind? Goodness, Corrie, I know if I had the chance to snag a husband as good-looking as that man of yours, I'd waste no time about it! I'd get his ring on my finger before he had the chance to think twice about it!"

As if getting a husband is more important than having a good and solid marriage—or more important than the will of God!

I tried to tell her that I *wanted* you to know everything bad and selfish and inconsiderate about me before we were married. I loved you too much to try to deceive you, I said—especially about myself. If it is God's will for you to change your mind, then that's exactly what I *want* to happen. I would never dream of wanting to marry unless it was what God desired for me. And what harm is there in remaining unmarried, whatever people think of me or call me, if I am the daughter of my Father in heaven?

Laura laughed when I said that. Everything I said sounded ridiculous in her ears, just like her reasoning, which completely omitted any thought of what God might want, sounded to me.

How could we have grown to be such different people?

Christopher, why is it so difficult for people like Laura, who goes to church just as much as I do, to understand when I try to tell her we are trying to order our lives by God's design, not our own? Sure the first question we ought always to ask—about everything and anything . . . in every situation . . . every moment—is: *God, what do YOU want me to do, to say, to think?* Not that I always listen to him or get the message right or obey perfectly. But I want to try. I want God's will to be the first priority of our life together.

So few people seem to think that way, Christopher! Are you and I so odd, so out of step with the rest of the world?

Then just this afternoon I happened to see Jennie in town, and I suppose our talk prompted all this. She's been married now about six months. And all the happiness and excitement she felt a year ago when she was telling me about the young man who is now her husband—and when I was trying to tell her how different it was with you and me—all that is gone now.

I knew the minute I saw her downcast face that something was troubling her. I asked her what was wrong. She said that being married was harder than she'd thought it would be. Then she started crying.

I put my arm around her and took her into the back office at the Supply Company and we sat down. She needed someone to talk to, and she started telling me how it was without my saying another word.

The poor young thing! Christopher, I feel so bad for her— yet what can I do? It is too late. Now they're married and have to make the best of it. I'm sure they will, but they never had the chance we did to get to know each other ahead of time.

"I should have waited," she told me. "My pa told me it wasn't a good idea to get married so soon." That's Patrick Shaw, you remember, a good friend of Pa's—the one who played the banjo at the Christmas Eve gathering.

"But I *wouldn't* listen, Corrie!" Jennie was sobbing now. "So finally Pa gave his consent, though I know he didn't want to. I wish he hadn't given in to me, though I was being pretty stubborn about it at the time."

I asked her what the problem was.

"I just didn't know him, Corrie," she said. "I thought I did, though Pa said I didn't know him as well as I thought I did. He used to be so talkative and considerate, always being nice to me, doing things for me, bringing me presents and flowers. But almost as soon as we got married he stopped doing things for me or even talking to me. After a while he got gruff and then started going out with all his old friends like he used to before he met me. All he wanted out of me was to cook his meals and wash his clothes and . . . well, you know. He seemed so different, like he'd changed. But

Ma says people don't change—that he'd just been putting
on his best for me and now that we were married he didn't
have to bother. She and Pa'd seen it, she said, and that's
why Pa had told me to wait. But I was so sure that the way
he was with me was the real him, though now I see it
wasn't.

"I suppose he didn't know me too well, either. I got upset
yesterday, and before I knew it I'd raised my voice and told
him that he'd changed and he wasn't making it any fun to
be married. He got really mad at me and yelled back, 'I ain't
the one who's changed, Jennie,' he said. 'You're the one
who's different—all grumpy and glum all the time!' Then he
turned and stormed out of the door. Oh, Corrie, what am I
going to do!"

I didn't know what to tell her, Christopher. She should
have listened to Mr. Shaw.

I'm sure we'll have lots of things to get used to about
each other too—but at least we'll know each other better
than they do. And if, at the end of the year, Pa says we don't
know each other well enough yet, then I hope we'll both
have the good sense to listen to him!

I plan to anyway. I don't want you to have to yell at me.
I don't ever want to do anything that would make you yell
at me!

I am full of so many other thoughts, but it's late and I
have to get to bed.

Corrie

Dear Corrie,

Yes, I plan to listen to your father too!

That's the whole idea behind this arrangement—to en-
trust our young and inexperienced judgment to someone
older and wiser and who can counsel us with more wisdom
than we can muster even between the two of us!

I know exactly what you mean about watching the paths
of life diverge as you gradually find yourself separating from
people you have known for years and at the same time
drawing closer to people you hadn't known before. We are
a good example! Two years ago the name Corrie Hollister
would have meant nothing to my ears . . . now it means the
world to me! Our paths came together, just as yours and Jen-

nie's and Laura's have diverged.

I have thought about this for years, trying to get to the bottom of just what draws certain people together and likewise moves them apart without allowing a close proximity of soul to develop. There are relationships and friendships and associations that seem to last for a season, but even these often gradually drift apart, while others become permanent, stand the test of time, and remain deeply part of one's life forever.

What is the difference? It has seemed an important question to me somehow. More specifically, why do some people come to the point in their lives where they begin asking that question you raised—*God, what do YOU want me to do, to say, to think?*—about everything that comes along . . . while others never seem to begin asking it?

I have come to think it has to do not just with having things in common, but with the choices and decisions every man and woman makes.

Sharing things in common, it would seem, is the first circumstance that draws two people together—a shared interest, a shared goal, even some chance commonality of location or need. For example, your father and Patrick Shaw are friends first of all because by accident they both happen to live in Miracle Springs, and second because they share nearly adjacent plots of land north of Miracle Springs. You and Laura and Jennie were friends because your fathers knew each other. You and I first shared the common goal of getting you well after you were shot and brought to Mrs. Timms' farm.

But there comes a point, it seems to me, that having things in common—even if they are common interests and common attitudes and even common spiritual perspectives—is not in itself enough to keep two people close and moving the same direction in life.

You see, living always involves movement. When we talk about "life's road" and "paths" diverging or coming together, we talk about *walking* down those roads and paths. It's a step-by-step process. We are constantly taking steps, moving farther along whatever *road* or *path* we happen to be on.

Those steps we take are our choices. Every step represents a choice or a decision we make—ten, twenty, fifty a day. Some are large steps, some are so tiny we don't even realize we've made a choice at all. But each one represents a movement, a direction.

And having things "in common" with another person doesn't necessarily mean you are going in the same direction. The roads may have crossed one another briefly, or they may twist and turn in such a way that for a while they appear to be similar. But after both people continue to make dissimilar choices—in behavior and attitude and how they relate to people and how they respond to God's leading— eventually the disparity in direction begins to show itself.

In other words, as you and another person keep walking along and continue to develop the spiritual personalities that choices naturally develop, pretty soon you realize that, though you crossed paths for a while, you never were really on the same road at all!

At the same time, people whose motivations and choices are similarly directed will, in time, nearly always find themselves drawn *closer* together. If they are heading toward a common goal, how can it be otherwise? No matter how far apart they may be, the distance between them will continue to shrink as they each approach that destination toward which their inner choices lead them. Two individuals whose sole motive is to make choices that, as the old book says, are an "imitation of Christ," cannot help but draw closer together in spirit.

Choice and *life direction* "in-common-ness" is the thing that draws individuals together, be they men or women, not the lesser kinds of in-common-ness that cannot help but fade away in time if the paths are differently pointed.

So many people marry because for a short and temporary season of life their pathways cross and they seem, to their star-crossed eyes, to have *everything* in common. Alas, when the further passage of time reveals, by the ongoing direction of their character-producing choices, that their life's roads could not have been more different. Then does marriage become a burdensome thing indeed!

Such, I fear, is the sad case with Patrick Shaw's daughter.

For us, it is exactly such a scenario that my apprenticeship plan is designed to prevent. If, after a year of being around each other and working together and seeing one another at our worst, we do not know beyond doubt whether our choices are leading us in a common direction, then perhaps we deserve to be miserable together!

I do not think that will happen, however. Your father is too wise a man—and he listens to One far wiser.

Bless you!
Christopher

Dear Christopher,

Everything you say makes so much sense.

Though it is difficult to feel I no longer have much in common with people like Jennie and Laura, discovering "a commonality of choice and life direction," like you call it, is so much greater a thing to be treasured.

I am feeling so wonderfully content!

Of course I desire with all my heart to be *Mrs*. Christopher Braxton someday. Yet I sometimes think I could go on this way forever. I am so happy. We are learning and growing and finding out so much about ourselves and each other, learning what it means to grow *together* and to live as Christians *together*. Why would we want to hasten an end to such a rich time? I know—don't you?—that we will look back on this year as one of the most wonderful years of all our life together!

Oh, I *am* content, Christopher.

I know that, as you say, our inner choices are moving toward a common goal. The rest of this year will only make that direction all the clearer. If that is true, then why must we be in a hurry about anything? We are going where we are going *together*—so what difference does it make how soon we marry? If Pa should say, "Braxton, you've got to work another year—"

I'm laughing to myself as I write, imagining Pa with a stern face saying it like that.

But even if he should say that, what is that to us? We are still walking alongside each other—our roads still lead in the same direction.

To see you every day is a delight. I do not need to have you all to myself. You cannot imagine how it stirs my heart and warms me inside to see you working and laughing and talking with Pa and Zack and Tad! How many young women enjoy the privilege of having their family truly *love* their husbands? And what a richness it adds to my sense of your love to know it extends to my family as well. I cannot imagine anyone marrying against their parents' wishes. What an incomplete marriage it would be!

Oh, Christopher, Christopher! You have made me so happy—not because you have swept me off my feet, but because you have always wanted the best for me . . . whether that best is you or not! How can you be so giving and unselfish?

But I love you all the more for it!

Corrie

Dear Corrie,

I don't know if I will have the courage to give you this letter! I am writing it late, just before retiring. As always at such times, my thoughts are filled to overflowing with you.

All this talk about it being "good" what we are doing and our being "content" to wait until the right time for marriage has caused me to think about the opposite side as well.

So here I will balance the scales—and perhaps confuse you altogether!—by saying that I *am* eager to make you my wife as soon as possible.

Do you ever find yourself thinking about what it will be like?

I'm sure you do, just as I do. Right this minute you are probably lying in bed dreaming of me and Jesus and his great work within us and of your love for me. In the same way I will soon be lying in bed dreaming about you and the abundance of my life with you in the Spirit of Jesus.

I am also dreaming—and here is the part where I don't know if I will have the courage to give the letter to you!—of the day when we won't have to say "good-night" and separate, but will just lie there together quietly and peacefully, praising our Father for his love and supreme goodness to us until we fall asleep in each other's arms.

Oh, Corrie, I do love you and long for you so much! We are already one, so I know I needn't explain my feelings every time they rise up within me.

I appreciate you so much, on so many levels. I appreciate

your willingness to go through this year of waiting when so many young women would have objected. Thank you for your patience. It won't be long before God has made of us a man and woman who are *ready* for marriage, not merely *eager* for it. He is now preparing me for you and you for me.

Why would we desire to choose something less by rushing God's plan for us? His plan is perfect, but it almost always takes more time than people are willing to give him.

Do you remember when I saw you washing your hair the other day? I cherish that look on your face when you looked up from the basin, water and soap dripping off you, and saw me standing there.

At first you were shocked. Then we both laughed.

I'm sure your friend Jennie made sure she was always perfectly presentable whenever she saw her beau. Most young couples only see each other at their best. But that's no preparation for a life together!

I want you to see me at my worst—when I'm dirty and my hair's not combed, when I'm grumpy, when I'm sweating from hard work, even when I'm impatient or frustrated or moody. I want you to know all of me—*especially* the bad side—so that you will know if you want to spend the rest of your life with it!

My dreams of you are becoming more and more God-centered. Perhaps that is an aspect of this year that I did not anticipate—the changes that would take place within our mutual loves. The more time we give him, the more he can shake from us the fleshly attributes that typically draw men and women together. Thus he can perfect our love on all levels, even that of the flesh, because it is rooted and founded on something more lasting and eternal—that is, the spirit.

Christopher

CHAPTER 39

INTO A BRAND-NEW TIZZY

At the end of the summer, a letter came in the mail that took me by surprise—not so much the letter itself, but my reaction to it.

Ever since I'd written back to Mr. Kemble, telling him that I couldn't accept his offer to become a permanent writer for the *Alta*, I hadn't thought nearly as much about writing as I always had before—professional writing, I mean. Of course I kept writing in my journal and to Christopher.

I had continued to get invitations and offers from time to time, but they were not something I paid much attention to. Other newspapers from San Francisco and Sacramento inquired about my writing for them. And there were more invitations for me to speak, especially as people began thinking more about the 1866 elections. Several Republican candidates contacted me, wanting to know if I would speak on their behalf or even campaign for them. I didn't pay them much mind either.

Then I had a letter from the governor of California:

Dear Miss Hollister,

I hear from the inevitable political grapevine that circulates through this city that you are now back in California after two years in the East. I want to take this opportunity to welcome you back to the Golden State and offer my congratulations for all your effective efforts on behalf of the Union and its cause. Your byline became rather widely known here during your absence, and I took particular pride in my association with you, even flattering myself that I might have helped in some small way to propel you onto the national stage.

I know that President Lincoln and many others in the East thought highly of you, and I want you to know that you had many admirers back home here in California as well, myself included. I read as many of your articles as came across my desk. I always felt you focused important perspectives as you viewed events, giving your readership more to ponder than the mere events about which you wrote. I certainly hope that we in California will be favored by more of your insightful journalism now that you are back home with us.

Remembering your help in previous campaigns, I hope it would not be presumptuous of me to ask whether you would help us out again in the upcoming elections. A number of our Republican candidates on the ballot this fall face stiff fights, and I know they would welcome any words that you could write or speak publicly on their behalf. There would be occasions where I would, no doubt, be joining you at the podium.

Finally, I am hoping you might be able to use your influence to convince your father to reconsider his decision not to seek reelection. He is a fine man, one of the most honest, humble, and straightforward legislators in all of Sacramento, and I consider it an honor to have served with him these past five years since I became governor. The Assembly will be poorer without him, and many of my colleagues join me in hoping that he will change his mind.

I look forward to seeing you one day soon. When you are next in Sacramento, please call at my office. I would enjoy talking with you again.

> I remain, Miss Hollister,
> sincerely yours,
> Leland Stanford, Governer

I showed the letter to Christopher. He read it very quietly.

"What are you going to do?" he asked with a serious look on his face.

"Nothing," I answered. "I have no desire to involve myself in

politics again, at least right now. My life is here in Miracle Springs
. . . and with you."

"But . . . but aren't you . . . don't you think perhaps you *should*
think about what he has said?"

"You mean as my duty to my state and my country?"

"Maybe something like that."

I thought a moment.

"My first duty is to you, Christopher, and then to my family,
and then perhaps to myself and to my community. There was a
time in my life when political involvement and writing for newspapers seemed a good thing and was what I felt was right to do.
But everything changed when I met you. No, I'll write Mr. Stanford back and tell him how things stand. And I'll also have to tell
him that Pa's decision is his own to make, that I'll convey his message but that I won't try to sway Pa's mind on the matter."

Despite my confident-sounding words to Christopher, however, I didn't sleep very well that night. I have to admit I was kind
of proud to get the letter from the governor. And just when I
thought I'd put to rest all the decisions of what to do about my
writing and my speaking, suddenly I found myself right back in a
tizzy.

What thoughts and confusing questions Mr. Stanford's letter
stirred up! All at once I began questioning all my resolutions of the
previous autumn.

I discovered that the desire to write and be involved in all the
exciting things that go along with it—especially politics!—wasn't
as dead as I'd thought. There was a part of me that wanted to rush
off to Sacramento the very next day and jump into that whole
world again with both feet.

I couldn't believe the things I found myself thinking as I lay
there tossing and turning. I wasn't thinking about Christopher at
all, but about writing and speaking and all the flattering things Mr.
Stanford had said in his letter. I was ashamed of myself . . . but I
couldn't help it!

The worst part was that I couldn't tell Christopher what I was
thinking. He would think I was having doubts about getting married—which I wasn't.

Or was I?

If I did accept Mr. Stanford's offer, what *would* that mean between Christopher and me? Christopher's plan included us being around each other every day—that was just as important as it was for him and Pa to work together. Could I just leave and go to Sacramento and then around to other places as I got involved in the election?

What if Christopher told me he didn't want me to . . . and I wanted to anyway? What if I did it against his wishes? Surely he would take that as a sign that his plan had worked and that I'd found out that I didn't want to be married as much as I wanted to do other things. He would say our arrangement had kept us from making a mistake and that it was better we discovered it now than later.

Knowing Christopher, he would probably be very gracious and loving about the whole thing. But then he would probably go back to Virginia . . . and I couldn't bear the thought of losing him!

Oh, I didn't know what to do!

I got up the next morning bleary-eyed and miserable, and I was sleepy and depressed all day. I was sure Christopher would know something was wrong and try to talk to me and find out what it was. But I *couldn't* say anything to him! So I tried to stay out of his way.

It was a horrible day. I hated myself for trying to avoid Christopher and for keeping something from him. We had always talked about everything, and now suddenly here I was hiding my innermost thoughts from him.

I know Christopher noticed. He was quiet all day too, and by the next day he seemed to be avoiding me. We hardly talked once, and both of us felt the strain in the air between us.

Once you're into a time of awkward silence like that, it's so hard to break out of it. One of you has to be the first to go to the other and say something, but you're both feeling so hesitant and nervous that you can't summon the courage to do it. Then feelings get hurt, and talking becomes all the harder.

After three days of avoiding each other's eyes and not talking at all, a big black cloud had come between us. I know Almeda and Becky felt it. It kind of quieted everything down around the place.

But still no one said anything. I didn't like that!

CHAPTER 40

THE INVITATION

Early the next week another letter came. It was just as surprising, yet it was almost a relief too, because it gave me something to talk to Christopher about. However, I didn't expect his reaction.

It was another invitation to speak, but this time not directly having to do with politics or the upcoming elections:

Dear Miss Hollister,

Some of us in the Marysville auxiliary of what was the Sanitary Commission during the war have continued to meet together to promote public awareness of social issues vital to our state. We have recently begun an organization called Concerned Women of Northern California.

Many of us are familiar with your writing and followed it while you were in the East, especially as you were working so closely with the Sanitary Commission itself. It has been women such as you and Clara Barton who have raised the stature of women all over this nation, and we are proud that a woman as important as you are lives right here in our own area.

We would be honored if you would visit us. The purpose of this letter is to invite you to be the speaker at our meeting next month. We would like to hear firsthand about your time in the East and would be eager for your perspectives on the war and how you view the future of our country as a result.

We can insure a large turnout to hear you, for your name is widely known among the women of our region. Many of us heard you speak during the election of 1860 and later when you were helping to raise money for the Sanitary Fund.

If you can join us, a twenty-five dollar honorarium will be paid.

Thank you very much for your consideration of this request.

Sincerely yours,
Cynthia Duff, President,
Concerned Women of
Northern California

I put the letter down and shook my head. What was the Lord trying to do—confuse me all the more!

But then I thought that this might be just what I needed to help me talk to Christopher. Since this was a straightforward yes-or-no request, I would show him the letter, ask him what to do, and do whatever he said. Maybe it would help dispel the cloud between us and get us back to talking again.

As soon as Christopher and the others came down from the mine for lunch, I showed the letter to him. He read it without showing much expression on his face.

"Are you going to do it?" he asked.

"I don't know. That's why I'm asking you."

"Asking me what?"

"Asking you if I should do it. Should I accept the invitation or not?"

"Do you want to?"

"I don't know," I said. "I want to know what you think."

"Does it matter what I think?"

"Of course it does," I said. "Why would you think it didn't?"

This wasn't working out the way I'd hoped! Christopher wasn't smiling as he spoke, and his voice sounded distant, like he didn't care.

"I figured this was a part of your life you could handle on your own," he said.

"What would make you think I didn't want you to be part of it?" I said, and I know my voice had a frustrated tone. "I want to do what you think I should."

Christopher was silent a minute, staring down at the ground.

"All right then," he said finally, "I'll think it over."

Without another word, and without even looking at me, he turned around and walked off.

I went in the house for lunch, and the others were waiting for us. I sat down at the table.

"Is Christopher coming?" asked Pa.

"I don't know," I said softly, staring down at my empty plate.

"Corrie," said Almeda tenderly, reaching out from beside me and placing her hand on mine, "is something wrong between the two of you?"

"I don't know—yes—oh, I don't know!" I burst out, then jumped up and ran from the table sobbing.

I hurried to my room and closed the door. I threw myself on my bed crying.

It was so awful! What was happening! Why had Christopher all of a sudden become so strange and quiet and cold?

I stayed in my room all afternoon and finally fell asleep.

When suppertime came, everybody was a little quiet, probably wondering what was going to happen. I guess this was what Christopher had wanted—everybody seeing everybody else when they weren't at their best.

We sure weren't now!

By this time I was almost afraid to see Christopher, and didn't think I could even look at him in the eye. How could this awkwardness have come up between us? I still didn't know what had even caused it! Did this always happen between people?

And now the one person I wanted to talk to about it—suddenly I couldn't talk to about anything at all.

Christopher came in with Pa as if nothing was wrong. We all sat down. I was nervous. I didn't know what to say.

"Did Corrie tell you about the letter she got today?" Christopher said to Pa as we started eating.

"No," answered Pa.

"Invitation to speak to a women's group."

"Where?" asked Almeda.

They all seemed anxious to have something to talk about!

"Marysville," answered Christopher.

"Why, that's only thirty miles from here. Are you going to do it, Corrie?"

"I . . . I don't know," I said hesitantly, speaking now for the first time.

"She asked me what I thought she should do," Christopher went on. It seemed like he was trying to put the awkwardness behind us.

"So what did you tell her?" asked Pa.

"Nothing . . . yet. I haven't had the chance. But I'm going to tell her now. Corrie—" he said, glancing over at me.

I looked up, still hesitant. But his face looked normal. His smile had even almost returned. I tried to smile, but it was hard.

"—I think you ought to accept their invitation," said Christopher. "I might even go over there with you!"

I breathed a sigh of relief and now smiled again. And just as suddenly as it had gotten gloomy and silent, now the conversation started to flow again around the table.

CHAPTER 41

MARYSVILLE

I wrote back and accepted Mrs. Duff's invitation.

Things became tolerable between Christopher and me again, though not the way they were before. We talked, but not deeply and personally. We both knew something had happened we couldn't explain, but neither of us was ready to talk about it.

Up till now I had thought Christopher and I could talk about anything. That's what made this whole situation so surprising. I didn't know what to think. I didn't know what *he* was thinking.

I guess we didn't know each other as well as I'd thought.

I took the opportunity of the time between now and then to make the yellow dress Becky and I had planned. We'd bought the fabric at the same time as the rose calico, and now I needed something to occupy me during the difficult days.

This dress took me longer than the other because it had fancy detail to it. It didn't go together quite as easily either, and I found myself getting frustrated every time I had to take out a seam and sew it over again. No doubt that had more to do with my mental state at the time than the dress!

Eventually I got it done though, and it turned out real pretty. It was a full-length dress, not just a skirt and blouse. The bodice had an inset white yoke with lace edging all around it. The lace also went around the neck, and about the height of my knees the same lace circled around the skirt. That lower part of the lace I had to take out twice. I had an awful time getting it straight.

The yellow fabric had tiny pink flowers all over it, and the lace was also pink. The short puffed sleeves were gathered together with pink and tied in little bows. There was a pink sash that tied in a bow in the back at my waist.

Much to my surprise, when the dress was finished, Mrs. Gianini—who I'd gone to for help at least a dozen times!—presented me with a matching hat she had made to go with my dress. It was a straw bonnet, and she had used the same yellow fabric to make a sash that tied around it and hung down the back. A flower of the pink ribbon was attached to one side.

When I first tried the whole thing on, I felt so good about what I had done. It was so pretty I was almost afraid to wear it, but it turned out to be the perfect thing to wear to the meeting in Marysville. I wouldn't wear it in the carriage all the way there. I'd change after we arrived.

Not too many letters passed between Christopher and me during that month. I was glad to have had the dress to occupy me. I kept writing, but mostly my letters were full of questions and doubts, and I didn't dare give them to Christopher. I didn't know if I ever would. Probably I'd burn them someday!

I don't know if he was writing to me or not. He didn't give me more than one or two, and they weren't about much more than everyday stuff. I was beginning to worry that Christopher had changed his mind about me. So a new cloud began forming in my mind. Every day I expected to wake up and find him packing his bags to go back to Virginia.

Christopher did go over to Marysville with me, but fortunately so did Almeda and Becky. A few months earlier I wouldn't have imagined anything more wonderful than a whole day alone in a carriage with Christopher. Now I was relieved to have other people along so we wouldn't have to sit there in awkward silence as we rode along.

There was a pretty large gathering in the church building where the meeting was held. It was mostly women who came. In fact, as Christopher pointed out on our way home, he was one of only five men in attendance.

I spoke to the group first about just what I had done, sharing some of my experiences working for the Sanitary Commission in the East, right where the fighting was going on. I talked about President Lincoln and General Grant and Gettysburg, and I told them about working with Clara during the fighting in Virginia.

Then I talked about some of the things I'd said in the last article I'd written about the war, the one I wrote on the train when I was going back to Pennsylvania after my visit to New York.

"I have read several articles in newspapers from around the country," I said as I began to conclude my speech, "that have used the term *defining moment* to describe the war. All of us who write about such things have been groping to find a way to put the war into perspective, and those are the words that some men are using to help them do so.

"But if the war was, as they say, a moment of definition in our national history, what does it define? Does it define who and what the people called Americans are? Does it define what this country we call the United States is all about?

"If so, I cannot say I altogether like what such a definition yields. That we could kill our own countrymen—what does that say about us? We pride ourselves on being a nation founded on spiritual freedoms and biblical values. Where have those values been for the last five years? We named this nation the *United* States of America, and yet when the first serious threat to that unity came, we were not united at all, but utterly divided. What does that make of us but hypocrites at the very foundation of what we call this country?

"I suppose this is why, though I pray that God will fill me with forgiveness, at this point I cannot say the anger is altogether erased from my heart toward those who precipitated the events that led to the war. They turned us all—Northerners *and* Southerners, Easterners *and* Westerners—against those biblical values that were our foundation. They made us hypocrites whenever we speak the words *United States*.

"Yet no American is without his share of the blame, because we *all* allowed it to happen.

"Can we look upon ourselves, upon the ugly scar of this war, and take accountability for the great wrong which has been done against our founding fathers and against our Constitution itself? It will no doubt take another generation or two before that question is answered.

"At the same time, however, we have discovered that this is no nation of cowards. Whatever sins may be laid to our charge—and during these last five years there are many—we have nevertheless found that to be an 'American' *is* something worth fighting for. It is no untarnished image, but it is a strong and courageous one.

"As I said in an article I wrote soon after the end of the war, we have spent the years of this war looking into a red-stained national mirror—looking at the enemy, but at the same time looking at ourselves. The images in that mirror are far from pleasant. Yet we also see in that mirror a strength of fiber in the word American. If the mirror has revealed flaws in our character, it has also revealed a valor that I hope will grow into an even greater national strength in the generations to come."

I paused. The room was still and quiet. I hadn't realized how emotional my talk would be, but a look around at the faces staring at me was sobering. Christopher's eyes were big and round, as if in disbelief to hear me talk like that. I guess he had never heard me give a speech before.

"One of my favorite passages from the Bible," I went on after a moment, "is John 15. The image of pruning is something I think a lot about because I love growing things. John says that the Father, who is the gardener, prunes every branch that bears fruit, so that it will bear even more fruit.

"Why is it that pruning makes plants grow and thrive? I find so many of God's ways curious and backward from what we might expect. Why does cutting a branch off a tree actually make that branch grow better and produce *more* fruit? It seems strange, but it really does work that way.

"I suppose that I am trying to look at this terrible war, which has meant so much loss of life in our nation, as a time of pruning from which good will eventually come.

"I do not as yet see much good beyond the fact that the Negroes are free, and there is no more slavery. I pray we will eventually be able to see more good results in the end. I confess that at the moment I find it difficult to see beyond the bloodshed, the heartache, the dreadful cost . . . and the loss of a great President and even greater man. Only time will show what good fruit has resulted from this terrible pruning.

"But I do not want to take this pruning image too far. According to the Bible, God prunes branches to make them fruitful. But I do not for a moment believe that *God* brought this pruning upon our nation to make it more productive and healthy in the end. We brought it upon ourselves.

"Nor do I believe that this pruning was necessary for our health, as it may be for a young tree. I will always look upon this civil war as a great evil, as a black mark upon our national soul. We should not have fought it. It was wrong of us—on both sides—to take arms against our own countrymen, although the southern political leaders who refused to acknowledge the obvious moral wrong of slavery must no doubt bear the heaviest weight of responsibility.

"So when I speak of pruning, it is with no sense of the inescapability of this war. It was *not* necessary, and I hate the memory of it. I cannot think of the day I spent on the Gettysburg battlefield and remember the faces of the young men lying there in blue and gray without tears coming to my eyes.

"But now, as we look back and try to find meaning in what happened, we must only hope and pray that good will come of the pruning, that fruitfulness and a restoration of our national health will be the result, no matter that we took the pruning knife in our *own* hands and did what no one but God ought to do—that is, take the lives of our fellowmen.

"I believe with all my heart that God is able to make good come out of bad and wrong and evil . . . *if* we allow him to. I only hope and pray that we as Americans will be able to do so."

I turned and went back to my seat between Almeda and Christopher in the front row. Everyone clapped so loudly that it began to be embarrassing. Mrs. Duff went up front, but when they kept clapping, she motioned me to come back up and join her. Finally the room settled down.

"Would you mind answering questions," she said to me, "if any of the listeners have any?"

"That would be fine," I said.

Immediately several hands shot in the air, and Mrs. Duff, who knew nearly everybody by name, began calling on people one at a time.

"What is it like being a woman writer?" someone asked. "Are you accepted by your male peers?"

"Some find a woman trying to do a man's job annoying, others don't seem to mind. After they get over the initial shock, most men try to be fair and judge you on the basis of what you do. Not all, of course, but most. Once the war was taking such a toll, there were so many woman doing so many things—Clara Barton and others like her, for instance—just because all the men were out on the battlefields, that men became more accepting of women doing all kinds of things."

"Will there ever be a woman President?" asked another.

"That is very difficult for me to imagine!" I laughed. "How could there be—we can't even vote!"

"Will women ever get the vote?"

"Certainly . . . someday," I answered. "At least I think so, though it may take another hundred years!"

"What about you, Corrie? Will you ever try to go into politics?"

"No. I like to write about politics, but I doubt I would ever seek office . . . even if women did get the vote in my lifetime."

"What about your father? Why don't you run for his seat in the legislature?"

The question caught me off guard. I hesitated momentarily.

"Corrie Hollister for legislature!" shouted someone. Then others joined in. I just stood there smiling, then finally breaking into laughter.

Finally the noise died down. Mrs. Duff took a few more questions, which I answered. Then the meeting broke up. We were there another hour, however, because everyone wanted to meet me and shake my hand and talk to me and thank me for coming.

I couldn't help feeling proud when one of the ladies complimented me on my dress and asked if I'd bought it when I was in the East. If she had only seen me gritting my teeth the second time I had to redo the lace around the skirt!

CHAPTER 42

WORKING THROUGH OUR FIRST BIG MISUNDERSTANDING

Christopher was quiet again all the way home. If it hadn't been for Becky and Almeda, the ride would have been unbearable. We three talked, but Christopher just sat with the reins in his hands all the way, hardly saying a thing.

We got home just about dark.

Almeda and Becky and I went inside, while Christopher unhitched the carriage and put up the horses. We quickly fixed up some supper, and I expected Christopher to come in at any moment, but he never did, and I didn't see him again that evening. He went straight to the bunkhouse and to bed without even eating.

Whatever the problem had been earlier—it seemed to have come back.

When Christopher wasn't at breakfast the next morning either, I resolved that I *had* to talk to him. This awkward silence could not go on forever. I was afraid. But I *had* to find out what he was thinking, even if it meant learning the worst.

Finally, halfway through the morning I got up my courage and walked up to the mine. I looked all around but didn't see him.

"Where's Christopher?" I asked Pa finally when he saw me and came over to greet me.

"Took off a few minutes ago. Said he needed a break. Must have—he's been working harder this morning than I ever seen a man work in my life . . . sweat pouring off him. If he kept that up, he'd collapse before noon."

I forced a smile, thanked him, and turned to walk off.

"Hey, what is it with the two of you lately anyway?" asked Pa behind me.

A lump rose up to my throat. How could I answer him?

I turned and tried to say something, though I can't even remember what I was going to say. But instead of words, tears came rushing out. I turned again and ran off toward the woods. Pa just stood there watching me, bewildered but I know hurting for me at the same time.

I wandered into the trees and finally got my tears to stop, then headed back down toward the house at the edge of the clearing between the wood and the pasture. Just as I was turning in toward the house, suddenly Christopher appeared from behind a tree, coming up from the woods in the opposite direction.

We both hesitated, then stopped.

His eyes were red. A pang stabbed my heart just to see the look of hurt and grief on his face.

"Hello," I said awkwardly, trying to smile.

He returned the smile, though it looked just as forced as mine.

"Just, uh . . . out for a little walk," he said. "Needed a break from swinging that pick."

"I know. Pa told me."

"You were up at the mine?"

I nodded.

"What for?"

"Looking for you."

"Me?"

"I figured it was time we talked. At least it was for me," I added. "I couldn't stand it anymore."

Christopher smiled again, though the expression on his face was one of pain, not humor.

"Yes, I suppose it is," he said. "You . . . uh, want to walk a little now?"

"Sure," I answered.

Without planning any direction, we turned away from the pasture and began walking aimlessly off through the woods.

Christopher was the first to speak.

"I'm so sorry about all this, Corrie," he said. "I . . . I just haven't known what to say."

"Why don't you just tell me why you got so quiet and quit talking to me all of a sudden."

"It's not that easy to say," he replied. "I don't know if I even know myself."

We walked on a few more steps. It was quiet and I was *so* nervous for fear of what Christopher was going to tell me.

"That was some speech you gave yesterday," he said at length.

"Thanks," I said.

"I had no idea . . . I mean, of course I knew you were a thinker and a writer—maybe I'd even say philosopher in your own way— but . . . that was a powerful and moving talk, Corrie. Those people were hanging on your every word."

I couldn't help laughing, though it was still nervously.

"I just try to tell what I'm thinking and feeling," I said. "It's no different than writing."

"No, you're wrong there, Corrie. I've done a lot of writing and a lot of speaking and I know about both of them. You have a unique gift to move people, even to sway their thoughts and opinions. I just . . . I'm sorry, Corrie . . . before . . . before this last month, even though I knew you wrote newspaper articles, I just didn't realize—"

Christopher was fumbling for words. I'd never seen him like this!

"I . . . I just didn't realize what an important person you are, Corrie," he went on. "I—"

"I'm not an important person," I interrupted.

"Of course you are, Corrie. Why else would the governor of the state and even the President . . . why would they write you? Why would they want you working for them?"

I kind of half shrugged.

"I saw why yesterday," said Christopher. "You are a powerful lady, Corrie. You are an influential person—whether in writing or speaking. They recognize that—Mr. Lincoln and your editor at the newspaper, the governor, those ladies over at Marysville. You've become an important figure in this state, Corrie. Even in the whole country."

As Christopher spoke, his voice rose in intensity. In spite of what he was saying, his tone wasn't that of trying to compliment me. Instead, he sounded frustrated and agitated.

"I don't agree with that," I said. "But . . . but even if it was true, what difference . . . I mean, why would that suddenly change everything between us?"

Now it was *my* turn to struggle hard to find the right words.

"Oh, but don't you see, Corrie!" exclaimed Christopher, turning away from me, then back, clutching at the air with his empty fists in frustration. "Don't you see? I'm not part of all that . . . I could never be part of that side of your life. That's . . . that's something you have done yourself. . . . And it *has* to be that way. . . . How else could it be?"

"What . . . what are you saying?" I asked slowly.

"I don't know!" he cried. "Don't you see what I'm getting at? How . . . how can . . . how could this ever work when . . . when you have another whole life . . ."

He didn't finish, but kept turning and gesturing with his hands in silent frustration for being unable to find the right words.

"How can . . . how can *what* work?" I said timorously, terrified for what he meant, but having to know.

"Between us!" Christopher burst out. "How can it work . . . how can a marriage work when . . . when two people have such different directions in life to pursue?"

The dreadful words fell like an anvil dropping out of the sky straight onto my head. He'd said the words—*how could a marriage between the two of us ever work!*

Christopher didn't want to marry me after all!

I should have known it would end like this! It was Cal Burton all over again. Who had I been trying to fool in thinking a man could be in love with me? I had made a complete fool of myself. I should have stayed at the convent. It was all a terrible nightmare!

All of a sudden I don't know what came over me. I started yelling like an angry little girl. The memory of those moments is mortifying.

"If you've changed your mind and don't want to marry me," I cried, "why don't you just say so? If I'm too ugly and you don't like what I write and speak about, then just tell me instead of getting all quiet and avoiding me like I had the plague!"

I burst into a fit of sobbing and ran off through the woods. I never wanted to see Christopher again. I never wanted to see any man again!

I ran and ran, I don't even know where—not along any path, just off through the trees wherever my feet happened to go.

Finally I stopped, exhausted, threw myself down onto the ground, and just cried and cried, as sick at heart over how I'd lashed out at Christopher as from what he'd said.

Never in all my life had I felt such misery as I felt in those moments. I lay there crying from deeper depths than I'd ever cried before.

Christopher *wasn't* another Cal Burton! How could I have even thought such a terrible thing?

I *loved* Christopher—that's why the pain went so deep. I loved him like I would never love another man.

To lose a man like him . . . to discover that he didn't love you as much as you thought . . . to place all your dreams of the future on a love you thought was mutual and so solid nothing could shake it—only to have it suddenly wrenched away. . . .

I felt like a great knife had sliced me right to the core and cut out my heart and then a heavy booted foot had stamped on it. The hurt was so bad I couldn't bear it!

I cried and cried! I don't think I stopped for twenty or thirty minutes.

Finally the tears subsided. I took several quivery breaths.

I lay on the ground another ten minutes. I smelled the scent of the pine needles so close to my face, but their fragrance meant nothing now. It only reminded me of a happier time of innocence, when all I'd had to think about was learning about God and nature and writing about it. Now I was learning about life and relationships and how painful they both could be, and even the warm and fragrant woods could not make the hurt go away.

If only I could fall asleep, I thought, and sleep for a year. If only I could wake up and find that by some miracle it had all been a dream, that I'd never gone east, never been involved in the war, never been wounded, never met Christopher Braxton—that it had all just been a story I had made up in my mind . . . and that here

I was at my home in Miracle Springs just like always.

If only . . .

Suddenly I felt a hand on my shoulder.

It startled me. I jumped to a sitting position and spun around.

"Go away!" I cried. For all my heartache over yelling at him before, I couldn't help doing it again. I was so full of hurt and anger and feeling sorry for myself that I wasn't thinking straight!

Christopher's face looked like it had been struck a physical blow. He winced slightly from my words, as if they'd actually hit him, then stood up from where he'd knelt, turned, and obeyed my command, walking away without a word.

The look on his face smote my heart, and I repented of my cruel and selfish outburst.

"Christopher, please . . . please wait," I said.

He stopped, but still did not turn around.

"I'm sorry," I said. "Forgive me for saying that. I . . . I don't really want you to go."

He turned. His face was wet. Tears were streaming down his face. Suddenly my eyes were full again. Whatever had happened, whatever had been said, I *did* love this man! I couldn't bear to see him suffer so much that he cried.

He walked over slowly and sat down beside me.

We sat a long time, each trying to get control of our tears, and trying to figure out what to say.

Christopher was the first to speak.

"Corrie, Corrie," he said softly—so softly I could barely hear him. "I am more sorry than I can ever say that you think I have changed my mind, or that I think you are not the most beautiful young woman in all the world, or that I don't like what you write and speak about. Oh, Corrie, Corrie—forgive me if I have conveyed such things to you!"

His voice was pleading and full of heartbreak.

"I . . . I'm sorry for what I said," I replied. "I don't suppose I meant those things. It was just that you said our marriage could never work . . . and I . . . I couldn't bear the thought that . . . that you didn't want to marry me after all."

I put my hands to my face and started weeping again.

Christopher reached out, touched the back of one of my hands tenderly with his fingers, then reached up and stroked my hair gently a time or two. I brought my hands down, but I still couldn't look him in the eye.

"I'm sorry, Corrie," he said. "I never said I didn't want to marry you."

"But . . . but I thought—"

"Oh, Corrie! I want with all my heart to marry you!"

"But you said—"

"Only that I didn't know how it could work. But I love you, Corrie!"

Oh, those words! How could they not suddenly fan the flame in my heart to life again. At last I looked up. Christopher's eyes bored straight in mine.

"I love you, Corrie," he repeated. "I *love* you!"

Tears again filled my eyes. Tears of happiness, yet I was still so confused.

Christopher saw it all, and understood.

"I was only avoiding you," he said, his voice full of compassion now, as if he was pleading with me to understand so as to undo all the misunderstanding he felt he had caused, "because I didn't know what to say or do."

"About what?" I asked. "I still don't know why it got so quiet and awkward between us all of a sudden. This last month has been so hard. I've missed you so much."

Christopher drew in a deep breath, then tried to explain.

"The moment I read that letter you received from Governor Stanford," he said, "something went astray inside me. I began doubting everything that had happened between us, all the things we'd written and said."

"Doubting . . . but why?" I asked. "His letter had nothing to do with you . . . with us."

"But it did! It had everything to do with us—because it had to do with your future. Suddenly I saw that by marrying me, perhaps . . . I don't know—I don't even know how to explain it! I saw that you had a potential future outside of me, one that has nothing to do with me. I saw . . . that you were a more important person than I'd ever realized . . . and that maybe you needed to do other things that would be impossible if you had a family . . . and maybe I began wondering if you *wanted* to do them. That's when I began doubting myself, doubting that I was the right man for you, and wondering if you would be better off . . . not marrying me."

"Christopher, how can you even say such things? "

"Then when you spoke at Marysville, Corrie . . . that was powerful. Your words rang with truth. You have a gift. You are an important voice. I . . . I don't want to be the one to stand in your way. What if . . . what if you *are* supposed to run for an office of some kind one day—"

"I don't want to do that, Christopher."

"But what if it could happen—that is, if you weren't tied down to a husband and family? I want the best and fullest possibilities for you, Corrie. I want your life to count for all it possibly can. What if you can influence and help more people in these other ways, through your writing and even politics . . . oh, I am just so fearful of being a detriment to all the ways God might have to use you! You are an important public figure, Corrie, whether you admit it or not . . . and I don't want to be the one to keep you from fulfilling whatever destiny the Lord might have for you."

He glanced away, blinking back tears again.

Now it was my turn to reach out and touch him alongside his cheek, which was still turned away from me.

"Christopher," I said. "All of that means nothing to me alongside you—don't you know that? I love you too. The only destiny I care about for myself . . . is being your wife."

He turned and looked at me, wiped at his eyes a time or two, then smiled. I smiled back.

"I'm sorry," he said. "I've never been through anything like this before."

"Neither have I," I said.

"Sometimes my self-doubts just get too strong to fight, and I succumb to what they tell me."

"Mine too. When you got so quiet and quit talking and giving me letters, I thought you had changed your mind about me. I thought your plan had worked so well that your time here was showing you that you didn't love me after all."

"Never! But the time here did eventually show me that you had another life that was pretty significant before I came along. It made me think that you would be better off without me."

"I'll say the same thing you did—never!"

We were quiet a while. At last the woods seemed peaceful again. I drew in a deep breath. Now the pine fragrance was pleasant again.

"I'm sorry for doubting you," I said at length, "and for the things I said back there. I should have trusted you enough to just come and talk to you. But why, if all these things were in your mind, did you tell me to go speak at Marysville?"

"Because we had to know if that was something the Lord might have for you in your future. You had to know, and I had to know. And I must admit I'm not altogether certain God wants you to put all that behind you. You obviously have a voice he can use. We just have to determine where Corrie Hollister the writer and speech-maker fits into our someday being Mr. and Mrs. Braxton."

"Almeda had to deal with the same thing when she married Pa. She was a successful businesswoman."

"We should probably talk to them about it."

We were quiet again for just a moment.

"You're always thinking of what is best for me, aren't you?" I said.

"I don't know. I suppose that is usually what comes to my mind."

"You're a good man, Christopher Braxton."

"I don't know about that. I still struggle with so many things within myself. I'm sorry for withdrawing back into my shell like I did," said Christopher. "It's one of my worst faults. I tend to get quiet and introspective when self-doubts attack me. I know it's hard for the people closest to me, but when it comes, I can't help it. I just ask for your patience if it happens again."

"I'll do my best to remember that."

"Whatever you do, please don't doubt my love for you."

"I'll try. But I get tossed about by self-doubts too."

"I guess we all do. But you and I have to learn to come *to* each other when things like this happen, not drift apart and quit talking. If we don't talk when doubts and questions come, then walls and barriers will grow between us—that's something we positively mustn't let happen. And please come to me when I get that way, because sometimes it nearly paralyzes me and I simply don't know what to do."

We both breathed a deep breath, as if resolving to put the misunderstanding behind us.

Christopher leapt to his feet, then offered me his hand and pulled me up. When I was beside him, he took me in his arms and held me tight.

"I love you, Corrie. I'm so sorry."

"I'm sorry I doubted your love. I should have known you wouldn't quit loving me so easily."

"I will never quit loving you at all."

After a moment, he released me and we began walking slowly back toward the house.

"Do you know the thing I feel worst about of all?" Christopher asked as we walked.

"What?" I said.

"That I didn't say anything about your new yellow dress."

I laughed lightly.

"I was being selfish to be so withdrawn, Corrie. Forgive me . . . again. I love the dress. You did a magnificent job, and you were absolutely beautiful in it."

"Thank you. I had to have *something* to keep me busy."

Now it was Christopher's turn to laugh.

"Well, I hope you can begin writing me letters once again."

"I will . . . if you will too."

"It's a bargain!"

By the end of the day, everyone else knew that the clouds between Christopher and me had blown away and the sun was shining again. They were all obviously relieved, though nobody asked what it had all been about.

For the next week, whenever Christopher and I caught each other's eyes, the smile that passed between us was a smile of love and trust on an even deeper level than before.

Christopher had been right. Getting to know someone you love was a matter of going down to one layer beyond another. And that was worth doing even when pain and temporary misunderstanding was the instrument used to chip the hard crust away so the two of you could to get down there.

We never forgot the difficult lesson in communication we had learned—that when doubts and questions and frustrations and difficulties came we had to talk *more*, not less.

CHAPTER 43

A RIDE, REFLECTIONS, AND MORE LETTERS

In mid-September I took Christopher on a long ride into the mountains east of Miracle Springs. We got up at dawn, packed two meals, and were gone the whole day. We didn't get back until dusk was closing in over the foothills.

We were sore for three days afterward! But what a time!

As we climbed up and began to gain a view of the higher Sierras east of us and the valleys below to the west, I couldn't help thinking about the ride I had taken with Cal Burton at the Stanford ranch. Could that have been only six years before? It seemed like a lifetime!

That had been a time when my outlook was expanding in many directions and I was eager for all life had to offer. Cal had fed my dreams too, with all his talk about having power and impact and about how I could be important and famous and sway people with my writing.

Yes, Cal's "road" had shot across mine right then and had nearly knocked me over—I suppose in a way he'd almost knocked me off my own road altogether. It wasn't just Cal, of course. All those years I'd been involved in writing and politics had shown me so much that was possible for me—and some of those possibilities had become reality. For a while, I suppose, I had tasted what it was like to be successful and important and to have an impact on the world.

But so much was different now.

Everything had changed for me the day I woke up and saw the face of Christopher Braxton staring down at me.

Well, maybe it didn't really change all that much. Maybe the direction of my life was already pointed similarly to his. I'm sure that's what he would say. And it did not take me long, after realizing Cal's deceit, to see how different we had really been all along. But knowing Christopher helped me begin seeing it all more clearly.

For so long my focus had been on all that I might *do*. That was all Cal looked at too. But what a different kind of man was Christopher Braxton! Because of his own perspective on life, he helped me focus instead on what I might *be*.

Riding up to the summit with Cal and looking out over the Pacific had filled my thoughts with all that the world could offer me. The desires he awakened all had *me* at the center of it. They were all about fame and fortune . . . and Cal's favorite word—opportunity.

Riding up into the Sierras on this day with Christopher made me realize my desires had changed. The opportunities that excited Christopher and me now were spiritual ones—opportunities to grow as God's children and to do his will and to put him at the center of our life together.

Governor Stanford's letter and the speech at Marysville had caused Christopher to think for the first time about where my speaking and my writing might lead me. But I had thought about all that at an earlier time in my life. Cal had confronted me with those same issues, as had my time in the East and even the decision to come back to California. And it was becoming clear that those kinds of opportunities didn't matter much to me anymore.

Even the difficult month of misunderstanding with Christopher had forced me to think and pray about it all over again.

Yes, I wanted to *become* something . . . but not in the way of what the world counted important. The question that now occupied my thoughts and prayers was: *What kind of woman do I want to be?*

Who cared what I did or whether anyone knew my name or whether my life was "filled with opportunity," as Cal would have said?

Life *is* filled with opportunity. Every moment is filled with opportunity . . . the opportunity to become more like Jesus.

How could Cal ever understand something like that? He would laugh at the very words.

I suppose a lot of people would scoff at someone like me, who had done what I had done and been to the White House and Gettysburg and all the rest, and who now said all she wanted was to be an obedient daughter of her heavenly Father.

Let them laugh, I thought. The people that mattered most to me wouldn't laugh. Christopher wouldn't laugh. Almeda and Pa wouldn't laugh. Zack wouldn't laugh. Neither would Rev. Rutledge or Harriet or Uncle Nick or Aunt Katie.

That *is* what I wanted to be. Sure, I wanted to live and have fun and do things . . . and maybe even write again. I wanted to laugh and ride horses and learn to sew better and have a home and raise a family. I wanted the same things other young women thinking about marriage would want.

But what I wanted most, deep down, was to be what God wanted me to be, because that mattered most of all. If people thought Christopher and I sounded too spiritual and introspective because we were always talking about trying to deepen our lives as Christians, then I would be sorry. But I still couldn't see that anything else mattered as much as that.

When we got back from our ride, I was too tired even to write about what I'd been thinking. I tried to tell Christopher about it the next afternoon, when he and I went on a short walk. The following morning he gave me this letter:

Dear Corrie,

It's late. Zack and Tad are asleep. I have my kerosene lantern turned down low so I can see the paper in front of me. After our walk and talk today, I must write you.

What is happening between us is so marvelous, so beyond my expectations for such a relationship, that I find myself wanting to talk and talk and talk about it. Every chance I get, whether in your presence or when I sit down to write, I want to describe in endless detail how I feel, just to let you know more and more how complete is my love for you. Everywhere I turn are new ideas, new thoughts, new realizations that I want to express to you. I am very excited about our life together.

Remembering last month—which suddenly seems like a year ago!—is so embarrassing. How could we have gone on so long without talking and writing to one another!

I for one have learned my lesson . . . I hope. I promise that I will talk to you next time doubts assail me. If I want to know what you are thinking—I will ask you face-to-face!

It seems like we are getting to know one another all over again on a deeper and more spiritual plane. Perhaps this is a result of my living around and among your family, of my working in such proximity to you while yet unmarried . . . even of going through what we did recently. It may even be the most important fruit of this grand experiment we have undertaken—our Jacob and Rachel arrangement.

I don't pretend to understand how it is happening, but I find my love for you increases every day. Oh, how I thank God for that love, and how I long for that moment when I can take you in my arms and hold you as my wife.

And yet this time is good! I see nothing but infinite worth in prolonging it in this manner, because in every minute of our present "separation," God is deepening and strengthening the bonds that are forming between our spirits. One of the most beautiful aspects of this is how God continues to show us truths that are practically identical. I see the whole foundation for our future together being molded and shaped by the blinding light of God's love for us and his plan for us.

Do you agree, Corrie, that being married is going to be one of the most highly spiritual experiences of each of our lives? In so many ways we are already "one," and our Father is taking us someplace beautiful together. So when the day comes when we are fully united, it will be such an experience of the Father's love and care that I hardly think I will be able to contain the joy.

I have experienced much in my life, some of it neither happy nor pleasant. But God's grace is sufficient, and I continue to discover that there really is a full and completely abundant joy waiting for those who are totally willing and obedient to follow him.

I thank God he has called us to such a life . . . and called us to share it together!

Christopher

Then I wrote him back that evening.

Dear Christopher,

You wrote about us getting to know each other all over
again, on a deeper plane. That's exactly it—just like you said
that day when we were walking around Miracle Springs. Do
you remember? It was the day after you arrived. You asked
me if I was disappointed, and I misunderstood you. Then
you talked about that very thing, about how we would have
to get to know each other again at deeper levels.

It has happened just like you said it would!

Those first few days, I admit, were anxious for me. I
wondered what you would think of me. It had been so long
since we'd seen each other, I had wondered if *you'd* be disappointed once you saw me. Whatever you say, you dear,
kindhearted, gentle, and gracious Christopher Braxton, I am
not beautiful. What if you saw me, I feared, and said to
yourself, "Ugh . . . what have I done? I don't want to marry
that!"

And then last month I thought all those same things
again—I say it again. You are right, it is embarrassing to remember how uncommunicative we allowed ourselves to become. I join in your promise!

All those doubts are now past, and now that I am learning—sometimes it is still a struggle!—that you really truly
do love me just as I am, love me for the person I am inside
and not what my features look like on the outside.

I am sure we will have more doubt, and more struggles,
and more misunderstandings, but I hope they will be progressive struggles. Do you like the term *progressive struggles*? I just made it up! It refers to struggles that help us to
progress in our knowing of each other.

I am finding the "getting to know" process so wonderful.
Every day we get to discover more of those deeper levels
with each other, just like you say. And just as I am getting
to know you, I am getting to know myself at deeper levels
too!

For so many years I have been learning and growing as
a Christian. At first Almeda helped me so much. I talked to
her about everything, and she would explain things I didn't
know or understand. Then gradually I began to feel my own

spiritual feet under me and take steps of growth on my own. I began to feel the Lord himself speaking to me and guiding me and helping me along.

Pa also helped me, but in different ways. Watching him grow and make choices that set his life going in a new direction was such an example to me. Though we didn't talk about it as readily as I did with Almeda, he was what I'd call a "living lesson book."

Now you have come along and we are able to help one another. It is difficult for me to believe that I really help you spiritually, though you are kind to say it, but I know you are helping me know myself and our Father better in so many ways. Much of this comes, I suppose, from having someone to share everything with—someone who is moving in exactly the same direction.

So besides the fact that I love you, Christopher, I am thankful for you too.

I will always thank God for giving you to me . . . as long as I live.

Corrie

Another letter came from Christopher a couple of days later. He handed it to me at breakfast with a wink.

"I couldn't help myself," he said. "Writing letters is habit forming. It's getting to be that I can't go to sleep unless I have written you!"

Dear Corrie,

Whether or not you believe it, it remains just as true—you have helped me spiritually just as much as I have helped you. I cannot define exactly how. Like everything else it is a process . . . a process of growth.

Surely you remember how confused and frustrated I was when you first met me? Can you think the changes in me—the smiles, the happiness that is now part of my countenance—have nothing to do with you?

Corrie, Corrie, they have everything to do with you!

I am confident, too, that I have grown from the misunderstanding of last month. Though I am older than you, and though I was once minister of a church, I am still very much a learner in some of the most difficult areas of life—especially those that involve learning to know oneself. That is where you are helping me most.

I am not merely happy because a beautiful young woman loves me. (Yes, I will say it, and I will staunchly defend my right to proclaim the truth—a beautiful young woman! *Beautiful,* do you hear! And I thought you put all that behind you in Bridgeville—your mother wasn't saying that you weren't pretty, but that she wanted you to be strong. You *are* a pretty girl, Corrie.) I am equally happy because this young woman is of godly fiber and has helped me see many spiritual truths through all that we communicate together.

So I too am deeply grateful to God for you . . . and likewise shall remain all my earthly days.

I spoke in my last letter about us being "separated."

We are hardly "separated"—we are able to see one another almost at will—although I trust you understand what I mean. Since I wrote that, however, I have been reminded of an earlier time when there truly was a separation between us. I mean last April, just after the President's assassination, when you left Richmond. I was so afraid I might never see you again.

Letting you go back north and saying nothing to you that might persuade you to stay was one of the most difficult things I have ever done. I wanted to ask you to marry me right then! But I sensed that the timing was not right and that many things had to be resolved within each of us before God could fully make us one as he intended.

I know that my decision to let you go, without saying anything encouraging to you with regard to the future of our relationship, made things difficult for you too. I am sorry to have had to put you through it, although I still feel that awaiting the Lord's timing was the best choice.

I was prompted to think about this again when flipping through my journal. My eyes fell upon the following entry, written, from the sound of it, as a prayer. It is dated the evening of the very day you left. I thought you might be interested in what I wrote:

"Henceforth, it is almost going to be like it was when I was asked to leave the church, so drastically has my situation changed. I've known it had to come, but suddenly Corrie is gone. I've already found myself just sitting, not knowing what to do with myself. Though I am 'at home' amid all the same familiar surroundings, I am lonely.

"What will God do in these coming months? I feel that he *will* do something great. But tonight I am so lonely for Corrie. I've gone this long without her before these past months. But this time I know she is not here . . . and is not coming back. I want her back! But, God, you have to accomplish that—I know it.

"I must wait. If there is love between us, it must be able to endure this time. So, Father, accomplish your will in me. Help me to *trust* (always trust) you and thank you. I want *so much* to walk with the humility of your Son!"

I don't know what you will think of that, Corrie, but I found it interesting. God *did* honor our willingness to wait—and will honor our willingness to wait still further this year.

Good things come much more often from patience than from haste.

I do love you, Corrie! And I thank God for you!

Christopher

CHAPTER 44

QUARTZ!

Pa and Christopher and the boys had been working hard on the new mine shaft all spring and summer. They had burrowed a long way into the mountain from the other side, but they still found only dust and some nuggets—no new rich vein.

By October it was obvious to everyone, including the miners, that they were beginning to get discouraged.

Now too that election time was getting closer, I wondered if Pa was having second thoughts about his decision. If he was, his friends in Sacramento didn't make it any easier. They still kept pestering him to reconsider, even though by now someone else was running for his seat. Pa held firm, but I know it would have been a lot easier if there'd been more gold coming out of that hill.

Then one day, only about an hour after breakfast, Tad came rushing into the house.

"Hey, everyone!" he cried out. "Come see what we found!" Before we even had the chance to ask him what he meant, he was gone again, sprinting back up toward the new mine.

The house emptied and we all hurried after him, sure that they must have struck gold. I imagined a big, wide vein of pure yellow glistening from the wall of rock.

When we reached the mine, no one was to be seen, but shouts and the clanking sounds of picks were coming from inside. The voices sounded excited!

We crept inside, calling out greetings as we entered the dim darkness.

"Here they are!" shouted Tad.

The picks stopped.

"Over here!" called Pa, coming toward us with a lantern and leading the way up to the end where Tad, Zack, Christopher, and Mr. Jones were all clustered around their most recent discovery. They parted to let us look.

Pa pointed to a white stripe about three inches wide and about six inches long, right at the farthest end of the cave wall.

"It's white," said Ruth. "I don't see any gold."

Pa laughed.

"There's an old expression, Ruthie," he said: " 'Where there's smoke, there's fire'—you ever hear that?"

"No, Pa," she answered.

"Well then, I'll give you another one to remember: Where there's quartz . . . there's gold!"

Behind him, all the men raised a cheer. To listen to them, you'd think they had found a vein of gold itself, not just a trail they hoped would lead to it.

"Tad found it about an hour ago," Pa said, now speaking to Almeda. "Since then we've been picking away at it, and sure enough, it looks like it's going to lead deeper into the hill. If this quartz vein keeps widening, then it'll lead us to gold eventually."

"Congratulations!" she said. "Congratulations to you all. It appears your hard work is not going to be in vain after all."

"Not in vain at all . . . because we *are* going to find that vein!"

Everyone laughed.

"Then we shall let you get back to work in pursuit of your dream," said Almeda.

We turned and left the cave. Before we were even back out into the sunlight again, the sounds of picks had resumed behind us.

———

The next day Christopher gave me a letter.

Dear Corrie,

I am exhausted after the day's work, yet full of thoughts.
Your father and brothers are tremendously excited about
the quartz line we found, and I must admit to being stirred

as well. Finding the vein has caused me to ponder anew whether there is a chance I will make any money from this mine eventually . . . or whether it is time I began thinking of other possibilities for employment in order to support us when the time comes that such a need presents itself.

I have been thinking for quite some time about the question you raised in one of your letters. You asked about our future. And I haven't responded because I haven't known what exactly to say. I do want to respond in some fashion, however, and so perhaps this is a good time, even though I have nothing very definite to tell you.

My answer is simply this:

Corrie: I do not know what the future will hold for us. But our Father does . . . and that is enough.

I would not be honest, however, if I told you I do not think about these things. Certainly I do. Any man who wants to build a good life for the woman he loves ponders about the best way to do that. So I think about the various kinds of work I know how to do.

I think, for instance, about our getting a place of our own and farming the land and raising livestock. If we find any gold in your father's mine—which I have found myself increasingly doubting as more rocks and dirt have passed through my hands!—perhaps we can use my small share to buy an acre or two that we can call our very own.

Whether or not that proves possible, of one thing you may be sure: I will always work hard, and I will provide for you and for whatever sons and daughters it may be the Lord's pleasure to bless us with. Whatever I do, I will do it unto the Lord.

Where might we live? I would probably say the same thing that you did: if I am with you, wherever it might be, I will be "at home." My heart belongs to you, and from now on that's what *home* will mean to me—not a city or a state or any particular location.

I strongly doubt that any large city such as Richmond or San Francisco or Chicago could ever be a place I genuinely called home. They are tumultuous cities, and I would not want to raise a family in any such place. With you beside me, I would submit to living there if I had to, but I pray that is not where the Lord sends us!

As you know, my own family ties are by now so thin and loose that they exert no pull upon me. After my father died I was cast adrift from any strong sense of family. Except for my affection for Mrs. Timms, I have had no personal attachments for many years . . . until now, with you and the Hollister clan of Miracle Springs. They have all made me feel so much a part of the family I could not imagine being away from them. I love them almost as much as I do you!

(Well, not quite, I suppose!)

If I were to speak to you about my own wishes in the matter, I would say that I am not eager to leave Miracle Springs or California. In a very short time I have come to love this locale. Even though I am from the East, I could happily live out my days here.

And yet men and women who have given themselves utterly and wholly to the Lord can never be allowed the luxury of becoming too attached to any one place. We must never forget that we are pilgrims and strangers in this land and that God does not want our roots to extend too deeply into this world. He is preparing for us another home, in another kingdom, toward which our eyes must ever be turned. We cannot know what he might have for us to do, where he might choose to send us.

You have given your writing into his hands. What might he yet want to do with it? I have given my desire to minister into his hands. How might he yet want to use it? In the same way, I believe, we must give our future home into his hands. If and when he says, "Go here" or "Go there," I want us to be ready.

We are in *his* hands, Corrie.

We are at home with each other, yes, and I marvel in this sense of belonging! But more than that, and fulfilling the love we have for each other, our home is in *his* heart.

We are, therefore, his—to go and do and be wherever and whatever he ordains for us according to his purposes.

That is the only future I am sure of.

Good-night. It is late, and we have a long day ahead of us tomorrow. The quartz vein has filled us all with renewed vigor!

Christopher

CHAPTER 45

COMMITMENT OR EMOTIONS

I could hardly believe how quickly the year had passed.

If I were to tell about all the things Christopher and I did—all the conversations we had, all the fun, all the serious times of prayer together, all the letters that passed between us, it would fill ten books!

I felt like I'd grown ten years' worth in that one year too. In so many ways, though I was just a year and a half older, I hardly felt like the same person who had come back to Miracle Springs from the East.

As November drew to an end, Christopher and I were both well aware that his apprentice year was nearly over. The work in the mine had yielded just enough results to keep them going, but still the quartz hadn't led them to the rich vein of gold they were sure was behind there somewhere. The quartz vein had widened, and they had followed it now another eight or ten feet without finding gold. They were still optimistic, but I knew they had hoped to find something more substantial by this time.

Pa hadn't said anything yet about me and Christopher. I *knew* he would say yes—how could he not think the world of Christopher after working alongside him for a year? I was still nervous, though. I guess I would be nervous until I heard the words from his own lips.

A few days before the one-year anniversary of his arrival, Christopher said he wanted to talk to me about something that was very important.

It was a chilly day, but we bundled up and went for a long walk. In the places where evergreen forest gave way to scrub and black oak leaves replaced the pine-needle carpet, and the trunks and branches were stark and bare.

"I think we should both realize and prepare ourselves," Christopher told me, "for something that will happen to us eventually."

"What is that?" I asked.

"One of these days," he answered, "some of the feelings we have for one another will probably fade and change. That doesn't mean our love will fade or grow less," he added hastily, "only that it will change and mature. In many ways, when that happens, love is actually deepening and broadening. It's very natural and probably inevitable. But when young people are unprepared for it, they often think the love that drew them together in the first place is going away.

"I saw this over and over when I was in the pastorate," he went on to explain. "People would come to talk to me about their marriages, and I heard them describe the same thing over and over. That's why I want us to expect it and even anticipate it—so that we will realize that it is just one more aspect in the natural progression of human love."

"I don't know if I like the sound of it," I said.

"It can't be helped," replied Christopher. "I'm not in a hurry to see it happen either. I like the way I feel about you right now. It feels good to be in love. I'm happy, content . . . sometimes when we're together I'm on top of the world! But I want to be a realist too."

"Does it have to be that way?" I asked.

"I don't know if it *has* to. I am just convinced it usually is. I'm not old enough to say it *always* is, but all my experience says so."

"But why, Christopher? Why does it change?"

Christopher thought a moment or two.

"I don't know . . . it's the way God designed it, I suppose. He intended the decision of marriage and the mutual *commitment* two people make to be the fuel that sustains the husband-and-wife relationship—not the *emotions* of what is commonly called 'love.' As I've thought about this, in fact, it has struck me that a marriage can be just as good with or without the emotions, as long as the mutual commitment is there.

"Perhaps that is why so many parentally arranged marriages worked in times past. There was never any question of emotion to confuse the issue of what marriage was all about—commitment. Nowadays, in a sense, the process of falling in love can actually detract from laying a solid foundation for marriage because it can take young people's eyes off the necessity of commitment. It becomes too easy to think that the emotions of love are enough."

"Does any of this have to do with your plan this past year?"

Christopher laughed.

"Ah, you are an astute one, my Corrie! Indeed it does."

"I'm listening!" I said.

"When I first began thinking of the apprenticeship plan, I thought it would be good for a young man and woman to be around each other long enough to get well past the initial stages of relationship. That way, if the emotions were going to fade, they could begin to do so before marriage rather than after. Then the couple would be able to see how much they *really* did in fact love one another. Did they still desire to spend their lives together, even though the emotional tingles associated with doing so were not as great as before? If so, then love would truly be beginning to blossom between them."

"How could love be 'blossoming' right when it's starting to fade?"

"It is not the love itself that fades, only the emotions attached to the beginnings of love. True love is deeper than the mere emotions. True love never fades, it matures. All through the New Testament, love as Jesus describes it has to do with actions, attitudes, behavior, and commitment, not any particular feeling of giddiness. That is why I am convinced that a man and woman do not really begin to progress into the depths of true love until this fading process is underway. There has been a form of love prior to it, but not the depths of New Testament love. The further a man and woman can progress into those depths before marriage, the stronger their ultimate marriage bonds will be."

Again he paused.

"In any event, that is what I hoped for between us. I want to love you as Jesus loves you, my dear Corrie, not only in the shallow way the flesh of Christopher Braxton is able to love you. *That* is my commitment to you."

———————

Dear Christopher,

I have been thinking almost constantly about our talk of a few days ago. You said there will come a time when the "feelings" will fade between us. You told me to expect it, that the high and emotional crest that we've felt—speaking for myself at least!—since knowing that we were beginning to love each other couldn't last forever at the same intensity.

At first your words seemed a bit frightening. I see the point of everything you said, but another part of me didn't want to believe it.

But just since then I think I have come to understand a little better what you were talking about. In fact, I had felt this fading a little already, but I hadn't said anything to you about it because I didn't want to admit that something might have changed in my feeling for you.

Could it be that the intensity we felt was almost too much for us, that perhaps we are wearying from it? Perhaps the oneness between us has been so total and our communication so fervent that it has almost drained us. (You specifically warned me of upcoming "lows" between us.)

But this is good. Isn't this exactly why we are waiting this year? I know we are doing it in part so that you and Pa can work together and get to know one another before Pa gives you his answer. But isn't it part of the plan that we will get to know each other so well—even if it means lows and sometimes fading emotions—that we don't depend on those emotions to sustain us through marriage? That is what I thought I heard you say.

More and more I see the wisdom in this arrangement. Marriage has to be based on so much more than just a romantic and emotional connection, doesn't it?

What am I saying—you told me that exact thing!

So again I say, this is a good time of testing and learning and growing. We are being sobered by it and are thus able to look peacefully and realistically toward the future.

Christopher, I love you so much for the way you communicate and share with me. You are a most unusual man! I don't think that most men are able to be as open with their feelings as you.

I am the luckiest girl in all the world!

We will be starting out many miles ahead of so many young couples who marry—not necessarily ahead of them in maturity, but in having learned how to really communicate about deep spiritual things. I have you to thank for that. I know, if we really listen to God, that we won't go wrong (or if we do, that the Lord will steer us right again).

Oh, Christopher, right now I want to be with you so much I think I might cry. I mean really be with you! I know there will be unemotional lows, but right now I am not feeling that way! I am feeling very pensive and romantic and I so long to feel your arms around me.

All in good time, I know you would say. And I trust you.

Corrie

Dear Corrie,

Am I really all that unusual as far as men go? You are right, I'm afraid, in that most men aren't as open with their thoughts and feelings as I am. But it's not because they *can't* be . . . rather because they *won't* be, or they don't know how to be.

Men "feel" just as much as women. But they have this ridiculous notion that it's unmanly to let anyone see what they feel.

I used to find myself so irritated by some of the men in my church when they would stoically hide behind their so-called manliness, never opening so much as a crack to show their inner selves. Then I would have to remember with a shock that I was one of their kind myself!

But forgive my soapbox. I suppose all preachers—even retired ones like me—have bees that buzz about inside their bonnets and that cannot help from coming out at times.

I don't know if it was from observing these stoic, silent parishioners of mine, or from keeping a journal that helped me clarify my thoughts and feelings, but for whatever reason I determined long ago that I was going to be a different sort of man. I would try to make of my inner self an open book that anyone could read who wanted to know me. Not that I thought I was anything so special in and of myself. But God was carrying out a work within me, and that qualified as significant—equally significant as his work in *all* men and women.

I crave knowing what the Lord is doing in the lives of others. I want to get inside those who pass my way just as much as I want to expose my innermost self to others. How else can there be unity between brothers and sisters unless we truly know one another?

I have so much enjoyed, for example, getting to know your brother Zack. He's got such quality of character—bolstered, no doubt, by his time in the desert, but begun long before that. If ever I imagined having a brother of my own, Zack is him.

So many marriages would be so much more wonderful, Corrie, if their men would make the decision to make the communication between husband and wife equal and flowing *both* directions.

I agree with you that this present time is the best foundation we could want for building our future. If I can say such a thing—I *want* your romantic and emotional feelings for me to fade somewhat so that we get all that out of the way *before* marriage. I probably said that poorly. I'll try again. Perhaps it is good that they fade. The same is true for me.

It is such a shock for so many who discover, after marriage, that their feelings are becoming different than they were. Not expecting it, they conclude that perhaps they didn't love one another after all, and that the marriage was a terrible mistake. Well, like you told me about Jennie.

We are so fortunate to be able to be near to each other like this, to go through the normal "fading emotions" phase of knowing each other and then go beyond that into the realization that we *do* love each other—*more* deeply, not less, through all emotions, high *and* low. Marrying too soon prevents people from testing their love as we are having the opportunity to do.

I too find myself, even in the midst of these lessons we are learning, longing to hold you forever. I can be a very emotional man in that way too!

The time will come, no doubt sooner than we think. I would work and labor to make you my wife for seven years . . . and even for seven years beyond that, so great do I deem the prize of your hand.

But I hope it will not come to that!

I love you, Corrie Belle . . . if not more than you can know, certainly more than I can ever say.

Christopher

CHAPTER 46

PA'S ANSWER

Another Christmas season came—and then the day that marked the end of the year Christopher had been working with Pa. I knew the exact hour! Whatever I'd said during the year about being content, which I was, I was still anxious to find out what Pa's answer was going to be!

I expected Pa to come and say something on that very morning, but the whole day went by without a word from him. At supper that night Pa was his normal self. I was watching his every move, but he never brought up the subject of our "Jacob" arrangement or our marriage.

I was dying of suspense!

Somehow I managed to sleep through the night. But the next day was just the same . . . and the next . . . and the next.

Finally I couldn't stand it any longer. When Christopher and I were alone, I asked him why he didn't say something to Pa.

"What should I say?" he asked, as if he hadn't even noticed the date.

"Tell him your year's up," I said impatiently. "That's what Jacob did after his seven years."

"I'm sure he knows."

"But he's not saying anything."

"If it keeps going another seven years, I'll be sure and say something then."

"Christopher!"

He laughed.

"Your father is an intelligent man, Corrie. He's more aware of the date than you think he is, and I'm sure he's giving the matter of our future a great deal of thought and prayer. If he hasn't said anything, it's because he's not ready to say anything."

My frustration must have shown all over my face, for he took my hands gently and went on in a serious voice.

"When I submitted the decision into his hands," he said, "I submitted the timetable to him too. It's out of my hands, Corrie. There's nothing I would do, even if I could."

"Oh, sometimes you are so maddeningly rational and logical!" I said, laughing, but with a hint of exasperation. Right then I didn't particularly want to be grown-up. I was in a hurry to know!

The days continued to go by.

Christopher and Pa kept working together and talking and carrying on as if nothing were any different. I was nearly beside myself, but I didn't dare say anything. I knew Christopher was right about leaving the matter in Pa's hands, though I could barely stand to do it!

Christmas Day drew closer.

We baked and planned, cut and decorated a tree, bought and made and hid presents. Everybody was caught up in the festive spirit once again, though I was too distracted to enjoy the season as much as I had the previous year.

Finally it was Christmas. Uncle Nick and Aunt Katie's family all came down for breakfast as usual and we opened our gifts.

By now I wasn't expecting to hear anything from Pa. At first I'd awakened every day thinking, "Today's the day when he's going to say something!" But after a while I had quit thinking that. I don't exactly know what I was thinking. Maybe I was slowly realizing that I could trust both Pa and Christopher to do the right thing.

At any rate, Pa caught me completely by surprise when he stood up after all the gifts had been opened.

"I reckon it's about time for me to deliver one last present," he said after he'd quieted all the youngsters down and gotten everyone's attention. "You may have noticed that I didn't give our new young friend Christopher Braxton anything. I've been saving his present for last."

Pa stopped and took a breath. I could feel myself suddenly getting very hot and red.

"When you came, Christopher," he went on, looking now at Christopher, "and said you wanted to ask me for permission to marry my eldest daughter, Corrie Belle—"

Everyone glanced over at me. I shrank down in my chair, my cheeks on fire now. Oh, this was so embarrassing right in front of everybody!

"—and then said you wanted me to wait a year before giving my answer," Pa went on. "At first I didn't know what to think. Sounded like the craziest thing I'd ever heard of—you wanted to work for me for a year, without pay, just so I'd get to know you well enough to be able to say one way or another whether I thought you'd make a fit man for my Corrie."

A little laughter went around the room. I think *everybody* had thought it was a pretty unusual idea!

"But after I thought and prayed about it some," Pa went on, "I saw what a lot of sense it made. And I don't deny it made me feel good that you and Corrie trusted me that much. So I reckon that made me take it a heap more seriously. I figured if you were going to put your future in my hands like that, then I'd better make the right decision!

"So I prayed all year long that God would show me what he wanted me to say. And I watched the two of you and how you were to each other. I listened to the way you talked and the way you treated each other.

"I especially had my eye on you, Christopher, watching not just how you treated Corrie, but what you were like to Almeda and Becky and Katie and other people. If there was a mean streak in you anywhere, I wanted to find it. If it came out toward anybody, then I knew it'd come out toward Corrie someday too, and I didn't want that. Anything that's in a man is going to come out at his wife someday, and if there was selfish stuff down inside you, I figured it was my duty to find out. I was even intentionally hard on you a time or two and put you in some difficult circumstances, just to see how you'd react. I'm sorry about that, if an apology's in order—"

"Think nothing of it," said Christopher. "I'm sure you did nothing without intending it for my good."

"Right you are there," said Pa. "That's what I intended, all right. I figured you'd given me a mighty important decision to make, and so I'd better know all I could about you so I'd make the *right* decision.

"So we worked and we talked, and I watched and listened and prayed. And I figure in the end I got to know you about as good as one man can know another in so short a time. You showed me you're a hard worker, that you're not mean or selfish, and that you know what you're about. You ain't without your faults, and I saw them plain enough. But then, we all got faults. If we didn't, wouldn't be much use of the Lord's having to work on improving our characters like he does.

"Well . . . so now it's been a year—little over, in fact, eh, Corrie?" added Pa, looking over at me with a wink. I guess he'd noticed my agitation these past couple of weeks!

"—and I figure that's about long enough to keep you two young people waiting. What I'm trying to say, Christopher—"

As he spoke, Pa went over and extended his hand to Christopher.

"—is that I'm proud to know you. You're a fine and honorable young man."

They shook hands, gazing into one another's eyes for a long moment or two. Then Pa turned and began walking toward me. Again, I felt myself getting hot and red.

He reached me where I was sitting, stood in front of me, then stretched out his hand toward me. I took it, and he pulled me up to my feet.

Slowly he led me back over to Christopher.

"So this is my gift to you, Christopher Braxton, on this special day. . . ."

Christopher stood. Pa put my hand into his, then stepped back.

"I present you with the hand of my daughter, Cornelia Belle Hollister. My answer is yes."

Shrieks and shouts and clapping immediately erupted throughout the room. But I was already weeping too much to hear what came next. I felt arms around me and people jostling. People were shaking Christopher's hand and hugging and kissing me. I know Almeda was beside me . . . there was laughter. . . .

But mostly I just kept crying for joy.

CHAPTER 47

ANOTHER PROPOSAL

That Christmas of 1866 is one I'll never forget, but the reasons don't have much to do with Christmas.

After what Pa had done, everyone was talking more about Christopher and me than Christmas. But Christopher and I only wanted to find a way to have some time alone.

About two o'clock, after most of the dinner fixings were ready and there was just about an hour more to wait for the last things to get done, Christopher came over to the kitchen and asked if the rest of the cooks could spare a certain young lady long enough for her to accompany him for a walk before dinner.

Even though it was all family, I couldn't help blushing. Christopher helped me on with my coat in such a gentlemanly way, and then we went outside. He took my hand in his and we walked out across the flat toward the woods. We didn't say anything for a while.

"What do you suppose they're all talking about inside?" said Christopher at length.

"Us," I said, chuckling.

"That's the way I had it figured too," he said.

We walked on again.

"Well," Christopher began again, "how does it feel to you?"

"What do you think?" I said quietly. "I'm happier than I ever remember being. But how do *you* feel?"

"The same. Quiet, I suppose—content, happy in a subdued and deep way. I feel my whole being is one big, contented sigh."

Soon we were out of sight of the house. Christopher led me into the woods and to a great boulder we sometimes sat on when we wanted to be alone. We'd had many long talks here, but somehow I sensed our talk today would be unlike any of the others.

After we'd climbed up and arranged ourselves next to each other on the hard stone, neither of us spoke for a long time. Christopher was looking off into the wood. I just waited. I suspected a little of what might be coming, though certainly not all of it.

We probably sat in silence for five minutes or more. Finally Christopher spoke.

"I feel so shy again all of a sudden," he said. "We've waited so long for this day—and suddenly I feel like we're back at Mrs. Timms' farm—I'm all tied up in knots about what to say."

I gave a clumsy little laugh. "I know," I said. "Why are we like that?"

"I don't know," replied Christopher. "Maybe it's just one more awkward stage—like we had for a day or two after I came to Miracle Springs."

"Oh, I hope it doesn't last a day or two!" I sighed. "Today is Christmas, and this is all too wonderful for us to have to tiptoe around not knowing what the other thinks."

"All right," laughed Christopher, "I'll do what I can to tell you clearly what I am thinking. I brought you out here to ask you an important question."

My heart fluttered and I caught my breath. I tried to say something, but after I opened my mouth no sound would come out. Luckily Christopher had glanced away. By the time he looked back at me, I'd regained my composure and was staring down at my lap.

"You know there were two purposes in spending this past year the way we have?" he said.

I nodded slowly, but I was really too preoccupied to be thinking clearly.

"I needed to give your father time to know me in order to decide upon my suitability as a son-in-law . . ."

I kept nodding slowly, still looking down.

" . . . and," Christopher went on, "we had to get to know each other well enough to know if *we* still wanted to be married to each other."

He paused and took a breath.

"Well," he said, "now that we have your father's answer to the first question, I want to give you my answer to the second."

I was trembling in earnest now! I dared not look up. I didn't know whether I might start crying, or jump down off the rock and run off through the woods, or throw my arms around Christopher and kiss him. So I just sat there, trying to be calm, but nearly ready to burst with a thousand emotions exploding inside me all at once.

"When I wrote you at the convent," Christopher said, "I told you I had to come to Miracle Springs upon two very important errands. I said I needed to see your father to ask if he would give me the hand of his daughter. That he has done. Now it is time for me to attend to the second item of business I told you about. . . ."

Again Christopher paused. I was so fluttery inside that I hardly noticed how short of breath he was too!

He drew in a breath of air and finally blurted out the rest of his sentence.

"Now it is time for me to ask *you*," he said, "if you will consent to do me the honor of calling me your husband. Corrie . . . I'm officially asking you to marry me and be my wife."

Suddenly my arms *were* around his neck, and I was laughing and crying and babbling something I don't remember!

"Do I take that as an answer in the affirmative?" laughed Christopher.

"Yes, yes . . . of course the answer is yes!" I cried.

"Then there's only one problem," said Christopher, trying to sound serious. "I don't have a diamond ring to give you—"

"I don't need a diamond," I said. "All I want is to be your wife!"

"Let me finish," insisted Christopher.

"All right . . . excuse me."

"Here is my third and final question with regard to this proposal of marriage. I don't know that I could afford both—that is, unless we strike that vein in the mine Alkali Jones keeps talking about. So here's my proposition: I've been doing some reading, and they're bound to get them working one of these days. So would you like a diamond ring . . . or would you like me to get you one of those new typewriting machines they're experimenting with someday?"

He stopped and stared at me expectantly.

"Oh, Christopher . . . you are the most amazing man!" I said, beginning to cry again for joy.

This time he put his arms around me and kissed me once, then again, then held me tight in his arms. We sat in perfect bliss for a minute or two.

"What would I do with a diamond?" I whispered at length into his ear. "Besides, I'm not the glamorous kind. I'll take the type-writing machine."

I could tell Christopher was chuckling, though he said nothing, only squeezed me all the more tightly to him.

"Does this mean I'm actually engaged now?" I asked.

"That you are, Miss Hollister. You are engaged to be married to one Christopher Braxton!"

Slowly we released one another and drew apart. Christopher hopped down off the rock, gave me his hand, and helped me scramble to the ground.

"Do you suppose we ought to go tell everyone else the news?" he said.

"I don't think it will come as a surprise to anyone," I answered, taking Christopher's hand as we began walking back to the house.

"I'm sure it won't. But it's nice to have it made official at last."

CHAPTER 48

THE AWKWARDNESS OF BEING "ENGAGED"

The rest of that Christmas Day was some happy celebration indeed! I can't think of anything more wonderful than to become engaged on Christmas!

I suppose I had already thought of myself as engaged, or halfway engaged, before that. But now I was *really* engaged!

We even started discussing a date for the wedding that very day. Christopher wanted Pa to help decide even that. He was trying so hard to be respectful and not to presume too much.

But Pa put his foot down and said, "I gave you my answer— now you gotta decide the rest on your own. The two of you can get married tomorrow or next year as far as I'm concerned. You got my blessing whatever you do."

Still Christopher was reluctant to be in too much of a hurry. So we talked with Pa and Almeda further and consulted with the Rutledges and discussed and prayed some more between ourselves, and after about a week we finally set a date for April 3 for the wedding.

Then we set out once more on the complicated adventure of getting to know one another—again.

From the very beginning, Christopher and I had talked about the increasingly deeper levels that love has to go through in order to get down to the solid bedrock foundation that is capable of sustaining a lifelong marriage and weathering the difficulties that are certain to be part of it. But that very process of going deeper carried its own difficulties too. Every time we had found ourselves opening some new door in our relationship and peering down into the unknown of what some new level was going to be like, we had also found a whole new bunch of uncertainties to go along with it. Just when we thought we knew each other pretty well, suddenly we'd feel like we were starting over.

At first it had been frustrating and confusing. Suddenly I would find myself wondering if the whole relationship was falling apart. Then we would find our way through the frustrations—sometimes quickly, sometimes painfully—and we would emerge with a deeper understanding.

After Christopher's letter to me at the convent when I left, everything changed. We began talking to one another so openly about our love. It was a much deeper level than whenever we'd been together before.

When Christopher arrived in Miracle Springs, we had to transfer all that letter-writing openness into face-to-face conversation. That had been awkward at first, but eventually that level had become comfortable too.

Then we'd had the misunderstanding after Governor Stanford's letter, and as painful as that time had been, it had opened up still new levels of trust between us.

And now that we were officially "engaged" and had actually set a date for the wedding, the same thing seemed to be happening *again*. Of course we were happy. But frustrations and confusions and awkwardnesses still crept in too. Each step we took toward actually being husband and wife seemed to bring a whole new bunch of complexities that could only be resolved by going deeper—not into the emotions of love, but into our mutual commitment.

At least now we had learned that we had to talk about these awkward things instead of letting them pile up inside and lead to silences and misunderstandings.

At each new level, what Christopher had said in the beginning turned out to be more and more clearly true. Our *commitment* to each other—our commitment to think of the other before ourselves, our commitment to put the other first, to serve one another, to talk and communicate and share our thoughts and feelings no matter how hard—was more important than the *emotions* of our love.

We had to be friends first, spiritual comrades second, and lovers third, Christopher said. The longer we were together, the more clearly I saw that this was the only order that could make a marriage really work the way God intended. And at every new getting-to-know-each-other level, the friendship and spiritual camaraderie between us grew greater. It wasn't that the emotional love part grew *less*—although Christopher did keep reminding me that would happen eventually—but it did become more a balanced part of the other two.

The months after Christmas, as we made plans for the wedding, were awkward in new ways. There had been no pressure on us before. We'd just been working, talking, and enjoying one another, all the while waiting on Pa's decision.

Now suddenly everything was on *our* shoulders.

A whole new list of questions presented themselves, and along with them new doubts and fears surfaced.

What was Christopher going to do for a job? What if the mine never turned up any gold? He didn't want to live off Pa and Almeda. I had saved some money from my writing, but it wasn't that much, and Christopher was determined that living off what I had in Mr. Royce's bank was no way to start a marriage. I know he was seriously concerned about that. He didn't want to be seen as a sluggard who couldn't support his wife. Not that anyone who knew him and had seen him work could think such a thing, but he was concerned for my reputation too.

What about my writing? Was that perhaps supposed to be part of how we supported ourselves? I was willing to do my share, but Christopher was reluctant to put me in the position where we needed the money my writing would bring in.

Pa kept telling Christopher not to worry, that his mine partnership wasn't going to end just because we got married. But the gold they were getting wasn't much, and Christopher couldn't help wondering what would happen after it dried up.

We also couldn't help wondering, each of us in our own way, whether we could be enough for each other—whether we were truly what the other person needed. This was hardest of all to talk about, because it was so deep and so personal and involved so many painful self-doubts. More than once the awkwardness and quiet grew between us, and we had to struggle our way back to the point of being comfortable talking again.

Opening up your innermost self can sometimes be about the hardest thing in the whole world to do! Making a commitment that's got to last every day for the rest of your life is a pretty fearsome thing!

Dear Christopher,

As the last year gradually passed, and now as we approach the day we have awaited for so long, slowly I am finding the ecstasy of what has happened between us wearing off. You were right in what you said to me earlier about feelings fading. I do not mean to imply that you are less special to me than always. Never! Only that I am becoming more accustomed to being around you. I am accepting our living in such proximity and our eventual future together as more normal.

I think it must be a good thing. Don't you think that being married is hard for some people—after the newness of it wears off, I mean—because it is so different from anything they knew before? I have heard it said by some that they wake up after weeks or months of being married and don't recognize their husband or wife because they are so different from the person they knew before.

With this change I see within myself is coming a more relaxed feeling about writing and talking to you. I know I don't have to explain every moment that I love you, and I don't have to explain in endless detail every feeling I have.

I am so glad we are learning some of these things *before* the stresses of marriage. I know there will still be a multitude of new things to learn. But the more we have behind us now, the more easily those future lessons will come to us.

And in all we are learning, of course, all that matters is that we become more like Jesus.

Do you understand me at all? If not, we can talk about it tomorrow, or after you have read this.

The joy isn't fading, just the urgent necessity to tell it all to you every second, the "restless urge to write." Even if we didn't see each other for a month and never wrote all that time—though I would miss you terribly!—nothing between us would change. We would just walk up to one another at the end of that time and quietly smile as we looked into one another's eyes, and then one of us might just say, "You too, eh?"

We would *know* without the need of words.

Anyway, that's how I feel right now. Don't blame me if I say something completely contradictory tomorrow. Women have to reserve that prerogative for themselves, you know!

Corrie

Dear Corrie,

What you raised in the letter you wrote me about people changing after getting married is so true. I encountered this time after time when I was in the ministry.

The reason, I am convinced, is the artificial nature of the relationship between most betrothed couples. They rarely have the opportunity to see and relate to one another under normal life circumstances. Thus, they are always on their best behavior.

Unfortunately, one's best behavior is the worst of all possible preparations for marriage. A man and woman ought to see one another on their worst behavior and *then* decide whether they want to be married or not.

That is why I feel so good about our present circumstance. They are anything but artificial. Your father's bringing me here to work and live has reduced the artificial quality even further. While I was living at Mrs. Gianini's I was still, in a manner of speaking, a visitor, a guest. But no more. Ever since I began working in the mine I have been here all the time, truly part of the household. There has been no hiding any of myself from you—as we painfully discovered a time or two!

But on to another subject you touched on in your letter—one I have been thinking and praying about for years. You write, "all that matters is that we become more like Jesus." But what might that really mean? Suddenly I am thinking through the implications of that prayer more than I ever have in the past.

Does it mean people will notice me someday, that I will be a famous pastor or will occupy a prestigious pulpit? If we follow the Lord more closely, will we "prosper" according to the ways of the world? Will more people read your words and listen to my voice?

No, I think not. All this is a false way of looking at it.

Being like Jesus isn't something the world—even the Christian world—can always recognize. I may never be well known. (Why would I want to be anyway? Yet sometimes vain ambitions cannot help flitting through the mind of any man!) I may never be popular. I may never even be well thought of. No movement may spring up around me. The world may never see anything of value attached to the name Christopher Braxton.

In marrying me, Corrie, you may be destining yourself to a life of ignominy. Are you sure you know what you are doing!

Perhaps the Lord will call us to give our lives to the service of a mere handful of people. But if that is the job he gives us, then that is enough. What could be more thrilling or more fulfilling?

Right now I feel more fortunate than anyone in the world! I love you!

Christopher

Dear Christopher,

Can you believe we're actually going to be married?

Sometimes I can't! I'm scared, excited, nervous, anxious, and thrilled about it—all at once.

We have learned so much and grown in so many ways together. That won't stop, will it? We mustn't let it. I want *always* to grow . . . with you.

I must stop. This has been short, but I never get tired of talking to you and telling you that I love you.

I do love you, Christopher . . . so much!

Corrie

CHAPTER 49

THE BLUE LACE DRESS

After Pa had given his official answer and Christopher had made his official proposal, you'd think the excitement would have died down for a while. But if anything it picked up all the more.

Suddenly there was a wedding to plan for!

All the other women in my life were even more excited than I was, I think, about getting everything ready for the wedding. Almeda, Aunt Katie, and Mrs. Gianini were all involved, of course, as well as Becky and several other friends, like Mrs. Shaw. Knowing that Emily would be coming back north for the wedding added even more to everyone's enthusiasm.

I guess you would say I was the center of attention, like brides always are. But in another way I felt strangely detached from all the bustle, like it was happening to someone else. I just wanted to be with Christopher, to walk and talk with him, or to be by myself so I could write letters to him and read the ones he'd written me.

Sometimes all the fuss didn't seem worth it. Why couldn't we just get married and get on with starting our life together? And then there was the nervousness too. How could I think of actually being *married,* and not be nervous?

On another level, of course I was tingling with excitement. Oh, there was so much to do—working out the ceremony itself with Rev. Rutledge, planning food to have in the town hall afterward, making arrangements for after the wedding and the time Christopher and I would be away . . . and of course the wedding dress. That took the most planning and the most work of all!

Becky and Almeda and I started talking right away about what I should wear for the wedding. Aunt Katie offered to let me wear the dress she'd worn in her wedding. I remember so well how nice Almeda had been, even though she loved Pa, when we thought Katie was going to marry him. She'd entered right in and had Mrs. Gianini make a dress for Katie.

Almeda said I could wear her dress from Boston, but I didn't want to look that fancy. I remembered what Ma used to say when she married Pa. She said she had only two dresses. When one was dirty, she'd wear the other. So when it came time to get married, she had worn the one that happened to be clean.

I asked Pa if he remembered what Ma wore on the day they'd been married. He got a kind of dreamy, faraway look in his eyes and said, "I wasn't looking at her dress, Corrie. I figured she was just about the most beautiful girl in the whole county."

He stopped and looked me over up and down, then smiled and nodded his head up and down.

"You remind me a heap of her, Corrie Belle," he said. "You're looking more like your ma every day. She'd be more'n a mite proud of the woman her daughter's become."

"Thank you, Pa."

He hugged me, and I savored the moment, especially knowing that before much longer I wasn't going to be a Hollister anymore. It was just about the nicest thing Pa could have said to me right then, because for some reason I'd been feeling real close to Ma lately. I really wanted Ma to be here sharing this time with me. I think Pa did too. Sometimes when I'd look at him staring at me, but kind of right through me, I knew he was seeing Ma in me, and then he was looking at me for both of them, thinking what their little girl had grown up to be.

The more I thought about it, the more sure I was that I wanted a wedding dress that I would be able to wear for other occasions too. I knew that's what Ma would have done. She was always so practical. Since I'd made two dresses recently, I decided to make a wedding dress myself—with help, of course, from Becky and Almeda and Mrs. Gianini.

I went to the General Store several times to look at fabric, but I couldn't find anything that exactly struck my fancy. Mr. Bosely told me he was expecting a new shipment in a few days.

Four days later, when I was working at the Supply Company, little ten-year-old Jefferson Bosely came in. His pa had sent him over to say there was some new cloth goods to look at. I went over to the General Store with Jefferson, and when I saw the sky-blue lace fabric, I knew it was what I wanted. When I picked it up, I was surprised it was so soft.

The very next day I took Becky and Almeda in to see the material, and they loved it too. We all sat down to look at patterns, and by the end of the day we had all the supplies we would need. I couldn't wait to get started on my dress!

I worked on it all through February and into March, mostly by myself, but getting help and advice from the others as I needed it. The dress took shape as the weeks went by, almost as if it were the calendar whose progress marked the days until April 3.

Since the fabric was sheer, I needed to make a lining to wear inside it. The full skirt didn't stick out at all, but hung down straight and simple, in gentle folds. I made a plain bodice with buttons down the front. The full sleeves matched the fullness of the skirt and ended in a simple cuff.

The dress didn't need any trim because the lace fabric, though simple in one way, possessed an elegance all its own. There was a stand-up white collar, and Almeda suggested a white satin belt that came to a point at the top and the bottom right in the center. Almeda embroidered blue flowers for the sides of it. She said that for other times I could make a darker blue belt, but that for the wedding nothing would do but white satin. Down the front, the buttons were pure white, matching the collar and belt, and looking like a straight string of perfect round pearls.

When the dress was finished and I'd tried it on a dozen or more times for all the little additions and tucks and alterations, we took it to Mrs. Gianini's for final approval. She made one or two further tiny alterations that nobody but a dressmaker would notice. Then we left it there, where I would get dressed before going to the church.

CHAPTER 50

BOX OF MEMORIES

The week before the wedding, Becky and I went out into the hills to collect greens to decorate the church. There had been so much to do that my thirtieth birthday had come and gone without much fuss.

Becky and I had grown close over the past year. We both admired each other for different things. A respect and love had grown between us since I'd returned to Miracle Springs that was richly unlike anything I'd felt with anyone else, I think, other than Almeda and Christopher. No more was she just my little sister, but a true friend.

Becky had watched all that went on with me and Christopher during the year, and now she told me that she hoped Pa would do the same thing for her when her own special young man came along.

"In fact," she said as we talked about it that day out in the woods, "I'm going to insist that they both do it!"

I laughed over my armful of ferns. What would Christopher think to hear that his marriage apprenticeship plan had its first convert?

I thought more and more about Ma that whole last week before the wedding. I wanted so much for her to be there to share my wedding day.

Then it occurred to me that even if I couldn't have her with me, maybe I could have something of hers.

When Ma died out there on the desert, we had buried her, and the wagon train had just moved on. When we got to Miracle Springs, we had emptied the wagon into Pa and Uncle Nick's cabin, and most of Ma's things had just become what we used for living. But there had been one little box of her personal belongings. When we'd found out who Pa was, I had given him the box, thinking he would want it. I hadn't seen that box for years.

That night, I asked Pa if he still had it. He smiled and nodded.

"If you can wait a day," he said, "I'll fetch it for you tomorrow."

The next day he arranged for us to go for a ride up into the hills, just the two of us. He brought along the box. It was about eight inches long, about five wide, and three inches deep.

After a long ride, we stopped at a clearing where the trees opened up. We tied the horses to a tree, then walked over to some fallen logs and sat down together.

Neither of us spoke for a long time. I knew Pa wanted to talk to me, not just show me what was inside the box.

We'd had lots of memorable moments together, Pa and me. We loved each other just about as much as I figure a father and daughter can. And now that I was going to get married in a few days, this was one of the most memorable moments of all. He'd already given away one daughter, so this wasn't the first wedding of the family. But I was Ma and Pa's firstborn, and that put a special kind of love between us. I know too that Pa wanted to tell me the kinds of things that Ma would if she'd still been alive. I felt Ma's presence that day stronger than I had since I'd visited Bridgeville.

"There's some things in this box that remind both you and me of your ma, Corrie," said Pa at last. "A couple of them you might want to take with you on your wedding day."

He paused and took in a breath.

"But more important," he went on, "I want to tell you something about your ma. I don't reckon I can say anything you don't know, but I gotta tell you anyway.

"It ain't been easy on any of you losing a ma like you did. All of you've had to figure out how to deal with it as best you could, and I don't suppose that right at first I was too much help. But after a while we figured out how to get by pretty good, and I'm sure Aggie's as thankful for Almeda's being part of our lives as all the rest of us are.

"Anyway, I know your ma's proud of you, Corrie Belle. I've told you that before, but it's important you hear it again now. She was a fine, honorable, hard-working, faithful, brave woman, and I know she saw a lot of herself in you. Even before I left, she told me that you reminded her of herself.

"And your ma'd be proud of the kind of man you're fixing to marry. A lotta girls marry fellers who're better looking than Christopher or who've got more money than him. Girls marry fellers for a lot of reasons different than why you love Christopher. But I know both your ma and me consider you a pretty wise and level-headed young lady to be able to recognize a man with the kind of fiber your Braxton's got. Aggie'd like him a lot, you can be sure of that. I can just see the two of them laughing and carrying on together."

A few tears began to creep quietly down my face as Pa spoke.

"Anyway," he went on, "I wanted us to come out here so we could look at the things in this box and remember your ma together one last time before your big day."

Slowly he removed the lid, holding the box on his lap. Together we peered inside. One by one he took all the items out, handed them to me, and told me something about them.

"I'm sure grateful to that Dixon feller for having the good sense to save these things before he buried her," mused Pa as he held up the few simple pieces of jewelry that Ma'd been wearing when she died.

"This here's the wedding ring I gave her the day she married me," said Pa, holding up the small gold band with one tiny diamond. He gazed at it several long moments, sniffed a time or two, blinked his eyes, then put it back in the box.

"I gave her this brooch on our first anniversary," he said. "Wasn't much—we didn't have money to spend on nothing expensive—but she always wore it like it was worth a thousand dollars."

He went on, showing me an embroidered handkerchief, some receipts that meant nothing to me that had to do with the farm in New York, some letters, several other smaller pieces of jewelry, and some other small trinkets and little cloth items that I recognized immediately, though I hadn't seen them for years.

"When I first saw these things after you got to Miracle," he said, "it was late one night. I held every one of them in my hand and remembered your ma. I don't mind telling you that I cried over every one of 'em. I'd probably be crying again right now, if I wasn't trying so hard not to. . . ."

"Oh, Pa!" I was crying enough by now for both of us!

"Seeing the letters was hardest of all. It was like hearing her voice again, like she was alive. Most of them were letters she wrote to me but never sent because she'd had no place to mail them to. Oh, Corrie, they were like knife wounds in my heart! She never stopped loving me, and it was years before I could forgive myself for what I'd done. And then here's the letter, too, from Nick, the one that gave her the idea to come West."

He put the letters back, then withdrew a small white Bible, the last item of all.

"Do you remember your ma's Bible," said Pa.

"Yes!" I exclaimed. "I knew something was missing from the mantel when I came home from the East."

"I took it down after you left and put it away with these other things. I figured it might be needed one day for just such an occasion as this one. It's getting a mite old and ragged by now—ragged not just from age, but because she read it cover to cover several times in her life that I knew her. Maybe part of why I put it away, too, was because it was just too precious to have out with the other books. I always figured on giving it to you when you was grown, and I reckon now that day's come."

He handed me the small book. What a treasure it was.

"Thank you, Pa," I said, my voice thick with tears.

"Actually," he said, "I want you to have everything here—well, except for two things."

He reached inside and took out the ring and the personal letters. Then he handed me the box and all the rest of the contents.

"You're the lady of the Hollister-Belle family now," he said. "You're about to start your own branch of the family. From now on we'll have to call it the Hollister-Belle-Braxton clan! So I reckon it's time for you to have what few heirlooms this poor family's got, to keep as a memory of the people that came before you. You can pass them on to your own daughter when her time comes, God willing, and tell her about the strong roots she came from."

"Thank you, Pa," I said shakily. "This means so much to me."

We hugged one another, both tearful now, then rose to go.

"I gave Christopher his answer, and the right to your hand," Pa said as we stood and faced each other. "But there's something I need to say only to you. It's just this—I think you're doing the right thing, I think you picked as fine a man as I could have chosen for you, and you're as fine and godly a daughter as ever a father would wish to have. You've been a good friend to me, Corrie Belle, as well as a fine daughter. A *friend*, do you hear me. I'm gonna—"

Pa's voice choked, and he looked away. I knew he was struggling to keep from breaking into tears as he spoke.

I could hardly stand it! Now the tears were streaming down my face.

"I'm gonna miss you, Corrie," Pa went on hesitantly, trying to clear his throat of the lump that kept trying to get up into his mouth. "That's the one thing wrong . . . with all this—that I'm gonna miss having . . . having you around so close by all the time, 'cause you made life rich and fun wherever you was."

"Pa . . . please," I said.

"No, let me have my say, Corrie," he said, wiping one of his eyes with the back of his hand. "I won't ever have this chance again, at least not while you're still a Hollister. So you listen while I tell you that I have loved you ever since the day you were born thirty years ago, and I love you still. I'll . . . I'll miss you . . . but you got my blessing, girl of mine. I . . . I want you to know—"

His voice finally broke.

The next moment we were in each other's arms, holding each other tight. It felt so good to have Pa's arms wrapped around me. Nothing more was said. I *did* know. And Pa knew it.

We stood like that for several minutes.

I'll never understand why happiness always seems to have a certain kind of pain attached to the other side of it. As happy as my coming marriage made me, it was hard to know that at the same time I was leaving behind a part of myself, a part of life I loved.

We rode down the hill slowly, neither of us in a hurry to see these special moments together end. As we neared the cabin, I knew that at last I was ready to become Mrs. Christopher Braxton.

CHAPTER 51

A QUIET KIND OF LOVE

April 3 would be a Saturday, and by Friday, the day before the wedding, everything was ready. At least everything *seemed* ready . . . until that evening. Then suddenly a whole new onslaught of doubts and worries flooded over me.

All that day an anxiety had been slowly growing inside me. I couldn't put my finger on it, but the happiness and joy that should have been there seemed to be slipping away.

I don't know if it was caused by an incident between Christopher and me just after lunch. But that's when I first started to notice the anxious feeling, and then it grew worse and worse as the day wore on.

We were walking out of the house together and Christopher made some comment. I can't even remember now what he said! In all the commotion and emotion of the next few days, so much time passed before I wrote about the day in my journal that I had forgotten what his words were. I think it had something to do with the lunch we had just finished, for which I'd fixed most of the food.

It was just an innocent comment, and Christopher had no way of knowing I'd take it wrong or even that I'd fixed the lunch myself. But his words went into my brain crooked. Even though I know Christopher hadn't meant it that way, I took his comment as criticism directed at me.

But the real problem wasn't Christopher's comment, but what happened next. His words irritated me, and I found myself annoyed at Christopher.

Then I got quiet. We walked on a bit. Christopher detected the change in my mood.

"What's the matter?" he asked finally.

"Oh . . . nothing," I said.

The minute the words were out of my mouth I felt awful. I had intentionally not told Christopher the truth!

We had promised not to get quiet, to always to tell each other what we were thinking and feeling, and never to let awkwardness or misunderstanding creep in between us again. Now I had done that very thing . . . and just the day before our wedding!

But even knowing all that, I couldn't make myself undo what I had done. I couldn't bring myself to apologize or say what I'd really been thinking . . . because another side of me was still irritated with Christopher and was still blaming *him* for what had happened.

How can such a *little* thing cause such a *big* rift between two people? I don't know . . . but it did.

Within an hour I was miserable, and my misery grew as the day went on.

Then about halfway through the afternoon, I realized something that nearly shattered me. It had crept up so slowly throughout the day that I hadn't even seen it coming. When suddenly I saw it for what it was, I could hardly stand the thought.

I realized that right then I wasn't feeling "in love" with Christopher at all. When I thought of him, my heart didn't flutter like it had a year earlier. When his face came to my mind, it wasn't with thoughts of how handsome it was. I had become so accustomed to his face that it just looked ordinary to me now. When he came back from working at the mine, I now noticed that he smelled just as bad as Pa and Zack sometimes did. Some of his mannerisms, which I'd never noticed at first, had begun to grate on me.

And I still couldn't help being irritated at him for what he'd said right after lunch.

I hated myself for thinking these things . . . but I couldn't help them. It was just like Christopher had warned me about—the emotional feelings of "love" had lost some of their luster. I'd been around Christopher for so long, day after day, that I guess I'd grown used to him.

Oh, I thought to myself, why couldn't this all have happened a

month ago . . . or even waited *another* month! Why now—the very
day before our wedding? I didn't want to get married when I was
keeping something from Christopher—and was annoyed with him
besides!

Evening approached. Everybody noticed how quiet and withdrawn I was. I think my family just thought I had come down with
a case of pre-wedding jitters. But Christopher knew me too well.
He knew something was wrong.

Supper was awkward. In the midst of all the excited talk about
the following day, I had pulled into my own introspective turtle
shell, silently wondering what I should do.

Should I call off the wedding . . . or postpone it a few days until
Christopher and I could work through this latest problem? Was all
this a sign that we weren't supposed to go ahead with our marriage?

How dreadfully awkward and embarrassing it would be to do
something like that! We had already met one final time with Rev.
Rutledge to plan out the whole ceremony. All the food was cooked.
The whole town would be there. Emily and Mike had come all this
way.

How could I possibly cancel or postpone our wedding! Yet how
could I go through with it feeling like I did! Both options seemed
impossible.

Oh, I didn't know what to do! This wasn't how I had thought
it was going to be!

It was after dark when Christopher and I met outside the barn.
We both knew we had to talk. This time it couldn't wait.

"Feel like going for a ride?" Christopher asked me.

"Now?" I said.

"There's a good moon, and the two-seater's all hitched up."

I nodded my consent.

He brought the buggy around from where he'd had it ready to
ride up to Uncle Nick's with his things. He'd made plans to spend
the night with them so as not to be around when I was getting ready
in the morning. He helped me up, then got in beside me and flicked
the reins. We started off in the moonlight toward town.

It was a quiet ride. We talked some, just trying to get the feeling
of communication back after the awkward day. We rode into town
but didn't even stop, turned around at the church, both of us think-

ing about what was scheduled to take place there the next morning,
and then headed back out toward home.

At last, as hard as it was, we began to share what we had been
feeling. Unknown to me, Christopher had been thinking many of
the same things. We didn't talk specifically about what had happened after lunch. By then I think I'd already forgotten what it was
anyway. Instead, we each confessed our anxieties and reservations
and even admitted that we were not feeling nearly so "in love" as
we had earlier. Christopher apologized for whatever he'd said that
had been insensitive to me. I apologized for getting quiet and for
not being honest with him and telling him how I felt.

We arrived back at home about ten o'clock. The house and the
bunkhouse were both quiet. Everyone else, I think, was already in
bed.

Christopher pulled up in front of the barn and stopped. We sat
there beside each other in the darkness, neither saying a word.
Nothing had been resolved by the ride, but at least we were talking.
The mood between us was still subdued.

"What are we going to do?" I said finally.

"What do you mean?" Christopher asked.

"How can we go ahead with it when we feel this way?"

"Are you suggesting we *don't* go ahead with it?"

"I don't know."

It got quiet a minute.

"I know what you have always said," I said after a bit, "about
us needing to rely on commitment instead of feelings, but I didn't
know it was going to be like *this*!"

"I know," sighed Christopher. "It's been a low day for me too."

"Have you had second thoughts?"

"Of course. I've been plagued with them all day."

"But you still think going ahead's the right thing to do?"

Christopher didn't answer immediately.

"Do you still love me?" he asked finally.

"I, uh . . . of course," I said.

"Though it doesn't feel like it did before?"

"I guess that's it."

"Well, I still love you too."

Again he hesitated.

"When we began this adventure," he went on, "I said to myself, and I told you later, that I thought it would be *good* for some of the feelings to fade so that we would *have* to rely on something deeper. Now that exact thing has happened, so why are we doubting that it is good? We ought to be rejoicing instead of moping around."

"Rejoicing that we're not as happy as before?" I said with a half laugh.

"Maybe in a way," laughed Christopher gently. I must admit it felt good to hear humor in his tone again. "And if we can't quite rejoice in it, at least we ought to *thank* God for it. I've always said that a marriage is stronger if it is established in solid commitment instead of more superficial feelings. Now God is giving us the opportunity to see if we really mean what we've been saying and writing to each other all this year."

"It's easier to talk about it when you don't *really* think the feelings will fade than to be thankful for it when it *does* happen, after all," I said.

"You didn't think they would?"

"Maybe intellectually I knew it was bound to happen," I answered. "But now that I think about it, I realize another part of me *did* think I would keep loving you the same way forever. I certainly didn't think anything would come between us so soon."

We thought quietly to ourselves a while.

"The most important thing of all," said Christopher finally, "is this: How can we ignore all God has done between us—how he brought us together, how we have grown, how he has knit our hearts and lives together on so many levels? How can we doubt him after all he has done?"

"God *has* led us to this moment," I said. "I guess down deep I do know that and nothing can change it. Whatever happens must be based on that fact, not the feelings that come and go."

"He has been preparing us this whole year, knitting and bonding us together in so many ways. It seems to me that we simply *have* to trust him."

"Even in the midst of these doubts."

"That's the only time it can really be called *trust*. If there are no doubts, then there's nothing to trust."

"So you're saying that you think we should go ahead?"

"I don't see that we have any choice . . . that is, unless you really have changed your mind."

"No . . . it's not that," I said. "It's just that it seems that on a girl's wedding day . . . oh, you know."

"Do we trust God even more than our own feelings? That's the question."

"I'm willing to, if you are."

"That's how I feel about it too. As long as you're with me, I want to go ahead . . . in faith."

"Are you sure it's the right thing?" I asked.

"Right now . . . no, I can't say I'm *sure*," replied Christopher. "But those are my feelings talking. My brain and my heart *are* sure, because I *do* trust in what God has done between us. I *believe* with all my mind that he brought us together and that we are to be married. So maybe in another way, I *am* sure."

"That's exactly how I feel. You've said it perfectly."

"Then let's agree—in faith—to stop doubting God's work."

I laughed, and the laughter felt good after this difficult day.

"Agreed!" I said.

We were quiet again. Our mood was still subdued, but the melancholy cloud that had been hanging over us all day seemed to have lifted somewhat. We knew that we loved one another, but on this night it was a very deep and quiet love. And I sensed that we had moved one more step down into yet a deeper, unseen level where love must dwell—a love based on faith.

Christopher reached over, took my hand in his, and began to pray.

"Heavenly Father," he said, "we need your help so much right now. Our limited eyes have grown weak, and the frailty of our human feelings have betrayed us. We lost sight of you today, and we join in asking you to restore our sight to see this union as something you have ordained.

"Oh, Lord, found this marriage in the deep commitment that Corrie and I have made to one another. If we doubt again, let us remember that we may trust you, and that we can believe beyond any doubt that you brought us together for your purposes."

He stopped.

"God," I prayed, "I am sorry for doubting you today, and sorry for doubting Christopher. Please forgive me. Help me be a trusting wife to him and a trusting daughter to you. Help me remember that Christopher loves me and that I love him, even when things may come up that make me apt to forget or to think something has changed between us. Help me remember that as long as our marriage is rooted in our mutual commitment to you, nothing will ever change."

Then Christopher prayed again.

"Lord, we want to join right now and—one more time, as we have already done in the past—give you our whole selves. We give you our pasts . . . and our future together. We give you all of our hearts, our thoughts, our feelings—our whole beings. We place ourselves, our marriage, and all you want to accomplish in us and through us—we place it in your hands, Lord, our Father."

"Yes, I agree, Lord," I said. "Accomplish your will and your purposes in us."

We were silent. After giving everything to the Lord once more, there was nothing else to pray. Now it was time to simply go forward . . . trusting him.

We sat there a long time, my hand resting in Christopher's.

"It's getting late," he said finally.

I smiled. "Pa is probably sitting inside waiting for me. This is my last night as his little girl, and he's probably feeling very protective."

"Then we'd better get you inside without delay."

Christopher jumped down, then helped me to the ground.

"Well," he said, looking me in the eye, "every day is certainly a new and unexpected adventure in getting to know each other, isn't it?"

"Unexpected it is indeed!" I laughed.

"I, uh . . . guess I'll see you tomorrow."

"At the altar, but not before."

"I promise you won't set eyes on me until you and your father walk through the door."

"I'd better not," I said joking.

"I'll be waiting for you in the front of the church."

Christopher walked me to the door, squeezed my hand, then

turned and ran back to the buggy, jumped in, and bounded off up the road.

I went inside.

If Pa was waiting up for me, I didn't see him.

CHAPTER 52

THE BIG DAY

April 3, 1867, fell just a week and a half after my thirtieth birthday. *A perfect age to be married,* I thought. I wouldn't have had it come a single day sooner!

The moment I woke and saw the sun shining through the window, all the previous day's doubts seemed to be a hundred years in the past.

It was a good thing too—I was about to be married!

We had scheduled the wedding for ten o'clock in the morning. By Thursday we'd decorated the church with the greens we'd collected. There were blue candles about the church in a few tall candleholders we'd borrowed, except in the front where three white candles stood. All the chairs next to the center aisle had blue ribbons tied to them, so that the aisle was bordered with blue as you walked in and looked down it toward the front of the church.

On Friday, right in the middle of my melancholy doubts, we'd taken all my wedding clothes into town to leave at Mrs. Gianini's. Saturday morning the other women in the family—Becky, Emily, Almeda, Aunt Katie, Ruth, and little Joan—all got dressed at home and then drove into town with me about nine to help me get ready at Mrs. Gianini's. We left the house to the men. Christopher stayed up at Uncle Nick's until we were well on our way to town.

As I was getting dressed, my mind kept flitting in and out of the present, almost as if I were somewhere else. I was aware of all the fussing about me. I'd heard somewhere that brides always looked pretty, so I wasn't distracted too much by the oohs and ahs I kept hearing from everyone.

It seemed that my mind went through everything that had happened during the last two years, since that day when I had awakened at Mrs. Timms' to see Christopher's face staring down so tenderly at me. Then there was all the time at the farm, while I was getting better . . . then all our letters . . . then his time here . . .

I felt like I was in a dream—everything going on around me was muted. I carried on conversations with everyone and laughed and went about the business of getting ready, but at the same time my memory kept bringing images and pictures and conversations with Christopher into my mind to think about.

Gradually, however, the present began to gain the upper hand.

I had Ma's embroidered handkerchief with me, and I tucked it inside the dress—I wanted it close to me. I would carry her white New Testament through the ceremony and would hand it to Rev. Rutledge for him to read the scripture from.

After I was dressed, Becky and Emily were fixing and decorating my hair and putting ribbons and little white daisies in it. I was sitting in front of the large mirror at the dressing table. In it I could see the reflection of Almeda and Mrs. Gianini talking on the other side of the room. I wondered if they remembered the first day we all came to town and spent our first hour around Mrs. Gianini's table eating apple pie and wondering what was going to become of us.

Again I found myself lost in reflections, until suddenly I heard Becky announcing to everyone else that I was all done and ready to meet my husband.

Hearing her say that word shocked me back to the present quicker than anything!

I stood up. There looking back at me from out of the mirror was someone I hardly recognized.

It couldn't be me! The lady in the mirror looked so grown-up and almost . . . pretty!

A silence fell over the room.

Almeda walked slowly toward me. Her eyes were full and sparkling. She hugged me gently, careful not to rumple my dress.

"Corrie," she said, "you are so beautiful. How I wish we had some way to preserve this moment forever."

"Thank you," I whispered.

Our eyes met. We loved each other so much!

"I am so proud of all you have become, dear Corrie."

Only a moment more we stood. Then, realizing this was no time to start weeping, we both looked away. Suddenly Mrs. Gianini and Emily and Becky, followed by Ruth and Joan, all came around to hug me, too, and to wish me the best. Then we all went into Mrs. Gianini's sitting room.

It was about twenty minutes before ten. Just a minute or two later, Pa arrived with the buggy.

"You all ready?" he asked as Mrs. Gianini let him in. "The church is filling up mighty fast. Gonna be people standing all around the walls the way it looks."

With final words and hugs and kisses, and a few tears, all the other women went with Pa.

"I'll be back for you in ten minutes, little girl," said Pa to me with a wink, then closed the door behind him.

Suddenly I was left alone in the quietness of Mrs. Gianini's house.

Slowly I walked about, trying to breathe deeply, thinking about so many things. It was right here, I remembered, while Mrs. Gianini was working on those first dresses for us girls, that Almeda and I had had our first real talk about God and how he works in people's lives. I had been so young then. I had understood so little about what being a Christian meant.

Fragments of that conversation came back to me now as I walked about the empty rooms of the house.

"Jesus didn't talk much about the outward things a person did," I remember her saying, "but about the inside, what a person is like in his heart."

I smiled as I remembered her saying that there were other things about living with God she hoped she would have the chance to tell me about someday.

Well, she had. We had had so many treasured and important talks together.

I remembered how I'd felt during those first years getting to know Almeda, and how she had helped the hunger to be closer to the Lord grow inside of me. I had wanted so much to be good, to be close to him, to know what truth was, and to obey him.

So many years had gone by since then—years of learning and growing and deepening my understanding of God's work in my life.

Slowly I got down on my knees. I didn't care if I put an extra crease in my wedding dress—I just had to give my Father thanks for the wonderful years of my youth he had given me. He had been so good, so protective, so generous. I wanted nothing more than to be all the more completely his every day . . . for the rest of my life!

I heard Pa's buggy drive up again. I glanced up at Mrs. Gianini's clock on the wall. It was four minutes till ten.

When I stood, there were tears on my cheeks. I was so full of God's love right then that I could not begin to keep it inside.

A moment later the door opened, and there stood Pa. He just stood there and stared at me, then slowly walked forward.

"I didn't have a chance to tell you a few minutes ago," he said, "but you are a beautiful bride, Corrie Belle."

"Oh, Pa," I whispered, barely able to make my voice work. Then I hugged him tight.

"You afraid?"

"No, Pa . . . just very, very happy. I was thinking of all God has done for us."

Pa nodded. "He's looked out for us all mighty well, all right."

He paused, then added, "And there's a young man waiting over at the church who wants to have a chance to look after you too. So . . . you ready to go?"

"Yes, Pa."

We turned and walked outside to the buggy. Pa helped me up, and we rode slowly to the church without another word. There wasn't a soul to be seen in the streets. Everyone was inside the church.

He pulled up outside. Music was already playing, filtering out through the building from the little pump organ the church had bought and that Harriet played for the services.

Hearing it, realizing that everyone who knew me in the whole town was inside waiting . . . for *me*, sitting there with Pa all alone in the still morning air . . .

Suddenly my heart started to pound.

This was it, I thought. The moment had come!

It was a beautiful spring morning, fragrantly warm but not yet too hot. The sun was bright but still only about halfway up the sky. A few clouds hung about in the blue, and it seemed as if the organ music was floating straight up to them.

Pa looked over at me and smiled. Then he got out the other side of the buggy, walked around, looked up, and stretched out his hand.

I took it, relishing in the feel of his tough, hard-working skin which yet was able to grasp a woman's hand in the most tender manner possible.

I stepped down to the ground, and slowly we walked across the grassy meadow to the church.

Pa stopped me at the bottom of the steps. He turned toward me.

"There's only one last thing I got to tell you, Corrie Belle," he said, "before I give you away and you're a Hollister no more."

He paused, reached into his pocket, left his hand there.

"I know what you told me about Christopher and the diamond ring and what you told him. So he'll be giving you a small gold band on your left hand. But before we go in there, I want to give you your ma's wedding ring, the same one I slipped on her finger the day I married her."

He now withdrew his hand from his pocket, holding the ring I had seen in the box several days earlier. He took my right hand in his, and slipped it gently onto my fourth finger. It fit perfectly.

"Let this remind you, Corrie, every day you live, that your pa and ma loved you more than they could ever say. You have been the best daughter to them that ever a girl was."

"Oh, Pa . . ."

I had tried so hard not to cry this morning. But it was no use. I could not keep the tears back now!

"Now you be as good and loving a wife to that man in there as you've been a daughter to me, and you'll have a happy marriage."

"Thank you, Pa. I love you so much!"

"I love you too, Corrie Belle Hollister."

He smiled broadly, then offered me his arm.

I took it. We turned and slowly walked up the steps together, pausing one last time at the top.

We looked at each other, smiling in a way that expressed more than ten thousand words could ever say. Then together we drew in a deep breath and let it out as if in final preparation.

Pa reached for the door, opened it, and . . . we stepped inside.

CHAPTER 53

A HOME FOR THE HEART

It was probably six or seven minutes after ten.

The instant they heard the door creak open, every expectant head in the church swung around toward it.

Harriet had been watching for us, and the moment we appeared in the doorway, the chords of music changed into the Wedding March.

Pa closed the door behind us. My heart was pounding so, yet the only feeling I can remember being aware of for the first few moments was the skin of my mouth stretching wide in a smile I couldn't help. There sat a hundred faces all smiling toward us, and what could we do but return them?

We stood at the back of the church two or three seconds as the wedding music began, then slowly Pa started to move forward down the center aisle with me at his side, still clutching his arm for dear life.

With small slow steps we walked . . . there was the blue ribbon stretching out down the center of the church on both sides of us. . . .

In the front row, Almeda was looking back toward us as we came, smiling wide with tears in her eyes. We were starting to pass smiling faces now, so close I wanted to stop and greet each person!

The organ was loud, Pa was standing so straight and tall and proud. Slowly we made our way forward. . . .

In my memory of that wonderful day, as I walked down the aisle—though it could have taken no longer than a minute—it was as if my whole life since coming to California replayed itself before my inner eyes ... then mingled with the words Rev. Rutledge spoke and the vows Christopher and I made later.

"Dearly beloved, we are gathered here today. . . ."

We had arrived in California alone, in search of a future we could not see. Our pa had been waiting for us, though we didn't know it right at first.

It could not have been more fitting than for me to be with Pa for these final seconds of my unmarried youth. He and no one else represented the beginning of my life in California, and now here he was sending me off to begin the *next* season of my life.

"Who gives this woman to be married to this man?"

Pa and I had been through a lot together. It had taken a while to put the past behind us. As we walked down the aisle toward my future, it was hard to believe we were the same two people who had looked at each other in bewilderment outside the Gold Nugget, neither of us, in those initial seconds, even knowing who the other was.

Oh, Lord, I thought, *how much you have blessed us since that day!*

It was such a feeling of fulfillment to now be a grown woman, yet still his "little girl," like he sometimes called me. What a feeling of safety and protection to have a loving father at your side. No wonder God used that very word *Father* to describe himself.

"My dear departed wife, Agatha Belle Hollister, my wife Almeda Parrish Hollister, and I, Drummond Hollister, all do."

As we inched forward in the midst of all the faces, the only one missing was Ma. I knew Pa was thinking of her too.

"When a woman's not of the marryin' sort, she needs to think of

somethin' besides a man to get her through life."

Oh, Ma, I thought, *if only you could see me now! Would you be proud of me?*

And I knew she would. Knowing it gave me a warm feeling inside.

"I reckon you'll do all right, though, Corrie."

How many times had I heard those eight simple words of Ma's in my memory. Just being reminded that she believed in me had gotten me through some rough times of self-doubt.

You ARE here, aren't you, Ma? I thought.

As I did, I realized that she was just as much a part of this day as Pa was . . . and that she was smiling as she looked down from heaven upon her daughter, now a bride, though neither she nor I had ever dreamed such a day would come.

"Do you, Christopher . . ."

It was my father—this man walking beside me now—that I had discovered first after arriving in this place fifteen years ago. But soon other people began to become part of my life and growth.

Almeda—she was Mrs. Parrish to me then—was the first spiritual friend I'd ever had. She helped get me started along the pathway of life as a Christian. I can't imagine what my life would have been like had she not been there during those early years when I had so much to learn! God would no doubt have found some other way to teach me about himself, but I'm glad he used her!

". . . take this woman to be your wedded wife . . ."

Almeda once called me a daughter of grace back then. It was another of those things, like Ma's words, that stuck with me and helped me figure out who I was supposed to be as I grew up.

How well I remember the day she and Pa were married!

As they said their vows to each other, I could hardly believe what was happening. Now I was about to say those very same words myself.

That was even harder to believe!

". . . to have and to hold from this day forward, for better, for worse, for richer, for poorer, in sickness and in health . . ."

It wasn't long before my sheltered world began to expand. As I started writing, and as my faith grew roots, the hunger to know the truth began to deepen inside me—both personally and as I wrote. I met lots of people and found myself in many circumstances that I suppose were mighty unusual, even frightening, for a girl my age. I did some things that women just didn't do. My hunger for truth had led me on many trails I never expected, but I was thankful for them as I looked back.

". . . to love and to cherish, till death do you part, according to God's holy ordinance?"

My twenty-first birthday, after I had been in California five and a half years, was a turning point in many ways. I think that's when I first began feeling like I might be an adult before long. As much as I'd done by then, I still didn't feel *quite* grown-up. But that's when I began to think there might be hope for me yet!

That was when I began to think seriously about what place God might have for me in his world and in his plan—as a grown woman someday, not just as a girl.

Where was he taking me? What was he going to do with me? I began to ask those kinds of questions in my early twenties.

I suppose that's when I first began wondering what and where "home" would be for me once I *was* grown—though I didn't start thinking of it in just that way for several more years.

"Do you, Cornelia . . ."

For so many years I assumed I would spend my whole life as

an unmarried woman. I had been used to the idea from before I could remember, so there was no real shame in it. I never thought of myself as a future old maid. I thought of myself as God's daughter who would live my life in companionship with him rather than with a husband and a family. It was an exciting prospect, not a depressing one.

Loneliness never worried me. I didn't even think about it. There were many times when I *was* lonely. But what did occasional loneliness matter when God was my Father and I was where he wanted me to be?

As writing led me into politics, rapidly my world expanded. Though heartbreak was part of it too, soon I was involved in important things and meeting important people. The whole country was filled with opportunities to write about things that really mattered . . . from one sea to the other.

". . . take this man to be your wedded husband . . ."

Then came the war, and shortly thereafter the incredible, fateful letter from President Lincoln. Before I knew it I was on my way to the East Coast. The war and my two years in the East gave me a wider perspective on so many things that I might not have been able to get any other way.

But how could I have known at the time that I would be gone from home for so long?

So quickly I was thrust into the very middle of that dark night of our nation's history, a night much longer and bleaker and redder with blood than any would have imagined.

It was during that time, while at the Convent of John Seventeen, that I began again, just as I had at twenty-one, to ask God about my future—about what he had in store for me, about where my home really was.

Little did I know that he was preparing me, even then, to meet the one who would soon be the answer to that time of questioning.

As my thoughts strayed back across the miles to the California that had been my home, and as I thought about my early days in

New York in what had been my birthplace, my very first home . . .
I was aware that it was not toward either of these places that my
heart was bound.

*". . . to have and to hold from this day forward, for better,
for worse, for richer, for poorer, in sickness and in health . . ."*

When I opened my eyes in that strange bed on a farm outside
Richmond, Virginia . . . though I had no idea where I was, *God*
knew!

He had been leading me there all along!

It wasn't until the conflict to make this brave land a free one for
all its people was over . . . not until I left Virginia, not until I returned to visit my childhood home in New York, and finally not
until I boarded the train holding the letter that would change my
life forever . . . that I realized where the home was that God had
been leading me toward and preparing me for all my life.

*". . . to love and to cherish, and to obey till death do you
part, according to God's holy ordinance."*

Suddenly I was back to the present, my memories of yesterday
blending into the images and faces of now. In front of me, Zack
and Tad stood on one side, and Emily and Becky stood on the other
side—all waiting for me. They were all smiling as we made our slow
approach.

Pa and I were nearly at the front.

Now we were passing Almeda. Tears streamed down both
cheeks all the way to her lovely mouth. She smiled and mouthed
the words with her lips as I passed, "I love you, Corrie."

Oh, Almeda, I love you so much!

I glanced quickly at Emily, Becky, Zack, and Tad.

But it was on none of my brothers and sisters that my eyes finally rested. My gaze was riveted on the man standing right in
front of me, and suddenly it was just like that day at Mrs. Timms'

farm when my eyes opened and that wonderful face filled my vision.

God had led me *there* . . . and since then he had led us both *here*, to the altar of marriage!

Here was the *home* to which God had brought me . . . standing right in front of me!

Our eyes met.

Oh, Christopher . . . Christopher! Is it possible for a woman to love a man as much as I love you?

Pa and I reached the front and now stopped. So did the music from the organ.

The church was silent a moment.

All eyes were upon us, but Christopher and I had eyes only for one another.

After addressing the congregation briefly, Rev. Rutledge spoke to Pa, who gave me away, then took his seat beside Almeda.

I took a couple more steps forward and took my place at Christopher's side. Rev. Rutledge led us through the simple ceremony.

Never had three letters possessed such power to take my life in a new direction as when I heard Christopher's wonderful, resonant, confident, and smiling voice say the words: *"I do."*

Tears filled my eyes immediately.

He actually loved me so much he wanted to marry me!

How can any woman hear those words, realizing what an astounding truth and what a lifetime of commitment they contain, and not weep at the very idea of being loved that much!

Now the moment had come for me to repeat my own vows. I was afraid I would open my mouth and a little croak would come out that no one could hear.

But I followed Rev. Rutledge through the words, and though they were no more than a whisper, I knew from the smile on his face and the look in his eyes that *Christopher* heard them. And he was the only one who mattered . . . for I was speaking them to *him*.

I tried so hard to say it as confidently as he had, but if anything the whisper of my promise grew even quieter. Yet never in all my life had I meant anything so much as when I now said to the man God had chosen to be my husband: *"I do."*

Christopher and I now stepped to one side.

"The bride and groom have asked me," said Rev. Rutledge, "to speak a few words to you about the spiritual dimensions of marriage, which is extremely important to them as they begin their life together. They are not only, on this hallowed day, committing their lives to one another. They are at the same time committing their marriage to Christ, for him to work in and through them according to whatever purposes he chooses to accomplish. These are no mere textbook words to this serious young couple. I have spoken to them both at length and they are in deep earnest in their desire to . . ."

Rev. Avery Rutledge, I thought, *what a wonderful man, and what a helpful part he played in my development as a Christian.*

Even though we had asked him to speak to all the people who came to our wedding about our life and commitment to the Lord, and though I did my best to concentrate on his every word, I could not keep my mind from wandering back over the past two years since I had left the East.

His words brought to such focus all that God had done to mature Christopher and me spiritually, through our hundreds of letters and our talks and times of prayer and through the year of "Christopher's plan," to prepare us for this moment.

How thankful I was to God . . . and to this man now standing at my side, to whom I had just given my whole being in sacred matrimony.

Suddenly I was aware that the brief sermon had come to an end. Rev. Rutledge was looking at Christopher and me as we again stepped around to stand in front of him. Why were his eyes glistening so?

Only a moment the silence lasted. When Rev. Rutledge began speaking again, his eyes swimming in tears, it was to complete the ceremony that had been interrupted by his brief address.

At last came the final words that resounded in my ears almost as loudly as the pounding in my chest.

"I pronounce you man and wife."

Was it really true! Had I really heard the words? Was my heart at last truly *home!*

"And now, sir," came the minister's words, "you may kiss your new bride."

Christopher bent down and kissed me lightly on the lips, so

gently it lasted but a moment—a kiss so perfect and gentlemanly that only a man of great love could have so tenderly kissed it.

I was home!

I had found a home for my heart.

"Ladies and gentlemen, friends of Miracle Springs," Rev. Rutledge now concluded, "may I take the honor of being the first to present to you Mr. and Mrs. Christopher Braxton!"

CHAPTER 54

BEGINNING OF THE FUTURE

We walked out of the church arm in arm, followed by Emily on Zack's arm and Becky on Tad's and Almeda on Pa's, while everybody clapped, a few people cheered, everyone smiled, and all the women cried.

We hadn't even made it all the way across the grass to the town hall—where the food and the decorations and the wedding cake Almeda and Mrs. Gianini had worked so hard on were waiting—before Tad and Zack were out of the church and running ahead of us, producing handfuls of rice out of somewhere.

Christopher yelled at me and we made a dash for it. But it was too late. The boys pelted us with a shower of rice and were soon joined by all the other boys and girls of the town.

I was too happy and laughing too hard to resist.

For the next hour we smiled and greeted more people than I thought Miracle Springs contained—shook more hands, kissed more cheeks, hugged more hugs, and smiled so continuously that I began to think my face would never recover.

At last we cut the cake, ate the first bites as gracefully as we could in the midst of our smiles and laughing in front of everyone, then watched while Emily cut it and Becky distributed it among the townspeople.

As soon as we were able, Christopher and I made our escape back to the house. There—he in the bunkhouse, me in the house— we changed our clothes. Even though we were now married, there were lots of things that would take getting used to, and now we were facing the hugest step of all in getting to know each other all over again!

We got our bags, which we'd packed and prepared ahead of time, loaded everything into the carriage, and drove back into town. Not a single person, I don't think, had left the town hall.

Our arrival caused a whole new round of rice-throwing and celebration. We remained another thirty or forty minutes, continuing to eat and visit and make merry with everyone. It was probably half-past noon or one before we finally got off and on our way to Auburn, where we would spend the night before going on to Sacramento.

The hugs, kisses, final words, and waves of goodbye brought fresh tears to all the women's eyes—mine and Almeda's probably most of all.

Pa and Christopher shook hands firmly, man to man.

"Welcome to the family, son," said Pa.

"I don't think I'll be able to call you *Pa* just yet," laughed Christopher. "But I appreciate what you say. It means more than you can know to have a family . . . and a place to call home."

Then Christopher flicked the reins, and we were off.

We rode across the empty meadow toward the deserted town. I gazed behind us, with the church building, the town hall, and a hundred waving hands slowly fading smaller in the distance, until we rounded the corner and I could see them no more.

A few minutes later we were riding out of Miracle Springs. As much as had happened to me since coming to California, I could not help feeling that I had been caught up in a new and wonderful story that was only just beginning.

AFTERWORD

There may be those who will say that this book is too "spiritual" to be called a "love story." To such an objection I would only reply, "Where did love originate but in the kingdom of heaven . . . in the very heart of God?"

How, therefore, can any love story be complete, independent from God's involvement in a man and woman's mutual life together? Without him there can be a shadowy form of what is called love . . . but not a thorough and fully integrated love.

"But no two people in love think and talk like Corrie and Christopher," someone might say. "Young people in love, even committed Christian young people, just aren't that spiritually motivated. They're not that introspective."

All I can offer in response is this: I cannot speak for the rest of the world, only from my own experience. And twenty-four years ago, a certain young man and young woman spoke and thought in just this manner in contemplation of their *own* future life together. Much of their destiny they were unable to see, and they both had a lot of growing ahead of them. Yet their motivations and heart's desires were well established, however immature their world outlook may have been. Some of Corrie's and Christopher's letters, in fact, passed almost word for word between these two I speak of— my wife and me.

So whether the *majority* of young people look to marriage as an opportunity to commit themselves mutually to God's purposes, I cannot say. But I know that *some* do, because I am intimately acquainted with one young couple that did.

And I here affirm how thankful to God I am, twenty-four years later, for that particular young woman whose heart, like Corrie's, desired what her Father in heaven wanted for her. And it was just that heart's desire that so deeply resonated with my own prayer that I might grow to reflect the character of his Son.

We have shared life fully ever since, first as the best of friends, then in the heart-knit journey of spiritual camaraderie, and finally in all the multitude of ways that commitment to the common goal of God's purpose (including the struggles, hardships, frustrations, misunderstandings, and all the soul-twisting pains involved in human relational growth) leads a man and woman to learn truly to love one another on steadily deeper levels of knowing.

No marriage road is without its bumps, potholes, twists, and unforeseen turns, and ours (we sometimes think!) has had more than our share. Ninety-five percent of the terrain we have traveled and the struggles we have encountered, we did not anticipate in the least.

Is any marriage "easy"? I have not encountered one. Ours has contained *great* personal struggles, as Corrie's and Christopher's will no doubt have. Yet our shared desire to discover God's perspective in all these "unexpectednesses" has made our life together an adventure that we look back on (and look forward to) with profound and quiet thankfulness.

Judy, my friend, my comrade, my love, though certain aspects of our youthful exuberance may have faded through the years, and though the gray hairs are becoming more numerous all the time . . . I love you now more than ever!

To you who have read Corrie's journals from her arrival in California at fifteen until her marriage now as a full-grown woman at thirty, I hope you *keep* reading.

Corrie's story is not over yet!

In the meantime, while you are waiting for the continuation of Corrie's journals, there are three other books with my name on them I think you may enjoy.

The first is *Grayfox,* the story of Corrie's brother Zack during his Pony Express days.

In the second you will encounter a young lady by the name of

Sabina who shares, in her own unique way, many things in common with Corrie, even though the settings in which the two live are altogether different. Sabina is sixteen when the story opens, and she is about to embark on an adventure—and a relationship!—that will change her life forever. The book is called *The Eleventh Hour*.

Then third, in the opening pages of the nineteenth-century Scottish romantic mystery *The Heather Hills of Stonewycke*, thirteen-year-old Maggie stumbles upon an ancient family mystery that will not be fully resolved even in her lifetime, though she herself is the one who will uncover the clues that in the end make the unraveling of the mystery possible.

Sabina and Maggie and Zack are as close friends to us in our family as Corrie is, and I hope you will come into an intimate friendship with them as well. I hope you will discover that knowing them is an enriching experience which will give you fun and pleasure and also cause you to learn, to think, and to grow.

By the time you have made acquaintance with these other three young people, perhaps there will be more from Corrie's pen ready for you to enjoy!

Finally, if you are interested in some of the perspectives I have come to hold in my own personal walk with God, you may want to read my nonfiction book, *A God to Call Father*.

If Corrie's story has spoken to you in some personal way, my wife Judy and I and our sons would love to hear from you. We cannot promise a response, but we will try. You may write us at: 1707 E Street, Eureka, California 95501.

In all things, never forget this truth, which holds the whole universe together: *The Father is good, he loves you, and he desires only the best for you.*

May the Father of Jesus be with you always!

Michael Phillips

ABOUT THE AUTHOR

Bestselling author, bookseller, historian, and publisher Michael Phillips has produced more than sixty books on a wide range of topics. Known chiefly for his historical fiction, Phillips is also the redactor primarily responsible, through his edited editions of MacDonald's books, for the current worldwide resurgence of interest in the nineteenth-century Scottish novelist George MacDonald.

In his own right, Phillips has written more than twenty books and co-written (with Judith Pella) another dozen. Fifteen of his books have been nominated for Gold Medallion awards and a dozen have appeared on bestseller lists, and nearly all have appeared as book club selections and been translated into several foreign languages.

Phillips lives on the coast of northern California with his wife Judy and three sons Robin, Gregory, and Patrick.

For a complete list of Michael Phillips titles available, please contact your favorite Christian bookstore, or write to Bethany House Publishers.

Michael and Judy Phillips

If you liked *A Home for the Heart,* you may also enjoy these other books and series by Michael Phillips:

THE JOURNALS OF CORRIE BELLE HOLLISTER (Bethany House Publishers)

My Father's World (with Judith Pella)
Daughter of Grace (with Judith Pella)
On the Trail of the Truth
A Place in the Sun
Sea to Shining Sea
Into the Long Dark Night
Land of the Brave and the Free
A Home for the Heart
Grayfox

Good Things to Remember:
333 Wise Maxims You Don't Want to Forget

The practical wisdom and spiritual perspectives that Michael Phillips' readers have come to associate with his uniquely insightful fiction are available now in this thought-provoking collection of maxims and quotable quotes from Phillips and other sources. Get to know Michael Phillips, the man behind the bestselling books!

Tales from Scotland and Russia (Bethany House Publishers)

Adventuresome, dramatic, and mysterious stories from the romantic worlds of nineteenth-century Scotland and Russia. Co-authored with Judith Pella, these books are packed with abiding spiritual truths and memorable relationships. If you haven't yet discovered the worlds of adventure and intrigue opened up by these series, a wonderful treat awaits you!

Scotland:
Heather Hills of Stonewycke
Flight From Stonewycke
The Lady of Stonewycke
Stranger at Stonewycke
Shadows Over Stonewycke
Treasure of Stonewycke

Jamie MacLeod, Highland Lass
Robbie Taggart, Highland Sailor

Russia:
The Crown and the Crucible
A House Divided
Travail and Triumph

The Secret of the Rose (Tyndale House Publishers)

This is the newest series from the pen of Michael Phillips, set in Germany before World War II—a page-turner with spiritual content and rich relationships you won't soon forget!

The Eleventh Hour
A Rose Remembered
Escape to Freedom

THE WORKS OF GEORGE MACDONALD (Bethany House Publishers—selected, compiled, and edited by Michael Phillips)

Twenty-eight books in all, both fiction *and* nonfiction, that will delight and edify both adult and young readers. Please consult your bookstore or write for a full list of availability. Especially recommended titles include:

Fiction by George MacDonald Edited for Today's Reader:
   The Fisherman's Lady
   The Baronet's Song
   The Curate's Awakening
   The Highlander's Last Song
   The Laird's Inheritance

Nonfiction From the Writings of George MacDonald:
   Discovering the Character of God
   Knowing the Heart of God
   George MacDonald, Scotland's Beloved Storyteller
      (a biography of MacDonald by Michael Phillips)